Out of the Shadows

DIANE GREENWOOD MUIR

Cover Design Photography: Maxim M. Muir

CONTENTS

ACKNOWLEDGMENTS

One of the most fun things about writing these books is getting to know all of you who read them. If you have a chance, find us on Facebook (facebook.com/pollygiller). If Bellingwood is a real place, this is where you'll find it.

Contests and giveaways are a lot of fun – especially when they help me write the books. This time, I needed names for a pair of kittens. There were so many great entries and I honed the list to two pairs. The runner-up names were Wing & Nut from JoAnne Schulte. As you read the book, you will meet May & Hem from Maryann Wenner Potts. Since these new cuties match a pair that just entered my own life – Mayhem is a perfect description of the chaos (and lots of love) they've brought to my life.

There are many different people who help me as I write. Rebecca Bauman reads as I do the work. I send her every chapter. Her job isn't to edit or criticize, she ignores the continuity issues and errors and encourages me to keep going. Without this, there are days I'd never be able to write another word.

My beta readers are more than just readers. They edit, find continuity problems, point out unnecessary words / phrases / thoughts, catch strange grammar and are such a necessary part of my process. Without them, I'd be lost. Thank you to these amazing people: Tracy Kesterson Simpson, Linda Watson, Alice Stewart, Fran Neff, Max Muir, Edna Fleming, Dave Muir, Linda Baker and Nancy Quist.

As I made final edits to Book 11, problems cropped up and were caught by several people. One woman, however, worked with me to fix them as quickly as possible and she came on board to do a final edit for me, catching things I messed up as I purged excess words and re-wrote sentences. Thank you to Judy Tew and Carol Greenwood for working quickly at the end of the process.

Writing these books is all about the people I get to know along the way. I am so fortunate! Thank you for being part of this.

.

CHAPTER ONE

Trying to open her eyes, Polly grew frustrated. She couldn't. Blackness was everywhere. Her heart raced and her throat closed up as panic threatened to overwhelm her. This couldn't be happening again. She tried to move her hands, but nothing worked. Screaming wasn't possible. Nothing came out of her mouth no matter how hard she tried. She wanted to cry, but even tears wouldn't come. Why had he taken her? Why was he torturing her? Why wouldn't he let her live in peace?

"Polly! Honey!"

There was that voice. She recognized it, but who was it and why was he calling for her? What was happening? What was wrong?

"Wake up, Polly. Come on. Wake up."

She tried to climb out of the thickness of sleep. Her body was being shaken and then a sloppy tongue lapped across her face. Polly opened her eyes to find Obiwan pressed against her on one side and Henry hovering over her on the other.

"What was going on up there?" he asked, gently brushing her temple. "You had a hard time hearing me."

"It was that nightmare again. I couldn't see anything or move or even scream. I really thought I'd be finished with it after yesterday." She slid to a sitting position, her back against the headboard, clutching her arms to her chest.

Henry reached over and flipped the light on beside her and she blinked against its brightness.

"I'm sorry," she said. "I'm so sorry."

Obiwan laid himself across her lap and she buried her face in the heavy coat at his neck. "You smell good," she said, holding tight to the warmth and comfort he offered.

"He smells like dog," Henry said. "He needs a bath."

"But he smells like *my* dog and it's normal and it's okay." She took a long, slow breath. "What time is it?"

Henry swiped his phone open and held it in front of her.

"Four thirty. Oh Henry, I'm sorry. I've wrecked your sleep again. Obiwan and I can go out to the sofa."

He climbed out of bed and turned the television on. "I don't know about you," he said. "But I could use a distraction. These nightmares are shaking me up. Ever since Joey's trial began, you've been a wreck."

"But it's over now." Polly shivered and pulled the blankets over Obiwan and up to her shoulders. "I hoped that when they finally sentenced him, I'd let this go."

"You haven't. Maybe now you'll talk to someone?" he asked.

"And tell them what, that I'm having a recurring nightmare? It's going to go away. I just need to quit thinking about Joey and quit listening to lawyers replay everything he did to me." She shook her head. "Over and over, ad nauseum. Like the jury didn't understand the story the first time. And that defense lawyer. Did he think I was going to change my story and tell them that Joey *didn't* obsess over me and kidnap me?"

Henry nodded at her, letting her talk it out.

She dropped her head to her chest. "I almost felt guilty when I saw Joey's parents. Like it was my fault that he'd gone crazy."

"His mother is waaay out there." Henry twirled his finger at his temple. "She was frightening."

"When she came charging at us down the hall, screaming that I destroyed her son, I wanted to crawl under that bench," Polly said. "His poor dad. He doesn't know what to do with either of them. I don't know why he stays married to that crazy lady."

"When the guards ran her down, I didn't know what to think," Henry said.

"Neither did she," Polly said with a small chuckle. "I doubt that she's ever had that much physical contact with anyone. She glared at me through the whole trial. I could feel her eyes burning holes in my back. When I was up front, she stared at me like she was trying to kill me herself. It was the weirdest sensation. No one has ever hated me that much."

"She isn't aware of what she's doing or saying," Henry said. "You knew it beforehand and now we've all seen it. She's as nutty as a fruitcake. Completely bonkers and out of control."

"I feel sorry for her. The committees and sororities she belonged to have shunned her. No one wants to be connected to a woman whose only son was linked with a serial killer."

"It wasn't just that," he said. "They've probably been looking for ways to be done with her for years. How many times can you ignore that level of crazy?"

Polly shook her head. "I don't know. She was high up there in the whole social echelon. This will probably destroy her."

"It's not yours to worry about, honey. You've done nothing wrong."

"I wish I had ignored him from the very beginning," Polly said.

"If wishes were horses..."

She nodded. "I know."

"Polly, honey, each step you took led you back here to Iowa. You've said that one of the motivations you had for leaving Boston was Joey. If you'd never met him you might still be working in the Boston Public Library and we wouldn't be married. You and I wouldn't even know each other."

"That's not true," she said reaching out for him. "We were going to find each other. It was only a matter of time. I can't imagine any other life than one with you."

Henry took her hand and brushed his lips across the top of it. He couldn't get much closer without dislodging a dog. "I love you too."

"He's going to be transferred tomorrow," Polly said. "The only thing he'll see for the rest of his life is four walls. He has such a brilliant mind. I can't imagine how much more this will break him."

Henry sat down in his chair with his feet propped up on the bed. Han climbed across the bridge his legs made to find a soft spot on Henry's lap. "I'm just glad it's over. Joey will never get out this time."

"It's strange to realize that he's in the same state as me now, though," Polly said. "It was easy to forget about him when he lived fifteen hundred miles away."

"Give it time," Henry said, clicking his remote through channels on the television. "It's still fresh for you. And to be honest, Polly, you didn't obsess over it or even think about it for the last six months. The only time it crossed your mind was when we spent time with Al preparing for the trial. Right?"

Al Dempsey, Polly's lawyer, was an old friend of Henry's. They'd become closer to him in the last few months. Between the upcoming trials for Joey Delancy and Marcus Allendar, and then the legal work surrounding their guardianship of Heath Harvey, she'd gotten to know him better.

"You're right," she said. "As long as there were other things going on, I didn't think about it. But this is only the beginning. I have to go through it all again when Allendar goes to trial."

"Al said that wouldn't take as long. The FBI has been putting that case together and they have a decade's worth of information to present. You're just one small part of the picture with that man. And, as far as we know, he isn't pleading insanity so you don't have to go through that again."

"Joey *is* insane," Polly said quietly.

Henry smiled at her and rubbed his dog's head. "I know."

She pushed Henry's pillows together and leaned over, propping herself up on her elbow so she could see Henry's face.

"There are a lot of things I can't do," she said. "I can't work in the medical field because I'd faint every time I saw blood and I can't imagine being a criminal prosecutor. Having to listen to people lie to my face or try to justify why they murdered someone would haunt me night after night."

Henry waggled his foot at her and moved it closer to her face. Polly swatted it. "Get that yucky thing away from me," she said.

"It's not yucky. It's clean and fresh. See?" He pushed it at her again.

"You do that one more time," she said, "and I'll bite it."

Henry laughed. "I know that neither of us is sleeping, but it's nice to just sit here with you in the quiet. These last few weeks have been hectic. I'm glad this part is over."

Polly nodded. "Heath is going to Ames this weekend. Hayden has tickets for the football game and they're going to make a whole weekend of it. Maybe I should ask Stephanie if she and Kayla would want to have Rebecca over. Or maybe Jessie. We could go away somewhere. Just you and me."

Henry leaned back and shut his eyes. "A weekend away with my wife. No pressure and no worry." Laughter burbled out. "Who are you kidding?"

"What?" Polly was confused. "We've never done that. It's not too much to ask of our friends."

"Honey, I love you more than life itself, but can you honestly tell me that you'd get in the car Friday night and drive out of town, knowing you'd be out of touch with all of this?" He waved his hand around.

"Sure? Why not?"

"The coffee shop. The kids. Your friends. Evelyn and Denis downstairs. Sycamore Inn and Grey. The horses and donkeys. Sal. You could leave them all?"

Polly pushed her lower lip out. "I had a good time on our honeymoon."

"That was a year ago. You're planning for Halloween, the junior high band concert is next week and Rebecca probably has another dance coming up. All of that and you can leave town?"

"Maybe." She stuck her lower lip out in a pout.

"And what would you do with the dogs and cats? Are we taking them with us?"

"I don't know. But we could. I just wanted to go away with you somewhere and not have to think about all that's going on. You're the one who says I never leave. Now I try to make a plan and you come up with a million reasons why we can't go."

He took a breath and smiled at her. "You're right. I'm a terrible husband. Where would you like to go this weekend?"

Polly shrugged her shoulders. "If we go to a fancy hotel, we can't take the dogs." She peered up at Henry. "Do you want to go to a fancy hotel?"

"I don't care. This is your thing. I'll go wherever you want."

"Maybe Sal and Mark could go with us," she said.

He smiled.

"Joss and Nate can't. They aren't ready to leave the twins for a whole weekend." Polly turned her eyes upward, thinking. "But if we took Rebecca, she and I could go shopping. Or we could go to the zoo. That would be fun." She put her arm around Obiwan. "If we went to Omaha to the zoo, Joss and Nate could take the twins. Sophie and Coop would love that. They took them to the Des Moines zoo and had fun."

Henry propped his elbow on the arm of the wing chair and leaned his head on his hand, smiling at her.

"What?" she asked.

"Are we taking the whole town with us on our just-you-and-me weekend? I'll rent the bus. You tell me how many."

Polly reached over and ran her index fingernail up the bottom of his foot, making him jump. "You're mean to me," she said.

"I know," he agreed. "I'm the worst husband ever."

"You're pretty hard to get along with. So you're telling me that we aren't going anywhere this weekend."

"No," he said patiently. "I'm not telling you that. If you want to get away, I'm all for it."

"I can't do it, can I?" she asked, dropping her head to the pillow. When he didn't respond, she looked back up at him.

"I'm not saying another word."

Polly drew a deep breath and snuggled closer to her dog. "Maybe we could set in supplies and hide."

"Hang a 'Do Not Disturb' sign on the doors?"

She nodded slowly, feeling drowsy again. Henry's scent wafting up from his pillows was relaxing her. "I'd miss the excitement, though. I can't do that."

Henry sat forward and put the dog on the floor, then reached over to stroke Polly's hair. "I know," he said quietly. "How about we try to take it easy this weekend."

"I love you," she mumbled.

"I love you, too. I'm going to take the dogs outside and start my day. You sleep. There's no reason for you to hurry out of bed. I'll wake the kids and get them going."

Polly lifted her head. "But I woke you up, too. That isn't fair."

"Don't worry. I'm wide awake." His voice grew softer. "Sleep. Nothing can disturb you here. You're safe. I promise."

~~~

The next time Polly woke up, she stretched her shoulders, trying to work out the ache. When she realized that she'd fallen asleep all twisted up, she rolled her neck. That position might have been a mistake. The animals were all on the bed with her. After Henry had returned with the dogs, she'd dropped into a sound sleep, oblivious to anything else happening in the house.

As soon as the cats realized she was alert, they leapt to the floor and stretched. Han rolled over on his back looking for belly rubs while Obiwan yawned and put his paw on her arm.

"I have to get moving," she said. "I can't waste the day away."

She didn't have to be anywhere today. They hadn't been certain when Joey's trial would be over and so she'd made no plans. By now, everyone in town that cared would know he'd be imprisoned for life. She and Henry had come back quietly, arriving in time for a late dinner with Heath and Rebecca. Polly didn't feel like celebrating, though she knew her friends might see it differently. It didn't seem right to celebrate the fact that someone she knew would be locked away for the rest of his life, no matter how horrible his actions were.

Picking her phone up, Polly made her way to the bathroom. She looked at the shower and shook her head. She wanted to sit around in her pajamas, drink coffee, read a book and hug her animals. She'd start in the living room and if she came back to the bed, no one was stopping her. Henry was at work and the kids were in school. Her plan was perfect.

She swiped the phone open and groaned at the number of texts waiting for her attention. Unless someone desperately needed her, she wasn't responding. That's all there was to it.

Most everything was from friends who wanted to let her know they were thinking about her. That was nice. She'd deal with them later. Jeff Lyndsay had texted to tell her that he was up at the coffee shop if she was looking for him. The nut. Stephanie would tell her the same information. He was only reaching out.

She smiled at the text from Jason. He'd been in court one day last week, giving his account of the night they caught Joey after the fire. He'd been proud to be part of this with her. And she'd been proud of him. He was composed and articulate on the stand, probably due in no small part to the time Al Dempsey had spent with him.

Sylvie had brought Rebecca and Andrew to the courthouse that day so they could see what the experience was like. Hopefully that would be the only time they were exposed to it.

Jason wanted her to know that he was glad it was finally over and she was safe.

Everything else could wait. Polly dropped her phone on the sofa as she went through the living room to the kitchen. Coffee was waiting for her and she poured a cup, then took a deep breath, inhaling its scent.

Leaves on the sycamore trees were turning and falling to the ground. The plants in the garden on the corner were dying and Eliseo had emptied the water from the fountain. It felt as if the world was tucking itself in for its winter's sleep. Polly yawned and walked back to the living room. Her book was still on the coffee table, so she sat down, drew a blanket over her body, and snuggled in. The animals curled up around her as she leaned back. She yawned again, pushed the coffee toward the center of the table and sighed.

Quick thoughts of Joey and the life he faced wouldn't leave her. Every time she relaxed, something else popped into her mind and she'd come alert. There was nothing she could do for him any longer. He'd made his choices and she couldn't fix it.

She reached up to touch her cheek and realized she was crying. "Why do I feel so guilty?" she asked out loud. "I didn't do anything wrong."

Obiwan nudged her leg and she stroked his head. After trying to relax one last time, Polly gave up. She tossed the blanket off, stood up and headed for the shower. If thoughts of Joey were going to haunt her all day, it would be better to be out with friends than trying to sleep here all by herself.

There was coffee at Sweet Beans. Lots and lots of coffee and lots and lots of people.

CHAPTER TWO

Han had two ideas about bath time and either or both would show up in any given evening. He either loved bath time and soaked Polly clear through while he played, or he hated it and soaked Polly clear through in his struggle to get away. She was never sure which Han would show up and when both of them did, she came out completely drenched.

Tonight, he'd settled on playful and after she rinsed him down one last time, she leaned back against the wall and brushed her hair away from her face. Henry had offered to help - once. He'd gotten so frustrated with water going everywhere that he stalked out and slammed the door. That wasn't long after Han had come to live with them. He'd apologized to Polly later, but never again offered to help with bath time. She could talk him into drying his dog down with a towel and tonight that was going to be his job.

"Henry, I'm ready for you," she called out.

He opened the door from his office and clicked his tongue against his teeth before Han could launch himself into Henry's arms. "Sit. Stay," Henry commanded and took the top towel from the stack of dog towels in the closet. They had a stack of dog towels. Polly could hardly believe it herself. But then, there were towels at the barn for the horses and donkeys and there were towels for the Sycamore House kitchen and more towels for the kitchen at Sweet Beans. Everyone had their own towels. It made her laugh. Did everyone have towels specifically for their dogs?

Henry wrapped a towel around Han and lifted the dog into his arms, snagging a second towel on the way. "Do you want help cleaning up?" he asked, giving her a sidelong glance as he left the room.

"No. Thanks," she said. "Don't worry. I've got it."

"I'll be back in a few minutes if you change your mind."

The door leading to the media room opened and Rebecca stood in the doorway looking at the mess. "Polly?"

"Yes, Rebecca." Polly pulled herself up and took two more towels down, then dropped the toilet cover and sat down so she could rub Obiwan dry. When Rebecca didn't respond, she peered at the girl. "What's up?"

"Do you believe in ghosts?"

"There's no such thing." Polly held the towel between herself and the dog as he gave himself a shake, then chuckled at herself. She was already wet. Who cared? She rubbed the towel down his back and bent over to smell his head. "You're so much better now. You *were* a stinky dog." She let him shake once more before using a fresh towel to fluff him up. When she looked back up, Rebecca was gone. She didn't know what that was about. Hopefully Sarah wasn't haunting her daughter. She laughed to herself again. Ghosts weren't real. It was just junior high silliness.

As she wiped out the tub, Polly thought back to her junior high days. Someone had told her that ouija boards would scream if you burned them because they had a spirit inside, guiding the arrow. She'd only played with a board once after that and it had given her nightmares for a week. When Mary found out what was scaring her, she promised not to tell Everett, but made Polly promise to stay away from that stuff. Polly had. She didn't need those nightmares. She didn't need the nightmare she'd had last night either.

That might have been behind the grand dog-washing extravaganza. She wanted to be able to pull Obiwan close tonight if necessary. And though she'd never admit it to Henry, the dog had gotten pretty smelly.

After putting the towels in the washing machine, Polly stuck her head into the media room. "You two have your homework done, right?"

Heath had draped himself over one end of the sofa to watch football, his feet propped up on the coffee table. They'd had more than a few discussions about leaving his shoes in his room and not putting them up on furniture. Polly's directions about being polite had gone right over his head. When Henry made a remark about where his shoes had been and the number of animals that did unspeakable things on the ground and bug guts and everything else, it finally clicked. Heath's shoes were no longer an issue.

"Toss me the towels, Henry," Polly said and put her hands out to catch them.

Henry whispered to Heath. "Watch this." He formed the first towel into a ball and lobbed it straight at Polly. She went high for it and the towel smacked her in the face and then fell to the ground. Heath smiled hesitantly.

"One more," Henry said. He tossed the next towel to her and though she reached out for it, that one also fell to the ground.

"Not fair," Polly said. "You didn't aim well."

"He..." Heath spoke up to defend Henry, but Henry stopped him.

"It's okay. It's one of her things. She can't catch."

Polly scooped up the towels. "You can't throw." She put them in the machine and turned it on. "I get no respect," she muttered. "No respect at all." She finished cleaning up the bathroom and went back into the media room. "Nobody said anything. Is homework done?"

Heath nodded and Rebecca looked up from her sketchpad. "I did everything after school with Andrew and Kayla."

"Everything?" Polly pressed. "And you practiced your flute, too?"

Rebecca rolled her eyes. "Yes."

"You have a concert coming up," Polly said. "I want you to be ready."

"I'm ready now."

Henry coughed and looked at the two of them.

"What?" Polly asked.

He tilted his head at the television screen and pursed his lips.

"I didn't tell you to be quiet last night when we were watching the movie," she protested.

"We've seen *Back to the Future* nearly as many times as *Star Wars*," he said with a sigh. "You have the dialog memorized. It's not the same."

"Fine. I'm leaving." Polly crossed in front of the television and waved her hands up and down, then put her hand in front of Henry's face before walking away. He didn't react or respond, but released the dog from his lap. Obiwan and Han chased each other around Polly's legs and she grinned. She'd asked for it.

She pulled a blanket from the back of the sofa in the living room and threw it over the cushions before sitting down. Okay, that was ridiculous. She protected the couch from wet, clean dogs, but let them up on it the rest of the time with no concerns. She sat down and reached over to pick up a book. Neither she nor Henry had done anything about planning for the weekend, so maybe they were staying home. She hadn't even talked to Rebecca about staying somewhere else. A sense of malaise had followed the nightmare and Polly still hadn't shaken it.

"Heath, have you packed for the weekend?" she yelled back to the media room. "Is Hayden picking you up in Boone after school or coming here? Or do you want me to take you over to Ames?"

She waited for a response and when she turned to repeat her question was startled to find Henry standing over her.

"What?" she asked, with a grin.

"You're yelling across the house and the television is blaring."

"Yeah? So?" She laughed until she snorted.

"You didn't grow up with a sibling. That is blatantly obvious."

"What do you mean?" she asked coyly.

"Mom would have had our head if we yelled across the house."

"So it's a bad thing?" Polly put the book back down and stood up. She wrapped her arms around Henry's waist. "Are you yelling at me?"

"No, but maybe you should get face to face with the boy if you have questions."

Polly glared at the media room. "You guys don't like it when I bother you during a football game, remember?"

"Okay," he said. "You're right. We don't. But, listen..." They both stopped and listened. "It's a commercial." He stepped back into the room and said, "Heath, could you come here, please?"

As the boy stepped into the living room, Henry said, "Did you hear what Polly asked?"

"I'm just taking a couple of shirts," Heath said. "I don't need much. Hayden has everything."

"Do you need a ride?" Polly asked. "We probably should have talked about this earlier."

"There's some guys going to Ames after school tomorrow. I can hitch a ride with them."

"I know you don't like riding the bus, Heath, but I'd rather you come home and I'll take you," Polly said. "Let me make up cookies and brownies for the weekend."

"You don't have to do that."

She scowled at him. "Boys in college never get homemade goodies. Let me do it?"

Heath shrugged. "If you want to. And I don't mind the bus. At least for now. I'm saving for a car."

"For now, I'll take you to Ames, if you'd like," Polly said.

The announcers came back and both Henry and Heath looked toward the media room.

"Go," she said and they were gone.

Polly started to sit back down on the sofa in the tiny space that the dogs had left her when the clock in the dining room chimed. They'd finally gotten her father's wall clock back from being repaired. While it had taken time getting used to hearing the chimes throughout the night, it was a source of comfort to her.

She opened her mouth to call Rebecca's name, then remembered Henry's admonition. Why had he come up with this? The apartment wasn't so big that they couldn't hear each other, but it was probably about respect. If his parents hadn't allowed him and Lonnie to yell at each other, that was more than likely it.

Rebecca knew that nine o'clock was her bewitching hour and Polly waited a few minutes to see if the girl would come out on her own. Rebecca hated going to bed. She was a night owl and would do whatever she could get away with in order to stay up longer. Polly wasn't ready to give up on her bed time yet. Sleep was too important for these kids.

A couple more minutes passed and Rebecca still hadn't come out, so Polly pulled herself back up off the couch and went into the media room. Rebecca was studiously ignoring her, sketching on her pad as fast as she could, head down. Polly walked across to the back of the sofa, bent over and whispered in Rebecca's ear. "It's time. You have to start your evening routine. One more night and then the weekend will be here, okay?"

"Just let me work out this ear," Rebecca said. "I almost have it."

It was always something. An ear, a tree, blending the right color for a dragon or a tiny little dot that was a fly being swished by a horse's tail. Every night there was something that Rebecca had to finish before she would put her artwork down.

"You have until the quarter hour chime and your time is up. Fair?" Polly asked.

"Not really, but okay. I wish I was a professional artist so I could be creative any time I want," Rebecca grumped.

"Someday," Polly said. This was an old argument. "But quarter after. No later. I don't want to come back for you." She winked at Henry. "And I'm not yelling for you either."

~~~

Polly was nearly asleep when Henry and Han climbed into bed.

"Did they win?" she asked.

15

"Do you care?"

She yawned. "I want you to be happy."

He rubbed her shoulder. "You're so good to me."

Polly turned to face him. "Darned right I am. I'm the best wife you've got."

"Yes you are. I couldn't ask for anyone better." He leaned forward and kissed her nose. "I need to talk to you about something."

"Now? I was nearly asleep."

"I'm sorry. But we're rarely alone."

Polly sat up and crossed her legs in front of her. "Is something wrong? You sound serious."

"No," he said, patting her knee. "It's just something that you need to make a decision about."

"Well then, what?"

"Your truck."

Polly poked her lower lip out. "Is there a problem with my baby? Don't take it away from me."

"Not that truck, you nut," he said with a laugh. "The other truck."

"I don't have another truck in my life." She stretched her arm out and put her hand in front of his face. "I'm not acknowledging its existence. It's dead to me."

Henry sighed. "Then I'm not sure how to deal with this."

"You promised I would never have to drive it again. I don't want it in my life."

"We own the truck, Polly," he said. "We need to make decisions about it."

"I thought we collected insurance on it because it was stolen."

"No," he shook his head. "We didn't. We own that truck."

"Sell it."

Henry wrapped his hand around her foot and held it tightly. "Please just listen to me. Can you do that?"

"I guess," she said with a pout. "What?"

"What if Heath drove it to school? Jason and he could ride together and both boys would be able to stop riding the bus."

Polly looked off into space. "It's not the worst idea. Does he have a driver's license?"

Henry nodded. "He's driven my truck a couple of times. I wanted to make sure he knew what he was doing. He does okay for a kid."

"Jason and he don't get along all that well," Polly said. "They hang out in different crowds and Heath hasn't shown any real interest in the horses. He's down at the barn because we pay him to work with Eliseo, but I don't think he cares. He'd rather be mowing or cleaning up the yard than spend time with the horses and donkeys. Jason is pretty much offended by that."

"So, this is a bad idea? I thought maybe the boys could avoid the bus."

"How do I keep an eye on him if he's loose in Boone with a vehicle?" Polly asked. "It's not like school is here in Bellingwood. And I don't want his buddies riding with him. That whole gang mentality. That's when kids get stupid. That's when *he* got stupid. He's barely out of trouble with the Sheriff now. What if he does something ridiculous and hurts somebody with the truck?"

Henry waited quietly.

"Aren't you going to say something?"

"Everything you say is true. It was just an idea. We can sell the truck."

Polly pushed at his shoulder. "Sometimes you give up too easy. Talk to me about this. Don't just let me blather on and then agree. Tell me what you're thinking."

"Your concerns are valid. Heath has only been here a couple of months and before that he was nothing more than a common hoodlum. Nobody trusted him. Who knows if he could handle this responsibility? I certainly don't."

"We'd have to put him on our insurance," she said.

Henry nodded. "He already is. Since he has a license, I wanted him to be insured to drive our vehicles just in case something happened."

She bent over and kissed him. "You're so smart. Am I being too fearful?"

"Look," Henry said. "Nobody even knows this truck still exists in our lives except you and me. We can do whatever we want. Aaron stopped me yesterday and told me that they'd be releasing it in the next week and wondered if I knew what we might want to do with it."

"Raising kids is hard," Polly said. "How can I say that I don't trust Heath to do the right thing if I haven't given him the opportunity to make the choice? That's not fair. He's been good since he moved in. His grades are decent and he's helpful and Rebecca really likes him."

"So you want to do it?"

"You're still not talking to me," she complained.

He took a deep breath. "I hated riding the bus and as soon as I could, I talked Dad into letting me drive. If Heath's parents were alive, he'd probably have a car. It's his junior year and he's going to be seventeen. These last couple of years have stopped a lot of his social maturation and I just hate watching him have nothing. He needs something that says he's a young man. And he needs to be responsible for something."

"Will you teach him how to do maintenance on it?" Polly asked.

Henry nodded.

"Can we set down ground rules and will you back me up if I have to take the truck away because he's broken them?"

Henry grimaced. "The only thing I hate about that is we'd be responsible for transporting him again, but yes."

"I don't want him taking the kids anywhere yet. At least not until he's driven for a while. I don't want any of his friends or kids his age in the truck except Jason. Not for any reason."

"That makes sense," Henry agreed.

"He can drive it to school and back. After he drives you or me to Ames to his brother's house a couple of times, then we can talk about him driving it over there. And I want him to be responsible financially for this thing. I know we won't make him pay for insurance since it's already in place..."

Henry interrupted her. "No, if he starts driving regularly, he can be responsible for his portion. And he puts gas in the truck. If we ask him to drive anywhere for us, we give him gas money. I'll teach him how to do maintenance, but he'll pay for the supplies."

"Wow. Okay," Polly said. "Now I have one more thing to ask."

"What's that?"

"Are we doing this?"

Henry smiled as he looked up at her. "If it falls apart, we'll deal with it. I hope that he'll take on this responsibility and be successful."

"Me too. Can I tell him tomorrow?" she asked.

"Okay. Why so soon? We won't get the truck back until next week at the earliest."

"I'd like him to drive to Ames to start getting a feel for it."

Henry nodded. "Sure. You'll have him trapped in the truck and you can scare the stuffing out of him while he drives."

"I'm good at that." Polly slid her legs back between the sheets and stretched out, snuggling up against Henry's chest. "I like keeping y'all on your toes."

"Yes you do. I'll call Aaron tomorrow."

"I'm wide awake now," she whispered. "Are you?"

CHAPTER THREE

Every day, Heath went to school and then helped in the barn during the evenings and on weekends, but he detached himself from personal involvement. He responded to Polly and Henry when they spoke to him and seemed to enjoy watching football, but there was nothing that made him interesting or unique. He'd shut every bit of his personality away from the world. He wasn't sullen, he didn't get into trouble, he wasn't happy. After he'd separated himself from the group of people he had run with, he didn't have any other friends. The poor guy didn't seem to care and wasn't about to make an effort to put himself out there again. He just existed.

The best conversations he had were with Rebecca. He was quite taken with her and treated her exactly as a big brother should. He was polite with her, responded to her questions with actual conversation and it was only because she pressed him about it that he did any school work.

It broke Polly's heart that she couldn't find a way to break through his shell, but Henry told her to be patient. That wasn't one of her best things, but she knew he was right. After losing his parents, Heath had been thrown into a less-than-loving situation with his aunt and uncle, so he'd never been allowed to grieve. His older brother was too caught up in his own grief as well as worrying how to stay in school. He'd hoped that Heath would be safe, but had no way to make things better for the boy.

Heath loved his brother. They hadn't spent any time together after school started, so she was glad Hayden invited him to spend the weekend. When Heath asked Polly and Henry if it would be okay, it was the first time she'd seen any sign of life in him.

Polly held her hand over the plate of brownies to see if they were cool enough to slip into a bag. There hadn't been much going on downstairs, so she'd spent the entire day cooking and baking. Lydia would be proud. She'd made cinnamon rolls and chocolate chip cookies, lemon-poppyseed muffins (something she'd discovered Heath liked by accident), blueberry muffins, brownies and cream-filled cupcakes. Then, she'd gone up to Sweet Beans, purchased a pound of ground coffee, a loaf of Sylvie's sourdough bread and a half-dozen French rolls. She hadn't packed it all, there was plenty left in the house, but this was her first opportunity to mother Hayden and she was going to attack it with all she had. Heath would probably kill her.

The kitchen was a mess, but Polly didn't care. If she had to spend all day Saturday cleaning, this would be worth it.

Both dogs jumped up from their pillows on the floor in the dining room and Polly glanced at the clock. It was time for Andrew, Kayla and Rebecca to be home. She arranged the goodies on a plate and put it on the dining room table.

The three kids barreled into the dining room, faces flush with excitement and pulled up short when they saw what she'd done.

"Are you impressed with the food or the mess?" Polly asked.

Andrew was the first to speak. "What did you do?"

"I baked. A lot."

"For us?" he asked.

Rebecca swung her backpack at him. "It's for Hayden Harvey, you dope." She took in the variety on the table. "Did you lose your mind or find a new recipe website?"

Polly pursed her lips. "Maybe both. I couldn't stop myself once I got started. Cookies weren't enough and then I had time on my hands while the dough mixed up for the cinnamon rolls, and then I went on a tear. But there's plenty for everyone."

"Have you taken any of this down to Eliseo?" Kayla stepped closer to the plate on the table. "You should work at the bakery."

"Not me," Polly said. "I do this once in a blue moon. And no, I haven't taken any of this anywhere." She pointed at the containers on the counter. "If you want to share, that would be wonderful. I'm driving Heath over to Ames, so I can't help, but take a plate to Evelyn and Denis and another to Stephanie and Jeff. Eliseo and his crew would probably like a break, too. Mix and match and share. We certainly don't need all of this in the house."

Andrew dropped his backpack on the floor and pulled out a chair at the table. "I'm starving," he said. "Do you care what I eat?"

"I don't care. But will your mother?" Polly asked, scowling at him.

"I won't tell her. As long as I eat my supper, we're cool."

Polly chuckled. "Just be careful. It will still be here tomorrow."

"Is it supposed to be a nice day tomorrow?" Rebecca asked quietly. She slipped past Polly into the kitchen and took down three glasses from the cupboard. Kayla took them out of her hand and Rebecca opened the refrigerator.

"It should be beautiful," Polly responded.

"Can we have pop?" Rebecca asked.

Polly shook her head. "There's lemonade, milk and juice in there. No reason for pop."

Andrew gave a loud sigh. "Mom doesn't let me drink it either. And I like that Mountain Dew. You drink it all the time, Polly. Why can't we?"

She lowered the lids of her eyes at him and said, "Seriously?"

He thought about it, his eyes darting back and forth and then he said, "Yeah. Seriously. Why can't I if you do?"

"First of all, you don't get to do everything that adults do. I won't be pushed into that game. Secondly, your body is still trying to figure out what comes next. The less garbage you put into it while you're young and adapting to the world, the better. Your brain is building connections that will serve you over a lifetime. Thirdly, it's a rule in your house and you know that, too. Would you like me to keep going?"

He had hung his head while she spoke. "No, that's good. It isn't fair that you get to have something and nobody else does."

"Do you see me drinking pop right now, Andrew Donovan?" she asked firmly.

"No, but you probably did earlier."

"And because I put a bra on this morning, does that mean you should do that too?"

He looked up at her, his face twisted up in shock. "No!"

"Exactly. And by the way, whoever told you that your perception of fair was how life was going to be lived, lied to you. Fair has nothing to do with life, no matter what you might think. Are we done with this conversation yet?"

"Yes," he said quietly.

Rebecca and Kayla had stood stock still through that encounter. Rebecca finally made a noise in her throat and said, "Lemonade?"

Polly burst out laughing and put her arm around Rebecca's shoulder, then took the pitcher of lemonade out of the refrigerator and put it in Rebecca's hands. When she looked back up, Heath was standing in the dining room door.

"There you are," she said. "Do you want anything to eat before we leave?"

"No, I'm fine," he responded. He nodded to the plate of goodies on the table. "Did you make all of that?"

"Maybe." She pointed at the two grocery totes. "Those are for you and Hayden."

"It's only two days," he protested.

"You can leave the rest with him. He should have home baked goodies every once in a while, don't you think?"

"Well yes, but, all of that?"

"She lost control," Rebecca said. "You just need to go with it. How did your test go?"

Heath shrugged. "It was okay."

"What about your speech?" Rebecca asked. "Wasn't that today?"

Polly had no idea any of this was happening in his life, but Rebecca didn't miss a beat.

Heath shrugged again and turned to leave. Rebecca jumped out of her chair and ran to catch up with him.

"It's a good thing he's her brother," Kayla said in hushed tones. "Or Andrew would be way jealous."

Andrew opened his mouth to protest, but since it was full of chocolate cupcake, he waggled his tongue at her.

"You're gross," Kayla said.

Rebecca and Andrew had finally dealt with their relationship in time for the first dance of the year. The three of them had gone together that night and the teachers had been ready for the kids, teaching line dances and even dragging out a few square dance routines. There hadn't been much opportunity for the girls and boys to dance together, much to Andrew's relief. Rebecca confided in Polly that she had worried about it all week long. She wanted to dance with Andrew, but wanted to have fun with everybody else, too. It had all worked out.

There were two more dances to come. One in January and one last dance in April. Polly knew they had more consternation on the way, but the longer she could put it off, the better.

Heath and Rebecca came back into the dining room. She sat back down with Kayla and Andrew. "Polly, do we have plans for tomorrow?"

"No," Polly said. "Why?"

"Kayla and Andrew and I want to do some exploring. Since it's going to be such a nice day, can we take a walk?"

This was highly suspicious. "Where do you want to walk to?" Polly asked.

"Just around," Andrew said.

Polly glanced at Heath. He gave his signature shrug.

"Around where? You guys never want to just explore."

"Well..." Andrew started and then he looked at Rebecca. Kayla bent over and picked up her backpack, busily taking things out.

That too, was suspicious. They knew they didn't have to do homework on Friday afternoons.

"Fine," Rebecca said. "We want to go to the cemetery. Somebody said they decorate it for Halloween and we want to see what they do."

"Nobody decorates the cemetery for Halloween," Polly said. "Where did you hear that?"

"Just kids at school. Can we go, please?"

"We'll talk later. I need to get Heath over to Ames."

"But if we don't make a plan, Stephanie won't let Kayla come over and Andrew might have to stay home with Padme," Rebecca pleaded.

"Uh huh," Polly said. "Both of them are over here every Saturday afternoon. You'll have to do better than that. I promise, though, we'll talk about it and if you're worried that they won't show up, you can call them tonight."

Rebecca dropped her hands on the table, making a loud sound which startled the dogs.

"Do you have everything you need, Heath?" Polly asked. It was better to ignore whatever Rebecca was doing.

Heath held up his bag.

"I know I'm going to sound like a mother hen, but you and I haven't talked much about this weekend."

His shoulders went up and Polly continued. "Are you sleeping on the floor, on a couch, in a bed? Do you need a sleeping bag or an air mattress?"

"That's what you wanted to know?" he asked, surprise evident on his face.

"Sure. What else is there?"

He shook his head. "I don't know. Maybe you were going to tell me not to drink or anything like that."

"That's a given. You're only seventeen and Hayden isn't stupid. He's got a scholarship to maintain. I don't need to tell you not to do things that you're already not going to do."

Confusion was evident in his face. That had obviously never occurred to him.

"So where are you sleeping?" she asked.

"I don't know. It doesn't matter."

"We have a sleeping bag if you want to take it."

"Nah. It's fine. He has one."

"When you get back on Sunday you'll tell me if you guys need anything to make your next trips easier, okay?"

"Yeah. You want me to carry those?" He nodded at the tote bags.

Polly handed one to him and took the other. "You three have fun. I'll see you later."

When they got into the truck, Heath said, "You didn't tell them to take the dogs out. Will they remember?"

"I hope so," she replied. "They do it every day after school whether I'm upstairs with them or not. I don't have to micro manage every part of their lives."

He pulled his seatbelt on and sat back in the seat, his body stiff as a board. "Thanks for letting me do this."

"You and Hayden should spend whatever time you can together," Polly said. "Someday your lives are going to be too busy and you'll be glad for these memories. Have you spent much time with him in Ames?"

"This is the first time," he said.

Polly took a deep breath. The poor kid. There had been many times she wanted to knock his aunt and uncle's heads together. This was just another on the list. "What are you doing tonight?"

He shrugged again. "I dunno. He said we might get pizza. There are some parties we might go to." He put his hands up quickly. "I promise, though. I won't drink. And neither will Hayden. We're just going so I can meet his buddies."

"I trust you," Polly said. "But do me a favor, will you?"

"What?"

"Not just this weekend, but always. If something happens and you or Hayden needs one of us to help you out, you'll call. Okay? It will take time for us to get there, but we'll always come."

"Yeah. Okay."

"I know it sounds weird, but you aren't alone anymore."

26

He nodded.

They rode in silence until they were north of Boone. "Have you ever driven in Ames?" she asked. Then she laughed. "I guess not if you've never spent time with Hayden. That was a dumb question. The better question is, did you do much driving while you lived with your aunt and uncle?"

"No. They were afraid I'd wreck something. At least that's what they always said."

"Would you want to try?"

"Driving in Ames? In your truck?"

She nodded. "Yeah. Today. Do you want to give it a try? If you want to bail at any time, pull into a parking lot and I'll take over."

Heath visibly gulped. "No. Not today. You find where Hayden lives and I'll pay attention to everything. I didn't even think about this."

"Is it because it's my truck?"

"Well yeah. This is nice. I don't want to mess it up."

"Tell me what happens if you mess it up," she pressed.

"I don't know. You get mad at me and never let me drive again."

"Does that sound like me?"

He dropped his head. "No."

"What happens is that we fix the truck and move on. It's just a thing. Are you sure you don't want to try?" Polly hit her turn signal and pulled into a parking lot. She stopped, turned off the truck, and put her hand on the door handle.

"I can't believe you're letting me do this," he said. "I've driven Henry's truck, but I know how much you love this thing."

Polly smiled at him. "I know it makes no sense to you, but I love you more than I do my truck. Let's switch seats. You'll be fine and I know where we're going."

Heath jumped out of the truck and Polly lifted herself across the console and into the passenger seat. She belted in and waited for him to climb in and get settled.

"There are buttons on the side of the seat to move it," she said and waited while he made adjustments. He checked the mirrors and flipped the turn signal off and on, then put his hands where the key should have been.

"Press the button." Polly held up the fob. "The truck needs to know this is here, but you're good to go."

Heath put the truck into gear, looked behind him and pulled back out onto the highway. They drove a few miles as he brought it up to speed and he said, "This is nicer than Henry's truck."

"Yeah. Don't tell him that. He gets all jealous and stuff."

"But he bought this for you, right?"

"That's right. He still gets jealous. He wants a new truck, but he's has to wait. We have too many vehicles right now."

Heath nodded, keeping his eyes on the road in front of him. He was driving stiffly, his hands in the right place on the steering wheel, his eyes darting from the road to the mirrors and back to the road.

"You're doing fine, Heath. Relax. I wasn't kidding about the truck."

By the time they got onto Highway 30, he began to relax. Polly released her grip on the underside of her right leg and rubbed her hand against her thigh. She really was okay with this, but until he relaxed, she was tense.

"Take this exit," she said. "It's the easiest way to get to your brother's apartment. Luckily for you he lives out here on the west end of town."

"How do you know this?" Heath asked.

"Google and I are very good friends. Okay, turn left here," she directed and pointed to the street he should take.

Heath took a deep breath and pulled off onto a side street and parked under a tree.

"What are you doing?" she asked.

He turned to face her. "This is probably the only time I'm going to have the courage to say anything, but thank you for trusting me. I don't deserve it and I know it. Hayden and I've talked a lot about what I did these last two years. He didn't know everything so he made me tell him. And Rebecca never lets up. She's always telling me that I can be a better person. That it's my choice."

"She's right, you know," Polly said.

"Maybe. I never had choices."

Polly started to speak, but he put his hand up to stop her. "I know. I made bad choices. But they seemed like the only ones I could make. I don't know why you took me in. Hayden still can't figure it out. I don't know why you let me drive down here today or made all that stuff." He gestured at the bags in the back seat. "But you don't stop. And it feels like you never will."

These were the most words she had ever heard him say and all Polly wanted to do was keep him talking. Now wasn't the time to talk about the other truck. He'd had too much family input up to this point. And besides, maybe it would be better coming from Henry. Who knew, maybe Heath would get interested in cars. They could always use another gearhead.

She'd waited too long. Heath was staring at her. "You're right. I'll never stop. And sometimes it will drive you out of your mind." She looked him in the eyes. "I want to hug you now, you know."

He laughed. "I've heard that about you. Andrew complains."

"He's getting used to it. I won't hug you now, but someday soon you won't be able to stop that either." Polly did reach over and touch his leg. "Thank you for talking to me today. Can we try to do that again?"

Heath shrugged again and Polly knew that the moment was over. If that was all she got, it would be enough for now. "After you turn around, we need to go down two blocks and turn right. It's the second building on the left."

He pulled into a driveway, backed up and headed back the way they'd come, then followed her directions to the apartment complex.

"Do you want to call your brother?" she asked.

He nodded and swiped his phone to make the call. He jumped out of the truck as he spoke to Hayden, then swiped the call closed and opened the back door. "He's coming down. I told him there was a lot of food here."

Polly got out and walked around the truck to where Heath was gathering bags. She touched his arm. "I hope you have a great weekend. I'll be back at five o'clock on Sunday to pick you up. If you need anything, please call us, okay?"

"We'll be fine," he said. "Thanks for this."

"I love you, Heath Harvey. Don't you forget that this weekend."

He stared at her and then his concentration was broken. "Hay! She made brownies and cookies."

Hayden strode over and pulled his brother into a hug. "You got everything you need?"

Heath nodded and handed him a tote bag. He bumped the back door shut with his hip and said, "Thanks, Polly. I'll see you on Sunday."

She watched the two brothers walk away. Hayden had Heath in a headlock. This was going to be okay.

CHAPTER FOUR

Polly told Rebecca they could go on any adventure they wanted to in Bellingwood, as long as they stayed safe and were home by five. Rebecca called Andrew and Kayla as soon as she could and the three talked for over an hour on video chat while Polly cleaned the kitchen.

Since they weren't going away for the weekend, Henry made plans to move Nate's shop into the building at his new house. The Mikkels' house wouldn't be ready until next spring, but Nate was ready to give up his rented shop space and make things permanent. The two men were like kids in a candy store, they were so excited. Henry's dad had been building boxes for cabinets and they'd been busily sketching plans to finish a small office and bathroom. From what Polly could see, the office was more like a lounge with comfortable chairs, a flat screen and a tiny kitchen. Yes, there was a desk drawn into a corner, but that could hardly be called an office.

Henry hadn't returned home until after eleven o'clock Friday night and then was up and out early this morning. Rebecca and Polly got up late, had a quick breakfast and after Rebecca's lesson with Beryl, Polly was on her own. Kayla and Andrew showed up, both carrying backpacks and before Polly could ask questions, Rebecca threw hers over her shoulder and they'd taken off down the back steps. They weren't giving her any opportunity to change her mind.

She'd spent time that morning thinking about who she could take on an adventure of her own. Since Nate and Henry had plans, Joss would be busy with the twins. Polly loved them, but that wasn't who she wanted to gallivant around the county with. Sal and Mark were in Minneapolis for the weekend, spending time with his family; Sylvie was just plain too busy and Lydia was in Dayton with Marilyn's kids. Andy and Len were doing something romantic and Beryl had seemed glad to wave goodbye after Rebecca's lesson. She was preoccupied with other things.

Polly could usually talk the kids into adventures, but they had their own thing going on today and Jason was busy with Eliseo. All of these friends and she found herself pouting because there was no one to play with.

"Apparently I need more friends," Polly said to Obiwan who was sitting on the sofa beside her. He rolled over to show his belly and she rubbed it. Han looked up from the bone he was gnawing, saw that nothing important was happening and went back to his task. "I could take you two for a walk, but everywhere we go is no longer an adventure. It's known territory. What should I do?"

Obiwan made a noise in his throat and Polly stroked his chest. "You're right. We could do that. It sounds like a great idea. Let me change my clothes and then we're outta here."

It was a gorgeous sunny day, but the air was cool enough Polly wanted a sweatshirt. She changed her clothes and pulled her heavy-duty boots out. This walk was going to be bigger than a pair of tennis shoes. The dogs were both waiting, wagging their tails as she came back into the living room. "I can't believe I'm doing this. I just gave you two a bath."

They went down the back steps and Polly took two leashes, but didn't bother to put them on the dogs. She rolled them up around her hand. They walked down the tree line through sycamore leaves that crunched underfoot. Fall had taken a long time to arrive, but it was glorious now. With only a couple of weeks until Halloween, the property was beginning to put on its colorful fall garb.

Jason was in the pasture, throwing a big red ball into the air for the horses and donkeys.

"Hey there, Polly," he said, coming over to the fence. Tom followed and nuzzled her hand.

"The dogs and I are going exploring," she said. "I'd invite you to join us, but I know you're busy." She laughed and pointed at Demi trying to get his nose under the ball.

"Eliseo said we were all driving him crazy, so I thought it would be more fun out here. We got everything done this morning even without Heath." He grumbled out the last words and Polly glanced at him.

The two walked along the fence to the gate.

"What's up with that?" Polly asked as she waited for the dogs to enter the pasture.

"What?"

"You and Heath. Why don't you like him?"

Jason shrugged. It must be a high school boy thing. "He's fine."

"Fine seems like a bad thing."

"He's just..." He let it hang.

"Just what? Tell me, I'm trying to understand," Polly said.

"He doesn't do anything. He doesn't care about anything. He works here because he has to, but he doesn't like it. I can't believe anyone can be around these horses and not like them. He's never gotten close enough to one of them to find out if he does or not."

"It hasn't..."

Jason interrupted her. "I know, I know. It hasn't been easy since his parents died, but he should get over it. They aren't coming back and it's like he died too. How's he going to live if he just floats along?"

Polly glared at him. "You're one to take that stance. After all you've been through?"

"I figured it out, didn't I?"

"With a lot of help from everyone around you," she said. "Give the guy a break."

"Hey," Jason said. "I give him a break. You're the one who asked."

"Okay. You're right. I asked. Just be patient. Deal?"

"It's not my problem with patience," Jason said. "I don't care what he does. If he doesn't have friends or want to do anything with his life, that's his problem, not mine. I've got my own life to live."

Polly bit her tongue. If he wanted to be obtuse about this, fine. "I'm taking the dogs through the other field to try to find my way to Mikkels' new place. We haven't done that yet. See you later." She stalked across the pasture to the gate on the other side. It opened onto a bridge that spanned the creek. Eliseo had spent months working with the horses to teach them it was safe to cross that bridge. When she finally set foot in the south field, she stopped, took a breath and turned to look back at Jason. He pushed the ball with his foot toward Nan, gave it a small kick and she bent forward to lift it with her nose.

"I wanted to yell at him," she said to the dogs. "It's like he doesn't have any idea what people did for him when he was in trouble. That entitled freakin' brat. Not his problem, my ass." She kicked a clump of dirt and it broke apart. "How would he feel if I said that the next time he needed something. 'Not my problem, you selfish kid. Figure it out yourself.'"

Han must have seen something because he barked and leaped, running after it. Obiwan was close behind him and the two dogs chased whatever small animal was running for its life until they came to a sharp stop. Han started digging at the ground in front of him.

Polly chuckled. "Fine. I work myself into an emotional lather and you two want to play. Put me in my place, will you?"

They hadn't been in this field much and that meant there were new smells everywhere. The dogs could barely contain themselves as they marked territory and chased mice. Polly picked her way across the field. There wasn't a lot of land, but it was a long plot. Eliseo had tilled the north end for planting next spring. This south end he was leaving as pasture land for the horses. He'd mowed it down earlier in the season, but the grasses had grown up and the ground was uneven. She was glad she'd put her boots on. Walking was treacherous.

Nate and Joss's land backed up to theirs at a corner. There were only a few feet that they had in common. Directly to the west was farmland owned by Dan Severt. He'd sold this piece to Polly because it was useless to him. Though they'd met because one of his coyote traps had injured Obiwan, she'd enjoyed getting to know him and his wife, Leona.

Polly pulled up on the barbed wire fence to let the dogs through onto Nate's land, and then crawled through herself. Dan farmed right up to the edge of the property that bordered Nate's and Polly smiled as she looked out over the harvested corn field. She loved the fact that yards and fields were practically interchangeable. After living in the city for so long, it was still fun to see working farm land right on the edge of town. For that matter, there were a couple of small cornfields in strange places throughout Bellingwood. This was the life.

Obiwan and Han took off across the cornfield, chasing another small rodent and Polly watched them run. This was a great idea. Those two would be exhausted tonight and even if she had to give them another bath, the dirt would be worth it. She wandered over to a fence post and found a place between barbs to lean against it, watching the dogs chase each other.

She wasn't going to worry about Jason. He and Heath would have to work this out. Neither of them was going anywhere and it had only been a couple of months. She had to keep reminding herself of that. It felt like Heath had been with them forever. But he hadn't and he was still a messed up kid. She wasn't seeing discernible changes in him every day, but if she thought about it, he was better now than when he'd first moved in.

And when she dropped him off to spend the weekend with Hayden last night, she'd seen a glimmer of his potential. She needed to make sure those brothers spent more time together.

Obiwan started barking, an insistent bark, much different than his playful yipping and yapping. Polly looked for them and saw him standing in front of Han about seventy-five yards away. The younger dog was trying to get to something that Obiwan was protecting.

"Obiwan. Han. Come here," Polly commanded. Obiwan looked at her, snapped at Han and then barked again, refusing to move. Polly called again and when neither dog obeyed, walked across the field toward them.

This was even worse than the pasture she'd walked through. The ridges from the corn, the broken stalks and the debris didn't make walking easy. She continued to call the dogs and as she got closer, clicked her tongue against her teeth the way Henry had taught her. It was enough to make Han obey and he dashed for her side, wagging his tail the entire way. She reached down, caught his collar and snapped the leash on.

The closer she got to Obiwan, the more she realized that this was going to be bad. "What have you found, boy?" she asked softly, holding tight to Han's leash. Dirt and cornstalks made it nearly impossible to see what Obiwan was protecting until she was practically on top of it. She looked down, spun in her tracks and walked away, then dropped to her knees in the dirt and took deep breaths, willing herself to regain control of her esophagus.

Han rushed up, trying to lick her face.

"Stop it," she choked out. "Sit." He sat.

Polly collapsed to a seated position. "Why me?" She looked upwards. "Why me? Why? Why? Why? I hate this job. Can't you give it to someone else?"

She bent forward and propping her elbows on her legs, dropped her head into her hands. "I can't look at it again. I can't even think about it." She gulped once more. "Obiwan, come here, now." When he didn't move, she clapped her hands together. "I said, Come."

He looked down and then to her and slunk over. Polly snapped the other leash on his collar and pulled him in close so she could bury her face in his neck and shut everything else out.

"I have to make a phone call," she said. "Who would have thought?" Then it hit her. She should have realized. Anyone else in Bellingwood could walk into unknown territory and never encounter anything out of the ordinary, but not Polly Giller. All she had to do was wander away by herself.

Polly lifted her head and holding on to the two leashes with her left hand, dug the phone out of her back pocket. "He won't want to hear from me. Someday he's going to quit answering my calls."

She swiped the phone to place the call and waited as it rang.

"Beep. Aaron Merritt's phone. If this is anyone but Polly Giller, simply say hello, but if this is Polly Giller, you've done it again, haven't you. Beep."

"Stop it," she said. "I know it's you. I've heard your voice mail before."

"Are you calling me for your regular reason?" he asked.

"Yes and this is a bad one."

"What do you mean bad? Bad as in you know the person really well - bad?"

"No. There's no way I can tell who this is - bad. It's horrible, Aaron. I nearly puked my guts out."

"Oh Polly, I'm sorry. Where are you?"

Dan Severt's cornfield."

He gave a pathetic chuckle. "What are you doing in Dan's cornfield? The one behind your land? Why in the world are you there?"

Polly heaved a huge sigh. "Apparently I needed to find this body. I told the dogs I wanted an adventure today. I found one."

"Tell me how to find you. I'm on my way."

She described where she was and they both agreed that it was easier for him to come at it from the Mikkels' entrance. It was still quite a hike to get to the field, but there were no fences in the way and it was flat ground.

"Can you stay near the body or is it too awful?" Aaron asked.

"I'm about fifteen feet away from it," Polly responded. "I can stay here. I might even be able to stand back up by the time you arrive. This is really awful, Aaron. I think coyotes got to the body. All that's left of the head is..."

"Stop right there," he said. "Don't do it to yourself. I'll see it soon enough. Did your dogs get into it?"

"Han wanted to, but Obiwan wouldn't let him. I'm sure it smells like interesting meat to them."

"That dog of yours is amazing, Polly. I'd keep him around for as long as possible."

"I intend to," she said. "I'm not sure how I was so lucky, but I should probably tell Doug and Billy thank you again for finding him. He stood guard until I got there to snap a leash on Han."

"So why are you out and about by yourself today?" Aaron asked.

Polly huffed. "Because everyone else is busy. Even the kids were too busy to do something with me. Henry and Nate are moving Nate's shop, your wife is in Dayton." She chuckled as she realized what was happening. "Are you trying to distract me until you arrive? Because I'll be fine. I know you need to call this in."

"You know me too well," he said. "Are you sure?"

"We're fine here. I'm far enough away that I don't have to look at it and I can keep myself from thinking about it too intensely. Just hurry."

"I'm heading up R27 now. I should be there in fifteen minutes or less."

"Thanks, Aaron." Polly swiped the call closed.

Han was lying down, his head on her leg. Obiwan was in front of her, on full alert, watching the area where he'd found the body.

Polly hadn't taken much time to look, but she'd seen enough. Of *course* the goriest body she'd ever seen had been found just before Halloween. She shuddered. Rebecca had asked about ghosts the other night and then yesterday she was asking to spend time in a cemetery. Polly hadn't put those two things together until just now. What was happening with those kids? What had they seen? She should be proud of them for confronting it on their own. Now her own curiosity was setting in. What were they getting into?

"Maybe I should have sent you with them, Obiwan," she said, tugging him back to her. "Of course, I wouldn't have found this poor person today, but they might need you if there are ghosts and ghoulies out there." He sat back on his haunches, craned his neck to lick her face, then turned back to face the body.

"You're such a good dog," she said, stroking his back. She gathered her legs under her and stood up. Polly stopped herself from trying to look at the body again. She couldn't help it, even though she didn't want to see it.

Fortunately, she was saved by the sight of Aaron's SUV driving across the ground. He stopped in front of the field's edge and started across toward her. Han barked with joy at the sight of another human being. He was such a happy, goofy dog. Obiwan recognized Aaron and still refused to turn away from the body.

"I think I can tell where it is," Aaron said, pointing at the dog.

"He's intent on not losing sight of it," Polly responded. "I'm sorry to drag you out on a Saturday afternoon."

Aaron scowled. "Don't ever be sorry about that. If someone needs you to find them, I'll always be here to back you up. Stay here while I check this out." He walked away from her in the direction that Obiwan was pointing, coming to a slow stop. He stayed in place and took in the entire scene, then backed up and retraced his steps. "You were right," he said, exhaling loudly. "That's a bad one." He lifted his head at the sound of a siren. "That's my team. They'll be here in a few minutes. You can leave."

"Thank you," Polly said. "I didn't do anything around the body and you practically took my same steps in."

"I did take your steps," he said with a grin. "And I've learned to trust you." He patted her back. "I'm proud of you for not losing it, though. Not many would be able to keep it together."

Polly shook her head. "I got out of there so fast that my body wasn't sure what to experience. That was probably my only saving grace. We'll get out of here before everyone else arrives. Thanks for coming so fast."

Aaron stuck a colored flag into the ground where she'd been sitting, then stood back up and gave her a quick hug. "I'll walk with you over to the grass. Do you want someone to give you a ride home?"

Polly took a moment and then said, "No, we'll walk back across the pasture. I'll try to shake this off before I get home."

She held the barbed wire up for the dogs to pass under, transferring the leashes between her hands. Aaron parted the wire for her to crawl through and turned away to go back to his task. Polly held the dog's leashes until they crossed the bridge and were back in home territory. Jason was nowhere to be seen and for that she was thankful. All she wanted to do was go back to her apartment and sit in silence.

CHAPTER FIVE

Awakened by the sound of feet on the back steps, Polly sat up and patted herself down to make sure everything was in order.

"Polly?" Henry asked.

"In here on the couch," she replied.

He rushed into the living room and sat down beside her. "Are you okay? Why didn't you call me?"

"I didn't want to bother you when you were having fun with Nate. And no, I'm not being a martyr. This is old hat, right?"

Henry opened his arms and she leaned in, letting him hold her tight. "It's not old hat, though, and you know it. No matter how often it happens, you still have to face it. You should have called."

"How did you find out anyway?" Polly pulled back to look at him.

"When we drove in, there were emergency vehicles on Nate's property. It took twenty minutes to find Aaron so he could tell us what happened. He said it was pretty awful for you." He pulled her in against his body and leaned the two of them back on the sofa. "What were you doing over there?"

"I thought maybe we'd come see you. I hadn't found the

connecting point between our land and Nate's yet, so when everyone left today it seemed like the perfect time to go exploring. Do you know how wonderful it is out there? The dogs were chasing mice and playing with each other." Polly swallowed hard. "Until I saw what Obiwan was protecting. Then things turned ugly. Did Aaron say anything else to you? Do they have any idea what happened?"

"No. He didn't tell me. Someone called Dan Severt and he came over."

"What did he say?" Polly asked.

"He's upset that it happened in his field and asked if you needed anything."

"Did his combine tear up the body? It was a mess."

"He finished that field three weeks ago and someone said the body hadn't been there that long. Dan was quite concerned."

"I'll bet. I can't imagine how horrible that would be for him. At least he doesn't have that hanging over him. Did you hear anybody say anything about why the body was such a mess?"

"They were assuming exposure and animals."

She chuckled to herself.

"What's so funny?" he asked.

"We need one of those television forensics people to show up and look at their bones, maybe build a computer image of the face. You know, flashy TV stuff."

"You're a nut. Aaron's friend from the Department of Criminal Investigation was there. They'll deal with it. You've done your job, they can do theirs."

"I hope I'm done this time," she said. "And I hope it isn't someone we know." Polly sighed. "I don't mean that. It's someone's child or friend or spouse or parent. They know this person well. It's so sad."

"And you've made sure that they were found and the family can have closure, no matter what's going on."

Polly relaxed and breathed him in. Was it odd that even when he'd been working, his scent was still her favorite thing? "What time is it?"

"Four o'clock," he said. "Nate and I are done for the day."

"You didn't have to stop so early. I told the kids to be back by five. They'd have kept me occupied tonight."

He stroked her hair and ran his hand down her back - over and over as she continued to relax. "It's one thing when I can't be there for you if I'm working, but on weekends like this, you are still my priority. Will you ever understand that?"

"Don't be silly," she mumbled into his flannel shirt. "I can take care of myself."

"Of course you can." He continued to rub her back and Polly breathed slower and slower.

~~~

Polly stirred awake again when Henry moved.

"I'm sorry," he said. "I didn't want to wake you."

She sat up. "It's okay. I didn't even know I was tired. How long was I asleep?"

"About twenty minutes. The kids are coming up the steps."

They'd been gone a long time. Polly couldn't imagine what had occupied them for so long. If they weren't in the apartment, they were usually down at the barn so today's adventure was new territory for them. The dogs leaped down to say hello and even the cats were interested in the return of the explorers.

"I'm okay," she whispered to Henry. "I promise. Thanks for coming home." Polly kissed him and stood up.

The three kids were standing in a row across the doorway.

"How was your afternoon?" she asked.

"We need to talk to you guys," Rebecca said. She took a step into the living room and then turned to make sure Kayla and Andrew were following her. They hesitated, but soon all three kids were sitting on the sofa across from Polly and Henry.

"This sounds serious," Henry said, taking Polly's hand and pulling her back down to the couch.

Rebecca wet her lips and then glanced at the other two kids. Neither were interested in speaking - it was up to her. "We might have done something stupid today and then we broke a window and we didn't mean to, it just kind of happened. I don't know if anybody saw it, but just in case, we wanted you to hear it from us first. Polly, are you sure you don't believe in ghosts? Because we saw one today and this isn't the first time."

"Whoa," Polly said, putting her hands up. "Back up. Where have you been today?"

All three kids hung their heads.

"One of you is going to tell us what's going on," Henry said. "But first, is anybody hurt? When you broke the window, did anyone get cut?"

They shook their heads.

Polly turned to Henry. "Are you seeing what I'm seeing?"

He chuckled. "Hear no evil, see no evil, speak no evil? If I position their hands, will you take a picture?"

"You're not being serious," Rebecca chided them.

"We don't know what you're talking about yet," Polly said. "Tell us the whole story. And maybe you don't start with today, but earlier this week. I seem to remember you asking me about ghosts one night."

"I did. Because we saw one. I'm sure of it. And everybody knows the house is haunted. They were talking about it at school this week."

"What house?" Polly asked.

Henry sat back and crossed his legs. "It's the old Springer House, isn't it?"

Andrew nodded. "It's really scary there."

"You know about this?" Polly asked Henry.

He nodded. "It's been a source of spooky campfire tales for decades. Even before *I* was in junior high." He glanced over at the kids. Apparently, the fact that Henry knew something cool like this gave them newfound respect for him.

"What's the story?" Polly pressed.

"As the story goes - Muriel Springer hung herself from the upstairs banister after she received notice that her husband had died in the war. But then he returned. There'd been a mix-up in paperwork and transfer orders and he was alive after all. He didn't realize what had happened until he arrived in Bellingwood and discovered she was dead. It was all very tragic.

"After a proper mourning period, he married another woman and they started a family. But," Henry paused and looked at each person in the eye. "Then the second child was born. It was too much for poor Muriel and she came back in a fury. She gave them no peace, screaming through the house at night. They'd never know when she would show up and just about the time they believed she'd moved on, she was back. The poor family couldn't sleep safely in their own home. Muriel knocked family pictures off walls and tables and broke china and crystal that had been the second couple's wedding gifts.

Henry stopped again and waited to make sure they were all paying attention. Andrew's mouth was wide open and he'd moved forward on the couch, ready to pounce. Kayla had slid closer to Rebecca and was leaning against her friend. Polly had been completely taken in by the story and watched as Henry held the kids in his thrall.

He continued. "And then one night, John Springer went into the nursery to check on his baby before going to bed and he saw Muriel hovering over the child, her ghostly hands wrapped around its neck. He grabbed the baby and ran for the front door, yelling at his wife to wake up and get their son out of bed. He put the baby in the car and then ran back. Muriel stood at the railing, her hands holding the rope that was tied to the banister and around her neck. As his current wife ran for the front door, he watched as Muriel threw herself over the railing and died in front of him. He put his hands on the front door, looked up and she repeated the entire scenario again and again, screaming his name each time she fell. They left the house that night without taking anything but the clothes on their backs. No one knows where they moved to and the house was left to sit."

Polly tucked her legs underneath her and patted her side for Obiwan to get closer. Goosebumps had risen on her forearms and she rubbed her hands across them. "That's creepy. I had no idea."

"It isn't true," Henry said. "Yes, the house was owned by the Springers, but my grandfather told me that John Springer received an incredible job offer from a company in Chicago. He was given less than forty-eight hours to get there. It was such a good opportunity, they packed only what they could fit in their car, left everything else and moved on. Muriel's death had weighed heavily on him and his new wife was never truly accepted in Bellingwood. People couldn't see past the fact that she'd replaced a popular young local woman who had died tragically at the news of her war hero husband's death." He looked at Polly. "You know those busybody types who are always critical. They still live here."

"Surely not the same busybodies," she said. "They'd be ancient."

"They had kids. Lots and lots of kids. It was the fifties and everyone was glad the war was over. But they learned how to be busybodies from their parents, that's for sure."

"Now I know the story of the house. What does this have to do with you three?" Polly asked.

"Muriel is real," Rebecca said. "A bunch of kids at school saw her. And you know, it's been seventy years since she died. Penny Crosby's grandmother told her that she killed herself on Halloween and comes back every ten years to see if John is here."

Polly smiled. "Oh honey, it's only a ghost story. Henry just told you that there is a much more reasonable explanation for why the Springers left town. Were you at the house this afternoon? Is that where you broke the window?"

"She's really real," Rebecca insisted. "We saw her the other night."

"What night?" Henry asked. "You're home every night."

"No, after school. We went by the house and saw her in there." Rebecca looked at Andrew and then at Kayla. They both nodded in agreement.

Henry scowled. "That house isn't on your way home. Did you tell Polly you were going to be late?"

Rebecca dropped her head again. "You guys were in Boone at the trial and didn't come home until late. And we just walked up there and then came straight home."

"Well," Andrew interrupted. "We stopped at the bakery to see when Mom was picking me up."

"And your sister wasn't worried that you were late?" Polly asked.

Kayla looked at the floor. "We called from the bakery. She thought we were there the whole time."

As little rebellions went, this wasn't a big deal and the kids were shook up by whatever had happened to them today. Polly found herself biting her upper lip to keep from scolding them. Kids were kids and she'd much rather they tested their limits in ways like this.

However, Henry stepped right in. "If something had happened to the three of you, no one would have known where you were. When your families expect you to be here at Sycamore House, we're responsible for you. It's not fair to any of us when you lie."

"I'm sorry," Rebecca said, her lower lip quivering.

"Yeah," Andrew echoed. "Sorry."

Kayla nodded, her eyes brimming with tears.

"It's okay," Polly said. "You all know better. Don't do that again. It makes me less inclined to say yes when you want me to trust you when you ask to go off on your own. Got it?"

They nodded again.

"Now, tell us about what happened today," she said, putting her hand on Henry's leg. She felt his muscles clench and knew it was going to take a moment for him to calm down. This next story probably wouldn't help. Polly slowly rubbed her hand back and forth, trying to soothe him. "Was the story about decorating the cemetery true or did you make that up?"

Andrew looked at Rebecca. "Kids were talking about it. Someone said that it would be a good idea to hang sheets from the trees and make them look like ghosts."

"Who in the world said that?" Polly asked.

He gave her a weak smile. "Me."

She couldn't help herself and laughed out loud. "Did anyone else at school think that was a good idea?"

"Not really," he said.

"So you lied to Polly again," Henry said, his voice lower and quieter than usual.

"We're sorry," Rebecca said. "We just had to go to the Springer House and see if it was true. There were a bunch of kids that were going to meet up there today. We thought it had to be safe in the middle of the afternoon."

"How many are a bunch of you?" Polly asked, her hand still rubbing Henry's leg. He put his hand on top of hers and gripped her fingers. This dad thing was going to be hard for him. He'd only seen Rebecca's acquiescent, obedient side. Polly was going to have to remind him that she was still a kid and there were going to be plenty of things she did that would make him mad as hell.

No, she'd have a talk with Marie and see if maybe his mother could remind him what he and Lonnie had been like at this age. Polly knew for a fact that they were as normal as anyone could be.

"Maybe six or seven," Rebecca responded. "Some didn't show up."

"So you met at the Springer House this afternoon and spent three hours there and broke a window?"

"No, we didn't spend the whole afternoon there. We went to the coffee shop first to meet. We were all supposed to get there by two o'clock. Some of them were late though, and we didn't leave until like three or something. And then because we didn't get started on time, everybody else had to go home, so it was just us."

"Just the three of you?" Polly asked.

Rebecca nodded. "We packed flashlights and stuff. First we went to Andrew's house and got a pair of hedge clippers. That yard is way grown over. When we tried the gate the last time, we couldn't get it open. We had to cut some of the bushes. That took forever. I don't think anyone has been in there in seventy years."

Henry took a breath to speak and Polly squeezed his hand.

"Go on," Polly said.

"Have you seen that place?" Andrew asked. "Like up close? There are boards on the windows and the porch is sagging and it looks like there is an old garage, but there are vines all over it. It is one creepy building. If someone cleaned up the yard and did something about the house, it would look cool. It's huge – like a mansion."

Polly put her hand up to stop him. "How did you break a window if they were boarded up? And for that matter, how could you see a ghost if you can't see in the windows?"

"I broke the window," Kayla whispered. "I'll pay for it."

"We walked around the front of the house," Rebecca said. "And there are windows in the upstairs that don't have boards anymore. But the door on the breezeway wasn't boarded up either."

Kayla continued for her. "I didn't mean to break it. I was shining the flashlight into the room, trying to see and I thought something moved. I jumped and the flashlight hit the window and it broke."

"That's when we ran," Andrew said. "But when nobody came out and chased us, we went back and looked in. I tried to open the door and it's locked. Rebecca wouldn't let me pull on it. She said we were probably in enough trouble since the window was broken."

"Did you see the ghost?" Polly took her hand back from Henry and rubbed it against her other hand, trying to restore blood flow. He'd finally relaxed again.

"I saw a white dress in the upstairs window," Rebecca said. "It had to have been her. There was dust on the front porch and nobody had been on the back steps either. So it couldn't be a person. It has to be a ghost."

"How about you two?" Henry asked. "Did you see the ghost?"

"I was busy looking inside," Andrew said. "By the time Rebecca showed me which window to look in, she was gone."

"And you, Kayla?" Polly asked.

She shook her head. "I was too scared. I just wanted to leave."

"Are we in big trouble?" Rebecca asked. "It's all my fault. They shouldn't be in trouble. I'm the one who wanted to go up there today and I'm the one who wanted to go up there the other day, too."

Polly and Henry looked at each other. If he was thinking what she was thinking, it was that neither of them knew quite how to

49

set a punishment for something as silly as this. He nodded at her. Great. This was her job.

"Here's what I expect you to do. Kayla and Andrew, you have to tell Stephanie and Sylvie the whole story. Not part of it, the whole thing. If they want to punish you for any part of it, that's up to them. And trust me, you don't want them to hear this story from me, am I right?"

They nodded enthusiastically.

"Rebecca," Polly continued. "There will be consequences for lying to us in the first place. They're somewhat mitigated by the fact that you're telling us everything now. We will discuss that later. As for the window, Henry will check into it. We have no idea who owns the house or what will be done about it. If we have to replace the window, the three of you will work off the cost. Sound fair?"

Andrew took a deep breath and slumped back on the couch. "I thought we were dead meat," he said.

CHAPTER SIX

Soaking rain poured out of the sky as they got ready for their Monday morning and Polly drove Rebecca the few blocks to school. She watched her daughter run for the front door, then turn and wave before going in. These little moments still pulled at her heart strings.

Hayden had brought Heath back to Bellingwood last night and though he couldn't stay for dinner, came up for a few minutes to hear the story Polly told to Heath about her encounter with the dead body on Saturday. News had traveled fast, getting to them in Ames early Saturday evening.

Since Hayden hadn't been there since before school started, Heath showed him the property. Polly watched the brothers walk through the back yard from her bedroom window. Heath had playfully shoved his brother and Hayden returned it by wrestling him to the ground. Polly backed away from the window so they wouldn't catch her spying on that relaxed moment. There hadn't been enough of those in the last few years for either one of them.

After Hayden left, Heath listened as Rebecca described the haunted house to him, actually involving himself in the conversation. Polly hoped that was the beginning of positive change for him.

This morning, though, he'd returned to his quiet, uninvolved personality, eating breakfast and then hiding in his room until it was time for the bus to arrive.

Polly drove away from the elementary school and headed straight for the Springer House. She had to see this place for herself. She'd driven past it once or twice, but it was off any major road, so she'd never spent much time looking at it. When she turned the corner, she laughed out loud and pushed a button on her dash.

"What's up, hotstuff?" Henry asked after answering the phone.

"I'm right behind you. What are you doing over here?"

"What?" he asked with a laugh. "I'm at the office."

"Liar, liar," she said. Polly pulled up beside him on the street and lowered her passenger window, waiting for his to open.

"It's raining. I'd rather talk to you on the phone," he said, brushing raindrops off his shirt.

"Why are you here?"

"Same as you," he said. "I was looking the place over before making some phone calls. No one has thought about this house in years."

Polly pointed to the second story. A room jutted out over the main porch. "What's that room? A sun porch?"

"Probably a tuberculosis solarium. I can't believe we have one of those here in Bellingwood. This is a classic old house. How has it been ignored?"

"There's a *ghost*?" Polly said, laughing.

Henry nodded. "Actually, that's probably right. Unless they want the experience of it, people won't choose to buy a home where there's been a violent death. I'm surprised the city hasn't taken over the land and done something here. Dad and I are going to ask more questions today."

"Do you want me to do anything? I can go down to Boone and look through documents," Polly said.

"If we can't find the information in a hurry, I'll let you know."

Polly leaned on her console. "We didn't talk about Heath yet. I'm worried about him. He was doing so much better last night and then it all turned around this morning."

"It's going to take longer than a couple of months, Polly," Henry said. "He'll have ups and downs and then someday the ups will be longer than the downs and none of us will realize what kind of transformation he's made. It will just have happened."

She nodded and then shook her head. "I'm worried that it will go the other way. Or that something will trip him up before he's able to stabilize. We only have a couple of years with him and then he'll be gone."

"Stop it," Henry said. "Just because he graduates from high school doesn't mean he's going away. And don't waste the days he's with us by worrying. We'll figure out more ways to be proactive with him. This weekend was a step in the right direction. He'll take more of those."

"Whatever." Polly sat back up. He drove her crazy when he was pragmatic. Sometimes she wanted to freak out.

Henry looked over at her and smiled. "I love you, you know."

"Yeah. I know."

"And you love me."

"I know that, too." She couldn't help herself and smiled back at him. "Roll your window up. I'll talk to you tonight."

He waved as she drove off. They needed to talk more about Heath. If there was one thing Polly enjoyed doing it was connecting people with their passions. She hadn't been able to unearth what it was that Heath enjoyed. She wasn't ready to go back to Sycamore House, so drove downtown and parked in front of Sweet Beans Coffee Shop and Bakery. Caffeine would help. She'd only had one cup of coffee so far this morning.

There were a few people in the shop when she walked in. Camille had hired two other part-time employees to work early mornings during the week. Most of the retired farmers still met at Joe's Diner. They would never draw that group away from their morning watering hole, but the coffee shop was seeing increased business. Jeff and Camille had put together a nice package for teachers at the elementary school and were surprised to discover that several of them enjoyed spending late afternoon hours in the coffee shop, grading papers and writing out lesson plans.

"Hello Polly," Camille said, coming out from behind the counter. "You're here early."

Polly grinned. She usually met Joss up here early afternoon before the influx of kids at the library. "Dropped Rebecca off at school and don't feel like going back to work yet."

"May I introduce you to someone?" Camille asked.

Polly looked around the room. She recognized most everyone. "Sure," she said.

Camille led her straight to that table and said, "Polly, I'd like you to meet Jen Dykstra. She's planning to open a quilt shop next door." Camille touched the woman's shoulder. "Jen, this is Polly Giller."

The woman stood and smiled. She was in her late forties or early fifties with curly brown hair and bright blue eyes. "I've been hearing all about you," she said. "Come, sit with us. We're looking over plans that Sandy sketched out. Do you two know each other? And this is Sonya Biederman." She pulled a chair out and waited for Polly to sit.

Camille smiled and leaned over. "Your regular?"

"Double shot of espresso this morning," Polly replied. "Please."

The other two women leaned forward to shake her hand and smiled at her. Sandy whoever-she-was pushed pieces of paper in front of Polly. They looked like professionally done CAD drawings of the space next door.

"Did you do this?" Polly asked.

"Architect in another life," Sandy replied. "We just had a baby and I chose to slow down until I couldn't stand it. So far, that isn't happening."

Polly had a flash of a memory. "Is your husband Benji?"

Sandy grinned. "I didn't think we'd ever met before. But yes, we're the Davis's. How do you know us?"

"You won't even believe it," Polly said, shaking her head. "Lydia Merritt had to come rescue me one day this summer and she was making a casserole for you because you'd just had the baby."

"I can't believe you remembered that."

Polly continued to shake her head. "I can't either. That was a weird day though, and sometimes little things get stuck in my head. How's the baby?"

"He's good. Benji's mother has him today so I can do this." She smiled at Jen. "It's wonderful having a grandmother available who will help out. And she's so good with the baby. Everybody needs a grandma in their life."

"We love it as much as you do," Jen replied. She turned to Polly. "I have two little ones who come to my house in the afternoons so their mother can work. She likes being independent. I guess that's the way I raised her."

Camille put a mug in front of Polly, winked and walked away.

"I had no idea this was happening in Bellingwood," Polly said. "It's exciting."

"We've not said much to anyone in case things fell through, but we closed on the building last week and now we're ready to move forward," Jen said.

"The three of you are doing this together?" Polly asked, looking around the table.

"It's all Jen's baby," Sandy replied. "She had the idea and she's the creative one. I'm the organized one." She turned to Sonya, who had been quiet through the chatter.

"I don't know what I am," Sonya said. "But I'm having fun." Sonya Biederman was in her early sixties, with shoulder-length, silver hair. Her face still held a tan from working in the summer sun and the wrinkles around her eyes creased when she smiled.

"She's an amazing seamstress," Jen broke in. "And you should see her quilts. They're amazing. She's going to be teaching classes. If you don't know how to sew, Sonya is the one who will give you confidence in a short period of time."

"I've never even owned a sewing machine," Polly said. "But I'd give anything to change that." She pointed at the wall. "You're moving in right next door?"

Jen nodded. "That's us. Coffee next door, pizza across the street. I'm going to have to put out hand wipes everywhere so people won't mess up the fabric."

"Are you just doing sewing and quilting or will there be other things too?" Polly asked. "We have a couple of knitting classes that meet at Sycamore House and I know they'd love to have a better place to work. Somewhere downtown and somewhere there might be an inventory of yarns and supplies. That's probably the hardest thing for them. Everyone has to always be prepared and do their craft shopping in Boone or Ames." She pursed her lips. "I was actually thinking that we should open a craft shop, but if you're doing this..." Polly let her thought trail off.

Sandy looked at the other two ladies and laughed. "We've talked about it and right now, fabric is going to take up every square inch of our space, but if we're lucky and things go well, the bay on the other side is open and we can always expand."

"Show me," Polly said, looking at the pages in front of her. She pointed at a sheet. "What's this?"

"We're going to use the second floor, but I want to open it up." Sandy pointed at the back of the shop. "We'll put stairs in the front, but an elevator back here. I know a lot of older women whose knees are shot and can't be traipsing up and down stairs for classes and fabric. They won't show up if it's uncomfortable. They can park out back, we'll put a ramp in and then they can go right up the elevator. We'll have two classrooms and then I want to cut out the floor in the middle and put a railing around it."

"That should be awesome," Polly said. "Who's doing the build-out?"

Jen Dykstra didn't miss a beat. "Well, lucky that we're chatting with you today. We've heard that Sturtz Construction is too busy to take on any new jobs."

Polly sat back, "They are? I don't think so."

"That's the word around town," Sandy replied.

"Let me ask the horse," Polly said and took out her phone. She stood up and walked toward the front door and watched the rain come down.

"Hello, sweet thing," Henry said.

"Are you too busy for new work?" she asked.

"Uhh, what?"

"I'm at the coffee shop, talking to three women who bought the space next door and want to build out a quilt shop. They said you're too busy to take on anything new."

"Oh. Well, yeah. We're busy."

Polly shook her head. "That makes no sense to me. It's just construction. Hire more workers and take on more jobs."

"And then what am I supposed to do with them when the work goes away?" he asked.

"Okay, I suppose you know your business. It seems a shame to let a job like this flutter away."

She heard him heave a deep sigh. "You're going to be the death of me. Who is it that you're talking to?"

"Jen Dykstra, Sandy Davis and Sonya Biederman."

"That explains where the money's coming from."

"Which one?" Polly asked.

"Dykstras and Biedermans. There's a lot of money there. I don't know Sandy Davis. Unless she's married to..."

"Benji," Polly said.

He chuckled. "For heaven's sake. Benji Davis." Henry laughed again.

"What's so funny?"

"I went to school with him. He's a good guy. Didn't think he'd make much of himself, but he surprised us all. He's a lawyer in Ames. I heard he met his wife in college. She's not from around here. I didn't realize they moved to Bellingwood."

"She seems nice," Polly said. "They want you on this job. And it looks cool. Sandy is an architect."

Henry took a loud breath. "Fine. Tell them to call Jessie and set up a time to meet. We'll see what we can do. This kind of puts off a surprise I was going to give to you, though."

"What?" Polly asked.

"Nope. I only discuss one building project a day with you. This was your limit."

"Come on," she pleaded. "Tell me."

"I love you very much. Have them call Jessie. I need to go to work." Henry ended the call, leaving Polly standing there with her mouth open.

She texted back to him. *"You rat. You know you're in trouble tonight, don't you?"*

"I love you," he replied.

"Henry says to call his office manager, Jessie, and set up a meeting," Polly told the women as she went back to the table. "Apparently, he is busy, but I have my ways." She winked at them and then giggled.

"Really?" Sandy asked. "You had to pull the wife card?"

Polly shook her head. "No. He said he'd be glad to talk to you. However, he also told me that it was going to push off a surprise he'd planned for me, so you owe me."

"If this happens and he builds out the space for us, your first sewing class is on us." Jen patted Polly's hand.

Sonya leaned in and said quietly. "If he does the work, she can take as many classes as she wants. Right?"

Jen laughed. "That's our negotiator. She'd give away the shop if we let her. But if he agrees to do this for us, we know it will be done right and done well."

"Henry said he went to high school with your husband," Polly said to Sandy. She tried to place the young woman's age. They'd waited a long time to have children.

Sandy watched Polly processing and chuckled. "I'm three years younger than Benji and yes, we waited to have a child. Honestly, I didn't think I'd ever want this and when I got pregnant, I was as surprised as anyone."

"And you chose to give up your career?"

"Not completely. I still do freelance work for them, but I don't go into the office every day and it's okay. I'm happy."

She didn't sound that happy, but Polly let it go. People made choices in their lives and she barely knew this woman.

Sandy gave her head a quick shake and bent over toward Polly and in a conspiratorial whisper, asked, "So is it true about you?"

"Is what true?" Polly knew what was coming, but she liked to make people ask.

"You know," Sandy said. "You find dead bodies?"

"That's me. Grim Reaper."

"So you found that body in the field the other day?" Sonya asked.

Polly nodded.

"Do they know who it is yet?" This from Jen Dykstra.

"Not that I've heard. The sheriff doesn't tell me much unless I get up in his face. And then it's only because I pester him," Polly said. "Or I sic his wife on him."

"Lydia's been good to us," Sandy said. "We live down the street. I couldn't believe it when she showed up with food and then arranged it so other people from church did, too. It made those first weeks a lot easier. I was so not used to being at home and having to learn how to feed myself, Benji and a baby. Benji and I never ate at home before the baby. It was either over at his mom's house or we met after work in Ames. All we did was come home, collapse and go to work again."

"This is a big change for you, isn't it?" Polly asked.

Sandy nodded. "I'm trying to get used to it. It's getting easier and working with these two has been fun." She chuckled. "Everyone's on a mission to teach me to be more relaxed."

"I need to introduce you to Sal Kahane," Polly said.

Jen looked around. "Doesn't she own this place?"

"Yeah, but she grew up in Boston. Sometimes Bellingwood drives her absolutely out of her mind."

"I grew up in Denver," Sandy said. "This has taken some getting used to, but I've lived in Iowa since college." She glanced up. "We moved to Bellingwood after I found out I was pregnant. Benji thought it would be easier if we were closer to his mother. He was right, but I was so glad when you opened the coffee shop. Even if I couldn't drink caffeine, I knew someday I would again and at least I could come in and sniff it."

Polly laughed. "Yes, you need to meet Sal. You'll hit it right off."

DIANE GREENWOOD MUIR

Jen gathered up the papers from in front of her and gestured for the others to be pushed her way. "I'll set up a meeting with Polly's husband," she said. "Sandy, you and I need to find a time when you're available. Sonya, do you want to be there?"

"Maybe not at the first meeting. You girls have this in hand." She stood up. "I have a quilt to finish for a new grandbaby who's going to show up any day now, so I should be home and sewing. It was nice to meet you, Miss Giller."

"Polly. Please," Polly said.

She nodded and smiled before walking away. Jen stood up and slid the papers into a portfolio. "You two sit and chat. I have things to do before my kiddos come. I'll be in touch, Sandy." She shook Polly's hand and followed her friend out of the shop.

"What do you do on Sunday evenings?" Polly asked Sandy.

"Nothing." Sandy shrugged. "Why?"

"Sal and Sylvie, myself and Joss Mikkels all eat pizza together over at Pizzazz. Nearly every week. You should join us. It's no big deal; just a chance to get our heads on straight before a new week."

"Sylvie Donovan, the baker?"

"Yeah. And Joss is the librarian. We're friends who eat pizza. Sal's boyfriend is Mark Ogden, the veterinarian. Do you have animals?"

Sandy shook her head. "Are you kidding? I can barely take care of people in my life. I'm much better with lines and drawings than I am with living things."

"Anyway, his sister runs the dance studio in town and her husband, Dylan, owns Pizzazz, so we hang out."

"You know everyone, don't you," Sandy said. "If it weren't for these two ladies and Mrs. Merritt, I wouldn't know a soul in Bellingwood."

Polly laughed. "That's funnier than it should be," she replied. "I spent two years feeling like I didn't know anyone at all. Every time I turned around, I was meeting someone I should have already known. It will get easier. So, Sunday?"

"Let me see if Benji will be okay if I'm gone. He's not any better

60

with humans, and try as he might, this daddy thing is about to push him over the edge. We were not cut out for this."

"I know some baby sitters," Polly said.

"Do you have kids?"

Polly laughed again. "Oh, Sandy, if you only knew how crazy that question is. You are only a couple of years younger than me. I have two kids, but not because I gave birth. My daughter, Rebecca, is twelve and we adopted her after her mother died last spring. We're also guardians of a high school junior whose parents were killed a couple of years ago. So, yes, I have kids, but no I didn't have babies."

"Wow."

"I guess that describes it. You'll love Sal, because she'll get you, but you'll also love Joss and Sylvie. Joss wants a big family. She and her husband." Polly glanced at Sandy. "That's Nate Mikkels, the pharmacist at the drug store. Anyway, they adopted twins last year. I can promise you that she will help you in any way she can. Sylvie has two boys, a sophomore in high school and a seventh grader. She's on the opposite end of the spectrum as you. She's just getting started with her professional life and loves being a mom, too." Polly reached out to touch Sandy's arm. "You need to know us. We might not give you a lot of help, but we'll have fun."

"Okay. I didn't expect this."

"Have you gotten to know Camille?" Polly asked, waving the coffee shop manager over.

"I just met her today," Sandy said.

"Camille, you need to know Sandy, too," Polly said. "And you should probably come have pizza with us on Sunday nights."

Camille smiled. "Sal and Sylvie asked if I'd come. I think this next week I will finally be available. So yes, I'll be there. Are you coming too, Sandy?"

"It sounds like I'd be crazy to miss it," Sandy said.

CHAPTER SEVEN

The three kids - Andrew, Rebecca and Kayla - were at Polly's dining room table working on homework when her phone rang.

"Hey Eliseo, what's up?" she asked.

"Heath didn't come back on the bus. Jason didn't see him."

"Is Jason there? Can I talk to him?"

"Just a sec."

Polly waited for a moment and then Jason said, "Yeah?"

"Heath didn't say anything to you?" she asked.

"No, why would he?"

"I don't know. You both come to Sycamore House and you work together in the barn after school."

"I'm not his keeper," Jason said. "He does what he wants."

Polly was done. "Look, Jason. I'm not asking you to be his keeper. He can take care of himself, but I do expect respect and compassion out of you. People have extended themselves to you a lot over the last couple of years and for you to take this attitude with anyone is out of line. I'm tired of it."

"He didn't get on the bus. He didn't talk to me. That's all I can tell you," Jason said.

"You know we aren't finished with this conversation, right?"

"I figured," he muttered. "Here's Eliseo."

"Trouble?" Eliseo asked.

"Nothing we can't work out. I'll call Heath and see what's going on and let you know. Thanks for telling me," she said.

"We'll be fine here this evening without him. No worries."

"Thanks." Polly hung up and looked at her phone. She knew it had been too good to last.

After scrolling through her numbers, she landed on Heath's and swiped the call. It rang and rang and went to voice mail. "Heath?" she said. "This is Polly. You can't not show up and not tell me either. Call me as soon as you hear this. You don't want me to worry, right?"

She swiped the call closed and then re-dialed. If he was ignoring her calls, she was going to pester him. How in the world did her dad live without knowing how to reach her? She remembered Mary telling her that it wasn't fair of Polly to make her father worry about finding her dead in a ditch. It had only taken one incident of him being white with worry when she showed up late one night. She'd discovered that making a quick call was better than the other consequences.

This time Heath picked up. "Hello?"

"Heath, it's Polly. Are you okay?"

"Yeah. Sorry. I didn't mean to scare you."

"Where are you?"

"Still at school."

"Are you doing something?"

"Yeah. I'll catch a ride back to Bellingwood. No biggie."

She took a deep breath. "Are you going to tell me what you're doing? You do know who you're talking to, right?"

"It's cool. I'll talk to you later."

"No, Heath. That doesn't work. Around here you ask permission before doing something, you don't ask forgiveness later. Eliseo was expecting you at the barn and you aren't there. That's irresponsible."

"Sorry."

She took a breath. "When do you expect to be home?"

"I'll be there before supper."

"You know we're talking about this tonight, right?"

He sighed. "Yeah. Okay."

The second conversation she'd had like this in ten minutes. High school boys were going to make her nuts.

"Be safe."

"Bye."

She glanced at the kids around her table. The cats were sprawled out in a sunbeam on the floor beside Rebecca and both dogs were asleep on the sofa. Polly was so frustrated at the last two conversations she'd had, she wanted to scream. She knew she shouldn't let those stupid boys get to her, but dang, they drove her batty.

"I'm going out," she said to Rebecca. "I'll be back."

"Where are you going?" Rebecca asked.

Polly scrambled to think. She didn't know. But she needed to say something. "Maybe to the grocery store, probably to the library to see Joss. Do you need anything?"

The kids shook their heads and Rebecca looked up at her. "Everything okay?"

"It will be," Polly said. "I'll be back in a while."

Rebecca followed Polly to the back stoop. "You know it's Monday, right?"

Polly turned and looked at her. "Yeah. Why?"

"The library isn't open. The little kids are downstairs."

"That's right." Polly dropped her head. "I'm going to run to the grocery store to get inspiration for supper tonight." She patted Rebecca's hand on top of the newel post. "I'll be back later."

"Believe the best about him, okay?" Rebecca said.

Polly chuckled. "Go back to your homework, Miss Intuitive. I'll see you later."

She ran down the steps and out the door to her truck. In just a few minutes, she parked in front of the grocery store and went in. Nothing sounded good right now, so she hoped great inspiration would overtake her before she'd gone through the aisles.

"I understand you made a new friend today."

Polly spun when she heard Lydia's voice behind her. She stepped into a quick hug, holding two tomatoes in her hands. "I didn't see your Jeep," she said.

"It's in back. Gotta keep you on your toes. I stopped at Sandy Davis's house and she said that you invited her to join y'all on Sunday nights." Lydia patted Polly's hand. "That was a nice thing to do."

"I like her," Polly said. "She'll have fun with us. Camille is coming, too. Soon we'll fill the place with young career women."

"As opposed to us old stay at home ladies?" Lydia asked with a chuckle.

Polly clutched her heart. "Oh, you got me. Right here where it hurts." She grimaced. "You know what I mean."

"Yes I do. I think it's wonderful you're finding ways to meet more friends. And Sandy could definitely use some of those, too."

"Did you hook her up with Jen Dykstra?" Polly asked.

"Who me?" Lydia grinned. "Would I be so conniving?"

"Absolutely. It's what you do and you've perfected your technique."

Lydia put her hand on Polly's cart and pushed it out of the way of a young woman with her little son. "How are you doing? Aaron told me how bad things were on Saturday. I haven't had time to check on you. I haven't had much time to do anything lately." She gestured around the shop. "As evidenced by the fact that I'm here trying to decide what's for supper."

"That's what I'm doing too," Polly said. "Well, that and I escaped the house before I screamed. Young boys will be the death of me."

"Heath?" Lydia asked.

Polly nodded. "Yes. And Jason. They frustrate me. Some of it's because I didn't raise Heath and now I'm trying to force him into a mold that makes me comfortable. He stayed in Boone for some reason and didn't call me first. I would have thought that was common courtesy, but I would have thought wrong."

"You are the guardian and you get to make those kinds of

rules," Lydia said with a smile. She picked up a batch of bananas. "Two days and they'll be perfect for bread."

"I know I am, but I feel like such an ogre when I push him. I don't have to know everything, but I want to know enough so that I can take care of things before they fall apart."

"No you don't, dear. Sometimes things falling apart is the only way kids learn. Let him fight his battles, let him fail, let him grow up. Don't do it all for him."

"Hasn't he already been through enough?" Polly asked.

"He had a crisis and faced down what most of us would call abuse. But don't let those things cause you to treat him with kid gloves. If you expect him to call you first, be consistent and insist on it. The boy isn't broken, he's wounded. Give him boundaries, follow through with expectations and be consistent. That's what he needs."

Polly sighed. "I don't like being a parent."

"It's not an easy job," Lydia said. "But you're fine. Trust me."

"So can I ask you something even though I'm not supposed to?" Polly asked.

"Sure, what's that?"

"Has Aaron said anything about the body I found on Saturday? Do they have any idea who it is yet? Is there anyone missing?"

"He hasn't said anything to me," Lydia responded. "But that's not surprising. They probably don't have much information yet. Things are slow on Sundays and I haven't seen him yet today. Do you want me to have him call you tonight?"

"No, that's okay. I shouldn't press. It's not my business."

"Fiddle faddle," Lydia said "You found the poor soul, the least Aaron can do is keep you up to date on what he knows. But the truth is, you always seem to be part of the investigation anyway. You'll know more than I will in a day or two. Right?"

A sheepish grin stole over Polly's face. "Yeah. You're probably right. I'll be good.

They'd pushed their carts around the store and while Lydia had filled hers, the only thing Polly had was a few tomatoes and a package of pork chops.

"That's going to be sparse eating," Lydia said, pointing to Polly's cart.

"I knew I wasn't paying attention. I'd better walk through again," Polly said. "I'll see you later."

"Andy and I are going to start bringing things in tomorrow for the Haunted House. We need to dig through the shed and make sure everything is still in good shape."

"What's the new addition this year?" Polly asked.

Lydia smiled and put her groceries on the counter. "You'll have to wait and see. We never get to surprise you."

Polly gave a little wave and turned back into the canned goods aisle. She needed to focus on one thing now. Dinner.

~~~

After dinner, Henry said, "I can either clean the kitchen or walk the dogs, Polly. You choose." He grinned at Rebecca. "You get to help the winner."

"I'll take the dogs," Polly replied. "Heath, you're with me."

Henry winked at Rebecca. "That's what happens when you take a shower early. You get to help with the dishes."

She sat back in her chair, her mouth agape. "I don't know how this happened. I only took a shower because Andrew spilled orange juice on me."

He laughed at her. "And look. You get to spend the next twenty minutes hanging out with your favorite man in the world. See how things work out?" Henry picked up Polly's plate and put it on top of his, then stood and headed for the kitchen. "Hurry up, little girl, or I'll make you lick the pan clean."

Polly beckoned to Heath and the two headed for the back door. She patted her thigh and both dogs raced toward them, running for the steps. She handed Han's leash to Heath and he snapped it on the collar. Polly did the same to Obiwan. They were taking the trail this evening and she didn't want to run into any trouble.

As soon as they were outside, Heath stopped and looked at her. "I'm sorry for not calling," he said.

"You should be. We're responsible for you, Heath, and you need to let us know what's going on. If you have things you want to do or friends you want to spend time with, that's great. But I still need to know. The last thing I want is to get a phone call from the sheriff, telling me that you're dead in a ditch somewhere."

"Wouldn't you be the one to find me if that happened?" he asked, tilting his head, a smirk on his face.

Polly glared. "Not funny. Are you going to tell me why you were late this evening? And you owe Eliseo an explanation, too. If you commit to a job, you can't just not show up."

"I'll talk to him," Heath said. "That was my bad."

They crossed the street to the swimming pool parking lot and headed for the trail. "It's not just 'your bad,'" she said. "You can't make it go away by flipping a quaint phrase. What was so important that you blew him off and couldn't be bothered to let me know where you were?"

"It's stupid."

"Then tell me about it."

"It was Libby's mom. Her car broke down and we took it into the shop. She needed new filters. Mr. Drummond drove us to the hardware store and we got what she needed. And she needs an oil change. But I told her that I could do that another time."

Polly took in everything he said and it clicked. "Libby?"

"Her mom's car."

"Who's Libby?"

"Just a girl at school."

This was going to be like pulling teeth.

"Is Libby in your class?"

"No, she's a sophomore."

"Does she live in Boone?"

"Nah. Bellingwood. That's why I knew I could do her mom's oil change another day."

Polly shook her head. "So you got yourself in trouble because you were doing a good deed and then you couldn't tell me that?"

"When you called, they were right there and I didn't want to sound like I was doing anything special. Her mom was embarrassed. They don't have very much money and the car is a wreck. It needs a lot of work. But I told her that I can do the labor if she buys the parts. It will be cheaper that way."

"Do you like working on cars?" Polly asked.

"Yeah."

"Why didn't you say something before? You know Henry and Nate are rebuilding those Woodies." She couldn't imagine how much they'd missed out on with Heath because he refused to talk to them.

He huffed. "I didn't want to bother them. They wouldn't want me around."

"You kids are such dopes." Polly ran her hand through her hair. "Of course they would. Don't you realize how much fun it is for us to share what we know with you? Sometimes I want to hang you out a window by your toes."

"I'd probably deserve it," he said under his breath.

"Stop that. You don't deserve any such thing. You have to talk to Henry about the car thing, but I want to return to Libby. Is she a good friend of yours?"

Heath shook his head. "You aren't letting that go, are you?"

"Well, I'm Polly. I like to know these things. Do you want to ask her out?"

"Her mom won't let her date until she's sixteen and besides, I don't even have a car."

"Oh Heath," Polly said. "This is Bellingwood. You can practically walk everywhere in town. But if her Mom says she can't date, that kills that. What about school dances and things like that?"

"No car. Remember? Would you let me borrow your truck?"

"If it was special I would. But why don't you ask her to help with the Halloween things at Sycamore House and see if her mother will let her come to the party next Saturday." Polly paused. "Unless of course you don't want to ask her out."

They had arrived at the point she usually turned around, in front of the winery. She turned him toward the hotel. They could make it home faster by taking the sidewalk along the highway.

"I dunno."

"Ask. For all the communication options you kids have these days, no one talks to each other. Don't text or email or Facebook her. Ask her in school tomorrow. Face to face. We need tons more help with the Haunted House. Both of you could be doing things there."

"We'll see."

Polly put her hand on his forearm. "How much do you hate working down at the barn?"

"I don't hate it," he said.

"Okay, how much would you give to not work there ever again?"

"Just about anything. The horses are okay, but it's all gross down there. Everything I do is gross. And I don't think Jason likes me. Who could blame him? It's not his fault. I was a jerk. Eliseo's cool, though. I don't mind working for him."

"That's funny, though," Polly said. "Eliseo is introducing more and more horse-powered equipment. There isn't much down there that uses a motor or engine."

He shook his head. "Nothing at all."

"You should have talked to me about this," she said.

"Hayden says I can do anything for a couple of years and I owe you guys big-time. You didn't have to take me in. And I need to make money so I can buy a car. Even if I could find a place to put an old beater together. I could make it nice."

They crossed the highway and approached the front door of Sycamore House.

"You have to start talking to us," Polly said. "I'm totally serious. You don't have to put up with a job that you hate because you feel like you owe me. Find something you enjoy. Life doesn't have to be a struggle and you certainly don't have to be a martyr to live in it. You can have some fun, too."

"It's a lot better than it was. I don't want to complain. At least you guys aren't screaming at me all the time."

"We try not to do a lot of screaming around here. Sometimes I freak out, but I try to keep that to a minimum."

Heath opened the front door and waited as she and the dogs went in. "Thanks," he said.

"For what?"

"For letting me explain and not jumping to the conclusion that I was getting into trouble again. I figured that's what you assumed."

"Honestly, I was only mad that you didn't call first. The whole getting into trouble assumption would have come if you hadn't shown up for dinner."

He smiled at her. "Well, thanks."

CHAPTER EIGHT

It surprised Polly to see Alistair Greyson walk past her window. She caught up with him outside the main office door. "Good morning," she said. "What are you doing here?"

He gave her a slight bow of the head. "The sweetest of mornings to you, Miss Polly. It is good to see you." Grey gestured to the side door. "Master Denis and I will spend two hours in the great outdoors. Your beautiful backyard, the sun shining on our faces and friendly conversation is a perfect antidote for a young man confined to a wheel chair." He smiled. "It has the added benefit of offering a moment of relief to Mrs. Morrow, a woman of great generosity of spirit."

"Do you have a minute for me?" she asked.

"Oh, my dear. I have more than mere minutes for you. How might I be of assistance?"

They walked into the lounge and she pointed to a chair, then sat down in another next to him. "First of all, do you need any help at the inn? Heath isn't cut out to work in a barn and he's miserable."

Grey smiled at her. "I believe you are making things too easy on the boy. He's turning into a young man. Do you not think he can find an afternoon job on his own?"

Polly sat back, surprised at his words. It hadn't occurred to her that she might be doing this all wrong. If there was a person in her life and she could help them, she just did it. But Grey was right. She needed to back off and let Heath look for a job on his own. He'd probably find something he enjoyed.

"Okay," she said, nodding. "Wow, you're right. Thank you."

"That was simpler than I expected. You indicated that was the first query, did you have another?"

" I don't know if you can help or not," she said. "But it hit me in the middle of the night that maybe you'd know something."

"About?"

"About the person I found in the field back here on Saturday. Lydia tells me that no one in Bellingwood is missing and maybe Aaron found something out yesterday, but I'm pretty sure I would have heard from him by now. Then I wondered if maybe they'd stayed at the inn. Have you had anything strange happen there lately?"

Grey paused and then spoke. "That's very interesting. We have a young man who has been with us for several weeks. He rented the room until the end of the month."

"Is he missing?"

"I wouldn't have thought so. He has been in and out, staying away for a day or more at a time. He asked us not to clean his room unless he called first, so I put it out of my mind. But now that you speak of it, we have not been asked to clean in quite some time and I do not believe that I've seen his car in that same amount of time."

"What's his name?" Polly asked.

"Jeremy Booten. What a pity if your young man in the field was our guest. Do you suppose it might be?'

"I'd bet everything I have. Did you talk to him much?"

Grey grinned at her. "Why of course I did. You know how I enjoy meeting the good people that cross my path. Jeremy Booten was quite interesting. He's working on his first novel and was researching haunted places throughout central Iowa. As a budding photographer, he also carried expensive camera gear. He thought that if he was quite fortunate, he might run into a few ghosts that would allow him to take their picture."

"You're kidding, right?" Polly asked. Her laugh was stilted. This was nuts.

Grey tilted his head. "I fear that I am not. He spent a good deal of money on his gear and insisted that he was not leaving Iowa until he found the proof that he looked for." He turned his wrist to look at his watch. "As many minutes as I would like to offer to you, I must relieve Mrs. Morrow. She is taking a much needed respite and I do not want to make her late. If you have other questions for me, might we continue this at another time?"

"That's all I had." Polly stood up and waited as Grey pushed himself out of the chair. "Is your knee getting any better?"

"Good days and bad days. This is not the worst of the bad days, so I shall not complain, but move on until another good day. Thank you for asking."

When Polly got back into the office, she opened her phone to call the sheriff's office in Boone. Maybe if she didn't call Aaron directly, she wouldn't frighten him into believing there was another body.

"Boone County Sheriff, this is Anita, may I help you?"

"Hi Anita, this is Polly Giller in Bellingwood. What are you doing answering the phone?"

Polly had gotten to know Anita Banks, Sheriff Merritt's favorite tech goddess, last year. She'd hoped that a relationship might develop between Anita and Doug Randall, but the poor boy had never gotten his act together and they'd gone their separate ways.

"I don't know why the phone rolled to me," Anita said. "Things must be busy up front. Do you need to speak with Sheriff Merritt? It's not another body, is it?"

"That's why I called the office," Polly replied. "I hoped to avoid that question. Guess if it's me, that's going to be the assumption, isn't it!"

"I'm sorry," Anita said.

Polly laughed. "Nothing to be sorry about. It's my reputation and I can't change it. But no, there isn't a body. I might have information on the person I found last Saturday, though. Have you guys gotten anything?"

Anita whispered. "You know I'm not supposed to tell you, but they're still waiting for tests. Those crazy television shows always make it look like information comes back from laboratories and coroners overnight. Everybody is working, but that's all that's going on. Sheriff Merritt isn't going to like it if you solve his case again. You have a better track record than any of the deputies."

"I try to tell him everything first," Polly said. "I don't want him to be mad at me."

"He never is. But no one wants to take your cases. You always show them up."

"Big babies," Polly said. "Maybe I'll get my Private Investigator license and then they'll have to put up with me in their faces."

"That would be hilarious. I'm afraid you'd give Sheriff Merritt a heart attack, though."

"And his wife, too," Polly said. "She'd have my head. That makes me think. Halloween is coming up. Are you going to come to the Masquerade Ball again?"

"I don't know," Anita said. "I had fun and I love dressing up, but I'm not dating anyone right now and I don't want to come by myself."

"That boy is an idiot," Polly said.

Anita chuckled. "Doug? He just doesn't have any experience. He's such a nice guy, but I had to do the work. Once I stopped, he went away. And then he was embarrassed when he realized that he'd let me fade off into the sunset."

"It's like there should be a class in junior high about how to properly court a girl," Polly said with a sigh. "Not sex ed, but how to talk to a girl and what to do about her parents and how to be respectful and all that."

"For girls too," Anita said.

"You're right." Polly laughed out loud. "Maybe that's what I need to do. Teach etiquette courses. I can bring Mark Ogden in to teach everyone how to dance and ..." She stopped herself. "Yeah. Can you transfer me to Aaron?"

"Absolutely. And Polly?"

"Yes?"

"If Doug ever gets his act together and asks me out again, I'd go. I like him."

Polly processed on that information. She wasn't sure how she would use it, but there had to be a way. "That's good to know," she said. "Maybe we can convince him to pull his head out of his backside."

"I'll send you through to Sheriff Merritt. Just a moment." With that Anita was gone and Polly heard the BeeGees coming through her phone.

"Anita tells me you have no body," Aaron said, interrupting the song.

"No, but I might have some information for you. I spoke with Grey and there is a guest who hasn't been back to his room for a while. The young man does go out and about and asked them not to clean the room until he called for it, but it's probably been longer than it should be."

"That's interesting," Aaron said. "Do you have his information?"

Polly had already pulled it up on her screen. "Of course. His name is Jeremy Booten. He drives a red 2002 Honda Accord and he's from Duluth. Grey said he's in central Iowa to write a story about haunted houses. He could tell you more since he talked to the kid. He's a photographer and author."

"Is the car out at the inn?" Aaron asked.

"I don't think so."

"Even more interesting. But then we haven't been looking for that car. With this information, we'll be able to dig deeper into who the kid is. At least we'll be able to say for sure if it's him or not. Thanks, Polly."

"Anita says that I embarrass your other deputies and they won't take my cases because I always show them up. I don't mean to do that."

He laughed. "They do whatever they need to do and so do you, Polly. Don't feel bad about being in the middle of these things. I've learned that you can't help it. Things come at you and there's nothing you can do. It's easier for everyone if I let it play out. Now, don't think for a minute that I approve of you doing anything that puts your life in danger. But just this little piece of information moved the case forward quite a few steps. That's helpful and thank you."

"Okay," she said. "I like your people and don't want them to hate me because I'm just doing my Polly thing."

"You're doing fine. Now let me get this information where it belongs and maybe we can find out what happened."

~~~

Polly spun in her chair at the sound of tapping on her outside window. Lydia and Andy waved as they passed by on their way to the storage shed, probably to check on the Halloween sets and props. She couldn't wait to see what Lydia was adding this year. Last Halloween, they'd added a living head on a table. Doug Randall had enjoyed frightening people by opening his eyes and screaming at them. The illusion hadn't taken that much to create, but it had garnered some great attention.

She still couldn't believe how much pleasure Lydia took in this project. Three hundred and sixty-four days out of the year, the woman did everything in her power to care for people. This one day, she let her wicked sense of humor take over to scare the wits out of young and old alike.

"I'll be out in the shed," Polly told Stephanie on her way out of the office.

Stephanie smiled and nodded. Polly chuckled. Stephanie didn't care where she was or what she was doing. In fact, most of the time, the girl had no idea. If she needed Polly, she called her cell phone.

The door to the shed was propped open and Polly couldn't see her friends, so she crept in and stood quietly, hoping to hear where they might be. When she identified their location, she tip-toed toward them. Lydia was head down in a box of props while Andy was separating set pieces from each other, looking them over.

"Boo!" she yelled.

Both women jumped and Lydia cursed.

"Why would you do that to me?" Lydia asked. "How would you explain to Aaron that you'd given me a heart attack?"

Andy had taken a seat on a stack of boxes, glaring at Polly.

"What?" Polly asked. "It had to be done."

"I don't think so," Andy replied. "That was rotten. But at least I'm breathing again. What are you doing out here?"

"Do you need help?"

Lydia shook her head. "Not today. We're taking stock and checking to make sure things are ready to go. If we need to make any repairs, I want to be sure to have plenty of supplies on hand."

They had less than a week to pull this off. The crew would pull things out of storage Sunday afternoon and then the main foyer of Sycamore House would transform little by little until Saturday evening when trick-or-treaters and their families arrived to tour the Haunted House. Since Halloween was on Saturday this year, they planned to attempt both the Haunted House and the Masquerade Ball on the same night. Jeff insisted it could work. People would go through the Haunted House and either leave or enter the auditorium for the rest of the festivities. It made Polly's head spin. But there were more people than ever who were digging in to make sure that both events were successful.

"What are you doing this afternoon?" Andy asked.

"Not much. But I do have a question for you," Polly said.

Andy was peering at the front of one of the flats. "We need more black paint. Some of these are scuffed."

Lydia wrote that down on a notepad. "Question for who?" she asked.

"Both of you. I thought about Andy because she lives near the cemetery, but you probably know as much about it as anyone. What can you tell me about the Springer House?"

Andy stepped away from the flats and smiled at Polly. "How long have you lived in Bellingwood? Nearly three years now? I can't believe this is the first time you've heard about it. Things get wild and spooky every October. Kids tell the story of the haunting and there are always a few who insist they've seen a ghost on the second floor. Some of them are certain that the ghost has chased them off the property."

"Why hasn't it ever been lived in since they left town?" Polly asked. She looked at Andy, who in turn looked at Lydia.

Lydia shrugged. "I don't know. There are a few stories from when I was a kid about people who tried to buy it, but got scared away before the sale closed. It's a beautiful old house, but it's tucked back in there and nobody ever thinks about it."

"It's creepy enough that people put it out of their minds," Andy said.

"There are houses right across the street," Polly reminded them. "Are those people bothered by the ghost?"

"Who lives there?" Lydia asked. "The Dexters and Walters are the two houses right across the street..."

Andy interrupted. "Burnsides and Thierrys are in that neighborhood. They've never said anything."

"So it's a hoax," Polly said.

Lydia smiled. "Of course it is. Nobody believes in ghosts." She gave a slight shudder. "But you wouldn't catch me spending any time in that house."

"So you do believe in ghosts?" Polly asked.

"No, of course not. But I'm not foolish enough to test that belief either," Lydia replied. "Why are you asking?"

"Rebecca, Kayla, and Andrew were there on Saturday. They broke a window trying to see in. Rebecca insists there was a ghost. Henry shut the story down, but she hasn't slept well the last few nights. It was better last night. Maybe she's letting it go. You're right, though, Andy. The kids are talking about the story again. And then, Grey told me that there was a young man in town who was here investigating stories of hauntings around the area for a book he was writing."

"People want to believe," Lydia said, nodding. "Those ghost hunter television shows are popular." She grimaced. "As if real life weren't haunting enough for people."

"It's across the cemetery from you, Andy," Polly said. "You've never seen anything weird at the house?"

Andy pursed her lips. "I don't look. I've never looked. If there is something going on over there, I don't need to know about it. My kids think it is strange enough that my yard backs on to the cemetery. If they thought I was interested in a haunted house, I'm pretty sure they'd make me move."

"But the cemetery is a beautiful place," Lydia said. "It's not dark and scary at all."

"That's what I tell them. Mr. Tanner takes good care of the grounds. It is always lovely and it's very peaceful." She gave them a wan smile. "And I know that it sounds odd, especially since I'm married to Len, but it's nice to know that Bill is so close. Sometimes I talk to him. He's right there and..." This time, her grin turned wicked. "And he can't contradict me, so I always get the last word."

Lydia paused, giving Andy time to collect her memories and then asked, "Why are you so interested?"

"I don't know for sure. Yeah, some of it has to do with the kids messing around up there. Some of it is just plain curiosity. I can't believe I'd never heard of it either. Henry knows all about it. But that house is absolutely gorgeous and it seems such a shame that it just sits there."

"At this point," Lydia said, "it would take a lot to restore it. With a history like that, there aren't too many people who want to invest their money that way. Are you thinking about it?"

Polly shrugged. "I don't know. Henry and I haven't talked about it, but I caught him over there looking at it yesterday morning. I don't know if he was there because of the broken window or something else."

"Your family is getting bigger," Andy said with a smile. "And people used to talk about how big that house was. There were five or six bedrooms upstairs and then there's that solarium off one of the rooms. It would make a nice home for all the kids you're going to take in."

"Stop it," Polly said. "Heath is only going to be here for a couple of years."

"Uh huh," Lydia taunted. "In one short summer, you added two more members to your family. This might be only the beginning."

Polly scratched her head. "I'm so not a mommy. This is the strangest thing I've ever done."

"And this coming from the woman who renovated an old school house in a town where she knew no one," Andy said.

Lydia grinned. "Or the woman who finds dead bodies."

"Okay, okay, stop," Polly said. "I'm a weird person who does weird things. Maybe I should investigate purchasing that house."

CHAPTER NINE

Sucking in a deep breath, Polly answered the call from the elementary school Thursday afternoon. She still wasn't used to being a parent. Anything could go wrong and some days it felt like she was just waiting for the world to fall apart around her.

"This is Polly Giller," she said tentatively.

"Ms. Giller, we're calling about your ..." the receptionist paused. "We're calling about Rebecca. We'd like you to come to the school. There's been an incident."

"An incident?" Polly asked. "Did Rebecca do something? Has she been hurt?"

"She'll be fine, but we'd prefer it if you could come speak to us in person."

Polly was scrambling to gather her things so she could run out the door. "I'll be right there."

"Just come straight to the office, please," the woman said.

She ran for her truck and backed out of the driveway, forcing herself to look both ways. Her brain was barely functioning. Why would she be called to the office for Rebecca? Of all people. Polly tried to maintain a sense of calm as she pulled into the school parking lot and looked for a place to park. Of course it was as far away from the front door as possible, leaving her even more time to worry about what had happened. She took a deep breath at the front door, pulled it open and strode to the office. When she opened the door, two boys and Rebecca were sitting on chairs - Rebecca with a clump of bloody towels held in front of her nose.

"Honey, what happened?" Polly asked, rushing to Rebecca and crouching down in front of her.

"Miss Giller?"

Polly stood up to greet the principal. She hadn't spent much time with Mrs. Bickle, but had never liked her. She was a sharp-tongued elderly woman who held some antiquated ideas about education. Why she'd been hired by the district, many parents didn't understand. Mrs. Bickle had only been here for a year since the previous principal had moved out of state with her husband. People hoped the woman was only a temporary replacement until they could hire someone better, but she didn't seem to be going anywhere.

"Mrs. Bickle." Polly put her hand out to shake the woman's hand. "What happened and why does Rebecca have a bloody nose?"

"Would you and Rebecca please come into my office?" Mrs. Bickle indicated that they go through her door and then spoke to the receptionist. "If Master Evans's parents arrive, please interrupt me and send them in."

Polly had done everything in her power to stay out of trouble when she was in school. But today, at the age of thirty-five, she suddenly felt as if she were ten years old and in trouble. She took a deep breath. This wasn't about her. It was about Rebecca who looked like she'd gotten the wrong end of a very bad deal.

She and Rebecca had taken their seats in two of the four chairs directly in front of Mrs. Bickle's desk. When the principal rounded her desk to sit down, Polly did her best not to chuckle. She'd raised her chair so that she would look down on those in front of her. Not difficult to do with elementary students, but this was meant to be intimidating even to adults. Polly's hackles went up.

She wasn't going to be bullied by anybody. Rebecca was under her protection.

"Your ward was part of a fist-fight this afternoon. Each of my students and their parents and guardians were informed at the beginning of the school year that fighting is unacceptable behavior in my building," Mrs. Bickle said.

Polly looked at Rebecca, waiting for her to protest. The boys in the other room didn't look as if they'd been in a fight. Rebecca was the only one with a visible wound.

Rebecca simply looked at Polly, gave a negligible eye-roll and shrugged her shoulders.

"Exactly what happened?" Polly asked, glancing back and forth between Mrs. Bickle and Rebecca. When Rebecca demurred, Polly turned her gaze on the principal.

"We have not been given all of the details regarding the fight as of yet. We are still in the investigation phase," Mrs. Bickle said. "But nonetheless, she was part of the altercation and that is grounds for, at the very minimum, a one-day suspension. You will take her home this afternoon and she will not be allowed to attend classes tomorrow."

"Wait," Polly said. "She's being suspended simply because she got hit? That isn't fair. Why don't you wait until you know what happened?"

"I will not tolerate any type of violent behavior among the students in this school. If she was part of the altercation, she is responsible for her actions."

By now Polly was furious. She wanted to talk to Rebecca and find out what had actually happened, but didn't want to do it in front of this woman. Every bit of trepidation she'd had when she first walked in was long gone. She stood up, reached for Rebecca's free hand and said, "We'll be back in a moment. I'm going to speak with my daughter and find out what has happened. If she carries no responsibility for what has happened, I will ask you to reconsider."

Rebecca's eyes had grown wide as she silently followed Polly out of the office. They met another woman coming in and Polly turned back to the receptionist. "We'll be right back. If Mrs. Bickle wants to move forward without us in the room, fine, but we aren't finished."

As soon as they cleared the office door, Polly dropped onto a bench and pulled Rebecca down beside her. "Okay," Polly said. "Spill. What in the world is going on here? Did you get into a fight? And tell me the truth because I don't want to hear a different story from someone else and then find out later that you were exaggerating or lying."

"I took the punch," Rebecca said. "You know, like you do. I heard you say before that sometimes it's easier to take the punch and make the other person get punished for hurting you. So I took the punch." She turned her poor battered face up to Polly. "It hurt more than I thought it would. How come you never complain?"

Polly gave a sad laugh and hugged Rebecca's shoulders. "You poor thing. It hurts like the dickens. Now tell me why you had to take a punch?"

"You didn't recognize the other kid in the room, did you?"

Polly hadn't been paying attention. "Who was it?"

"That was Bean Landry. You know, Gina's older brother? The Evans kid was pushing him on the playground this afternoon and I told him to stop. Bean's always getting hurt. But everybody picks on him." Rebecca patted her nose with the damp cloth. The bleeding had stopped. "Chris and two of his friends were pushing Bean back and forth, calling him a mama's boy and a baby. Some of the other kids were talking about it. I didn't see it happen. Anyway, Andrew and I were coming back from band when Bean came around a corner and totally ran into us. He hit the floor and then Chris Evans came next. Andrew pulled Bean up, Evans was teasing him again and I told him to stop. Bean's only in fifth grade and Chris is in my grade. I don't know why he has it in for the kid. Anyway, Bean said something stupid about Chris picking on someone his own size and then I saw it coming. I knew he was going to hit Bean and I just stepped in and took the punch."

Rebecca put her hand on her forehead. "I need to rethink that maneuver next time. This really hurts."

"Okay, where is Andrew now?" Polly asked. "Why isn't he here as a witness?"

"Mrs. Bickle made him go back to class."

Polly rubbed Rebecca's shoulder. "Now I have a strange question for you. Have you done anything at all in the last year or so to make Mrs. Bickle angry? Is there any reason she isn't going to be fair with you?"

"She's just mean. Nobody likes her," Rebecca said. "I might as well take the suspension. It's easier not to cross her. If you do, things get worse."

"That's no way to live through junior high," Polly said. She wanted to say more, but not in front of Rebecca. "There's no reason that you can think of why this should go badly for you?"

Rebecca lifted her shoulders and shook her head. "I don't think so."

"Then let's see what we can do. If you have to get into trouble because someone else is being a bully, we'll deal with that."

"This isn't going to go the way you think it should," Rebecca said. "I promise."

"Let's see." Polly took Rebecca's hand again and they strode back into the office. She looked down at Bean sitting on a chair by himself. His mother had shaved his head which was why Polly didn't recognize him. "Hi Bean," she said. "Staying out of trouble?"

He looked up at her and shook his head. "No ma'am," he said.

"That's what I hear." Polly turned to the receptionist. "We're going back in. I might need to ask you to call for Andrew Donovan, but I'll wait and see."

The young woman nodded, glancing furtively at the principal's office door.

Polly opened the door and walked over to the woman and her son. "Are you Mrs. Evans?" Polly asked. When the woman nodded, Polly put her hand out. "I'm Polly Giller and this is my daughter, Rebecca. It appears that your son had the audacity to hit someone today in school. What are we going to do about that?"

Mrs. Bickle stood up. "Please take a seat, Ms. Giller. I will manage this investigation. We're nearly finished and though

Rebecca may have been on the receiving end of this trouble, she was still part of it and my decision stands. All three children who were involved will receive a suspension."

Polly remained standing. "You can investigate all you like, but I refuse to acknowledge that Rebecca did anything wrong. She stood up for a boy who was being bullied constantly and then, when young Mr. Evans took a swing at that boy, stepped in to take the punch. She did nothing to instigate the fight or perpetuate violence."

"I'm sorry," Mrs. Bickle replied. "My decision has been made. Maybe next time Rebecca will make a different choice and bring about a peaceful resolution to the situation."

"I'm sorry too," Polly said. "This was unnecessary and unfair. Is there anything else?" Without waiting for an answer, Polly spun on her heels and dragged Rebecca with her.

"I need to go to my locker," Rebecca whispered. "I have homework."

"Do you need a hall pass?"

"Probably."

"Just a second." Polly went back into the office and said, "Rebecca needs to get her things from her locker. Will you give her a hall pass?"

The receptionist nodded and mouthed, "I'm sorry" to Polly while writing something out on a pad of paper. She handed the pass to Polly, who handed it off to Rebecca.

The two of them walked down the hallway to the seventh grade lockers and Polly waited while Rebecca stuffed things into her backpack. She took the heavy pack into her own arms and waited a few more moments while Rebecca contemplated the rest of her belongings.

"Take your flute," Polly said. "You'll have time to practice tomorrow."

"My nose?" Rebecca asked.

"Oh right," Polly said. "Fine. Leave it. A weekend off won't hurt."

They were silent as they walked through the halls of the school.

Rebecca took the pass back into the office and then rejoined Polly as they walked outside.

"How mad are you?" Rebecca asked.

Polly gritted her teeth and then said, "I'm fine. I'm not mad at you. You did the right thing and I'm infuriated that you were punished for it. If you had done anything wrong, I would have completely backed her decision. You know that, right?"

Rebecca nodded. "I don't know why I feel so guilty. I didn't do anything wrong."

"I should ask about your nose. We'll go see the doctor."

"No!" Rebecca exclaimed. "I'm fine. It only hurts a little now. The nurse said it wasn't broken."

"All the same. I'd feel better if I knew that a piece of cartilage hadn't chipped away and was slithering its way into your brain."

Rebecca looked up at her in shock. "That could happen?"

Polly chuckled. "No. But we're going to run in and let the doctor look at you. You're too young to start this whole taking-a-punch thing, don't you think?"

"Maybe. All I could think was that you'd had this happen before and always got through it."

"You're a tough little girl, Rebecca," Polly said. "But Henry is going to have to bring home ice cream tonight for both of us."

~~~

Polly looked in on Rebecca one last time before going to bed. They'd gotten a prescription for a mild pain killer so she could sleep tonight and Doctor Mason said the cartilage hadn't been broken. She was lucky.

Andrew and Kayla had come in with the news that the story had gone all around the school and they thought they should organize a protest. Rebecca told them she could deal with it. Since she was going to be black and blue anyway, she preferred not going to school. The kids promised to get her homework assignments to her the next day. Kayla took Rebecca's math homework with her so she could turn it in on time.

When Heath came upstairs, he took one look at Rebecca's face and turned bright red. He'd been ready to take on the world for her. Polly tried not to feel proud of the fact that he was so protective of Rebecca, but she knew she had less to do with that than Rebecca did. Those two had grown close as sister and brother because Rebecca had dug in and insisted. She'd been relentless with Heath all along. Polly and Henry had done nothing to help that relationship - the two kids had done it themselves.

Obiwan jumped up onto Rebecca's bed. He'd become more and more comfortable there and spent many nights sleeping with the girl. Polly nodded and stood for a long moment watching them in the light of the moon. She was proud of that girl.

She quietly slipped into her own room. Henry was reading a woodworking magazine and the cats had taken up residence on her pillow. Han was sleeping up against Henry's legs, leaving barely enough room for her on the bed.

"How's she doing?" Henry asked.

"She's asleep and Obiwan is keeping watch," Polly replied.

He put his book down and reached out to take her hand. "How are you doing?"

"I'm still mad as hell. I don't know what to do about this. I can take on a battle and complain about her to the school board members I know, or I can let this be a learning experience for Rebecca. I don't know exactly what it is she's learning - nothing like what I'd teach her about situations like this, but at some point she needs to learn how to discern whose authority is trustworthy and whose isn't." She smacked her leg, startling the dog. "I'm so pissed. It wasn't fair. Rebecca didn't do anything wrong. At. All."

"She's learning that life isn't fair, but you still have to do the right thing," Henry said quietly. "If you want to raise a ruckus, you could probably get a large number of people to back you up, but is that the battle you want to take on? And, secondly, is that how you want to use your power in the community?"

"I don't have any power."

He laughed. "Of course you do. You're a respected business owner. You are seen as fair and reasonable. You're generous and caring and genuinely give back to Bellingwood. You have power. What are you going to do with it?"

"So you're saying I could get this woman fired?"

"If you want to, you probably could. It seems to me that she has enough bad press. Maybe they're looking for a reason to make her go away. I don't know what her contract with the district looks like."

Polly sighed. "But I don't want to be seen as that person. And I don't want Rebecca to think that anytime something isn't fair to her, I'll step in and get the person who messed with her fired. Sometimes life stinks and you have to keep living through it."

Henry nodded.

"If I have power in the community, I don't want to throw it away on something negative like this either," Polly said. "I'd rather fight for something good rather than against something bad. And just because she screwed with my kid doesn't mean that she can't do her job. If nothing else, she was committed to her belief in the situation. Even if I'm just as committed to the fact that she was wrong."

"Rebecca saw you be respectful today," Henry said.

Polly interrupted him. "Well, not terribly respectful. I walked out."

"But you didn't scream or shout. You didn't throw a tantrum. You didn't threaten the woman in front of the kids. None of that. And you never said anything bad about her to Rebecca, no matter how angry you were. That's a big deal, Polly. Not a lot of kids see that type of behavior when things don't go their parent's way."

"I'll probably have to have another conversation with Rebecca about respect, even when it doesn't seem fair," Polly said. She found a space for her head among the cats. Luke finally leaped to the floor and then jumped up on the first ledge of the cat tree.

"I'm thinking about Heath and his work down in the barn," Henry said quietly.

"Yeah?"

"He said something to me tonight about hating it and wondered if I had any work for him."

Polly turned on her side to face him. "What did you say?"

"I told him that I needed time to consider it."

She slumped "I told Grey that I was staying out of this. He said I fix too many things and make it too easy."

"That's why we love you," Henry said. "Does Grey have anything out there?"

"No. Not yet. Unless..." Polly propped herself up on her elbow. "Are you guys doing that hockey ice thing? We could pay Heath to help Grey get it dug out and start the work."

Henry nodded. "That's not a bad idea. It would give him something to do. I'm not sure if Heath is ready to be proactive about this, but we should help him."

"We're going to fix it, aren't we?"

"It's our job as parents. That's my story and I'm sticking to it," Henry said with a laugh.

"Whew. Thanks. I didn't want to be in this one all by myself. I'm glad you're as bad as me."

Henry reached across the dog and kissed Polly's lips. "We should be bad together."

"Your dog is in the way."

"Your cat is too."

CHAPTER TEN

Her own nightmares were fading, but Rebecca hadn't slept well again, so Polly let her sleep the next morning. The fear of being kidnapped and the memory of what Joey and Marcus Allendar had done to those other young women was no longer vivid in her memory, but Polly still woke up in a sweat in the middle of the night.

Fog had rolled in overnight and didn't seem to be in any rush to clear off. Polly thought about dressing in her sloppiest clothes and a warm robe and curling up under a pile of blankets with a good book. Some days she hated having to be a responsible adult.

She poured another cup of coffee and looked out the front windows, though she could barely see the highway. Jeff drove in and a few minutes later, Stephanie pulled in and parked her car beside Jeff's. The two other cars in the parking lot belonged to new people Sylvie had hired to work in the kitchen with Rachel, especially on weekends. It was still only Friday, but that probably meant there was something going on in the auditorium today.

Heath had been quiet again this morning. He'd asked about Rebecca and had offered to take the dogs out for their morning walk, but any breakthrough conversations they'd had apparently didn't carry over from day to day. He was going to have to figure this out. Polly was all out of words.

That made her chuckle. She was never out of words. It's just that sometimes they were more difficult to put into the right order. One of these days Heath would start communicating. She hoped it happened before he left their home.

"Polly?"

She turned around and cringed. Poor Rebecca. Her face was swollen and she was going to sport a heck of a shiner. "Yes, honey. How are you doing?"

"It hurts." Rebecca brought her hand up to her face, lightly touching it while grimacing.

"I know it does. I'm so sorry. Maybe next time you bring up a book to block the punch instead of using your face."

"Next time?" Rebecca asked.

Polly shrugged. "You never know. You're my daughter now. Anything can happen."

Rebecca gave her a weak smile. "Are you trying to scare me?"

"Is it working?" Polly dropped two slices of bread into the toaster. "Do you want scrambled eggs this morning?"

"No. Just jelly. Is there any bacon left? I can smell it."

"Bacon and jelly sandwich. That sounds horrible."

Rebecca scowled at her. "Yes it does. You know what I mean."

Polly took the plate of bacon out of the oven and put it down on the peninsula, then took a piece for herself. "Do you want to do anything today? The weather is weird, but we can go out if you want. Do you want to go see Jessie and Molly? Or maybe we can call Joss and spend time with the twins. It's up to you."

"I don't want anybody to see me like this," Rebecca said, touching her face again.

The toast popped up and Polly put it on a plate in front of Rebecca, moving the butter and jelly in front of her.

"We can stay home all day. But, if you have a black eye, shouldn't you show it off? I mean, it's a sign that you're courageous and a little tough, don't you think?"

"But I look horrible."

"You look like someone hit you. It's not something you can change. Be proud of it. If people stare, scowl at them. If they ask questions, answer them. You have nothing to be ashamed of."

Rebecca looked up at her. "You don't let us get away with feeling sorry for ourselves, do you?"

"That's just a waste of time," Polly responded. "By now the story of how you got that black eye has been told and retold in town. You might as well make the best of it. Take the attention, let people feel sorry for you. Maybe we can convince Camille to give you a free hot chocolate."

"Whatever," Rebecca said. "You'd pay for it anyway."

Polly chuckled. "Okay, maybe. But let's not hide away. Okay?"

"Okay then. Can we go where I want to go?"

It felt like this was a trap. "Where is that?" Polly asked.

"You aren't going to like it. But it's what I want to do."

Polly bit her lip, paused and waited. When Rebecca didn't continue, she asked, "Where are we going?"

"I want to go to the Springer House again. With you."

"That would be trespassing. It wasn't right when you kids did it and it certainly wouldn't be right for me to do that."

"Can we go and park in front of it? I want to look up at that window and see if the ghost will show up again. Please?"

Polly shook her head. "It's not fair. You look at me with that broken up face and I can't say no. But I want to wait until some of this fog lifts. It's much too spooky to be looking at a haunted house with this kind of weather."

Rebecca's face lit up. "Thank you! You're the best. Can we take your good camera?"

"Sure. We'll take the camera. It would be nice to get some photographs of that house anyway. I can't believe it's still empty. Somebody should fix it up and put it on the market."

"But nobody will buy a haunted house, will they?" Rebecca asked.

"There's no ghost," Polly replied. "There has to be a very real explanation for what people have seen in that house. It's just an old house with a lot of character. If you fix the front porch, put real windows back in, clear up the yard and paint the house, it would be gorgeous."

"If you can put up with an angry ghost," Rebecca said. "Maybe it's never been fixed up because she scared off the workers and nobody will set foot on the land again."

"You never know," Polly said with a shrug. "You never know."

~~~

By noon, most of the fog was gone, but the gloom of the day held on. Dark clouds blanketed the town and the sky looked like it could burst with rain at any moment. Polly smiled as she and Rebecca got in the truck. If there was a good day to check out a haunted house, today was it.

"We aren't trespassing," Polly reminded Rebecca. "We're just looking. Okay?"

Rebecca had found a pair of Polly's old sunglasses. With their immense rims, they covered her black eye and then some. She lifted them up and glared at Polly. "You keep telling me that. I promise to be good."

"Fine then. We're just looking. We aren't going to see anything because there's nothing to see." Polly wasn't sure whether she was reassuring Rebecca or herself.

When she turned on to Beech Street, she saw the big house ahead, foreboding in the gloom. The large overgrown trees were shedding their leaves and the bushes that had obviously been planted for privacy now rose high and sprawled into the yard. Someone had trimmed the outside of the bushes to keep them away from the sidewalk, but they were still out of control. Once-white siding was now grey, dingy and sometimes missing from the walls of the house.

"Polly," Rebecca whispered.

"What?" Polly parked in front of the house across the street from their target.

"More of the boards are gone from the windows upstairs. Do

you think other people broke into the house to see if it's really haunted?"

Polly nodded. "Maybe. That's too bad. It would be sad if they got in and destroyed things. But it wouldn't surprise me."

"If there was only a husband and his wife and she lived alone there when he was in the Army, why did they have such a big house? It's like a mansion."

"Maybe they thought they'd have a big family when he came home," Polly said. "But you're right. It's a mansion."

"Wouldn't it have been awesome to sit in that porch on the second floor in the winter? Especially if all those windows were glass. You could watch the snow come down all around you and still be warm." Rebecca pointed to the solarium. "I'd love to have a big couch out there with lots of pillows and blankets. The dogs would curl up with me and I'd draw." She gasped. "I'd paint there! That would be awesome! I could look out over Bellingwood and see trees and houses and birds. I'd paint them all."

"That *would* be nice," Polly said, enjoying listening to Rebecca ramble.

"Maybe if Andrew and I get married someday, we'll buy this house and hire Henry to fix it up for us." Rebecca stopped herself and gave Polly a surreptitious look. "That's silly, isn't it? I'm too young to think about that."

"You're never too young to start dreaming about your future," Polly said. "Just don't try to make it happen before the future actually gets here. When I was young, I used to fall asleep picturing my dream house. I had the rooms drawn in my head. I knew where everything was going to be; how the kitchen was laid out, the bedrooms. Everything." She smiled. "One of my dream houses had a giant tree in the middle with a big courtyard. I built the house around that tree. There were covered walkways all around the inside so that animals and bugs couldn't get inside, but it was beautiful. I had a little difficulty imagining the odd shaped rooms, but I made it work."

"How old were you when you did this?"

Polly thought for a moment. "Probably after the first time I went to a dance with a boy. That's when I started thinking about growing up and living on my own." She chuckled. "Of course my future looks nothing like I ever dreamed it would be."

"What happened to that boy? Is he still here? Have you ever seen him again? How long did you date him?"

"Hmm," Polly said thoughtfully. "We went steady for maybe six months." She laughed. "But I look back and it was so sweet and so innocent. We barely ever talked to each other. We never dated, just saw each other at school and then he asked me to go with him to a couple dances."

"Why did you break up?" Rebecca asked.

"I don't even remember," Polly said. She huffed a laugh. "It would have been so important at the time, but I truly have no memory of breaking up. And I only have vague little snippets of memories about us going steady. I haven't seen him since we graduated from high school. I have no idea what he's doing now."

"Do you ever want to see him again?"

Polly looked over at Rebecca. "No. We were never friends. We didn't run in the same crowd and neither of us had any reason to spend time together after junior high. Now it's one of those sweet memories of a life I lived years and years ago. Why are you so curious?"

Rebecca shrugged. "What if that happens to me and Andrew? We quit being friends and then when we graduate from high school we never see each other again." Her face screwed up as if she wanted to cry. "I'd hate that. I don't want to stop being his friend."

"Oh honey," Polly said. "You two have so much in common and you're good friends now. I was never friends with this boy. I still have no idea why he asked me to that first dance. But I promise, whether or not you and Andrew become close enough to be girlfriend and boyfriend, you'll never lose your friendship. I'm friends with Sylvie, Jason works at Sycamore House, and Andrew will probably always come to the house after school. Your relationship won't fall apart."

"Polly look," Rebecca whispered, pointing up to the solarium.

Polly followed Rebecca's finger and said, "I don't see anything. What am I looking for?"

"I just saw something inside."

Polly chuckled. "No way. You're just scaring yourself."

"No," Rebecca protested. "I really did!"

"What did you see?"

Rebecca's continued to speak in a whisper. "I think it was the ghost. It was a girl in a white dress and she was floating."

"She can't hear you clear over here," Polly whispered back.

"But it's creepy. Now do you believe me?"

"I didn't see anything, honey."

"That's because you weren't looking. Quit staring at me and watch the house. I know I saw her."

A tap at Rebecca's car window made both of them jump and squeal. As soon as Polly took a breath, she wound Rebecca's window down to an older gentleman who was dressed in a wool jacket and carrying a Chihuahua.

"Are you girls looking for the Springer ghost?" he asked. "It's a tad early in the day for her."

"You've seen her?" Rebecca asked, her voice filled with awe.

"I know she's there. That's why Brutus and I walk on this side of the street. No one ever walks in front of that house. She's made it very clear over the years that she doesn't like trespassers. The best time to see her is at dawn. That's when she killed herself, you know. But the poor girl doesn't show up every day. It must be exhausting to never find your eternal rest. I imagine she has to gather her energy so that she can show up when she does."

"How often do people see her?" a very entranced Rebecca asked.

"We don't see much of her in the fall until the anniversary of her death approaches. She likes springtime and stands in the windows of the solarium as the sun rises. But when the mornings get darker and later, she isn't around as much. We like to believe that she's building up the energy to show herself to the world again, to remind us what terrible things happen when you give up hope. Poor thing."

"Did you know her when she was alive?" Polly asked.

He nodded. "I was just a lad. It was a sad day in Bellingwood. It was even sadder when her young man came home and discovered what had happened. But when she forced him and his young family out of the house, we were glad to see that old place boarded up."

Polly glanced at the house again. "I can't believe no one ever tried to purchase it and fix it up. It's such a beautiful building."

"There's a very good reason for that," the old man said. He lowered his voice. "Young Mister Springer was so upset that he'd been forced out, he didn't want anyone to encounter his wife. He was so angry that he wanted her to be alone for a long time. No one was allowed to buy that house or the property for seventy years after her death. By then he'd be long gone and wouldn't have to read or hear about her harming anyone else."

"That's this year," Rebecca said quietly. "Someone can buy it this year."

"By golly it is," the man said. "Who knows, maybe someone with some sense can finally get into that place, put the poor girl to rest and fix it up. It would be nice not to have that dark specter looming over the homes in this neighborhood. The folks who live here are hardy people. They've had to be. When Mrs. Springer gets in a snit, sometimes they lose their electrical and if she's really upset, the water turns off.

"That's ridiculous," Polly said. "I have never heard about any of that happening in Bellingwood."

He tsked her with a forefinger. "You haven't lived in town long enough to know the stories. While it hasn't happened in the last ten years, people remember the days when she'd go on a tear. The power would go down for a block all around this house and there wasn't anything anybody could do until she calmed down."

Rebecca looked from him and then to Polly. Behind those sunglasses, there had to be some very wide eyes.

"Brutus and I should be about our business," he said, putting the dog back on the ground.

"I'm Polly Giller and this is my daughter, Rebecca," Polly said.

"I know who you are, miss," he said. "Be careful." He walked away without introducing himself.

Polly pressed the button to roll the window back up and said, "That was weird."

"He knows about the ghost," Rebecca said. "He's seen her."

"He never said that he saw her," Polly said. "He told you the story, but he never claimed to have seen her."

"What about when the ghost got angry and turned off the power?"

Polly turned the truck back on and checked the street before driving off. "I suspect that if we were to ask the right people, we'd find that Bellingwood was in the middle of putting in new power lines. You notice they haven't had any trouble in the last ten years? You'd think that if there was a ghost, she'd have an inkling about the rumors regarding the length of time she was going to be alone and might step up the activity now."

"But what if ghosts don't have any idea of the passage of time?" Rebecca asked. "How would she know? Maybe today is the same as the day after she died. And I did see her. When I get home I'm going to draw a picture. Then you'll have to believe me."

"That's a good idea," Polly said. "I'd like to see what you saw. Now what would you like to eat for lunch?"

Rebecca leaned against the door of the truck. "My head kind of hurts. Can we go get a hot chocolate at the coffee shop? And maybe a croissant or something that Sylvie baked?"

"That sounds great. It's warm in there and filled with normal people. It will be the perfect remedy for chilly ghost stories."

"It's not just a story, Polly," Rebecca said. "I think there's something to it."

Polly nodded. "I know you do. And I'm not discounting anything that you've seen. But I believe there is a rational explanation behind all that you've seen and all that has happened."

Rebecca grinned and echoed Polly's earlier words, "You never know."

CHAPTER ELEVEN

After work, Henry was stopping to pick up pizza for dinner. It would only be the three of them. Heath had called to tell Polly he was staying in Boone for the football game and would be home before eleven.

The gloom hadn't lifted from the day and Polly and Rebecca were wrapped up in blankets on the media room sofa when Henry walked in.

"Did you save me a blanket?" he asked. "It's cold out there."

"We used them all up," Rebecca said, pulling another off the back of the sofa to wrap around her legs. "See. There's nothing left for you."

He turned to walk back into his office.

"Wait," she said.

Henry looked over his shoulder.

"Leave the pizza. We're hungry and we've had a rough day." Rebecca put her arms up for the pizza box.

"Rough day?" Henry asked. "What could the two of you have been doing that was rough? Did you sleep late and then live in your pajamas until you could take a nap? If you left the house did you go up to the coffee shop? What could possibly have been so rough?"

Rebecca patted the bruise on her cheek. "I've been in terrible pain all day long. It's the worst thing I've ever experienced."

He looked at Polly and she shrugged. "Whatever she says. She's the one who was wounded."

"I think I'm being played," Henry said, putting the pizza box on the coffee table in front of them. "But since Rebecca looks so bad, I'll be the good guy." He pointed to their glasses. "Do you need refills on anything?"

"No, but maybe Cheetos from the pantry?" Rebecca asked, continuing to use a whine in her voice. "Please?"

"Polly?" he asked.

"I'm good. We brought napkins and plates out." He left the room and Polly looked at Rebecca. "You're rotten."

Rebecca giggled. "I know, but he's so funny. He didn't buy it, did he?"

"Maybe a little bit," Polly said. "You do look sad and he's got a huge heart."

"I'll apologize," Rebecca said, hanging her head in mock shame. "But he is funny."

Henry came back in, dressed in a sweatshirt and jeans, got what he needed from the kitchen and came back. "So really, no blankets for me?"

"You can have this one," Rebecca said, pulling off the top layer and handing it to him. "I was just teasing. I'm okay. Really."

He sat down in a chair, drew the blanket across his lap and stuck his lower lip out. "Just see if I wait on you hand and foot this weekend. Just you wait and see." He flipped the top of the pizza box open and put his hand out for the plates in front of Polly.

She reached down and passed them to him, their hands brushing for a moment. It made her heart leap. How was it that this man still did that to her? Polly glanced at him to see if he'd reacted the same way and discovered him staring at her.

"Oh please," Rebecca said with disdain. "Save it for later. I'm starving."

"Sorry," Polly said. She opened the bag of Cheetos and put them in Rebecca's lap. Han tried to jump up between them and Polly pushed him back down. "No, you beggar. No food for you tonight. You know better."

"Come on, little guy," Henry said, patting the seat of his chair. "Sit with me. The girls aren't in a very generous mood tonight."

"We did have a strange encounter today," Polly said.

"Where?" he asked. "Did you actually leave the house?"

"We went up to the Springer House," Rebecca said. "And I saw the ghost, but Polly didn't. And there was an old guy who told us even more about her."

"He was odd," Polly interrupted. "Maybe you know him. He lives near there and walks his Chihuahua through the neighborhood. He has to be in his eighties."

Henry chuckled. "That's old Jim Bridger. He's a kook and the self-proclaimed archivist of all things Springer House. Whenever he sees someone in that neighborhood, he stops to tell them about the hauntings. He's tried for years to get the city to make a big deal out of that house and turn it into a tourist attraction. He hasn't been happy with those who proclaim that it's all hooey."

"He said that she used to turn the electricity and water off to the neighborhood when she was mad," Rebecca said.

"I'm sure he did. I'd forgotten about that rumor. It's interesting that he's the only person who ever tied those events to the ghost. Most people accepted them as normal power outages when the electric company was working on lines in town."

"He also said that the house was never on the market because the husband didn't want anyone else to live there and be hurt by his dead wife. And apparently, that clause will be up after Halloween this year," Polly said quietly.

"That's right," Henry nodded. "I don't know what the family's reasoning for it was, but I did some checking this week. The trust releases it for sale on November second this year."

"I wonder if there are many interested buyers," Polly mused.

"Who knows?" Henry said. "It will be interesting to see how much they'll ask for it."

They held each other's eyes for a moment, then Polly nodded and took another bite of her pizza.

"Let's back up," Henry said. "Did you see the ghost, Rebecca?"

She nodded enthusiastically. "Yes I did. And when I got home this afternoon, I drew her picture. Do you want to see it?" She'd thrown off her blankets and was off the couch before he had time to answer.

"I'd love to," he said quietly, grinning at Polly. "She's a riot."

"She's definitely a force," Polly agreed.

"Did she really see the ghost?"

Polly shrugged her shoulder. "She insists that she did and I've never known her to lie or to make things like this up. I don't know what to think."

Rebecca returned from her bedroom, carrying a sketch pad. She flipped through several pages and handed it to Henry. "That's her. I saw her floating in that room upstairs. What did you call it, Polly?"

"Solarium," Polly replied.

"The solarium. And there were more boards taken down today than when we were there on Saturday. It's like she wants us to see her. Mr. Bridger says that she shows up more often when it gets close to her death date. And supposedly the best time to see her is at dawn." Rebecca turned to Polly. "I wonder if she wanted us to see her today and that's why she showed up."

"Maybe," Polly said. She pointed at the nearly empty pizza box. "Anybody want more?" When there was no positive response, she stood, took plates from Rebecca and Henry, put them on top of the box, and took it to the kitchen. "Does anybody need anything while I'm out here?" she called back.

"We're good," Henry said.

Polly re-packaged the pizza and put it in the refrigerator, then poured popcorn she had purchased earlier in the week into a bowl and returned to the sofa. "Are we ready for a movie? You know we're only a week away from Halloween. Shall we watch something scary?"

"Like what?" Henry looked pointedly at Rebecca.

She caught his glance and laughed. "I like scary movies better than Polly does," Rebecca said, rolling her eyes. "My mom loved them. She said I was too young to watch them, but as long as I knew they weren't real, I'd be fine." She reached over and patted Polly's knee. "You know they aren't real, right?"

"Brat." Polly's phone rang and she grabbed it up. "It's Lydia, I'll be right back."

She swiped it open as she stood back up and walked into Henry's office. "Hi there, what's up?"

The background noise was deafening. "Hi there, dear," Lydia shouted. "How's your Friday night?"

"Where in the world are you? Why is it so loud?"

"Aaron and I were invited to come down to Boone for the football game. We like to do this every once in a while to remind ourselves why we don't do it very often."

Polly laughed. "So what's up?"

"Just a minute. It might be quieter over here," Lydia said. The noise lessened and she continued. "I had to call and tell you what I saw tonight. It's the sweetest thing."

"Okay," Polly said. "I'll bite. What's that?"

"It's your Heath. Polly, he's a lothario."

"A what?"

"We have seen him with no less than five young girls swarming around. Wherever he goes, at least one of them is there. I watched two walk away and come back with food for him. Another girl brought a blanket with her so she could sit next to him and keep them warm. Dear, it's adorable! And I know he'll never tell you about this, but that boy is popular with the girls."

"I had no idea," Polly said. "Five?"

"And they aren't competing with each other, either. He's keeping them all happy. Back when I was in high school, we had a boy like this. He was very popular with everyone, but the girls loved him because he was safe. We always accused him of having a harem. I think your Heath is growing his harem."

"Lydia, you have no idea what this does to my heart," Polly said with a sigh. "Thank you for telling me. He's had such a rough time of it and it's wonderful that he is attracting girls. He's a good looking, nice boy."

"These are very pretty girls and they seem to be popular with a large group of people. They're all having fun."

"Thank you," Polly said again.

"I thought you could use good news. Now I should go back to those wonderfully comfortable bleachers. Those things aren't made for anybody over the age of eighteen. But here we are. Have a good evening, dear."

Polly smiled. "You too, Lydia. Stay warm."

"Oh, I have my big ole snuggly man to keep me warm."

"Stop it," Polly said. "I'll talk to you later."

"Good night."

Polly stood in the quiet of the office for a moment. This was good news. Then she chuckled. Of course. That's why Jason doesn't like him. He was jealous. That dirty little rat. They were going to have to work this out on their own.

~~~

"That's Heath," Henry whispered to Polly, jostling her awake.

Rebecca had gone to bed early, taking the cats with her. It would take time for the swelling to go down and Polly knew from experience that it was sometimes exhausting trying to keep your eyes open when you hurt that badly. Polly and Henry had curled up on the sofa together with the dogs to watch another movie.

"Do you remember your parents waiting up for you?" Polly whispered back. "I feel like such an adult."

They both looked up when Heath entered the room.

"I'm not too late, am I?" he asked.

"You're good," Henry said and pointed to the chair. "Tell us about your evening. Did we win?"

Heath shook his head. "No, but I had a good time anyway. Thanks for letting me go."

"Of course," Polly said. "There's nothing better than football in the fall, right?"

"I guess." Heath leaned forward. "I need to talk to you guys about something."

Polly swung her legs around to sit up, disturbing both dogs.

Han jumped to the floor and sauntered over to Heath for attention, while Obiwan jumped back to where she'd left a warm spot on the sofa and snuggled in beside her.

Henry pushed the blankets at Polly and said, "What's up?"

Heath took a big breath. "I appreciate you guys letting me work at the barn, but..." he paused and looked back and forth between Polly and Henry, then looked down at Han and rubbed his head.

Polly wanted nothing more than to jump in, but she remembered Grey's comment and thought it best to let Heath tell his story. So she waited.

"I hate that job," he blurted out. "I mean, Eliseo is great and all, but I hate it. I'm ready to do something else now."

"What do you want to do?" Henry asked.

"I don't care. But anything that doesn't involve cleaning up animal crap."

Polly chuckled. "So maybe not working at Doc Ogden's vet clinic."

Heath looked at her in shock. "Don't tell me he's got a job available." He shuddered and gave his head a quick shake. "No. I'd hate it. I need something else. I'll walk all over town tomorrow and see what's available if that's okay. I just need out of the barn."

"Working with animals isn't for everyone," Henry said. "I get it. I was very grateful when Polly hired Eliseo. If I'd married her before he came on board, she'd have had me down there shoveling crap and hauling hay bales. Those are beautiful animals, but I like my horses to be able to rev and hang out under the hood of a car."

"Me too!" Heath exclaimed. "I've always loved cars. Dad promised me and Hayden that when we got old enough he would buy an old muscle car for us to all work on together." He dropped his shoulders. "That never happened, though."

"You don't have to keep working in the barn," Polly said. "Just because you live here doesn't mean you have to work here, too."

"I know." Heath shrugged. "It wasn't my place to complain. You guys were doing all of this stuff for me and Hayden told me I need to suck it up for a while. But when you let me drive last weekend and were so good about me hanging out with him in Ames, and then you didn't freak out when I was late this week, he said maybe I could ask about looking for a different job."

Henry looked at Polly and then said, "How hard will you work?"

"I'll do anything. I'm strong. I've been hefting hay bales for the last two months."

Polly squeezed Henry's hand. When he glanced at her, she nodded.

"I have several ideas," Henry said. "But they aren't just one job and you'll be all over the place."

"Anything. I'll do anything. I really want to get a car."

"Okay. Here's what I can do for you," Henry started. "We need extra help in quite a few places and you're going to have to work out a schedule so you can do everything. First of all, I want you to go see Mr. Greyson at the inn tomorrow morning. He's been working with Eliseo to clear a space for a small ice rink at the hotel. He needs someone to level the ground, haul dirt, all sorts of things. Then, we're getting busier at work and I could use someone after school. You'll be a gopher, nothing more. The guys will tell you what to do and how to do it and you'll have to pay attention. It won't be easy work and sometimes they won't be easy to get along with, but the pay is good."

"Are you kidding? I'll do it. I'll do it all!"

"But there's one more thing," Henry warned.

"Okay?"

"You're going to need a vehicle."

Heath slumped in the chair. "I know. That's why I can't get a job in Boone, I don't have a way to get there."

"If you work for me, I'll provide a truck for you. It's not here right now, but Polly's old truck is coming back to us next week. You and I will work out gas. When you're driving for me, I'll pay for it, but you'll pay for your own miles. And as part of driving this truck, you're going to learn how to do the work on it. Nate's shop is down the road and we'll teach you what's going on under the hood. You and I will split the cost for parts - for oil and filters. And as for insurance, I've already put you on our policy, but I want you to pay the difference between now and adding another vehicle. Seem fair?"

Heath had sat back in his chair while Henry talked, making room for Han to join him. He wasn't paying attention to the dog, but absentmindedly stroked Han's head. "Are you serious?" He looked at Polly for her reaction.

She smiled. "If you drive the truck to school, I want you to ask Jason if he'd like a ride," she said quietly.

"Donovan? Why?"

"Because he hates taking the bus as much as you. And both of you have to get back to Bellingwood for afternoon jobs. There's no reason to stay in Boone after school, is there?"

"No, but..."

"But nothing," Henry said. "That's part of the deal. And you can't have other kids in your truck for a while. For that you need to build up trust with us. If you can handle this responsibility, we'll revisit that conversation, but for now, this is what you've got. Any questions?"

Heath sat for a moment, staring off into space. "If I buy a car that needs work, will you let me do that here?"

"No," Henry said with a smile, shaking his head. "But we can talk to Nate about parking it at his shop. When you have free time and if one of us is there, you can work on it. You'll like that place. He's got cool tools."

"Someday I want to work in a garage," Heath said. "That would be so awesome. There's nothing better than listening to an engine purr."

"Gearheads," Polly said. "I'm surrounded by gearheads. But one of the first things you're doing with that truck is painting it. I'll pay for that myself. I will not have that thing in my driveway looking the way it does now."

"What's wrong with it?" Heath asked.

Henry shook his head and grinned. "She has ugly feelings about that truck. It's the one used by the serial killer last spring."

"Oh!" Heath said, his eyes growing big. "I don't know if that's cool or creepy."

"Creepy," Polly echoed. "It's creepy. If you want to change the seats in it, I'm fine with that, too."

"We'll take care of it," Henry said. "Don't worry. So what do you think, Heath? Does this sound like a plan?"

Heath sat up and put his hand out, startling Han. "It's a great plan. Thank you."

Henry shook it. "Talk to Grey and find out how many hours he wants. Then, you and I will put together out schedule. Look at your school calendar and decide what types of things you want to do and when you'll need to be free. I don't want to stop you from having fun with your friends, but I want you to be deliberate about this. If there are extra-curricular activities you should be participating in, tell us. Don't miss out on high school because you need a car. Hayden played basketball and look where that got him. A scholarship and a lot of good buddies."

"I'm not like him," Heath said. "I was never into sports and I don't have a lot of buddies. At least not anymore." His head shot up after he heard what he said. "And I'm glad about that. Those guys weren't good for me. I wasn't complaining."

"You're fine," Henry said. "It's late and tomorrow is the start of another day."

"Do I need to tell Eliseo?" Heath asked.

Henry glanced at Polly.

"That's the right thing to do," she said. "I could do it for you, but when you resign from a job, it's best if you're up front about it. Eliseo knows that you've had a rough time of it. He'll understand."

That knocked some of the wind out of his sails, but he smiled when he lifted Han to the floor and stood up. "Thank you guys. I know you've been trying to let me tell you that I want another job, but tonight Libby told me I just needed to be done."

Before Polly could open her mouth to ask about Libby, he was already walking away. She waited for him to clear the threshold into the living room. "I hate that," she said under her breath.

"What?" Henry asked.

"I wanted to ask more questions about Libby. My opening came and went in a split second. Dang."

"He's finally talking to us, Polly. It will come again."

"You were great with him," Polly said. "Thank you."

"He made it easy. We'll see if he can hold up. It's a lot to take on."

"At least he isn't getting yelled at and disrespected every time he walks into the house," she said. "He's finally starting to relax. Can you imagine how bad things had to have been getting?"

"You're right, but he's never had to be responsible for this much. It makes me nervous."

"Why don't we deal with that when it comes up?" Polly poked his side "Aren't you always the one telling me to be patient?"

Henry grabbed her hand and pulled her close, kissing her lips. "Don't you throw my words back at me, missy-girl. I'll have to make you pay."

"Oh horrors," she said. "Whatever will I do?"

CHAPTER TWELVE

"Unless you have a really good reason, I'm not smiling." Rebecca was slumped over the table, still in her pajamas when Polly came into the dining room.

She was surprised that everyone was already up. Heath's hair was wet from the shower and he was dressed and ready for the day.

"What's the plan for today?" Polly asked.

"Heath's already been out," Henry said, pointing at the window. Rain was coming down in torrents.

"Out there? Why?" Polly asked.

Henry nodded to Heath, who responded. "I went down to talk to Eliseo as soon as I saw him drive in. I didn't want to wait."

Polly smiled. "And?"

"He was cool. Told me that if I needed anything, he was always around. I offered to work this morning since it was so last minute and he said he had plenty of help. So I came back."

"He was back and showered before I came out," Henry said. "We're making breakfast. French toast and sausage casserole. That's in the oven and will be ready in ten minutes."

"Why are you up, little miss?" Polly asked Rebecca, rubbing the girl's back.

"Stupid cats," Rebecca mumbled.

Polly laughed. "Their morning playtime? Don't you love it?"

"No. They played all over my bed until I finally got up."

"That's why you don't take the cats to bed with you," Polly said, moving her fingers up to massage Rebecca's neck.

"I'll remember that. They kept me warm last night, though. The bottom of Leia's paws are like little furnaces."

Henry handed Polly a mug of coffee. "Here's your go-go juice. Drink up. You look rough. I thought you slept well last night. What's up?"

"You fell asleep long before I did," Polly said. "I don't know what my problem was. There weren't any nightmares."

"Might have had something to do with that nap you had about nine thirty."

"Don't let me do that again, then. It's your fault."

Henry nodded. "After breakfast, Heath and I are headed out. Since it's raining so hard, I'm going to run him over to the inn to talk to Grey and then I want him to meet Nate and see the shop. I'll check with Aaron and see if they'll release the truck to us today."

"Wow." Polly sat down in a chair beside Rebecca. "I don't have near that many plans. Rebecca and I are thinking that there might be several naps today, right?"

"Uh huh." Rebecca still hadn't lifted her head out of her arms on the table.

"How's your noggin this morning?" Polly asked.

"It's throbbing and I don't want to open my eyes. I just want to take a pain killer and go back to bed."

Polly leaned in. "Are you interested in breakfast?"

"It smells kind of good," Rebecca whispered back.

"You nut." Polly laughed and stroked her hand through Rebecca's hair. "You can go back to bed after breakfast. Are you up for your lesson at Beryl's?"

Rebecca lifted her shoulders. "I don't know."

"If you get another couple hours of sleep, maybe you'll be in better shape. We'll see how you feel."

Heath put butter and syrup on the table beside the stack of plates and silverware. "OJ?" he asked Rebecca. When she didn't respond, he looked at Polly.

"Hey missy, he's talking to you," Polly said.

Rebecca lifted her head. "What? Oh sorry. Yes, please."

He filled a glass and put it down in front of her. "You look worse this morning than you did yesterday."

"Thanks," she said with a grimace. "That's just what a girl likes to hear." Rebecca dropped her head back into her arms. "But I feel worse today, too."

"The doctor said you might," Polly reminded her. "This is going to pass. I promise."

"Am I being a drama queen?" Rebecca asked.

Henry's shoulders shook as he flipped the French toast on the griddle. Heath turned so no one could see him grin.

"A little bit," Polly said. "But we'll let you get away with it this morning. This afternoon will be a different story. Okay?"

"Maybe I'll be dead by then. A cool, dark coffin," Rebecca said. "That would be okay." She lifted her head enough to wink at Polly.

Heath brought the hot casserole dish to the table and placed it on a dish towel he'd folded. Henry handed him a spatula and Heath set it in front of Polly.

"Plates," Henry said. "I need plates."

Heath grabbed up the stack and put them on the counter beside the stove. Before long, they were back on the table in front of everyone's place.

"Sit up straight," Polly said to Rebecca. "No slouching at the table."

Rebecca sat up and pulled her chair in closer, then leaned on the arm of her chair and picked at her French toast.

Polly dished up the sausage and egg casserole and sat back to enjoy what she had. "This is a great breakfast, guys. I like Saturday mornings with you all." She grinned at Heath.

"Especially when you two cook. Thank you." She tapped Rebecca's hand. "Tell them thank you and sit up and eat."

"Thank you," Rebecca said. She pulled herself up and promptly placed an elbow on the table, resting her head in her hand.

"Honey, if you don't want to eat now, you can be excused," Polly said. "But either sit up and eat with the rest of us or go on back to bed. You can have leftovers later."

"Really?" Rebecca asked.

"Really. Go to bed. Shut the door so you aren't bothered by the animals."

"Thanks." Rebecca pushed her chair back and started out of the room. "It smells good. Sorry."

"Is she going to be okay?" Heath asked.

Polly nodded. "She'll be fine. It's going to take time for her to heal."

"Polly's seen much worse in the last couple of years," Henry said, smiling across the table at her. "I think she asks for people to beat her up just for the sympathy."

"You've been beaten up?" Heath asked, his eyes huge. "In Bellingwood?"

"A few times," Polly said. "And you and your buddies thought you might get physical with me and Mr. Greyson."

Heath dropped his head. "I'm sorry." He put his fork down and the excitement of the morning drained out of him.

"Wait," Polly said. "I shouldn't have teased you about that. It's in the past, right?"

"Uh huh."

"My only point was that stuff happens in Bellingwood like anywhere else. I didn't mean to tear you down. You're doing a very good job of turning your life around."

"I can't believe we were so stupid," Heath said. He put his hand over his mouth and gulped. "And I can't believe Ladd killed those girls. It makes me sick when I think about it. I didn't know how to stop him."

Henry reached over and put his hand on Heath's arm. "Son, when a life is as out of control as yours was, sometimes you can't see what's right in front of you. We don't blame you for what happened. You need to stop blaming yourself."

"Other people blame me," Heath said, his head still down. He couldn't bring himself to look into Polly and Henry's faces. "Sometimes they still talk about it at school. How I should have told someone about Ladd. But there wasn't anybody to tell. Who was going to listen? Hayden was the only person who cared and he was hundreds of miles away. Then they took my phone away and the only time I could talk to him was on Sunday nights with them in the room." He shook his head and pulled deeper into himself. "It's like it was all some black nightmare. I didn't think I was ever going to wake up." He let out a breath. "I can't believe those people are my relatives. I never want to see them again."

"I hope you never have to," Polly said. "And as for the kids at school, there is no way that you can un-hear what they say to you or about you. Bullies won't go away, they will probably always be part of your life."

Henry interrupted. "You should hear some of the things people say about Polly here in town."

"I have," Heath said with a nod and then very quietly, "I said some of them."

"But it doesn't stop her from being who she is, does it?" Henry asked.

"No, but I'm not as nice as Polly."

Polly grinned. "See, Henry. I'm nice."

He chuckled. "Yes you are. Heath, you can make choices every day about what kind of person you want to be. Your character is a result of your own behavior, not what anyone else does."

"Uh huh," Heath said.

"Getting too philosophical?" Polly asked.

Heath looked up with a small smile.

"Eat more of this great breakfast you and Henry made," she said. "It sounds like you have a big day ahead."

"What about you?" Henry asked. "Big plans?"

Polly shook her head. "Nah. Rebecca and I will probably stay here. I'm going to cancel her lesson with Beryl. Andrew and

Kayla's arrival this afternoon will probably be enough activity for the day."

~~~

"Grey?" Polly called out when she walked into the lobby. He didn't immediately pop up from behind the counter, so she called again. "Grey?"

"Good afternoon, Miss Polly," Grey said, coming out from his apartment. "How are you this rainy afternoon?"

"I got cabin fever," she said. "The kids are all snuggled up in front of the television with the animals and I had to get out." She lifted the tote bag she'd carried in. "We made a shepherd's pie for lunch and I always make two, so I thought maybe you'd eat the second."

"That would be wonderful." He had come out from behind the counter to walk beside her and took the tote from her hands. "There's more than just a shepherd's pie in here."

"I made homemade bread, too. There's nothing like the smell of bread baking to warm up a house."

"This is a very generous gift," Grey said. "Thank you. I will enjoy it. Come on in to the apartment. I have coffee if you'd like it."

Polly followed him. "I've had plenty for the day," she said. "But I'd take a glass of ice water."

"Ice water for the lovely lady." He put the tote on the floor and held a chair for her at the kitchen table.

This was her father's table and it felt odd to see it in another's home. She wouldn't want it anywhere else; it just felt odd to sit at it with someone else.

Grey filled a glass and put it in front of her, then took the bread and pie out of the tote and placed them on the counter. "I have pastries from the bakery," he said. "That has been a wonderful treat for our guests in the mornings. We don't often have much left over, but Mrs. Donovan makes extras on Saturdays and Sundays. Those are usually our busiest mornings."

Polly nodded. Adding Sylvie's baked goods for a continental breakfast had been Grey's genius idea. Guests could tell that they were fresh from the oven and they'd received rave reviews for that one simple addition.

"Has the sheriff cleared out Jeremy Booten's room?" she asked.

"Not completely," Grey responded. "They continue to treat it as a crime scene."

"Was his camera gear here? His computer?"

"Yes, the computer was still there, but the cameras are gone. I suspect that when they find the young man's car, they will also find the cameras. Those were very fancy pieces of equipment. He'd converted one to see across the visible spectrum, from ultraviolet to infrared and everything in between." He gave her a conspiratorial look. "Just between you and me, I believe that he was searching for a lost cause, but maybe he found something and then it found him."

"I hope not," Polly said, her body reacting to the thought with a shudder. "Did he ever say anything to you about the Springer House here in town?"

"He did," Grey replied. "In the weeks before he died he spent time with an elderly gentleman who knew a great deal about the house."

"Rebecca and I met him yesterday. He knows a lot about Muriel Springer, her death and the surrounding mystery. Whether or not any of it is true remains to be seen," Polly said.

"Young Jeremy hoped to spend a night in the house if he could get permission. I do remember that he was having difficulty with that. No one in town knew how to contact the owner. Barring that, I don't know about his intentions. He did mention that the ghost was rumored to rise at dawn. He was often up before daybreak. He came back to his room during the brightest part of the day and then would be gone late into the nights." Grey smiled at her. "I don't like to wait up for the guests, but I generally see automobiles coming and going throughout the night. Bellingwood is very quiet and there is not much traffic on these roads. One or two cars gets a person's attention."

Polly grinned. "Don't I know it. When I first moved back here, the silence was surprising."

"It is certainly something to be treasured. 'Tis a shame that I often fill it with the noise of my television." His eyes lit up as he changed the subject. "Thank you for sending young Heath to my doorstep this morning. I look forward to spending time getting to know him. We will put in a great deal of hard labor, but during that time, I believe we will become fast friends."

"He needs good friends," Polly said. "I'd like them to be closer to his age." She stopped, thought about it and said, "You know what? I don't care. Only a few of my friends are my age. The rest are all over the place. Some are older, some are younger. What is it about school that limits us to a specific age group?"

"One of the conundrums of our educational policies," Grey acknowledged. "If we would learn together, we would learn so much more. But that's a conversation for another day."

"Or never," Polly said. "I get into those types of conversations and they frustrate me. There's nothing I can do to change the system and everyone has a better idea than the one that's in place." She huffed a laugh. "That's true, too. Nearly everyone's ideas are so much better, but then we are all reminded of reality."

"You are quite right," Grey said. "Do you believe Heath might consider learning to skate?"

"I don't know," she said. "But if he takes some ownership with the ice, maybe it will come naturally. I do believe, though, that he will not allow himself to look foolish while he learns. He's had enough of that in his short life."

"Those are things I will help him with as we go along," Grey said. "Now let's hope that freezing temperatures arrive in Bellingwood soon so this might come to pass."

Polly looked around. She hadn't been in the apartment since he'd moved in and though it was still sparse, hints of his personality were showing through. He'd rearranged the living room and a tall walking stick stood by the back door, the head of it carved as a gnarled burl.

"I see you got a new walking stick," she said, pointing at it.

"Your father-in-law created a wonderful piece for me. He's quite a master carver. The gentleman who works with him, Mr. Specek?"

Polly nodded.

"He turned the piece on his lathe and then we worked together to make sure the head would comfortably fit my hand. I'm quite proud of it and don't believe I've ever owned such a beautiful piece." Grey stood and walked over to the stick, then brought it back so Polly could hold it.

She rubbed her hand across the smooth length of it, admiring the patterns. "You found a nice piece of wood," she said.

"The masters are the ones who brought out its beauty as they worked." Grey took it back as she handed it to him.

"Is there anything else I can do for you, Grey?" she asked him. "Sometimes I worry about you living here all alone. You have to work the worst hours of the day and I know it doesn't leave you much time to be with people."

He took a deep breath. "It is best this way for now, Miss Polly. I've required a great deal of healing myself this year and though I am grateful for the opportunities which come my way, I am still not prepared to fully reintegrate myself into a life filled with people."

"And their problems?" She finished his thought.

"And the depth of their problems. Young Master Sutworth is in such desperate need of my help that I couldn't live with myself if I didn't spend time listening and speaking with him. He's come a long way since the accident, but his growth is only beginning. However, to maintain my own path toward wholeness, I am only able to take one young person like him on right now."

Polly stayed silent. She desperately wanted to know what had broken this man, but he didn't seem to be inclined to tell her his story yet.

He brightened up. "There is one thing I might ask of you in the next week or so." He stopped. "I believe it can wait until after your extravaganza on the thirty-first, though."

"What's that? I'd be glad to help with anything."

"I believe that I can no longer proceed without a vehicle. After a bit of online research, I will attempt to find one to suit my needs, but I fear that I cannot walk to Boone or Ames and will need to procure a ride."

"I'd be glad to take you wherever you need to go," Polly said. "Just tell me when."

"It is quite embarrassing to me that I must call upon you for assistance, but this will be the last time. Once I have a vehicle and my freedom again, feeling the wind in my hair will give me a sense of independence."

"Wind in your hair? It's getting colder," Polly said with a laugh. "I hope you keep your windows rolled up."

"At the very least, I will be able to answer the call of the open road." Grey smiled again. "I understand there are some very interesting highways in rural Iowa."

"Some of them scare me to death," Polly said. "Between the winding curves, the hills and the limited shoulders, those roads aren't something you take at high speed, even when you're quite familiar with them."

"I look forward to the experience." A bell clanged and he looked up. "Ahhh, the first of our evening's guests have arrived. If you'd like to wait, I will be back shortly."

"No," Polly said. "I should go home and check on my family. I just wanted to bring something warm and homey over for your dinner."

He held the front door open for her to walk through and waved at the customers who were approaching the counter. "I am grateful for your friendship, Miss Polly. Thank you for stopping in and for bringing such wonderful gifts."

Polly smiled at the guests and waved goodbye to him. She was glad she'd come and needed to make sure she did this more often on the weekends.

CHAPTER THIRTEEN

Next to Joey Delancy's face, the pickup truck he and Allendar had taken from her and used during their serial kidnapping and murder spree was the last thing Polly wanted to see. She shuddered when she drove into the driveway. Henry and Heath were standing at its rear gate, Heath leaning against the truck. Henry gave her a small wave as she drove in.

"You got it back," Polly said after jumping out of her own truck. "Joy."

"We're already making plans to paint it," Henry said. "Were you serious about splitting the cost for new front seats?"

Polly had a flash of a dead girl sitting in that seat. After trying to maintain another shudder and hold back the bile that rose in her throat, she nodded. "I'll pay for the whole thing. Just make sure the leather or whatever you choose is a completely different color."

"Are you okay?" Henry met her as she walked toward the back door. "Your face went pale."

"Flashbacks," she said. "I'll be fine. I just don't want to look at that thing right now."

He opened the door. "Should we have not done this?" Henry spoke softly so Heath couldn't hear.

Polly led him inside and closed the door. "I know that I'm being irrational. It's only a truck. And I also know that given time, this will pass. When the next trial is over, I'll put nearly everything behind me. But today, seeing that truck again and just coming off Joey's trial, it was too much. You know I don't like to make decisions when things are still emotional. We need another vehicle, we can make cosmetic changes to help me deal with it and..." she smiled and blew out a breath. "In five years will I still react so badly to the truck? No," she said, shaking her head. "I'll go upstairs and snuggle my animals and put this back in the compartment where it belongs."

"You're sure," he said.

"I refuse to make major decisions just because I freak out over something. Don't worry. I'm fine."

"Heath's pretty excited to have a vehicle to drive."

"You know," Polly said. "We didn't warn him about keeping his grades up. That's as important to me as him being responsible to the work he's taking on."

"We talked about that today. Driving the truck isn't based on keeping his grades up, but keeping his jobs where he can make the money he wants to make in order to pay for gas, insurance, and save for his own car is. That's what will give if his grades falter."

She chuckled. "That's kind of underhanded."

"Yep. I learned from my mother. She's as sneaky as they come."

Polly shook her head. "I never saw Dad that way. It was all right out there with him."

"You were probably a better daughter than I was a son," Henry said. "I pushed Mom into decisions she might not have made otherwise."

She kissed him and headed for the stairs. "Tell Heath it's okay. But would you mind parking it at the other end of the front parking lot until after it's painted?"

"On it."

Polly went up the steps and stopped to kiss the top of her dogs' heads before wandering into the media room. She was more than a little shocked to see Rebecca and Andrew snuggled together on the couch under a blanket.

"Where's Kayla?" she asked.

Andrew tossed the blanket aside guiltily and jumped up. "She had to go home. Stephanie wasn't staying. They had plans to go to a show or play or something at Iowa State."

"Ahh," Polly said, nodding her head up and down. "And what have the two of you been doing?"

"Nothing!" he exclaimed. "We were watching a movie." He glanced at the blanket. "And it was cold."

She didn't reply, but went over to the thermostat. "Seventy-two degrees. That's not cold. In fact, it's quite warm in here. So, do you want to tell me again what you thought you were doing?"

"I'm cold," Rebecca said, affecting a weak, sickly voice. "We weren't doing anything else."

"Sit," Polly said, pointing at Andrew. He sat back down on the couch, putting as much room as he could between the arm and Rebecca. The look of guilt on his face told her enough.

She took the chair next to him, lowered her head, drew in a deep breath and let it out. She repeated the action twice more, then looked up at the two of them. She remembered a conversation she and Eliseo had before he had taken Hansel and Gretel in to be fixed. They were such cute little kittens, playing with each other and always finding ways to be together. He'd taken them in as soon as Doc Ogden would do the surgery with a flip comment that "Cute kittens grow up to be randy tomcats if you don't snip it in the bud." They'd laughed uproariously at his joke.

The cute little kids that Polly had known and loved for the last two years were growing up. She was going to face this now ... out loud. It wouldn't be the last time they'd have this conversation and she knew it. Why couldn't they stay cute little kittens forever?

"You know that I trust you both, right?" she asked.

They nodded their heads.

"And I think the world of you. In fact, you are two of my favorite people ever."

They continued to nod and watched her face for what was coming.

Polly took another deep breath. "I don't know how to have this conversation with you."

"Then don't?" Rebecca tilted her head and looked at Polly, pleading in her eyes.

"Gah," Polly said. "I'm not ready for this." She stood up and walked behind the sofa. "You two are supposed to stay little kids forever. Well, not forever. When you turn twenty-one, you can do all of your growing up. But nothing until then, okay?"

They followed her pacing with their eyes, neither daring to move.

"I swear, Polly. We were just sitting here. We didn't do a thing," Andrew said.

"Then why the guilt?" She bent over quickly and looked him in the eyes.

"I don't know." He dropped his head.

"Rebecca?" she asked.

"We didn't do anything wrong."

Polly sat back down, leaned forward and rested her elbows on her knees. "I want to trust you to be alone in the house."

"You can," Rebecca said, interrupting her.

"But for how long?" Polly asked. "I know this is a runaway train and it scares me to death for you."

"We aren't stupid," Rebecca muttered.

Polly knew full well that smart kids got themselves in just as much trouble as anyone else. Probably even more because they were smart enough to avoid detection. But she didn't want to make a big deal out of this. The funny thing was, even though they denied that anything had happened, they still knew exactly what she was accusing them of doing. Or at least, something along those lines. If they hadn't been doing anything, both of them were thinking about doing something. She'd been so happy that Kayla was part of their crew. At least with a third person, things would stay aboveboard. This sitting alone under the blankets thing was a bad omen.

"Do you believe us?" Andrew asked.

"I do," she said. "But that doesn't mean I'm comfortable with you two being here by yourselves."

"That's not fair," Rebecca said. "Andrew's my best friend. We've been alone as long as I've lived here."

"And yet things have changed, haven't they?" Polly asked.

The two dropped their heads again.

Oh why, oh why did Polly have to be friends with both kids? If she was having this conversation with Rebecca or with Andrew, it would be one thing. This wasn't easy.

"Here's the deal," Polly said. "I know I can't keep an eye on you all the time, so I have to trust you. But I don't want to come home again and find you together under blankets. If you get cold - separate blankets, separate ends of the couch. Okay? I don't want to separate you and I know you're just beginning to think about being a couple. There are rights and responsibilities that come with a relationship. The responsibility part is the most difficult thing to deal with. Whether I tell you not to do this doesn't matter. You'll do what you want if no one's around. But I can tell you that if you wreck my trust, new decisions will be made about how you spend time together. Am I making myself clear?"

"You'd kick Andrew out?" Rebecca asked.

"Or you," Polly said, keeping as straight a face as possible.

"You can't kick her out, she's your daughter now," Andrew said.

Rebecca swatted his arm. "You're so easy. But you'd really not let him come over?"

"He has a nice house with a dog that loves him. If I can't trust you, that's where he'll be after school and on Saturdays. Easy as that."

Rebecca blanched and Andrew stood up.

"You can trust us, Polly. I don't want to stay home by myself." He looked down at Rebecca. "You're my best friend. We can't screw this up."

The dogs bolted for the back stairs and Rebecca looked at Polly in a panic. "Don't say anything, please?"

"You know I don't keep secrets from Henry," Polly said.

"But not in front of everyone. Please?" she whispered.

Polly nodded. "Cross your hearts?" she asked.

Both kids crossed their hearts.

~~~

"This is one of the perks of having Heath living with us," Polly said.

Henry put his hand out on the truck's console. "You don't trust Rebecca to take care of herself?"

She chuckled and put her hand in his. "No, that's not it. But I always feel guilty leaving her alone. Like I'm out having fun and she's stuck in the house all by herself, sad and lonely, a poor waif."

"With four animals there, how could she be lonely?" Henry asked.

"I didn't say it was rational. I hate not taking her with us. But with Heath there, even if they aren't in the same room, they know someone is around."

"Why didn't Andrew stay?"

Polly pursed her lips, glad that it was dark and he couldn't see her reaction. She didn't want to talk about the two kids with him just yet. He'd been so upset a few months ago at the thought of Andrew and Rebecca trying to create a relationship, she didn't want him to worry until it was necessary. Rebecca could just wonder how much Henry knew. In fact, more than anything, Polly hoped Andrew worried about Henry. That might keep him honest. But tonight she wanted to enjoy being out and about.

"I don't know," she finally said.

He glanced at her and then back at the road. She probably hadn't pulled that one off.

They'd gone to a sports bar on the southwest side of Ames for hamburgers. It was nice spending time with Henry. They'd talked about the silliest things, from political candidates to the World

127

Series, and an old friend of Henry's who had found him on Facebook. Polly didn't even realize he spent much time on social media. He'd caught her up on some of the idiotic things his guys did on job sites, admitting that he was going to have to fire one of them for falsifying company records. He hadn't stolen much, but it was a path Henry wasn't willing to go down with the man. After blatant lies and insubordination, Henry knew it was time to let the guy go, but it was never easy.

"I'm not ready to go home yet," Henry said when they got back in the truck.

Polly agreed. "Just drive, then. Nobody needs us to be anywhere. We could always find a park and make out."

"My luck you'd find a dead body."

"Not if I stay in the truck. Come on, Henry. Let's act like stupid kids. Just this once."

In the end, he'd driven up Highway 17 to Webster City and they'd gone to Dairy Queen for ice cream. Now they were meandering their way back to Bellingwood. Polly couldn't believe how well she'd gotten to know these country roads. She didn't ever know the area around Story City as well as she knew these roads. She'd gotten good and lost that first summer she moved back to Iowa, but there was no way that would happen again. At least not in the counties surrounding her home.

"It is my home, you know," she said.

Henry squeezed her hand. "I know that. What are you thinking about?"

"How well I know these roads. And even if I haven't been on all of them, I know where we are and what it takes to get back to one I'm familiar with. We drove around all the time when I was in high school and I barely remember any of that."

"You've had a lot happen between high school and now," Henry said.

"I can't imagine what it must be like to have lived in one place for your entire life. Nothing surprises you."

He chuckled. "You surprise me all the time. Maybe that's why I married you."

"Pull over," she said.

"What?"

"Stop the truck."

Henry slowed down and pulled over onto the shoulder. "What's going on?"

"Can you turn around? I saw something back there."

"You have *got* to be kidding me." Henry did what she asked and made a perfect three-point turn in the highway and headed north. "Where am I looking?"

Polly pointed into rough land, marked with a winding creek, trees and brush. "In there. I thought I saw something."

"Something what?" Henry asked, driving slowly.

"Something like a car. What would a car be doing back there?"

"It's probably a turkey house or maybe a hunter's blind."

She puffed air out of her lips. "Whatever." Then, she pointed. "Right there. In the creek. Do you see it?"

Henry stopped on the highway, backed onto the opposite shoulder and aimed his headlights where she pointed. They reflected off something through the trees.

"I see it," he said. "What is it?"

"I don't even want to say," she replied.

"Just tell me."

"It might be that young man's car. They haven't found it yet and you know it's just my luck."

Henry shook his head. "I don't have a good flashlight so we can check it out."

Polly took out her phone. "Let's see if Aaron thinks I'm crazy."

"Maybe you shouldn't actually ask him that question. You might not like the answer."

She swiped the call open and waited for Aaron to answer.

"Polly?" he asked with hesitation in his voice.

"It's not a body. At least I don't think so," she said.

"What do you mean by that?"

"You can do what you want with this, but I have a feeling that I found Jeremy Booten's car. The only problem is that it's in a ravine and I can't get to it tonight."

"Don't you dare go near it. Where are you?"

Polly gave him their location. They weren't that far north of Bellingwood, but she had no idea who owned this land. Aaron could worry about that.

"Someone will be there within twenty minutes. Can you wait?"

She giggled. "Oh goody. We have plenty of time to make out. Tell 'em to honk when they get close so we don't embarrass ourselves, okay?"

Aaron sighed. "Stop it. Please stop. Stu's on duty tonight. He'll be there soon."

"I'm not making out with you here on the highway," Henry said. "Don't even think about it."

"I can think about it all I want," Polly said. "It makes me laugh. You boys get yourself all worked up over the craziest things. Like I'd do that. Give me a break."

"And besides," he said. "There's this stupid console in our way. Remember back when we had wonderful bench seats in the front?"

"You mean like my dad's old truck?"

"Yeah. That. I miss those things."

Henry had re-oriented himself on the shoulder and lights from an oncoming vehicle flashed at them, followed by another flash of its emergency lights.

"That must be Stu," Polly said. "I'll get out and talk to him." She reached for the door, but stopped when Henry put his hand on her arm.

"Wait until he gets here and stops. You scare me to death, woman."

"What?"

"Don't *what* me," he said. "A million bad things could happen. It could be someone else, another vehicle could send him careening into you. Anything. Just be patient."

"You're a worrywart," she said.

"Someone has to worry about you," he muttered under his breath.

"I heard that."

The sheriff's vehicle pulled up in front of them, Stu Decker got out and walked up to the passenger side of Henry's truck.

Polly turned her window down and said, "Henry thought you might be a bad guy coming to hurt us."

"I did not," Henry said.

Stu just grinned at them. "So tell me what you saw."

"Can I get out of the truck now?" Polly asked Henry.

He rolled his eyes and opened his door, Polly followed suit. "It's right over there," she said, pointing off into the darkness. "But unless we turn the truck around so we can use the lights, we can't see it."

"I've got this," Stu said. "You point to where you saw it and I'll use my lights. They should catch it."

Polly was overwhelmed by the lights that his car had available. It lit the night up, showing everything in the vicinity.

Stu got back out of his SUV and stood beside her. She pointed and he followed her finger. "It's certainly something that doesn't belong there. The trees are in the way of me telling you for sure that it's a car, but I agree. It probably is."

"Can we stay and watch you pull it out?" Polly asked.

"Go home, Polly," Stu said. "This is going to take hours."

"But how am I going to know if it's that guy's car or not? Will you call me when you find out?"

Stu shut his eyes, measuring his words. "I'll ask Aaron to let you know. He's not coming out tonight, but we'll keep him in the loop. I promise. Take her home, Henry."

"Got it. She owes me a little something anyway."

"Do I want to know?" Stu creased his brow in confusion.

Polly giggled. "Nope. It's too much information." She poked Henry's side. "Since when do you start telling our secrets?"

"Ten dollars. What you owe me is money!"

She looked back and forth between the two men. "Now I'm confused. I owe you money?"

"Get in the truck," Henry said and put out his hand to shake Stu's. "Thanks for coming up. I hope your evening isn't too messed up with this."

Stu shrugged. "It was a slow night. Whenever Polly calls at least we're assured that something interesting will happen."

Polly put her foot on the running board. "And Aaron is going to let me know?"

"Go," Stu said, waving her off. "Just go home."

CHAPTER FOURTEEN

Turning into a parking place in front of Pizzazz, Polly took a breath. She wanted to arrive before Sandy and Camille, but once inside, found Joss in her usual place, a glass of red wine in place of her usual iced tea.

"Rough day?" Polly asked, pointing at the glass.

"Horrible weekend," Joss said. "I fought with Nate, the kids were complete brats and none of us slept last night. I can hardly wait for Tuesday when I get to go back to work and rest."

Polly smiled. "Then wine it is. I'm glad you came out tonight. We have two new people joining us. You already know Camille and then I met this great girl - Sandy Davis. You'll like her."

Joss took a drink from her wine glass, opened her wallet, drew a five dollar bill out and tossed it on the table. "I'm heading out," she said. "Talk to you later."

"Wait. What?" Polly jumped to her feet to follow Joss out of the restaurant. "Where are you going?" She glanced back at Bri, their regular waitress and held up a finger, hoping Bri would understand she'd be back.

"I've had the worst weekend in months," Joss said when they

got outside the front door of the restaurant. "All I wanted to do was get some sympathy and companionship from my friends and now you tell me I have to be social and nice because two people I don't know are showing up. I can't do it. I just can't do it."

Polly grabbed Joss's arm. "I'm so sorry. I had no idea it would hit you this way. We've talked about meeting more people and this all fell together."

"Well, it fell together on the wrong night for me. I know you didn't do it on purpose, but you could have given me some warning."

"I'm so sorry," Polly said. "Please don't go. We'll drink wine, complain about kids and husbands and I swear you'll love Sandy."

"Not tonight, Polly." Joss shook her head and pulled her arm out of Polly's hand. "I just needed a safe escape and since I'm not going to get it here, I'll go home and deal with my little mess of a life. It's fine. Nobody's problem but my own."

Polly followed Joss to her car and waited while her friend unlocked it, then climbed in on the passenger side.

"What are you doing?" Joss asked.

"I'm talking to you. I don't want you to go home and be mad at me."

Joss leaned forward and rested her head on the steering wheel.

"What in the world happened with you and Nate?" Polly asked, reaching out to touch Joss's shoulder.

"It's no big deal and it's probably all my fault," Joss mumbled.

"What's your fault?"

Joss sat back. "It's that damned, freakin' house. We never should have done this. We were perfectly happy in our little house and who knows whether or not we're ever going to have more children. If I hadn't let him talk me into that great big acreage with a great big house, none of this would be happening."

Polly understood this panic all too well. There was at least one point of freaking out in every building project she'd been part of since moving to Bellingwood. Now, sometimes the other people freaked out, but it always happened. "What's going on?" she asked quietly.

"It's one thing after another," Joss replied with a sigh. "We fight about flooring and windows. I want to enclose the porch so the kids can be outside and I don't have to be right on top of them watching their every movement. Nate thinks I should give them more freedom. We're arguing about fixtures and where to put electricity. I've never had this many fights with him."

"How long have you been fighting about it?"

"Mostly this weekend. And I feel like hell. My period should be starting any day and of course, you know that means I'm still not pregnant. I'm never going to be pregnant. I know that, but every single month it's like this shows up and slaps me in the face to remind me. Cooper and Sophie are into everything. They're terrors. Cooper fell off a chair yesterday and has a huge cut on his forehead. Then I caught Sophie trying to eat a clump of dirt by the back door. She'll put anything into her mouth. It drives me nuts."

Polly sat there, watching her friend fall apart. The biggest stress in Joss's life was that she couldn't have her own children. As much as she tried to be okay with that fact, it was never going to be easy. The house was a focal point for that stress and Polly chuckled to herself at the abuse Nate was taking for this. She knew him well enough to know that he was the last person in the world to be argumentative.

"Aren't you going to say anything?" Joss asked.

"You're in hell." Polly looked at her friend. "There, I said it for you. Is it better?"

Joss put her hand over her face and then rubbed her eyes. "Maybe. You think this is all my fault because I'm hormonal, don't you."

"No. I would never say that. Whether we're hormonal or not, the emotions still take us down. It probably has more to do with your disappointment every month than just your period showing up, though."

"I wish it didn't," Joss whispered. "It's not like I haven't been dealing with this for a couple of years and I love Coop and Soph. I love them so much I cry when I look at them. They're perfect and they're mine. And they're absolutely adorable when they sleep."

Polly chuckled. "That's what my dad used to say about me. And hey, I was a good girl. But you grieve for those babies you can't have every month. Have you ever talked to Nate about it?"

Joss was shocked. "No. I don't want to make it worse for him. He's so happy there are other ways for us to have children in our lives. I don't want him to have to worry about me and my inability to have babies."

"You're starting to think about adoption again, aren't you," Polly said.

"Yeah," Joss said, nodding. "But we don't want to do anything until the house is finished and we're settled in. That's too much chaos."

"I can't believe you and Nate are talking about flooring and fixtures right now," Polly said. "You don't even have a structure yet."

Joss rolled her eyes. "That's my fault. Nate doesn't even care. But I got some catalogs and started pushing him to make decisions. When he finally pointed at things on the page, it was all wrong."

"Of course it was. Men are stupid," Polly said.

"I probably should have gotten out of the house before tonight." Joss put her forehead on the steering wheel again and bounced it twice. "This was the worst weekend."

"You said that. Do you want to come in and eat pizza now?"

Joss tilted her head and looked at Polly. "You don't think I'm crazy?"

"Of course I think you're crazy. But no more than the rest of us. Especially no more than me," Polly said. "Come on in. Meet new people, drink wine, eat pizza and bread and when you go home, tell Nate that you're making all the decisions for the inside of the house and that's the way it's going to be."

"He'd be relieved."

"Of course he would. And by the way. I need to tell you something about Sandy based on this conversation. She just had a new baby this summer and quit her big architecture job. They moved to Bellingwood because her husband's family lives here."

"What does that have to do with me?" Joss asked, then it hit her. "Oh. She's not thrilled about a baby."

"She's doing her best to be happy with this life change, but it was a surprise. Are you okay with this?"

"Maybe another glass or two of wine would help," Joss said. She took a deep breath and sat up straight. "Okay. I'm ready to head into the fray. Don't say anything, okay?"

Polly shrugged. "There's nothing to talk about. If it comes up tonight, it will be from you. Come on, let's go. Everyone else has gone inside."

Before she put her hand on the door, Joss reached across. "Thanks for not letting me get away with this. I'm sorry."

"Nothing to be sorry about either," Polly said. "It was a bad weekend and you didn't want to face new people. I get it. You're better now, though, right?"

"Right."

~~~

"Do you really believe a ghost lives there?" Sal asked Polly.

Polly shrugged and pushed the last piece of pizza toward Sylvie. "You've been quiet. What do you think?"

"I don't know," Sylvie said, pushing the pizza away. "Every year about this time, people work themselves into a frenzy about it. When I was in junior high, it was the same thing. We'd walk by the house after dark, just to get a glimpse. Some of my friends said they saw her. They weren't usually the types who would lie either."

"But not you?"

Sylvie dropped her head. "I was too afraid to look."

"What?" Sal threw her head back in laughter. "You didn't even look?"

"No," Sylvie said, looking up with a wry smile. "I was such a chicken. Somebody told me that if we looked and saw her, we'd have bad luck for the rest of the year. I didn't want to chance it. My life was hard enough."

Sandy Davis sat forward. "Did it happen every year?"

"By the time we were in high school, we had other things to think about. I forgot about it until Andrew came home last week, asking questions."

"Did Jason get caught up in it?" Polly asked. "I don't remember him ever saying anything."

"You had just gotten here and his life became all about those horses," Sylvie replied. "He didn't pay attention to much else. And since it's been seventy years and the house is about to go up for sale, there's been a lot more focus this year. I think people kind of let it die." She snuffled out a giggle. "That was bad. Sorry."

"We should go over there tonight," Sal said in a whisper. "Do any of us have a car that will hold six?"

Sandy put her hand up and wrinkled her nose. "If we move the baby seat, I have a van." She looked at their laughing faces. "I know. One kid and I already have a minivan. Please don't laugh at me. Benji insisted. Said it would be a good idea if we have more kids. He sold my Charger."

Camille patted Sandy's hand. "That's the saddest thing I've ever heard."

Everyone broke out in laughter.

"You have to stop letting that man change your life. It's only one baby," Sal said.

"You're right," Sandy said. "It all came as such a shock that I'm afraid I just stopped thinking. For nine months I focused on being pregnant and tried to wrap my head around taking care of a whole other person. I lost myself."

"It doesn't have to be one or the other," Joss said. "Sure, there are changes, but you don't actually die."

Sandy nodded. "I'm learning that." She opened her purse and took out her wallet. "But if we're going to go see this ghost, I probably need to start now. Benji's mom is at the house because my husband is scared to death of staying alone with the baby. This is the first evening I've been gone from them."

The others took out their purses and divvied up the bill. It always seemed to get left to Polly to make sure there was enough.

She counted the cash and nodded. They rarely miscalculated. It was nice to be with people who could add.

"I'm right out front," Sandy said, standing up. "Give me two seconds to warm the van up and make sure there aren't any weird crumbs or gooey stuff there."

After she hit the door, Joss turned to Polly. "That husband of hers is a real pip. I'd deck him."

"Neither of them were ready for this and she shot right down the old-fashioned, traditional wife path," Sylvie said. "Benji was okay when I knew him. His parents are nice people. Probably a little overly involved with them, but all Sandy has to do is put her foot down. Once she realizes that she isn't the first person who's had a baby, she'll be okay."

Polly handed the money to Bri and they trooped outside. Sandy was in her van on the phone. She popped the side door open as they approached.

"I'll be home later," she said. "Love you, too. Bye."

"You were worried about crumbs and gooey stuff?" Sylvie asked. "This is cleaner than any mommy van I've ever seen in my life. Even the ones that come new off the lot."

"If I have to drive this thing for the next ten years, I'm keeping it clean," Sandy said. "I can't stand a dirty car."

Polly crawled to the back row of seats and scooted over so Joss could slide in beside her. "Is your house this clean?"

Sandy smiled. "I'm used to a high-paced job. Being a mom is crazy, but since I don't sleep much, I have a lot of free time."

When they turned onto Beech Street, several cars were already parked across the street from the Springer House.

"This is the place," Sandy said and pulled into an open space. "But we're late for the party."

Polly leaned forward and looked out the window and saw a small fire in front of the Springer House. "What in the world?" she gasped.

"Who knew there were this many paranormal ghosty types in Bellingwood?" Sal asked, laughing.

Camille, who was in the front passenger seat, said, "I don't think they're from Bellingwood. The license plate on the car in front of us is Pennsylvania."

"Don't they have enough ghosts in their own state?" Sandy asked. "They have to come to Iowa to bother ours?"

Three women were circling the fire, tossing something into it at regular intervals to make the flame spark and rise. They wore flowing white blouses over blue jeans. Six other people were seated on small stools, far enough behind them to be out of their way as they danced.

"Over there," Camille whispered, pointing further down the street.

Sure enough, there were two people with cameras, filming the entire event.

"Okay everybody," Sandy said. "Be quiet. I'm going to roll down the window."

Polly moved up to the front of the van so she was kneeling between the two captain's seats. She held her breath as she listened. They were chanting. Over and over the same thing:

Muriel Springer, to you we call.
Upon our face, let your visage fall.
We only wish to bring you peace
And from this plane, your soul's release.

She glanced at Camille and mouthed, "Seriously?"

The young woman smiled and shrugged.

With every third incantation, a young man on a stool would beat a drum, helping them maintain the rhythm of the chants.

Polly motioned to Sandy to raise the window and when it was back up, she said. "I wonder what the neighbors think of this?"

Sylvie leaned forward and tapped Polly's shoulder. "I wonder if Ken knows?"

"If they're filming for a television show or documentary, surely they had to get a permit," Polly said. She looked back at the houses on the opposite side of the street from the Springer House. The drapes in the large window of one of the houses had been pulled back and a small group of people were gathered, watching the action in front of them.

"Yeah, this is better entertainment than anything else they've got going on. And since they aren't being too loud, it isn't bothering anyone."

"Did you see it?" Sandy yelped, making Polly jump.

"What?"

"Something in the upstairs window. It looked like a woman in a long dress."

"You're kidding me," Polly said.

Sandy turned to her. "Yep, but every single one of you looked up, didn't you?"

"You're worse than any of us," Polly replied. "That was rotten."

"I have to take my giggles when I can get them. So how long do you want to stay?"

"I don't care," Polly said. "I've had my entertainment. Anybody else?" She turned to see what Sylvie, Sal and Joss had to say.

"It was an entertaining field trip," Sal said. "But I can stay out as late as you want."

Joss shrugged and Sylvie shook her head. "I hate to be the party pooper, but I have to get up early tomorrow morning. She reached up and touched Camille's shoulder. "Speak up. So do you."

"You're right," Camille said, "But I never get to have this much fun. Ghosts and weirdos and girlfriends. It doesn't get much better than this."

"Wine would help," Sal said. "Lots and lots of wine."

"Maybe we should go somewhere and cleanse ourselves with wine now," Sandy said. "I feel all weird about this. There are actually people trying to communicate with a ghost in the safest little town in Iowa." She turned and smirked at Polly. "And I'm with the person who finds dead bodies, so I feel even safer. If she hasn't found a body here, then it doesn't exist."

Polly swatted her arm. "We'll have none of that tonight. It's creepy enough with this going on just a few blocks from our homes."

"You should totally buy this house," Sylvie said quietly. "Fix it all up out here and make it into a bed and breakfast or something. That would put this haunting nonsense to rest."

141

"Maybe we should all buy it together," Sal said. "I'll bet it can't be that much. Things are in bad shape here."

Camille laughed. "That's just what I need in my life. A broken down, haunted house. I don't even have my own place to live yet. How can I afford that and be part of this?"

"You buy it," Sal said. "It would be great for your big family when they come visit."

"Yeah. No," Camille said. "I'm looking for a one-bedroom apartment, thank you very much. If I want to spend time with that big family, I'll go to Omaha."

"So are we done here?" Sandy asked.

Polly scooted back to her seat beside Joss and pulled the seatbelt back on. "Any time. I've had my quota of strange for the night."

Sandy pulled out and drove past the videographers before pulling her lights on. As she turned the corner, Joss said softly to Polly, "You were pretty quiet when they talked about buying this place."

"Uh huh," Polly said with a nod. "Let's leave it at that."

CHAPTER FIFTEEN

"I'm nervous," Rebecca said as Polly drove her to school Monday morning. "If people didn't know Bickle-Pickle suspended me, they'll see by my face that something is wrong." The poor girl's face was multiple shades of green, purple and red.

"It's a badge of honor," Polly said, patting Rebecca's arm. "And I don't want to hear you call your principal a name. We might not agree with what she did, but it was well within her rights and we have to live by it. The only way for you to not let this take you down is to rise above it. Treat her with respect, not because you like her, but because she's the principal. Got it?"

"It's not fair," Rebecca said under her breath.

They'd had this discussion several times over the weekend. With Rebecca, with Andrew and Kayla, with Heath. Polly wanted to scream. It wasn't fair. But that didn't matter. Rebecca had to move on.

"You did the right thing when you protected Bean from that older kid," Polly said. "If the kids want to poke fun at the way you look, just remember that in a few short weeks, you'll look normal again and they'll still be bullies. Okay?"

Rebecca finally smiled. "I never thought of it that way."

"It's hard to do it at your age," Polly said, "But always try to take the long view. Are you ready?"

"I am," Rebecca said, taking a deep breath.

Polly watched her walk into the school and relaxed when she saw Kayla run to catch up. There, a friend to help Rebecca walk through the front door. Man, it wasn't easy letting her grow up on her own.

Now, coffee before heading back into the fray. Lydia and her crew spent several hours yesterday moving props and set pieces from the shed into the foyer of Sycamore House and today construction began. Polly couldn't believe how excited those women got when it came to creating a haunted house. Every year, one or two more people came on board to help set things up - almost as if they couldn't wait to see the surprise; they had to be in on the secrets.

The regular meetings that were held in Sycamore House either chose to move to the coffee shop this week or agreed to meet even with the constant noise of hammers and saws.

Polly opened the door to Sweet Beans and stood for a moment to enjoy the amazing scents brushing across her nose. Camille had hung orange lights from the ceiling - Polly couldn't imagine how she'd managed to get them up there - and bright oranges, golds, deep reds and browns were found throughout the shop. From arrangements in the bookshelves, to gourds and pumpkins on the tables, the coffee shop had discovered autumn.

Skylar Morris waved at her from behind the counter and smiled as she approached him. "Do you want pumpkin spice in your latte this morning?" he asked.

Polly chuckled. "Nope. I'm not a fan. Are you selling a lot of it?"

"You won't even believe it," he said. "Pumpkin everything flies out of here. Sylvie can't keep the larder stocked."

"Larder?" Polly asked with a chuckle. "How old are you?"

He threw his head back and stood up straight. "Old enough to have a grandma who used those words. So there."

"Why aren't you in class this morning?"

"It's Monday. I don't have a class until tonight. So, does anything entice you?" He gestured toward the bakery rack with a sweep of his hand.

Polly thought about the crew back at Sycamore House and said, "Mix up a dozen of whatever. I'm taking it with me. And I want a mocha caramel latte with whipped cream. Lots of whipped cream this morning." She pointed to the hallway. "Is Sylvie back there?"

He nodded with his head. "She was grumbling about something this morning, but yeah. She's there."

"Happy workplace today?" Polly asked with a grin.

"It's good. I'll never complain."

"I'll be back in a few minutes. Thanks." Polly followed her nose to the bakery in the back. Sylvie pulled a tray of bread loaves from the oven and slid it into a rack before looking up to see Polly.

"Hello there, you rotten human," Sylvie said. She turned to the young man working with her. "When you're finished frosting those cupcakes, the muffins in Harold should be ready to come out."

"Harold?" Polly asked.

"We had to delineate, so we have Harold and Maude."

"Like the movie? That's weird."

Sylvie laughed. "One is old, the other is brand new. I couldn't help myself."

"So why am I a rotten human?"

"I didn't sleep last night and it's all your fault."

"My fault?" Polly asked with a laugh. "What did I do?"

"You took me to a real live haunted house and made me watch people dance around a fire. I dreamed about ghosts and all sorts of bad things. When I came in this morning, Camille said that she'd had bad dreams too." Sylvie swatted at Polly. "You're a bad influence."

"Whoops," Polly said. "I slept like a baby."

"Of course you did. The rest of us were a mess and you were just fine." Sylvie put her hand on Polly's arm. "How was your girl this morning? Andrew was nervous for her. He said she was pretty scared going back."

"She did it." Polly shrugged. "I wish it could have been different, but it wasn't and she had to face it."

"That poor girl has had an awful lot to face this last year."

"I know, but honestly, it's no more than most of us deal with. Hers came all at once," Polly said. "I'm just glad she has friends like Andrew and Kayla."

"And you and Henry. How is she doing with Heath in the house?"

"She adores him," Polly said. "And he wanted nothing more than to go to school and stand guard over her."

Sylvie smiled and flinched as something metal hit the floor.

"Sorry," the young man said. "Just a bowl. It was empty." He turned a mixer on and added ingredients.

"Do I know him?" Polly whispered.

"No," Sylvie whispered back. "Don't bother."

"Oh. I see."

"Uh huh."

Polly felt a tap on her elbow and turned to see Skylar there with a steaming to-go cup. "Thought you could use your caffeine in the dragon's den." He winked at Sylvie, handed the cup to Polly and ran back down the hallway to the front of the shop.

Sylvie laughed. "He's a hoot. We love him."

"And he's adorable," Polly said. "How do you even stand it?"

Sylvie looked at Polly over her glasses. "Are you kidding me? I'm old. Way too old for that."

"But not too old to look and pant a little," Polly said. "If not him, then when are you going to let Eliseo or Grey ask you out on a date?"

"I have no time for that," Sylvie said. She brushed back a non-existent tendril of hair. "And besides, neither of them has ever asked me. I don't have the energy to make the effort to be a modern woman these days."

Polly had leaned against the door sill, but stood back up. "Wait. You mean you'd accept a date if one of them would ask?"

"Maybe." Sylvie lifted her left shoulder.

"Well aren't you little Miss Coy," Polly said. "Who knew! You've been ignoring men like nobody's business and now out of the blue, it's their fault for not asking you out?"

"It's nobody's fault," Sylvie said quietly. "But maybe I'm getting ready to do something other than work and sleep. Jason and Andrew are busy with their own things. They don't need me. So ... maybe."

Polly reached in and gave her friend a quick hug. "Ahhh," she said. "Life's about to get interesting."

"Don't you dare do anything," Sylvie said, shaking her finger at Polly. "I will pulverize you. Just let things take their natural course."

"Uh huh. On it."

"I'm serious, Polly Giller," Sylvie said. "Don't you dare say a word."

Polly was already walking away. She lifted her hand and waved. "Have a good day, Sylvie. Have a good day!"

When she got into her truck, Polly heard her phone buzz and laughed at the text Sylvie sent.

"If you do anything about what I told you, I will behead you on Halloween. You won't be able to play the Grim Reaper, you'll be reaped yourself."

Polly sent back a smiley face and grinned.

By the time she got back to Sycamore House, Lydia and crew were in full swing. Polly took the treats to the kitchen and put them out on a platter, arranging napkins and paper plates. The kitchen was dark and Rachel was nowhere to be seen. Since that rarely happened these days, she wondered what was going on. The building was always busy during the day with Rachel and Sylvie serving meetings or prepping meals they were catering.

"Did I see you come in with treats?" Jeff asked.

Polly pointed to the platter. "Where's Rachel?"

"She's working in the kitchen over at Secret Woods. Some of our meetings are there while we're in chaos and she's training one of their cooks."

"You aren't worried about them stealing her from us?" Polly asked. "Or even worse, stealing our customers?"

He smiled at her. "That would be foolish on their part. They get our overflow business and can borrow Rachel whenever they need her." He smiled. "And besides, they're good guys. I've helped them enough with the business side of what they're doing that we have a good relationship."

"Okay," Polly said. "I wasn't too worried, but you know."

"Grey called this morning. Do you want to talk to Aaron or should I?"

Polly tilted her head. "About what?"

"That kid's room. His things are still there. It's not a huge deal, but Grey was wondering if he should pack it into boxes or if the sheriff wanted to send someone up..." Jeff paused. "Or are we keeping the room for them until they've find who killed him."

"I'll call Aaron," Polly said. "Do we need the room?"

He shook his head. "No. We were just curious. Have you heard anything more about the boy? People in town are talking."

"About him looking for ghosts?"

Jeff grinned. "Yeah. He'd been asking a lot of questions."

"Who knew we had a famous ghost? Have you been up to the Springer House?"

"I drove by it once. Got assaulted by some old guy when I stopped to look."

"Bridger or something?"

"Yeah. The resident expert on Muriel Springer."

Polly thought for a moment and said, "I wonder why I didn't see him there last night."

"Who?"

"Old Mr. Bridger. There was a film crew and people dancing around a fire. I would have expected him to be in the middle of it."

Jeff leaned forward. "Dancing around a fire?"

She chuckled. "I should ask Andy if there have been any strange happenings in the cemetery. It's right behind the house, too, you know."

"If I lived next to a cemetery, I definitely would not be looking out at it when it was dark. That's just creepy," Jeff said.

Polly shook her head at him. "Because zombies are real."

"Leave me alone. You never know." He took a last drink of his coffee before refilling the cup. "The only reason I don't like Halloween is because my imagination does too many strange things and people tell creepy stories that make me want to double lock all my doors and put salt across the entrances."

"Salt?" Polly asked.

"You know, to ward off vampires or witches or zombies or demons. All of those scary things."

"Do you read too many paranormal mysteries?"

Jeff picked up a muffin and took a bite, then mumbled something at her and turned to leave.

"That's a yes, right?"

He shoved another bite in behind the first and wrinkled his nose.

"Hello dears," Lydia said, coming around the corner. "Beryl thought she saw you bring some of Sylvie's goodies in. She'll be glad to know she was right. Would it be okay to bother Eliseo for a while this morning? We need ladders."

Polly walked into the kitchen and picked up the phone. "What do you need?" she asked.

"Two of his step ladders would be great. I don't know where they are or we wouldn't bother him at all."

"Just a second." Polly pressed the intercom button for the barn. "Eliseo, are you down there?"

"Good morning, Polly," he said. "What do you need?"

"Lydia needs a couple of step ladders. Can you tell us where they are?"

"I'll bring them to her. Ralph is here with me and the two of us might be able to offer our assistance up there for a couple of hours."

"Thank you, Eliseo," Lydia said. "You're a dear."

"We'll be right up."

"Easy as that," Polly said. "Do you want anything to eat?"

"Oh no, dear. Not yet. But maybe later." They walked together back toward the main foyer. "Jeff said we could move into the classrooms and lounge this year. That will be helpful, especially as we add more scenes. We were starting to compact too much."

"Whatever you want," Polly said. "I still can't believe we're going to have both a haunted house and masquerade ball on the same night."

Andy stepped out of the lounge. "It's going to be quite the extravaganza."

"You!" Polly said. "I was just talking about you."

"Why?" Andy stepped back. "What did I do?"

Polly explained the scene she'd observed in front of the Springer House the night before. By the time she told them about the women dancing around the fire, Beryl and Len had joined them, everyone fully engaged in her story.

"I'm glad they weren't naked," Beryl said in a hushed voice.

"Why are you whispering?" Andy whispered back.

"Because we're talking about hauntings and ghosts."

"That's what I was going to ask you, Andy," Polly said. "Have you seen anything strange in the cemetery lately?"

Len grinned. "With all of the talk about Muriel Springer going on again, Andy avoids the kitchen after dark."

"I do not," Andy said, pursing her lips and wrinkling her brow.

"Then you saw the ghostly light floating across the southeast corner last night?" he asked.

"There was no such thing." Andy scowled at him and went back into the lounge.

"Are you joking?" Polly asked.

He shook his head. "No. I saw something. Don't know what it was. About nine o'clock. I didn't think much about it. People go in there at all hours to talk to their family members. And then there are all those people who are doing research."

"Not so much anymore," Andy said from around the corner. "Once they got it all digitized, the genealogists don't come in very often. Usually only descendants wanting a picture of a gravestone or something."

"So, who knows what was going on?"

"Do you guys know Jim Bridger?" Polly asked. "It sounds like he's the one to talk to about Muriel Springer."

Beryl laughed out loud. "Old Jim? He's been telling her story since he was a boy. He wanted to write a book about it once. Asked if I would paint something for the front cover. He wanted a picture showing her hovering in the solarium. Since it was all boarded up, he asked if I could paint it as it was when she died. Make the house look pretty and stately again."

Lydia smiled at her friend. "Did you ever do anything about it?"

"Nah," Beryl said. "He thought I would be satisfied with a portion of the proceeds from his book." She cackled. "Since he never got the thing written, I'm glad I told him no. But he loves that story and I do believe that it gets more exaggerated every year that passes. He even went to the city council to ask them to put a historical marker up, telling the story. A long time ago he asked the city to purchase the land around it so they could turn it into a tourist attraction. If they couldn't get onto the land, at least they could build up around the house. The poor old guy was nearly laughed out of the meeting."

"That *was* a long time ago," Lydia said. "He wasn't a poor old guy back then. But he was always odd. And he always had a thing for that house."

"You don't suppose..." Polly let her thought trail off.

"Suppose what?" Beryl asked.

"I was just going to say, you don't suppose he might have killed Jeremy Booten. Here the kid was with all of his fancy camera gear and a desire to tell ghost stories from central Iowa. Maybe Mr. Bridger was jealous that someone else would make money from it." Polly thought again and shook her head. "No, that doesn't sound right. He didn't seem threatening when I met him. Just a lonely old guy who wanted to talk about his passion." She turned to Lydia. "Was he ever married?"

Lydia looked at both Andy and Beryl, who shook their heads. "No," she said. "He never was."

"Do you think he had a crush on Muriel Springer?"

Lydia stepped back and looked at Polly. "He'd have been in high school when she killed herself. He still lives in the house he grew up in. It's on the corner by the Springer House. Of course he did. From what I remember my parents saying when they talked about her, she was lonely in that big old house and she used to have neighborhood kids come over. They helped her with lawn work and washing windows and other things while her husband was gone. Mother always told me that if I wasn't good I'd have to help the ghost clean her house. I'd forgotten all about that." She gave a quick shudder. "There are so many little bits and pieces of that woman's story peppered throughout Bellingwood's culture. Most of them are probably apocryphal, but even those are often based on little truths."

"I can't believe I've never heard any of this," Polly said.

"Oh you have," Lydia replied. "You just didn't know it. People don't even remember why they avoid Beech Street during the weeks before Halloween, but we do. Well, unless you're a kid. Then it's a challenge."

Everyone wandered back to what they had been working on and Polly went to her office. There was a phone call she needed to make. What was it? That's right. Aaron. At least she didn't have to talk to him about a dead body.

CHAPTER SIXTEEN

"Need to talk. What are you doing this morning?" the text from Joss read.

"Not much now," Polly texted back. *"What's up?"*

Her phone rang and she answered, "Hey Joss. You okay?"

"I'm so sorry about my attitude last night," Joss said. "I'm glad I stayed."

"No worries," Polly replied with a chuckle. "Even you get to have a bad day every once in a while."

"Have you been up to the coffee shop yet this morning? I could use some caffeine."

Polly laughed. "I'd love to join you!"

"Why are you laughing?"

"Because yes, I've already been there, but that doesn't mean much. There is no limit to the amount of good coffee I can drink in a day. Are you bringing the kids?"

"Nate is home this morning. He's got a cold and isn't going in to work."

"And he's letting you out of the house?" Polly gasped. "How come you don't have to take care of him *and* the kids?"

"Because that's an argument we had a long time ago. He isn't going to die and I'm not going to coddle him unless he's truly unable to care for himself. But he told me to leave for the morning. The poor guy was probably glad I came home in a better mood last night and wants to see if we can hold onto it for a few days."

"You train husbands really good," Polly said. "There's a whole town of women who could learn from you."

"I'm not cheap," Joss replied. "There's been a lot of learning over the years. However, they have to have good husbands like Nate, too. He's wonderful."

"He's standing right there, isn't he?"

Joss laughed. "Fifteen minutes at the coffee shop?"

"I'll see you there."

Polly had one more phone call to make and she swiped to dial.

"Good morning, Polly," Aaron said. "I know you're at Sycamore House, so I felt safe in answering. What's up?"

"Jeff and Grey were wondering about Jeremy Booten's room at the hotel. His things are still there. Do you want us to box them up or do you need to keep them in the room? Either way is fine. Just let me know."

He hesitated long enough that she continued. "If you need to keep the room, that's okay too. Grey was curious."

"We've been through the room and his things several times," Aaron said. "And yes, that was his car that you found the other night, so we're going through that."

"Can you tell me if his camera gear was in the car?" she asked.

"No gear. We're still looking."

Polly's curiosity was piqued. "Do you think he took a picture of something and that's what got him killed?"

"Now Polly," Aaron scolded. "You know I won't make assumptions until I have better information."

"Then I will. If we find his camera, we'll probably find the killer."

"There's no *we* involved in this," Aaron said sternly. "Don't you dare go looking for it."

"I wouldn't even know where to begin. So, did you and Ken

know about the fireside séance in front of the Springer House last night?"

Aaron chuckled. "Why am I not surprised that you know about it as well."

"I wasn't involved, but we drove past it. That was weird. I can't believe the neighbors are okay with it."

"This is the last year for the weird stuff as long as that house sells next week. They've been patiently waiting for it all to come to an end."

"Do you believe there's a ghost in the house?" Polly asked.

He coughed. "How well do you know me?"

"Got it. So no ghost."

"If you tell me there's a ghost, Polly, I'll believe it. But otherwise, nope."

"Are the weirdos going to be here all week?"

Aaron let out a sigh. "Every night. They got permission from the neighbors and as long as they're respectful, there's no reason to make it any worse than it is. I'm afraid, though, that after a few days, traffic will become a problem. We'll have to revisit the question at that point."

"You have all the fun," she said, laughing. "Is Jim Bridger involved?"

"You've met him?"

"I sure have."

Aaron said, "I'm sorry, Polly. I need to go. We can talk about this later."

With no more than that, he was gone. Polly grabbed her keys and headed for the back, waving at her friends as she ran to the auditorium doors. Eliseo was running a vacuum while Jeff and Ralph Bedford were stringing lights from the ceiling. Okay, Jeff was doing the work while Ralph held a ladder.

"Are you leaving us again?" Jeff called after her.

"Back later."

She drove up to the coffee shop and decided that she and Joss were getting their coffee to go. There were a few things she wanted to check on before the day was out. The grey, dreary skies were gone for a few days and temperatures were heading for the seventies. It would be a beautiful day to be out and about.

Joss hadn't arrived yet, so Polly went on inside. Skylar was cleaning tables when he heard the door's bell ring and looked up.

"Not enough caffeine in the first drink?" he asked.

"Hush," Polly said. "I'm meeting Joss. But we're taking our coffee to go. I have hauntings to disprove."

He walked with her toward the counter. "I heard about the people from Pennsylvania who were in town last night. They're trying to raise a ghost?"

"Yeah," Polly replied. "I don't know why they're working so hard at it. From what I understand, she'll show up on her own."

He whispered. "Do you think it's true?"

Polly pursed her lips and scowled at him. "No. What I think is that there's an old man who has been telling ghost stories for the last fifty or sixty years until people accepted them as truth."

Skylar slipped behind the counter. "Caramel Mocha?"

She nodded.

"What would you do if there was a ghost in that house?" he asked.

"Tell her that she needed to leave and go on about her business. Her time on earth was finished and she should let go. And if she didn't like that answer, I'd make dinner for her and ask why she needed to stay."

He chuckled. "Dinner? Ghosts don't eat."

"See," Polly said. "That's where you get me. How do you know that? Have you ever invited one to sit down at a meal? We have all these assumptions. Maybe they're just hungry and can't make anyone understand that. I'd be angry too if I hadn't eaten for years and no one thought to set a place for me."

By now he was laughing at her and he looked up when the bell rang again. "Hello, Mrs. Mikkels. Do you want your regular?"

"In a large, please," Joss said. "And if you have any of Sylvie's sour dough rolls, I need one of those, too."

"Got it."

"What are you two talking about?" Joss asked.

"You and I are going ghost hunting as soon as we get our coffee," Polly said.

"Back to the Springer House?"

Polly took her cup from Skylar and pointed at the roll he was warming for Joss. "One of those for me, too," she said. "That sounds amazing."

She turned back to Joss. "Since it's a beautiful, sunny day, I want to go to the cemetery. Len said that he saw lights in there last night while that little fire dance was going on. It might be nothing, but let's check it out."

"If you let ghosts get me," Joss said. "Nate is going to be very angry."

"It will be perfectly safe," Polly said. "I promise."

They paid for their coffee and rolls and went out to her truck.

"You certainly take me on adventures I'd never expected to experience," Joss said. "Here I am on a beautiful Monday morning in October, about to head to the cemetery to look for signs of paranormal activity. Has anyone ever told you that you're crazy?"

Polly smiled. "It's not new information."

~~~

"So, what are we doing here?" Joss asked as Polly pulled into the drive.

Polly looked at her friend with a sheepish grin. "I have a feeling."

"One of *those* feelings?"

Polly wound around the cemetery drive, not sure what she was looking for. During the day, this was a beautiful, quiet, restful spot. Large trees gave shade to the grounds which were beautifully kept. Many of the graves had flower arrangements while a few even had Halloween decorations. It was always a surprise to her to discover the large number of people who maintained this connection to people they loved. She had never been much about cemeteries, but then, neither had her father. She wasn't even sure where his parents were buried.

"I hope not," Polly said, "but something triggered for me in a couple of conversations this morning and I want to drive through here." She grinned at Joss. "And you were the one who wanted to have coffee with me. Don't forget that, okay?"

"Mom always used to take us to the cemetery back home," Joss said. "After Grandpa died, we went out a lot. She missed him so much. On his birthday, we'd pick Grandma up then we'd all go to Dairy Queen and get ice cream cones. Grandpa loved ice cream. There was always one extra ice cream cone for him." She looked out her window. "I wonder how many stories there are like that here. We took lawn chairs with us and sat and told stories about Grandpa. It was a great way for us to get to know him, even though he wasn't there."

"Do you still go out when you're home?"

Joss nodded. "If we have time. I want Cooper and Sophie to know that connection exists." She chuckled. "I read something the other day about how we come from thousands and thousands of people who loved each other. Think about the families throughout history that our ancestors made. We are linked back to the beginning of time and all of those marriages and sisters and brothers and husbands and wives. And these cemeteries only tell short little bits of the story."

"Look there," Polly said.

"A dead body?"

Polly laughed. "No. The gravestones. These are all Watsons. I wonder if they're Beryl's family."

"It's kind of strange to think about the families that have lived in a town for generations. There's so much history right at their fingertips. My grandparents are buried in our hometown cemetery, but their family was all over the east coast before they moved to Indiana. We don't have generational family plots. My parents will be buried there, but I won't."

Polly turned another corner. This was all alien to her. She and Henry had never gotten around to talking about this stuff. She didn't know where his parents would be buried or even what Henry thought about it all. As many bodies as she'd discovered, you'd think they might have talked about their own end-of-life plans.

"What are you thinking about?" Joss asked.

"I don't know anything about Henry's family. Where they're planning to be buried or anything. His grandparents are still alive, but what about their parents. Are they in here or somewhere else?"

"Yeah. It would be kind of creepy to find a dead body resting against a Sturtz family plot, wouldn't it?" Joss asked with a wicked laugh.

"Stop that," Polly said. "I don't want to find a ..." She stopped the truck and laid her head back on the head rest. "Crap."

Joss looked out at the cemetery in front of them. "What? I don't see anything."

"You can stay here if you want. I need to take a walk."

"Did you find another body? How come I don't see it?" Joss scrambled to get out of the truck so she could follow Polly. When she caught up, she looked forward to where Polly was headed and said, "Ohhh. You have to be kidding me."

"If you want to go back to the truck, I get it," Polly said.

Joss stumbled over a hillock and grabbed Polly to steady herself. "This might be close enough for me. I always forget how real this truly is when you talk about it. Your stories make it seem so benign, but death really isn't, is it?"

"No," Polly said, shaking her head. "Go on back to the truck. I need to make sure it's not a silly Halloween prank before I call Aaron." She waited while Joss took a last look then turned and walked away. As she glanced down at the headstone, she shook her head. At least now she knew where Henry's great-grandparents were located. Harold and Mabel Sturtz. Polly ran her hand across the headstone. "Thanks for being part of Henry's long line of loving families. I'm awfully thankful for him. And oh, by the way? He's not going to believe this. But don't bother trying to tell him. I'll give him a call. If you showed up, that might scare him."

She laughed at herself, patted the headstone one last time and walked on toward the mausoleum in the center of this section. Two large angels stood on either side and Polly couldn't help herself. She'd watched too many episodes of Doctor Who and knew better than to blink in front of them.

In moments she was standing over old Jim Bridger's body. She wondered where his Chihuahua had gotten to, hoping the poor dog was at home and not lost in town. Aaron would send someone to the house today and she'd make sure to ask. Mr. Bridger was curled around the base of one of the angel statues as if he were hugging it, but the congealed blood on his head and pallor of his body assured Polly he was definitely dead. And besides, she rarely got to find people before they died.

"Maybe one or two of those," she said to the sky. "Let me find them first so they can be saved. That would make things less grim, don't you think?"

There was no answer, for which she was grateful and she stepped back onto the brick pad that circled the mausoleum. After taking a deep breath and gathering her thoughts, Polly swiped the call she hated to make.

"Can I call you right back?" Aaron asked after answering the phone. "I have someone in my office."

"Ummm, that's fine," Polly said.

"Is it what I think it is?"

"Jim Bridger."

"I'll only be a few minutes. Are you safe?"

"I'm in the cemetery."

He chuckled. "Perfect. Of course you are. Just a few minutes."

Polly took a last look at Mr. Bridger, decided he wasn't going anywhere and walked around the mausoleum and looked off toward the west. She could see Andy and Len Specek's house from here. From the front side of the structure, she could see the rooftop of the Springer House over the tall wooden fence.

Walking back toward Harold and Mabel Sturtz's headstone, she looked for signs of a struggle. Len said he had seen a light out here last night. Was that Mr. Bridger walking around the graves with a flashlight? What would have brought him here?

Polly took her phone back out and turned the camera on, recording the graves as she walked up and down the well-worn paths. Nothing stuck out at her, but then it wouldn't. She didn't know many family names. And then she swore and went back to the mausoleum. She hadn't even looked at the nameplates.

The family name was Hoffen; Hilda and Peter, the matriarch and patriarch. Their names were at the top and as Polly scanned, she found Muriel's name. Polly would have assumed she'd been buried as a Springer.

The door was closed and latched with a padlock. Polly put her hands on the lock, wondering if it was open and it dropped to the ground.

"Guess I answered that question for myself," she said quietly. Just as she put her hand on the door to press it open, the phone buzzed in her other hand and then rang.

"That's not fair," she said. "I'm in a cemetery, about to enter a mausoleum and you nearly scared me to death."

Aaron chuckled. "Don't tell me. The Hoffen mausoleum?"

This was the only one she could see. "Is there another?"

"No," he said. "It's the only one. Lydia's family is just over the rise there. So you found old Mr. Bridger?"

"He's curled around one of the angels."

Polly pushed the door open, trying not to shudder as it creaked.

"What are you doing?"

"The mausoleum door is open. I'm going in. But it's dark in here."

"Stop what you're doing," Aaron commanded. "Don't take another step."

"But..."

"No buts about it. Don't you dare go in."

"I'm not afraid of no ghosts," she said.

Aaron didn't get the Ghostbusters reference. At least he didn't laugh at it. "Neither am I, but if that is open, there could be evidence. I won't have you messing it up. Now back out. I want to hear that door creak again."

Polly pushed the door further open, making it creak again. What Aaron didn't know wouldn't hurt her. Right?

"Polly?"

"Fine. I'm out." She took a step backward, holding her hand on the door. If nothing else, she was going to look inside with her flashlight on once he finally hung up.

"Stu is heading to Bellingwood now and I'll be up there soon. Maybe I should give you a roll of crime scene tape so you can start preparing these for us when you come upon them."

"That's a great idea," Polly said distractedly. "Anything I can do to help."

"You haven't left the mausoleum yet, have you?"

"I'll see you when you get here. Poor Joss is back in my truck. I should check on her." Polly swiped the call closed and opened her flashlight app, then passed it back and forth inside the door. She knew better than to go inside, though it nearly killed her. She laughed at the thought. There were so many awful jokes around death and cemeteries and here she was right in the middle of it.

She put her butt against the door and stepped inside, then moved the light and found what she was looking for. She knew it had to be here. A backpack camera bag was tossed toward the back of the open space, its top flap lying open. Lenses and cameras were still neatly in their places. She bent forward to see if she could snag one of the straps and heard scuffling behind her.

~~~

"Polly! Polly! Are you okay?"

Polly sat up. Wait. Why was she on the ground? "Joss? What are you doing here?"

"Somebody hit you over the head."

Polly reached up with her hand and felt the back of her head. She'd been rapped good. That hurt. "Did you see who it was?"

Joss shook her head. "No, the person was wearing a black hoodie and I was too far away to see much of anything. But I saw you go down and then they ran away, carrying something.

"No," Polly said. The camera bag was gone. "They took it."

"What was it?" Joss asked.

"The camera bag. I'm sure it belonged to Jeremy Booten."

"The kid who was killed?"

"Yeah. I leaned forward to try to grab it. I heard something and then here you are. How long was I out?"

"Just a couple of minutes. I ran as fast as I could."

"Whew. Stu Decker will be here any minute and he'll insist on calling the squad if he thinks I was hurt. I'm not hurt, so don't say anything."

"But, he hit you and you fell over," Joss protested. "Look, you've skinned your hands."

Polly brushed them off on her jeans. "It's nothing. I've had worse. But please don't say a word. They drive me crazy. And I'm going to be in enough trouble when Stu and Aaron find out that the camera bag was here and now it's gone."

"But you're going to tell them it was here."

"Yeah," Polly nodded. She put out her hand and Joss reached out to help pull her up. "I'm not much for hiding parts of the plot, but they certainly don't need to think that I'm wounded."

"How are you going to explain that it's gone?"

Polly scowled at her friend. "I haven't gotten to that yet." She rubbed the back of her head again. "Damn. I'm going to have to tell him everything."

"You're a lousy liar," Joss said, laughing.

"Just back me up when I insist that I don't need an EMT, okay?"

Joss backed away and shrugged. "Don't look at me. I don't want to be responsible for the condition of your head."

"Some friend you are."

They looked toward the road as a sheriff's vehicle pulled in.

"I'd better call Nate and tell him I'll be late for lunch," Joss said. "He won't believe this."

"Sure he will. It's part and parcel of being my friend."

"Oh yeah. I forgot."

CHAPTER SEVENTEEN

Grabbing the doorknob to go upstairs, Polly jumped when her phone rang and Beryl's number came up. The woman should be busy with Haunted House setup.

"Hello, crazy lady," Polly said.

"You have to come over here right now," Beryl said. "Don't ask any questions, just come over."

"Can I ask one question?"

Beryl whimpered. "Okay, one question."

"Where are you?"

"Get your hiney over to my house. I need you. Right this minute."

"It's not a dead body, right?"

"Shut up and get over here."

Polly chuckled. Beryl sounded impatient and rattled, but not upset. "I'll be there in a few minutes."

"I'll pay for your speeding ticket. Just hurry."

She looked at the doorway. The dogs were going to have to wait. Beryl never called Polly for help. Back to the truck she went. Henry would hear about her adventure at the cemetery later today. She'd planned to text him once she got the animals settled again, but best-laid plans and all.

Polly fully expected Beryl to be standing at the front door of her house, but when the woman didn't come outside to greet her, she walked to the front door and rang the bell.

It took a few moments for Beryl to arrive and when she did, she pulled Polly inside and tugged her through the house and down the steps to her basement.

"What's going on?" Polly asked. "What is so urgent?"

"This," Beryl said, pointing to a basket on the floor. "What in the hell am I supposed to do with this?"

Polly laughed as soon as she saw what was in the basket - two tiny grey kittens.

"Where did they come from?" Polly asked softly.

"I have no idea. I came home because I need to work this afternoon. When I went out to the studio, I heard crying." She wrinkled her nose and took Polly's hand. "I prayed that I was hearing birds, but it was unrelenting. I found that little one at the back of the studio." She pointed at the smaller of the two kittens. "She was insistent. I couldn't leave her outside, so I brought her in. All I have is Miss Kitty's food, but she was hungry."

Polly nodded. "And the other one?"

Beryl scowled at her. "Once I had that first little bugger warming up, I had to go back to the studio. She wouldn't let me out of her sight, so I took her with me. We came back to the house to get her a blanket and there was another of these silly things wandering beside the studio, making as much noise as his sister." She looked askance at Polly. "I checked. He's a boy. So here I am with these little stinkers in my house. What in the hell am I supposed to do with them?"

"Love them?" Polly asked.

"I don't have time for this," Beryl said. "And besides, Miss Kitty is a one woman cat. Or we're a pair. Or whatever. She isn't going to be happy when she finds them here."

Miss Kitty usually had the run of the house. "Where is she?" Polly asked.

"Sound asleep upstairs in my bedroom. I pulled the door shut so she wouldn't hear the pitter patter of kitty paws." Beryl pointed at the basket again. "Polly, what am I to do? Will you take them?"

"Not on your life," Polly said with both hands raised defensively. "Henry would move back to his mother's house if I added two more animals."

Beryl dropped down onto the chair beside the basket. The smallest kitty stood up on her back legs and reached for Beryl's pant leg, pulling herself up until Beryl looked at Polly with a piteous look on her face and bent over to gather the kitten into her arms. "This is a very bad idea," she said, stroking the kitten's head as it nestled into the crook of her left arm.

"What about Lydia or Andy?" Polly asked.

"Lydia won't take cats in because of her grandkids. And Andy? She wouldn't take care of you like she should." Beryl cooed at the kitten, turning it on its back and rubbing its belly. The little girl fell asleep and Beryl looked up at Polly again. "Are you sure you won't take them home with you? Luke and Leia need a family to raise, don't you think?"

Polly laughed at her friend. "You're already falling in love with them."

"No," Beryl said, her protest weak. "I can't fall in love with them." She reached back into the basket and scooped up the little boy. He stiffened until he felt the warmth of his sister. She woke enough to lick his shoulder a couple of times and then they both fell asleep in Beryl's arms.

"Call Doc Ogden's office and make an appointment," Polly said. "I do believe your family just doubled in size today."

"I don't have time to integrate two new kittens into my household," Beryl said. "I wanted you to come over and take these little things away from me." Her right hand hadn't stopped petting the kittens and every once in a while she reached down and kissed one or the other on the head.

Polly reached out and touched the little boy. He was so soft. "You wouldn't let me take them even if I wanted to. Have you seen the mama cat?"

"We have ferals that come across those fields. Sometimes I see them, but most of the time I don't. They come from a couple of the farms. Every once in a while, I see them moving their kittens. Something must have happened for these two to have been left behind."

"Either that or the mama is looking for them."

Beryl nodded. "But they're weaned. Neither of them had any trouble eating kibble or drinking water. And both of them used the litter box when I put them into it."

"That's lucky," Polly said. "What are you going to name them?"

Beryl looked up at her and growled. "You think I'm keeping them, don't you."

"Of course you are, you silly woman. Look at you. It's about time you had some kitten fun in your life. You and Miss Kitty have gotten too old and boring."

"Who you calling old and boring?" Beryl asked. She bent over and put the kittens back into the basket. She had to unlatch the little girl's claws from her sweater, but they fell asleep in the blankets she'd provided.

"I'm calling you and your old lady cat boring. These two are going to remind you of how much fun it is to have young blood in the house."

Beryl took Polly's arm. "But what am I going to do if Miss Kitty hates them?"

"Give it time," Polly said. "She'll be okay. She loves you, doesn't she?"

"You brat. I call you to take these little lumps of fluff off my hands and all I get from you are insults." She took Polly's arm and led her to the staircase. "Do you have time for coffee?"

Polly shook her head. "I'd better not. I've been up to Sweet Beans twice this morning already. If I ingest much more, I might get the shakes."

"I'm not ready to let you leave," Beryl said. "It's been so long since I've had kittens in the house, I don't know how to start with them."

"There are two of them," Polly nodded back toward the basket.

"They'll take care of themselves. Just call Marnie and get in there as soon as possible so you don't have to worry about their health."

Beryl sighed. "I don't have time for this."

"Do you want me to take them to the vet?"

"Would you?" Beryl's face lit up and then she stopped. "No, that's ridiculous. If I'm going to be their new mommy ..." She stopped and grimaced. "Oh good grief, I'm talking like a crazy cat lady. New mommy, my ass. But anyway, they need to know that I'm the one who takes care of them."

"Is there anything else I can do for you?"

Beryl shook her head. "No. I'm going to have to do this all on my own. No one to help me or rescue me."

"Dramatic much?" Polly asked.

"Whatever." She looked back at the kittens. "I don't have a carrier for them. How am I supposed to get two kittens to the veterinarian? And I don't have any kitten food here. And Miss Kitty's old toys are hiding under a bed somewhere." She sat down on a step. "I'm useless. And I'm still not getting any work done."

Polly patted her shoulder. "Why don't you take the kittens out to the studio with you and start working. That's what's stressing you out, isn't it?"

Beryl nodded.

"Let me take care of those other things. You can pay me back later."

"Really?"

"Really," Polly said with a laugh. "As many times as you and your pals take care of me, I can do this. Go ahead. Take the kittens and go. Do you want me to wait a minute and open the bedroom door after you've gone?"

Beryl looked up and rolled her eyes. "I'd have totally forgotten about her. Would you?"

"Of course. I'll wait until you're out the door. But tonight when you come back in, you're on your own, okay?"

"Would Thing One and Thing Two be awfully strange for their names?" Beryl asked.

"They're your babies. Name them whatever you want."

Beryl shook her head. "No, that doesn't fit. I need more time." She stood up. "They are awfully cute, aren't they?"

"Yes they are. You know you're going to have a blast, right?"

"All I know is that you failed me in my hour of need."

"Whatever," Polly said. "Now get to work. You have a canvas calling. I can hear it from here."

Beryl gave her a quick hug. "Thanks for talking me down. Lydia would have made me take them to the Humane Society or something and Andy would have called me crazy."

"You are crazy and Lydia would not have made you give them away. You know that."

"You're wrong there," Beryl said. "She knows how busy I am and how often I leave town. But they're cats and they'll learn to put up with my cat sitters. Right?"

"I know a few kids who would love to come check on your cats for you when you're out of town. Don't worry, Beryl. We'll help where we can."

"Okay. I'm skedaddling." Beryl picked up the basket. "Don't tell anyone that I'm a crazy cat lady, okay?"

"No promises."

~~~

"I can't believe he's dead," Henry said, putting dinner plates into the cupboard. "All those years of him being the keeper of the secrets of Springer House and now he's gone."

Polly handed him glasses from the dishwasher. "If it's going on the market next week, it does seem odd. Once that place is sold and fixed up, he would have become superfluous. Without the battered look of the place, who would believe a ghost lives there."

Henry chuckled. "Maybe the new owners when they have to put up with Muriel's shenanigans."

She leaned her hip against the counter and glared at him. "Don't you start."

"I've spent my entire life hearing about Muriel Springer. I can't get rid of her that easily."

"Whatever," Polly said. "I haven't heard of one person who's actually seen her."

"Rebecca says she did."

Polly lowered her voice. "Rebecca is an impressionable seventh grader. Who knows what she saw."

"Do you think the chanting spirit callers are up there again tonight?" Henry asked.

"Probably." Polly slammed the silverware drawer shut. "I'll bet they're staying at the inn! I wonder what Grey has found out about them. You know he talks to everyone and this would be a great conversation for him to have. Could one of them be the killer?"

"Not unless they were here when Jeremy Booten died. I thought they just got into town last weekend," he said.

"Oh." She huffed out a breath. "It was a good idea, though. Maybe they've talked to people who might know something."

He laughed and closed the dishwasher door. "Maybe you need to get out there tomorrow and chat it up with them." Henry tossed the dishtowel he'd tucked into his waist band at her. "And I have football to watch. You can find me in our room."

"Wait," Polly said. "How did he do today?"

Henry nodded toward the living room where Heath was working on homework and Rebecca was working on something in her sketchbook. "Heath?"

"Yeah. At work. How did that go?"

"He did fine. It's nice having someone fresh show up at the end of the day. There are cleanup errands he can run and it gives the guys time to prepare for the next day."

"So every night of the week?" she asked.

He grinned. "No. Mondays and Wednesdays for now. I won't take Friday nights away from him and besides, we try to wrap up work and get out early anyway. He'll help Grey on Tuesdays and Saturdays."

"Did he say anything about being able to drive the truck?"

"Nothing. But I assume he got himself and Jason back and forth with no trouble."

"I wonder how long it will be until those two can be friends," Polly said.

Henry reached out, grabbed her waist and pulled her close, then whispered in her ear. "Stop trying to fix those two boys. It's enough that you insist they ride together every day. They'll either work it out or they won't. Don't make it worse."

"Whatever," she said and licked his cheek.

He pushed her away and snagged the towel back to wipe his face. "Why did you do that?"

"Because."

"Because I'm right?" He tossed the towel at the sink and pulled her back in, then kissed her on the lips.

It truly didn't matter how often he did this to her, whenever Henry surprised Polly with a kiss, it still made her knees weak. "Whatever," she whispered.

He released her and stepped back. "I'll be in the bedroom watching the game. Heath said he'd take the dogs out before bed. Maybe you should spend extra time with your girl tonight. She was awfully quiet at dinner."

"I should," Polly said, nodding. "We haven't talked today. I hope school went well."

Henry was inching toward the door and she waved him off. "Go. Turn on your game. I'll be in later."

"I love you, too," he said and left as quickly as possible.

Polly let him go and walked into the living room. Rebecca was in one of the chairs, her legs curled up underneath her and a cat nestled in beside her, while Heath was bent over the coffee table, typing away on the laptop.

"What'cha working on?" Polly asked.

Rebecca turned her sketch pad toward Polly.

"What's that?"

"I was working on drawing that ghost," Rebecca said. "I have a bunch of sketches of her. Do you want to see?"

"Sure." Polly put her hand on Heath's back. "Are you comfortable here? Would you rather use the desk in your room or the dining room table?"

He shrugged. "I'm nearly done. Do you care if I turn the football game on after I'm done?"

Polly glanced at her bedroom. "No," she said, shaking her head. "I don't care. Finish your work and don't stay up too late. You have another long day tomorrow. Come on, Rebecca. Come into the dining room and show me what you've got."

Rebecca slid away from Leia and followed Polly back into the dining room.

"Do you want anything to drink?" Polly asked.

"No. Did you really just want to look at my drawings?"

Polly smiled. "I do want to see them." Her voice trailed off.

"But?" Rebecca pressed.

"But I also want to find out how your day went."

Rebecca dropped her head. "It was fine."

"Fine?" Polly sat down beside her and reached over to take Rebecca's hand. "What does that mean?"

"It felt like everybody was staring at me and the teachers treated me like I was one of the bad girls. Mrs. Bickle stared at me every time I walked past the office like she was waiting to catch me doing something wrong again."

"Did any of the kids say anything?"

Rebecca shook her head. "Andrew and Kayla were with me most of the day. The others left me alone."

"And what about the boy that hit you?"

"He got a week suspension. He's out until Friday." Rebecca put her hand on her cheek. "I hope I look better by then."

"You will. It won't be perfect, but you'll be better."

"I still don't understand."

Polly rubbed the top of Rebecca's hand. "Understand what?"

"Why I got into so much trouble when I didn't do anything wrong. It just isn't fair. Everybody thinks I'm bad now and all I did was stand up against a bully."

"We've talked about this over and over, sweetie. Life isn't fair."

"But that's not fair," Rebecca grew weepy and took her hand back so she could cross her arms and put her head down on the table.

"I know it's not," Polly said, rubbing Rebecca's back. She'd had an inkling today was going to be rough on the girl and wished she could make it all better with a snap of her finger. "But you get to come home and have us all remind you how much we love you and how terrific we think you are. Right?"

Rebecca lifted her shoulders.

"Right," Polly said. "And tomorrow, you'll go back to school and things will get better because people are moving on. Don't forget, they all have their own stuff and probably aren't thinking about you at all."

"So?" Rebecca mumbled.

"So you live through this. And I honestly don't believe the teachers think you are bad."

"You weren't there."

"You're right. I wasn't. But I know several of those teachers and they aren't like that. And you know as well as I do that the story of what happened last Thursday got around school pretty fast. They know the truth and they know what you did. Don't believe the worst of them because you think they're going to believe the worst about you."

Rebecca picked her head up and looked at Polly sideways. "What does that mean?"

"It means that sometimes we expect people to act a certain way so we interpret everything based on our expectations. Your teachers were probably not judging you at all. They have a lot of other things going on during the day and what you did five days ago is the least of their worries. Am I right?"

"I dunno. It sure felt like they were."

"Did anyone say or do anything?"

"No," Rebecca said. "It's just the way they looked at me."

"Hmm, maybe because they were worried about you or saw your bruised up face and were concerned?"

Rebecca touched her face again. "Do you think so?"

"Of course I do," Polly said with a chuckle. "Go in tomorrow and try something different. Believe the best about them and see how your interpretation of their actions changes things."

Rebecca put her head back in her arms and they sat there quietly for a few moments. Finally, she pushed her sketchbook toward Polly. "Did you really want to see these?" she asked, her face still buried.

Polly flipped through the sketchbook, past pictures of horses, cats and dogs, a few of the barn and some pages of trees and leaves until she landed on the first of several images of a young woman in a flowing dress. Rebecca was consistent in how she drew the woman's face, looking at it from different angles.

"She was a pretty girl," Polly said.

"Do you think it might be her?"

"I don't know. I haven't seen this girl before. Maybe it is Muriel Springer. That Jeremy Booten had all of the photographic equipment he needed to shoot a picture of a ghost. I wonder if he has anything this detailed."

"Could we take it to that old guy who knew her? Mr. Bridger?"

Polly shook her head. "I'm sorry, we can't. He died last night."

"He died?" Rebecca asked. Then she grew quiet. "You found him?"

"I did. This morning with Joss."

"You should have told me. I'm sorry," Rebecca said.

Polly pulled Rebecca in for a hug. "Thank you. I'm okay." She stroked the girl's hair and rubbed down her back. "And you will be, too. This is all going to work out. I promise."

CHAPTER EIGHTEEN

"Tell me I can fix them all," Polly said.

Henry turned over in bed and tugged her close. "You have to let them live out their own lives."

"But what if they miss out on something terrific because they're too blind to see what's right in front of their faces?"

He nuzzled her hair. "You smell good."

"You're trying to distract me."

"Is it working?"

Polly turned so they were facing each other and kissed him. "Maybe. But what if Sylvie has scared both Eliseo and Grey so badly that they never get the courage to ask her out. She finally thinks it isn't a terrible idea and they have no idea. And what about Doug? He's such a dipstick. Anita is still single and probably one of the few people out there who understands him and what if he misses out on her?"

"The world will continue to rotate even if you aren't matchmaking." Henry ran his hand down her arm. "I promise."

She stuck her lower lip out. "But it would be more fun if I could."

"Sylvie would have your head and Doug would die of embarrassment. You don't want that, do you? The two of them are intelligent adults. And besides," he said. "What if you were to set them up because it was what Polly wanted, but it wasn't the right thing for them? If you'd tried to set me up with young single women while I was in my twenties, I would have missed out on the most amazing girl in the world."

"Who's that?" she asked coyly.

"Hagatha Dromvinica."

"Oh yeah. I know her. She's pretty wonderful."

"Leave this alone," Henry said. "You have to promise me."

"I'm inviting Anita to the Masquerade Ball. So there," she said, blowing a raspberry.

Henry kissed her lips just as she finished blowing air through them and Polly sputtered. "We don't have much time before the kids get up. Be quiet and tell me you love me."

"Which one?" Polly asked.

"Huh?"

"You told me to be quiet and then I'm supposed to tell you that I love you. One or the other, big boy. Which one."

He kissed her again, making the question moot.

~~~

By the time Polly got to the kitchen, Rebecca was the only one still there.

"Where is everyone?"

"Henry took Han. Said he had to be at the office early. Something about his dad lifting a dresser."

"And Heath?" Polly asked.

"He said Jason had to be at school early for a project meeting. I didn't pay attention."

Polly smiled. Two days in and at least the boys were communicating with each other. That was a start. "Are you ready for the day?"

Rebecca pulled out Polly's extra-large sunglasses and put them on, then threw her head back. "Will they let me get away with this?"

"Doubtful," Polly said, gently removing them from her daughter's face. The words still sounded strange, but she was going to keep saying them in her head until it finally felt normal. "Do you want a ride?"

"I can walk. It doesn't hurt that bad any more. Now it only looks funny."

"Can you remember what we talked about last night?" Polly asked.

"The teachers aren't judging me. They have plenty of other stuff to think about," Rebecca rattled off.

"That's right." Polly poured a cup of coffee. "Did you eat?"

"I made toast with peanut butter and jelly," Rebecca said.

Polly laughed. "I'm a horrible mom."

"We talked about that," the girl said, deadpan. "But none of us knows where to report you."

Polly chuckled as she sliced bread and dropped it into the toaster, then looked out the window. The forecast had called for sunshine today, but mornings were taking a long time to arrive. She already missed summer with its sunshine and warmth.

"Speaking of being a horrible mom," Rebecca said quietly.

"What have I missed?" Polly spun around. Everything was so new to her and just about the time she thought she had it all together, something else came along to remind her that humility was her go-to behavior.

"Halloween."

Polly tried to think of what she'd missed for Halloween. There was so much going on at Sycamore House in preparation for the weekend, sometimes she wasn't sure what was coming next. Then, it hit her. "You don't have a costume. Do you have any ideas?"

"I kind of thought about going as Black Widow, but Kayla heard that idea and wanted to do it, so I let her have it."

"Not Elsa from Frozen?" Polly asked with a grin on her face. She knew she'd hit the mark when Rebecca scowled at her.

"I'm not five."

"Got it. What is Andrew doing?" They hadn't talked much about Andrew since their last conversation. Polly had been looking for a way to rid themselves of all the tension surrounding that relationship and bring things back to normal.

"I don't know. He doesn't know."

"Do you want to be elegant and creepy or a superhero or a classic character?" Polly asked.

"I don't know. Maybe elegant and creepy?" Rebecca said.

"I have just the character for you." Polly leaned over and whispered in Rebecca's ear.

Rebecca smiled. "Do you think Andrew could...?"

Polly nodded. "Of course he could. Talk to him today and maybe we can go to the thrift stores in Ames tomorrow after school. I'm sure we can cobble together a couple of costumes. We'll ask Jessie to help with makeup and hair. You'll be perfect."

"You're the best," Rebecca said, jumping up from her chair and throwing her arms around Polly. "Thank you." She looked at the clock over the sink. "I'd better go. I want to talk to Andrew first thing. He'll love it."

"It's going to be cold today," Polly called. "Make sure you have your coat and gloves." It still killed her that she had to remind Rebecca every day to wear a coat. Surely when the temperatures dropped into the twenties, they'd get past the need for a daily admonition.

~~~

Tuesdays were Lydia's biggest day of the week, so they'd made no plans to work at Sycamore House, restoring quiet to the main level. Polly wasn't quite sure what to do with the silence. Jeff was at a Chamber of Commerce breakfast meeting and Stephanie was working away at her desk.

Polly found herself typing Jeremy Booten's name into social media sites and photo sharing groups, just in case he'd uploaded any pictures from his time here in Bellingwood. It bothered her that someone had gotten one over on her yesterday at the cemetery. She absentmindedly rubbed the back of her head and realized she'd never told Henry the whole story. Why bother him with details that would only upset him, right? And this was minor. The knot barely hurt today.

She searched Facebook until she found Jeremy Booten's page and discovered that many of his photographs were public. He'd uploaded a series of pictures from some of his cemetery trips. Of course cemeteries would be perfect places for hauntings. But these were regular photographs taken of the locations and various gravesites. He'd announced that he was saving the best shots from his infrared and ultraviolet cameras for the book. But Jeremy had done his research when it came to reported hauntings around Iowa. There were pictures from the community college in Iowa Falls and even some of the buildings on Iowa State's campus. There were more ghost sightings in central Iowa than Polly imagined.

Clicking through pictures, she stopped on one of Sycamore Inn. What? Oh. He'd captioned it as a quaint little town with a sweet hotel and a big ghost story, hinting that more information would be coming. There were a few photographs of the Springer House and some of the mausoleum at the cemetery.

Polly picked up the phone and dialed, trying hard not to grin. It wasn't meddling if she had another reason for calling, was it?

"Boone County Sheriff."

"Anita Baker, please."

She waited a few moments and then, "This is Anita, how can I help you?"

"Hey Anita, this is Polly Giller."

"Hi there! Stu said you'd been at it again, but this time you got beat up a little. Are you okay?" Anita asked.

"I'm fine. No worries," Polly said. "Say, I was on Facebook looking at Jeremy Booten's page. Have you seen it?"

"Yeah. I started going through his social media stuff last week. Why?"

Polly had a thought and checked his list of friends. Sure

enough. "Did you see that he was friends on there with Jim Bridger?"

Anita chuckled. "We hadn't put that together yet. But wasn't he like old as dirt? I can't even believe he's on Facebook."

"Words like that will get you into trouble," Polly said, scrolling through Mr. Bridger's page. There wasn't much there which probably meant he had his privacy set so she couldn't see it. It was interesting that his cover picture was of the solarium of the Springer House. There was no one in the windows. So weird.

"Polly?" Anita asked.

"Sorry. Got distracted." Polly closed the tab in her browser and then shut down the entire browser. "Anyway. Facebook is fairly timeless these days. If they have a computer, they're probably part of the global membership. Even old Mr. Bridger liked keeping up with his friends." Before she could stop herself, she asked, "Are you coming up for the masquerade ball on Saturday?" There. It was out.

"I wasn't planning to. I had a great time a couple of years ago, but it seems ridiculous to come up by myself and I don't want to put any effort into finding a date. I'll probably stay home, turn the lights off, lock the door and watch an old horror movie or something."

"That sounds awful," Polly said. "Don't do that to yourself. It's been a while since you've spent time in Bellingwood. It's gotten more interesting, you know."

"Aaron does have stories," Anita said with a laugh. "It sounds like you've been busy. The inn is finished, there's a new coffee shop in town. And always more dead bodies. Kinda impressive."

"Stop it. Come on, you have to come up. The haunted house in the foyer will be running before the ball and it's going to be great. Aaron's wife, Lydia, is setting that up and he'll be dressed as a scary monster. He was Frankenstein's monster a couple of times, but I'm not sure if he's doing that again."

"I don't know," Anita said. "Maybe I could get some of the people from work here to come up with me. It would be fun just to see that."

"Then I hope to see you Saturday."

"We'll see. I'm not making any promises."

"Okay," Polly said. "Is Aaron in this morning?"

"Sure. Polly, you should see him cringe when he sees your name come up on his Caller ID. We all know it's you. His face gets all screwed up and red, he starts running his hand through his hair and if he's sitting down, he leans back in the chair and then sits straight up before he answers. If there's more than one of us in a meeting with him, we all try to sign the ASL sign for "P" first. The first one to realize it and make the sign gets a free lunch that day."

"You guys are nuts," Polly said.

"Sometimes we do what we have to do for entertainment. Just a minute and I'll put you through."

Polly listened to the on-hold music and stopped humming when Aaron spoke. "Trying to fool me?" he asked.

"No, I wanted to talk to Anita before I harassed you for information."

He took a deep, loud breath. "Now, Polly..."

She interrupted him. "I know, I know. You can't give me any details pertinent to the investigation. Because I'm so untrustworthy and might blab everything you tell me to the whole wide world and then the killer will know that you're on to them and you won't be able to capture them without a lot of extra trouble."

"Wow," he said. "That's more than I was going to say."

"I have some questions. Will you answer them if you can?" she asked.

"Shoot."

"Bang."

"Funny girl," he said "What's your first question."

"Did Jeremy Booten's car careen off the road into that creek?"

"No."

"That's all you're going to say to me? No?"

She could almost hear the smile in his voice. "I answered your question. Wasn't that what I was supposed to do?"

"Was the car put there on purpose so it would be hidden?"

"Maybe."

"Oh come on, Aaron."

"Fine. We aren't sure if it was on purpose or what, but it was driven there. It didn't end up in the creek because of an accident. It was too far off the road. No amount of, to use your word, careening, would have put it where it was."

"How was Jim Bridger killed?"

"Gunshot."

"Really! How was Jeremy Booten killed?"

"Gunshot."

"Was the same gun used for both?"

"I don't know that for sure yet. We're still running tests. This isn't television crime scene investigation, you know. Some of these things take more than twenty-four hours."

"Sure. I get that. Did you find anything in the car or in Jeremy's room at the inn that points to a killer?"

"Polly..." Aaron's voice held a note of warning.

"I'm pushing too far?"

"You're getting close. However, no we don't have a suspect yet."

"Were you, by any chance, leaning toward Jim Bridger as a suspect before he showed up dead?"

Aaron laughed. "We hadn't yet ruled him out."

"Oh!" Polly exclaimed. "He had a Chihuahua. Did you find it?"

"A dog? No. We weren't looking for a dog."

"Have you been to his house yet?" she asked. "Maybe the poor thing is out of food and water."

"The dog wasn't there when we went to the house yesterday afternoon. I'm sure it will turn up. Maybe someone's already found it and called animal control. We can check on that. Do you want to take the dog in?"

"A Chihuahua? Here? With cats and those two big dogs. Isn't that funny," Polly said.

"Well, you are the girl who rescues the world. Maybe you should rescue the old man's dog."

"I'd rather not unless I have to," she replied. "But let me know if you find it."

"Will do. Are you finished interrogating me for the morning?"

Polly smiled. "I'm sure I'll have more, but you've answered my most pressing questions."

"I'm glad I could be there for you. Stay off the streets, okay? Two unsolved murders are enough for now."

"I won't make any promises," Polly said. "But I'll try."

"That's enough."

They ended the call and Polly put the phone down and looked at her computer. She reached over and turned off the monitor. Nothing was keeping her here.

"I'm going out for a while," she said to Stephanie as she walked out of the office. "Call if you need me."

"Wait," Stephanie said. "Can you run out to Sycamore Inn?"

"Sure. What's up?"

Stephanie stood up and went over to a cabinet, opened it and took out a box. "Grey needs more card blanks. They just came in last night."

Polly took the box. "No problem. Is he in a hurry? I have a stop I want to make before going out there."

"No," Stephanie said, shaking her head. "He's fine. I'll let him know you're stopping by."

The kitchen was dark again when Polly walked through. She loved having big events here, but at the same time, normal business was relaxing – everyone where they were supposed to be, doing what they were supposed to be doing.

Polly put the box on the passenger seat and backed out of the garage. Aaron couldn't kill her too badly, could he? She was going to call this a strictly humanitarian visit - or a canine rescue. Or something like that. She drove past the Springer House, shaking her head at the fire pit and the insanity of the people who would do the craziest things in hopes of seeing a ghost. How many of them truly believed they'd see Muriel Springer and how many were there simply because they'd gotten caught up in something they didn't know how to escape?

She drove past Jim Bridger's house, peering at it to see if anyone was there. Of course no one was there. But if the dog had come home, it would be too cold for that little thing to be outside. And if it knew how to get inside on its own, it would be lost without its owner. Who would give it food or water or make sure that its messes were cleaned up?

One more time around the block and Polly could stand it no longer. She pulled into Jim Bridger's driveway and looked to her left and then to her right, just in case someone was watching her. "That's it," she said to herself. "Look suspicious. Get out of the truck like you belong here. You know better than this."

She put her hand on the door handle and said, "What was the name of that stupid dog? It was too big for a Chihuahua. Beast? Brute? Brutus. That's it."

"Brutus," Polly called jumping to the ground. "Are you here, Brutus?" She walked through the back yard, hoping that the dog would show up and she could get out of here before she embarrassed herself and did something stupid. There was no sign of the dog.

Polly knocked on the back door and chuckled. "Stupid woman. He's dead."

She raised her voice. "Brutus, did you get inside? Are you here?" She tried the door handle and was shocked to find that it opened. Did people never lock their doors? She looked at the handle when she got inside and realized there wasn't even a lock on this door.

Wait. She was inside. This was bad. This was very bad.

"Brutus? Are you here?" Polly looked around the tiny kitchen, clean and neat. At least old Mr. Bridger wouldn't have been embarrassed to have people in his house after his death. "Come on, doggie. If you're here, please come out."

She walked into a small dining room and looked around. An old buffet stood against a wall, its top filled with old photographs. She found herself drawn to them and the progression of Jim Bridger's life. There weren't many of him as an old man, but they went back through the years, mostly him with his dogs. When she got to the pictures of his youth and childhood, she realized that quite a few of him were taken in front of the Springer House.

One of the photographs practically leaped off the buffet into her hands. She picked it up with a gasp. The young woman in the picture with a teenaged Jim Bridger was the same woman that Rebecca had sketched. Polly gulped. She didn't believe in ghosts. She didn't believe in ghosts. This couldn't be true.

CHAPTER NINETEEN

How in the world had Rebecca seen Muriel Springer? Polly sat in her truck with the engine running, trying to warm up. The outside temperature was sixty-seven degrees, but she'd been chilled to the bone. She took a deep breath and turned around to look before backing up, then remembered the backup camera. She'd gotten more used to using it, but it still wasn't second nature.

Just as she pulled the gear shift in place to reverse, she caught a glimpse of something in the corner of the camera. She opened her door and turned to look and saw a small dog limping toward home.

"Brutus," she called, and the dog looked up at her. He gave a small tail wag and Polly jumped out to grab him. He looked as if he might run away, but she talked quietly, calling him by name and approached slowly enough that he stayed still. When she could grab him, she did and gathered the poor, shivering dog into her arms. "It's okay, little one. I've got you now."

She climbed back into her truck, holding him in her arms. Once in the truck, Polly tucked the small dog into her jacket, cranked up the heat and took out her phone.

"Bellingwood Animal Clinic, how may I help you?"

"Marnie?" Polly asked.

"Yes, this is."

"Hey, this is Polly Giller. Do either of the doctors have time this morning to look at a dog?"

"Did something happen to Obiwan? Doc Ogden's out on a call."

"No, this is Jim Bridger's Chihuahua. I found the poor thing and he's limping."

"Ohhh," Marnie said. "That's too bad. Are you keeping Brutus?"

Polly laughed quietly. "I doubt it, but for now I'll take responsibility for him. When can I bring him by?"

"Come on over. Doctor Jackson is with a patient, but he can free up some time."

"Thank you. We'll be right there."

Polly checked once more before backing out and headed toward the clinic. "It's a good thing I saw you back there, you little runt. You're awfully short."

Brutus's shivering didn't stop, but he reached up and licked her chin. "Yeah, yeah. We'll get you taken care of and then find a good home. I don't know if anyone will treat you quite as well as old Mr. Bridger, but we'll see what we can do."

She pulled into the parking lot and took out her phone one more time to call Aaron.

"Oh Polly, please," he said.

"No, it's fine. I wanted to let you know that I found Brutus. He's limping and I'm parked in front of the vet. Is there any reason you need them to not look at him?"

Aaron laughed. "No, I doubt that we're going to find the clue to lead us to the killer on the poor dog. If Doc Ogden does find something odd, tell him to let us know, but otherwise, take care of the dog. Are you adopting another dog?"

"No," she said resolutely. "But I'll take care of him until we either discover if Mr. Bridger made plans for him or someone else offers him a good home. The poor thing has been through enough. Nothing like losing your master and getting stuck outside in the cold, all in one day."

"You're a soft-hearted girl," Aaron said.
"Uh huh. Don't mess with my reputation."

~~~

Doctor Jackson checked poor Brutus out, took an x-ray and discovered that his limp was nothing major, probably a sprain or weariness from having walked all night. Polly took the dog home and after spending time introducing him to the crew, gave Brutus a bath and cursed herself for not looking for his dog food while she'd been in Bridger's house. She wasn't going back. Once was more than enough when it came to breaking and entering. Okay, entering, nothing had been broken. She laughed when she realized that Aaron hadn't even asked how she'd found Brutus. At least she didn't have to hem and haw her way out of that series of questions.

The cats were the most aloof of all the animals. Obiwan had taken Brutus's entrance into the house with a grain of salt and Han was still out with Henry.

Things had been quiet in the office and with no one else working in the building, she'd taken Brutus to the barn with her after lunch. Eliseo assured her the little dog would be perfectly fine with him, so she had saddled Demi and spent a couple of hours with him, wandering through the area south of Sycamore House. They'd traveled through Joss and Nate's land, back toward the field where she'd found Jeremy Booten. Crime scene tape still marked the area and it made her shudder to remember what that grisly scene had been like.

Once the kids had returned to school this fall, Polly made an attempt to get down to ride Demi at least a couple of times a week. It was easy to get busy with everything else, but once she climbed up on his back, she remembered the joy these horses brought her. Demi was steady and strong, never asking more of her than she could give. From the beginning, he'd been her horse. He was the one who taught her how to take care of them. In fact, her animals had all taught her what they needed. She'd never lived with so many different animals and had no expertise in any of it, but little by little, she'd grown comfortable with them.

When they got back, she found Eliseo putting finishing touches on the wagon for Saturday evening's festivities. Jason's two buddies from school, Scar Vasquez and Kent Ivers, were planning to ride in the back, dressed as grave diggers. According to Eliseo, they already had their costumes, having haunted a couple of the local thrift stores until they both found dark suits and white shirts. They'd purchased rubber old-man masks and had their shovels ready to go. She smiled. No one had any idea how she enjoyed watching people fall into roles that allowed them to participate in the fun at Sycamore House. Little by little, their cast of players continued to grow, each one bringing something new.

Brutus finally fell asleep on a pile of blankets Polly had arranged in the kitchen so she could keep an eye on him while she made dinner. It had been years since she'd made lasagna, but now was as good a time as any. While Kayla, Rebecca and Andrew worked on their homework and played with the new dog in the house, she boiled pasta, cooked hamburger, made a sauce and then layered ingredients.

She didn't feel like talking and playing with the kids, there was too much rattling around in her brain. She made molasses cookies and pumpkin bars, chopped vegetables for a salad, whipped up garlic butter for bread and thought that maybe with all this work, candlelight and a tablecloth would make dinner more fun.

Henry and Han came in first.

"What's up with this?" he asked, pointing at the table.

"Just something different. It feels like we should make more of an effort to be a family."

He kissed her cheek. "You don't need to make any extra effort. I think we're a perfectly normal family."

That made her laugh. "I love you, too. But get out of those smelly clothes. We're doing this up right tonight."

"Dressing for dinner," he said. "La-ti-dah!"

Heath came in the back door and walked into the dining room. "Am I late?" he asked.

"No," Henry said. "But we're under orders to clean up. You're a mess."

Heath looked down at himself. He was covered in dirt. "Yeah. Mr. Greyson let me drive the bobcat, but I still ended up with a lot of dirt on me."

"You both have time to take a shower and put on something clean," Polly said. "But hurry."

"Where's little girl?" Henry asked.

"She's in her bedroom with our newest guest."

He tilted his head. "Guest?"

"Jim Bridger's dog, Brutus."

Henry tilted it the other way. "Is it really a guest or are you adding a new member to this household?"

"A guest," Polly said. "I promise. It's on my to-do list tomorrow. Find that dog a good home. He's a nice dog, but I don't need a yip yappy thing in the house."

He kissed her again. "I'm impressed with you showing so much sense."

"Get going," Polly said, swatting his arm. "I'm setting the table now and you don't want to be late to dinner."

While Henry and Heath cleaned up, Polly finished setting the table. This had been a strange day. Not too much out of the ordinary had happened, other than breaking into Jim Bridger's house and finding that old photograph. But she hadn't called Aaron about it and she had yet to tell Henry what she'd done, so the secret was preying on her mind. She didn't want to spook Rebecca, because she still didn't believe in ghosts and didn't want anyone to think that she did, but the whole thing was creepy.

"I'm sorry I wasn't more help tonight," Rebecca said from the door to the living room.

Polly looked up, startled. "You're fine. How's Brutus?"

Rebecca put the little dog on the floor. "I think he misses his daddy. He keeps shivering."

"They do that anyway," Polly said with a laugh. "Don't worry too much. Doctor Jackson said he'll be fine. Now if we can find him a good home."

"He can't stay here?" Rebecca asked.

Han came bounding across the dining room floor at the scent of a new animal in the house. He skidded to a stop in front of Brutus, who planted his feet and growled at the bigger dog.

"He certainly has a big impression of himself," Henry said, coming in. He'd changed into a pair of jeans and a t-shirt.

Polly looked at his bare feet. She should be used to it, but she'd spent a lifetime with a father who always had his shoes and socks on. If he was truly relaxing, he'd take his shoes off. Everett always insisted that he had horribly ugly feet and the few times she saw them, she had to agree. He was much older when a doctor finally told him that he had athlete's foot and they could clear it up easily. But the training wasn't easily changed and the man still didn't like to go barefoot.

"Is this okay for dinner?" he asked. "Did I need to dress up more?"

"No" she said, smiling. "It's perfect. Would you mind taking the lasagna out of the oven so it can cool before we eat? Everything else is on the table. I'm just going to light the candles..."

"Can I turn down the overhead lights?" Rebecca interrupted.

"Absolutely," Polly said.

Heath came in as Rebecca was turning down the lights, dressed in his pajama pants and a sweatshirt and wearing slippers on his feet. "Whoa," he said. "I should change."

"You're fine." Polly gestured to the table. "I wanted to do something nice tonight. We're all here, I made a good dinner and it feels right to celebrate us."

They all sat down and Henry started to laugh.

"What's so funny?" she asked.

"Mom put candles on the table when she made a weird meal or when she screwed something up. Dad teased her that the candles were so we couldn't see that the food was burned."

Polly cut into the lasagna. "That isn't true. Your mom is a great cook."

"She had some bad meals. One night we had candlelight and bologna sandwiches because she made a bad meatloaf," Henry said. "If you ever want to see her blush, ask if she makes meatloaf. She still doesn't. It scares her."

"Meatloaf?" Rebecca asked. "Even I make that. Mom taught me how."

He laughed. "It's easy. I know. But that night Mom did something wrong and it was hard as a rock. And it bounced, too."

"How do you know that?" Polly asked.

"Dad got all funny about it and said that he'd throw it outside for the raccoons. When it hit the ground, it bounced. Mom was so mad at him. But it was gone by the next morning."

"Coons with indigestion," Heath said quietly. "That would be something to see."

"How was your afternoon with Grey?" Polly asked him.

"He's cool. Really easy to talk to."

She put lasagna on the plate that Henry passed to her, handed it back and took another. "What did you talk about?"

"Mostly hockey. He misses it. And he told me I should learn how to play. But I don't know if I'll have time."

"If you want to learn," Henry said, "you make time."

"Oh!" Heath said louder than usual, causing everyone to look at him. "Hayden and I were wondering if he could come to Bellingwood this weekend. I told him about the haunted house and the party. Can he come? He can stay in my room with me. He'll bring a sleeping bag."

Henry and Polly glanced at each other and he nodded at her, so she spoke. "Honey, Hayden is your family and that means he's part of this crazy little family. You two never have to ask permission for him to come. All you need to do is let me know when he's planning to be here so we can make sure there's plenty of food in the house for you two. And he can sleep wherever he wants. If you guys want to, we have the air bed and he can sleep on that. But we also have the extra room on the other side of the building upstairs. He can have that, too."

Heath nodded and looked down at his plate.

Rebecca put her hand on his. "She's telling the truth, you know."

He glanced at her and nodded again. "I know."

"Heath," Polly said, waiting for him to look up at her. "I'll talk to him, but I also want you to know this. We expect him here for Thanksgiving and Christmas break unless he has other plans."

"Really?" He looked back and forth between her and Henry.

Henry nodded. "Of course. I know it still seems strange, but this is your home now. Your. Home. That's kind of a lifetime thing. Polly and I didn't just sign up to be your guardian until you turned eighteen. We're here for the rest of your life. And we know Hayden is making his own life, but we're here for him, too." He chuckled. "As long as you two don't have fifteen or twenty other siblings hiding out there, we can absorb one more young man into our lives."

"I wish," Heath said.

"You wish what?" Polly asked.

"I wish we'd had more sisters and brothers. But they would have been in a bad place like I was, so maybe it's just as well."

"You have me!" Rebecca announced. "And at the rate Polly and Henry keep adding people, by the time you go to college, you could have fifteen or twenty siblings."

"Hey," Polly protested. "Don't even say that out loud. What in the world would I do with all of that?"

Henry chuckled. "We'd have to buy a bus. Can't you see it all painted with flowers and rainbows and hearts? You could take them on tour as a singing group. The Polly Family."

When Heath and Rebecca gave him blank looks, he put his hands up. "You know. The Partridge Family?" He looked at Polly, pleading for help. "Nobody?"

With her best patronizing smile, Polly said. "There, there, old man. The young 'uns just haven't been exposed to all of that excellent ancient television yet. It's okay."

"This is wonderful lasagna," Henry said. "You've outdone yourself. May I have more, please?"

She took his plate from him and added more to it, then held her hand out for Heath's plate. Polly remembered hearing Mary say that it always made her feel good when people wanted second helpings of food she'd made. It was nice to have a growing boy in the house who enjoyed eating.

~~~

Later that night, she and Henry were in their bedroom. He was in his chair watching television and she was across the room in her chair with her feet up on an ottoman and two cats in her lap.

"Henry, I need to tell you something," she said.

"I'm listening."

"No, I really need you to listen." Polly stood up and went over to the desk, pulled out the photograph, and handed it to him.

"What's this?"

"I stole it."

That got his attention. He pressed the button on the remote to turn the television off and looked more closely at the picture. "You stole it. From who?"

"From Jim Bridger's house."

Very slowly, he raised his head to look at her. "When were you in Jim Bridger's house?"

"This morning. Just before I found Brutus." Polly looked at the floor. "I went inside to see if the dog was in there and before I knew what I was doing, I was in the dining room. There were all of these pictures on his buffet and when I saw this one I had to take it."

"Why this picture? Is that Jim as a kid? Is he at the Springer House?"

"And that's Muriel Springer with him."

"Okay, so what's the big deal?"

Polly held out Rebecca's sketch pad, opened to the page where Rebecca had drawn her imagining of the ghost.

Henry looked at both of the pictures, then up at Polly, then at the pictures again. He flipped through the pages of the various drawings Rebecca had made and then peered at the photograph.

"What in the hell is going on?" he asked.

"That's my question. How did Rebecca see Muriel Springer?"

Henry turned to the bed and placed both items on top of the bedspread, unable to grasp what he was seeing. "Did she see a picture?"

Polly's body relaxed. "Of course," she said. "That's what happened. Maybe she saw a photograph inside the house when they broke the window that afternoon. Or maybe there's a picture in the library at school."

"That has to be it," Henry said.

"But would Rebecca lie to me about it?" Polly asked. "She said this was the person she saw in the house."

"Have you talked to her tonight and showed her this photograph?"

Polly shook her head. "No. It had me so freaked out, I wanted to talk to you first. I feel guilty about going inside his house."

He grinned up at her. "You're going to have to tell Aaron, aren't you?"

"Not right away. But yes. I can't keep this." She pointed at the picture. "And I'm not going back in there by myself again."

"Good." Henry stacked the photo on top of the sketchbook and handed them both back to Polly. "I'm sure there's a very reasonable explanation for the whole thing. We just don't know what it is yet."

"Right," Polly said.

CHAPTER TWENTY

Eerily quiet was how Polly felt about Sycamore House when she came down the main stairs the next morning. No progress had been made on the haunted house, but Lydia was a masterful planner and Jeff always had things well in hand for their events. She had to be fine with a quiet building.

The side door opened and Evelyn Morrow held the door for Denis Sutworth, who came through on a pair of crutches.

"Good morning, Polly," Evelyn said cheerily. "How are you?"

"I'm doing fine," Polly said. "It's good to see you out and about, Denis. How does it feel?"

He glanced at Evelyn and then back to Polly. "It's okay. Mrs. Morrow says I need to build my strength up. I'm not supposed to put weight on my leg, but I need to be ready for when I can."

"That's a good plan," Polly said. "Mrs. Morrow knows her stuff."

"We're heading into the office," Evelyn gestured for Polly to precede them. "Stephanie is training Denis on the reservation software. He is going to start putting in a few hours at the inn, giving Mr. Greyson free time to work on his hockey rink."

Polly's mouth dropped open. Why hadn't she thought of that? "What a great idea. He's a good man."

Denis nodded. "I like him. He's helping me a lot. Mrs. Morrow is almost done with me. When I can put pressure on my ankle, I have to move out of here."

"Oh," Polly said. "Are you going back home?"

She could have sworn he went pale at the thought. He wobbled on the crutches and finally said, "I don't know. It depends."

Evelyn stood behind him, rolled her eyes and gave a slight shake of her head.

"We'll miss you both when you leave," Polly said. "Evelyn, do you have a minute?"

Denis sat down in a chair to wait for Stephanie, who was on a phone call. "I'll be fine," he said. "Go ahead."

Evelyn followed Polly into her office and shut the door.

"Is he ready to go back home again?" Polly asked quietly, taking her seat.

Evelyn sat across from her and leaned forward. "There may not be many options. He can't afford to live on his own."

"How badly will that set him back? He's gotten so much better in the two months he's been here," Polly said.

"It took some doing," Evelyn said with a nod. "With the pain medications and other drugs, we've worked hard to re-balance his other meds. Doctor Greyson..." She stopped herself. "I'm sorry, Mr. Greyson. He doesn't want people to think of him as a doctor here. He said he left most of that behind. But it's only a matter of his title. He's fully credentialed, but he doesn't want to be known that way. Anyway, we've done good work together and I hate to see it all destroyed because Denis got back into old habits."

"Let me know if there's anything I can do to help."

"Thank you." Evelyn sat back. "You know, Polly, I wonder how serious you were about bringing other patients into that room. It is a perfect location. And to be honest, I've had several requests in the last two months. People interested in individualized hospice care and even one gentleman who needs to schedule back surgery, but would wait until I could be available to help in his rehabilitation." She grinned at Polly. "I never would have imagined that I could have this much life in my retirement, but it's exactly what I want to be doing."

"I already told you, Evelyn. We love having you here. The business end of it you need to work out with Jeff, but you're more than welcome." Polly slapped her palm across her forehead. "I didn't even think about bringing Rebecca down to see you last week when she was punched. The whole thing freaked us out and I wasn't processing on all four cylinders."

Evelyn smiled at her. "She needed to see a doctor. You did the right thing. And Rebecca's been down to see me a few times since it happened. She's doing fine."

"Thank you," Polly said. "That's a relief."

"She also tells me that Muriel Springer is back," Evelyn said.

Polly shook her head. "I don't know what to think. And now that Jim Bridger is dead, it seems even stranger. I can't make the connections come together. Did you ever know anything about that mystery?"

"No," Evelyn replied. "I didn't live here then. But every year, the stories get repeated and dear old Mr. Bridger made quite a living off telling those stories."

"He made money off of it?" Polly asked.

"Every time someone wanted to do a piece on haunted houses in Iowa, they'd come to Bellingwood and his star would shine once again. The poor old man had been infatuated with her as a kid and blew her death into something quite romantically tragic. He sold pictures he had of her..." Evelyn dropped her voice to a whisper. "And I don't even want to think about why he had so many. Personally I find it quite odd."

"He was odd," Polly said. "We have his dog upstairs."

"The Chihuahua? Story is, Muriel had a Chihuahua and when she died and her husband came home, he kicked that dog out because it was such a yappy little thing. Jim Bridger took it in and he's had one ever since. Always a male and always named Brutus."

Polly chuckled. "We all have our things, don't we?"

"There's a whole neighborhood that will be glad to see that ghost story die down," Evelyn said. "He brought in the weirdos. Have you heard what's been going on up there this week? That was all him. He contacted groups across the country about the Springer House, knowing that it was probably going to be sold. Once that property is cleaned up and the house either razed to the ground or completely renovated, it won't take long for the tales of ghosts and haunts to be nothing more than a page in the history books."

"I saw the fire dancers the other night," Polly said. "They're going to be there every night until Halloween." She laughed. "Maybe I'll have to talk Eliseo into riding past there Saturday night with me in my Grim Reaper costume and him with his coffin and gravediggers. That would spook 'em."

~~~

Evelyn went back to her room and Polly decided to go up town for coffee. This was much too convenient. She ran upstairs to see how the dogs were getting along. Adding another animal wasn't in her immediate plans, but she knew better than to question it. Whatever was going to happen, would happen.

Brutus was lying on the floor in front of the couch on full alert, while Obiwan and Han were sprawled out, wrapped in each other's legs on top of the couch.

"Not yet ready to trust them?" she asked. Every dog came fully alert when she spoke.

"You two stay put. I wouldn't want to disturb your beauty sleep. I'll just take Brutus with me. But I'll take an extra blanket. There's not much on him to keep a little dog warm."

She chased him around the sofa a couple of times before she finally sat down and waited for him to approach. Poor thing. He didn't have any idea what was happening. As soon as he got close, she picked him up, chuckling at his weight. There wasn't much to the dog. She tucked him under her arm and grabbed one of the blankets off the back of the sofa. If there was one thing Polly had plenty of in her life it was blankets. All shapes, sizes, colors, textures. It didn't matter. She was addicted to them and had more than most people she knew. But there were evenings when every single one of them was in use and that made it easier for her to justify the next purchase.

Polly took a leash off the hook once she got downstairs and snapped it on Brutus's collar.

She parked in front of the coffee shop and left the truck running while she went in. There weren't many people and Camille was the only person behind the counter.

"Pretty quiet in here," Polly said.

Camille smiled while she prepared Polly's order. "It hits a lull in the morning. We'll see a few people within the hour. This afternoon, more and more will sneak away from their offices. Things are going well, though."

"I haven't seen much of Sal up here. Am I just missing her?"

"She's not much of a morning person," Camille said with a grin. "She comes in late afternoons. If I'm alone and need help, she's always ready to pitch in."

"Afternoons." Polly shook her head. "What was I thinking? Of course! When we were in college, the worst days of the week were those she had early morning classes." She glanced outside. "Could I get a small cup of frothy milk for a dog who needs some happy?"

Camille turned to get a small cup. "Is something wrong with one of your dogs?"

"Oh no," Polly said. "It's a Chihuahua who belonged to the man who was killed. I want to find the perfect home for him, but until then, I can spoil the little bugger."

"That's sweet," Camille said.

"You want a dog?"

"I'm more of a cat person. And even then, until I get into my own place, I don't want to think about pets."

Polly gathered everything up and headed for the door.

"Say hi to Sal. I'll see you later."

She got back in the warm truck to a happy dog and sipped her hot coffee while Brutus lapped up the milk.

"We're going to do some investigating," Polly said to him. "Are you ready?"

Brutus responded to her conversation by wagging his bottom until he nearly fell off the seat. She gathered him back into the blanket and put her hand on his head. "I forget. You're a little excitable thing. Let's keep this calm."

She backed out of the parking space, drove down the street, turned and headed toward the Springer House.

"I know I shouldn't be here. There isn't a single soul in town that would think what I'm doing is a good idea, but I can't stand it. I want to know what people are seeing at that stupid house."

Polly parked across the street from the Springer House, hoping that no one was paying any more attention to her than they had to the other wingnuts in town to gawk at the ghost. She put the leash back on Brutus and took him with her. It was much easier to explain that she was walking a dog than that she was looking for proof of the existence of a ghost.

It was hard not to look sheepish as she crossed the street with the small dog scurrying along at her feet. She shouldn't be here. She didn't believe in ghosts and she'd already had much too much involvement with the people in this case. As she stepped up on the curb, Brutus tugged on the leash. Polly looked down, wondering if he had something important to tell her. No, he just needed to sniff a blade of grass and mark it as his own.

She looked closely at the homes on the other side of the street, hoping no one was paying attention. She didn't see anyone in the windows and looked up and down the street to make sure she was alone. Good heavens, she felt like a criminal, breaking and entering. Since she'd already done that once, her heart couldn't take it a second time. She wasn't going into the house, she was only going to look around the lot, just to see what she could find.

With that thought at the top of her mind, Polly pushed the creaky gate open. She and Brutus stepped through to the other side and she was surprised at how bad things looked. The bushes had grown up high as well as wide and were attempting to take over the yard. It was unimaginable that the city had allowed things to get so far out of control in here, but 'out of sight, out of mind' worked in a situation like this. The bushes hid what lay behind them. Several big old trees gave gorgeous shade to the house, but had dropped branches over the years.

She'd been holding the gate open with her body, and when she moved on in, it swung hard to close, banging as it hit, making Polly jump. Apparently those springs had held up well. The pavement of the driveway seemed to be the clearest, so Polly followed a path to it, finally picking Brutus up when he continued to lag behind. The garage was a separate building, but had been connected to the house by a screened breezeway. The screens were rotten and torn away. This must have been where the kids had gotten close to the house.

Polly stepped across the branches to the breezeway door, which was hanging open, bent on its hinges. She swiped at cobwebs that hung from the ceiling, shuddering at the sensation of them brushing her face and clutching her hair. As soon as she got her bearings, she looked for the broken window in the doorway. Henry hadn't found who to talk to about replacing it. But instead of broken glass, a fresh piece of plywood covered the window. Who would have done that? She approached the door tentatively, to test it. When she found it locked, she breathed a sigh of relief.

The door on the other side of the breezeway was just as damaged and the back yard was worse than the front. A cement path had once been there, but the overgrowth was deplorable and for some reason Polly felt really wrong about going any deeper into the lot. Brutus, still in her arms, looked up at her, out at the back yard, and growled.

"We shouldn't attempt that?" Polly asked.

He growled again and she backed away and headed for the garage. Its door was closed, but creaked open when she turned the handle. Polly didn't expect much and was surprised to find a car covered with a heavy tarp. That seemed odd. The tarp was eaten away in places and quite filthy. But why wouldn't Mr. Springer have taken this car when he left? Did it belong to Muriel and did her family refuse to let him have it? What a strange bit of history.

It wasn't dark in the garage, several windows in the overhead door and on the sides of the building allowed light in, but they'd grown grimy over the years and that light was limited. She flipped the flashlight on in her phone and proceeded to explore. When she got to the back of the car, she pulled back the tarp to find a name and smiled when she discovered it was a common Oldsmobile. She couldn't wait to tell Henry about her find and then giggled to herself when she realized she would have to tell him that she'd been snooping. He hadn't said too much at her admission of being inside Jim Bridger's house, but this might push him over the edge.

Brutus let out a low growl that sounded as if it was coming from his stomach.

"What do you hear, boy?"

He growled again and began to shiver more than usual.

"Is there an animal in here? That's fine. We'll get out. I'm not comfortable being in an enclosed space either. It's creepy."

She made her way back to the side door and went out, then walked back to the driveway. As her foot hit the concrete pad, Polly heard a scream and Brutus jumped out of her arms and ran into the brush of the front yard, barking and yipping. He'd carried his leash with him when he ran, but Polly hadn't been able to think fast enough to put her foot on it and stop him.

"Brutus," Polly yelled. "Come here."

A second scream and Polly found herself shivering. It was a haunting, mournful scream, full of terror and certainly meant to instill terror in those that heard it. She looked up at the solarium, praying she'd see nothing, but wasn't surprised when she actually saw the figure of a woman gliding across the room. The figure was far enough back that she couldn't get a good look. Polly took several short breaths and felt woozy.

"Slow down," she said quietly to herself. "This is nuts. There's no such thing as a ghost."

A third scream and Polly looked up again. Sure enough, the

features on the ghost looked much like those that Rebecca had sketched.

"I'm going, I'm going," she shouted. "Just let me get my dog and we'll be gone. I'm sorry!"

Polly scurried to the gate where she'd entered and yelled again, "Brutus. Come." She put as much emphasis into that command as she could, looking out over the lawn for any movement that might indicate where the dog was hiding. A quick glance up at the solarium, but she didn't see anything. Maybe the ghost had heard Polly's plea and saw her move to the gate. If Muriel Springer had loved Chihuahuas and she heard Polly call Brutus's name, surely she'd allow them to get out of here safely.

"Brutus, please come," Polly called. "Come on, baby. Let's go home. I'll give you anything you want. Just come to me."

She caught a glimpse of movement four feet in front of her and praying it was the dog and not some other creature, she stepped into the yard. Brutus yipped and the movement stopped. Polly gingerly stepped toward where she'd heard him and discovered that the leash had been caught on a downed branch. Brutus pulled toward her, unable to move any further. His yipping and barking grew louder and more insistent until Polly reached him.

Bending down to pick him up, Polly tugged on the leash. It wasn't going to give. With one last look at the solarium, she unsnapped the leash, grabbed him up, and ran for the gate. Once she got to her truck, she jumped in with Brutus, pulled the door shut, locked it and sat back, breathing heavily.

"What in the hell, little guy?" she asked.

Brutus jumped in the back seat and whined while Polly pulled her seatbelt on, pressed the button to start the truck, put it into gear and drove off. She wasn't sure where she was going, but when she pulled out onto the highway in front of Sycamore Inn, she made a quick decision to visit someone who was familiar and comforting. She pulled into a parking space beside the canopy. Grey was just going to have to take a few minutes to calm her down. That's all there was to it.

CHAPTER TWENTY-ONE

Polly called out, "Grey, are you here?" She was surprised at how tremulous her voice sounded. Those screams had shaken her.

After waiting a few moments, she approached the counter at the front of the inn and tapped the bell. She hated those things. It always felt as if she was so demanding and maybe even complaining that there wasn't anyone right there to assist her. But if Grey was in his apartment, she hated to bother him.

"Grey?" she called again.

"Hello, Miss Polly," he said from the front door, making her jump and squeeze the dog in her arms.

Brutus yelped and squirmed. She held tight to him, not wanting to let him go again. She'd found another leash under her truck's front seat. Those things were everywhere. She'd lost the dog once and that was enough.

"There you are," Polly said. "You scared me."

"I'm so sorry. I didn't mean to startle you." Whatever she'd felt inside must have shown on her face. Grey stepped closer to her and put his hand out to steady her. "My goodness, young lady. You look as if you've seen a ghost."

DIANE GREENWOOD MUIR

"Oh Grey," she moaned. "You can't even imagine."

He took her arm and led her to one of the wing chairs beside the fireplace. "What is going on, milady? I don't oft see you so shaken."

"I saw a ghost."

Grey sat down in a chair next to her and smiled. "You saw a what?"

"I saw a ghost. And it screamed at me."

"Polly, you are many things, but you are not easily taken in. You don't believe in ghosts."

She shook her head and dropped her chin to her chest. "Before today, I would have assured you that I do not believe in ghosts. But, Grey. I saw her. And she screamed at me to leave the grounds."

Brutus was still squirming in her arms and Grey reached out to take the dog. He held it in his lap and before long, the Chihuahua settled down. "Who did you see?" he asked.

"I saw Muriel Springer in the solarium. Brutus and I were exploring the grounds. I wanted to prove that there was no ghost. But instead, I was proven wrong. I saw her."

Grey scowled. "Ghosts do not exist. Our imaginations create scenarios in which they act out, but they aren't real. Might it have been a play of light across the glass windows?"

Polly looked at the front door. Cloud cover had shut out the bright sun. "There was no light to play with. And that's not all."

"There is more?" He sounded incredulous.

"Rebecca drew several sketches of the woman she saw there. It was the same woman," Polly said. "And Grey, I found a photograph of her in Jim Bridger's house and it was exactly the same as Rebecca's sketches." She heard her voice tremble again and took a breath to regain control.

Brutus had completely relaxed in Grey's arms, his eyes closed and his paws twitching as he ran through an imaginary field.

"Look at him," she said. "He was scared to death up there as well. At the first scream, he jumped out of my arms and got lost in the mess that was the front lawn. But I finally told her that once I

206

found Brutus, I'd leave and never go back. That's when she stopped screaming."

He nodded for her to continue.

"Brutus was Muriel Springer's dog," Polly explained.

Grey pointed at the Chihuahua in his arm. "This dog isn't nearly old enough."

"No," Polly said, smiling. "Jim Bridger took care of her Brutus after she died and then always had a Chihuahua and always named him Brutus."

"I see. And you think that she left you alone because you had her namesake dog."

"It all sounds so ridiculous now that I'm saying it out loud, but Grey, I saw someone in that solarium and I heard the screams. It was horrifying."

"You believe it was Muriel Springer's ghost?" he asked.

"Who else could it be?" Polly responded. "It looks just like her picture and these horrible things have been happening and..." she stopped herself, sat up straight and looked at him. "I have completely lost my mind. There must be a rational explanation."

"Of course," he said quietly.

"I can't for the life of me find it, but there has to be one, right?"

He smiled. "I would tend to agree with you. There are many strange and wonderful things in our cosmos, but I have difficulty believing that people stay on earth after they've died. It would seem there are much more interesting things to experience on the other side of death. Why would you want to stay in this singular place?"

"Unfinished business?"

"The girl's family left her and all she had was to spend her afterlife in a decaying house so she might scream at pretty young women and their dogs? After seventy years, that would become altogether tedious."

All of the arguments that people had been giving Polly to prove the ghost of Muriel Springer was real came pouring out of her.

"But other people have seen her over the years and there are stories of her frightening her husband so much that he had to rush his family out of town." Polly blinked. "There's even a car in the garage."

"What does that prove?" Grey asked. "Maybe you could tell me how many different people have seen her."

Polly sat back and deliberately forced her shoulders to relax. "I don't know how many different people have seen her. You're right, the only person that talks about this is Jim Bridger. You're saying the same things to me that I've been saying out loud to those who want to believe she's real."

"It is one thing for a group of people to come to Bellingwood so they might have an adventure at Halloween. The folks staying here at the inn wish to believe, and thus everything that happens promotes their belief in the supernatural." Grey leaned toward Polly, shifting Brutus as he did so. "But you, Polly Giller, are not looking for an adventure in the paranormal. You are surely grounded in reality. If you saw something that tests your imagination and heard things that you don't understand, you must look for truth rather than speculate on a myth."

"I'm not quite sure how that will happen," Polly said. "I won't go back to that house any time soon." She gave a weak chuckle. "I'm not usually one to run away from things that frighten or worry me, but I had the scare of my life this morning." She pointed at the dog in his lap. "I'm almost ashamed to say that I was prepared to leave him there if he hadn't shown up when he did."

Grey stroked the dog's back. "When he awakens, he must be reminded to be grateful that you rescued him from certain doom."

Polly looked at him in surprise. "Certain doom?"

"A jest, my girl. A jest."

"He's awfully comfortable with you. He hasn't been this relaxed since I picked him up yesterday."

Grey smiled down at the dog. "Brutus is quite the name for such a small beast. I imagine he has a heart of a warrior." He scratched the dog's ears. "It must have been quite alarming when that warrior awoke in such a small and fragile frame."

"You understand him better than most people," Polly said.

The front door opening attracted their attention. Grey stood, handed the dog back into Polly's lap. "Don't leave, please," he said. "I'd like to speak with you further." Grey gestured at the coffee pot. "It's fresh and if you were to peek under the linen cloth, you'd also find freshly baked croissants from Mrs. Donovan's oven."

He walked away. "Good morning folks, how might I help you?"

The older couple followed him to the counter, chattering away about the haunted house they'd heard about on the internet. They were surprised to find there were still vacancies at the inn, especially at this late date. They were looking forward to Halloween in Bellingwood and hoped it would be everything they could imagine.

Polly chuckled and spoke quietly to Brutus. "They have no idea. I certainly hope they're ready for the Sycamore House haunted parade."

Grey was good with people. He told them about Secret Woods Winery and their good fortune in having several wonderful restaurants, a brand new coffee shop and the interesting stores in the downtown area. When pressed about the Springer House and the deaths of people that had been part of that mystery, he graciously showed them how to find their way.

Polly wondered if she'd even finished the coffee she'd purchased from Sweet Beans, but another cup sounded like a good idea, so Polly carried Brutus across the room. After pouring a fresh cup, she sat down at one of the small cafe tables and looked outside. The clouds were breaking up and sunshine poked through across the sky.

"It's going to be a good day," she said to the dog, holding him close to her chest as the couple walked by, glaring at her. It made her laugh. They had no idea that she was the owner and in their quick judgment, made sure to let her know their disdain at a dog in the lobby. She desperately wanted to stick her tongue out, but thought better of it and then giggled when she saw that Brutus's tongue was hanging out between his front teeth. "Thanks, buddy. I'm glad you've got my back."

"I'll be right back," Grey said, as he followed the couple out.

Polly watched him walk past the front windows, pointing to the rooms along the highway. She turned in her chair and then stood up and went to the window. Not only did he show them to their room, but he unlocked the door, handed the wife the key card and helped her husband carry bags into their room. They weren't charging enough, nor were they paying him enough for this type of service. But she knew better than to say anything. This was simply his way.

She was back in her seat at the table when Grey returned. "It sounds like we're going to fill up with haunted house aficionados this week," she said.

Grey poured himself a cup of coffee and sat down. Both were surprised when Brutus strained to get back into his arms.

"I think he likes you," Polly said.

He put the coffee down and reached out, "May I?"

Polly handed the dog to him. "Of course."

"It's been a long time," Grey said, bringing the dog's face up to his. He tucked Brutus's head into his own neck and hugged the little animal. "I've missed out. Would you consider allowing me to bring a pet into this apartment?"

"Would you like this pet?" Polly asked. "And oh, by the way, I'd encourage it. I believe everyone should have pets. My menagerie grows on a regular basis."

Brutus settled back into Grey's lap and looked up at Polly as if he had claimed his person.

"I don't know what to think," Grey said. "I have nothing here to care for a dog."

Polly grinned and reached over to scratch Brutus's ears. "He's at home with you. I doubt that he'd be as happy anywhere else. And dogs are easy. All you need to get started is dog food, a water dish and a few toys. If you want to put him in a kennel or have a separate bed for him, you can pick those up another day. What do you think?"

"I think I am a new pet owner," Grey said.

"This is a good week," Polly said. "I helped Beryl Watson keep two grey kittens and now I've given you your first dog in your new home."

"My first?"

"They're like potato chips," she said with a smile. "You can't have just one. But this one will be sure to let you know what's happening. He's quite verbal. Once he's comfortable, he'll probably tell you what's going on before you're even aware of it."

"My boy," Grey said to the dog. "You and I are destined to become great friends."

Brutus snuffled and tucked his head into Grey's elbow.

"Would you like to see the work that your young charge and I completed out back?" Grey asked. "He will be a great help to me. If we can find one or two others to assist as this all comes together, we will have quite a rink."

"I'd love to," Polly said. She handed Grey the leash she'd brought in with her.

"Are you certain?" he asked.

Polly nodded. "You'll be glad for it in no time."

"How does he tell me?"

"I have no idea. But he didn't have any accidents in our apartment last night. He went out with Obiwan and Han, so we made sure he was taken care of. His records are with Doctor Jackson at the vet clinic. I took him in to see the Doc yesterday after I picked him up. All you need to do is tell them that you're taking care of him and they'll let you know when it's time for his annual checkup and vaccinations."

Grey nodded and stood up. Brutus did his best to stay attached to the man. "You are staying with me, young sir," Grey said. "Do not fear."

As they walked through his apartment to the central courtyard, Polly asked, "Are you coming to Sycamore House for the festivities on Saturday?"

Grey snapped the leash on Brutus and put the dog down. The dog's nose never came up from the ground, sniffing everything in its path. "I find myself in a quandary," he said. "As much as I would enjoy the company and entertainment, my duties here require that I remain in place."

"But won't the guests be out and about?"

"More than likely," he agreed. "But if one person needs me, I should be available. And perhaps I should ask if the inn is on the route for local children begging for treats."

Polly's mind was whirling as fast as possible. There had to be a way to get him to Sycamore House. Sylvie didn't want her to tell Grey or Eliseo that they should pursue a date with her, but if they were there, something could possibly happen.

"When are you bringing Denis Sutworth in to start working?" she asked.

"Mrs. Morrow will transport the boy here tomorrow and Friday so that we might begin his training. It will be quite pleasant to have someone in place so that I might avoid the guilt of leaving, if even for short periods of time. And having him here will also allow me to spend more time building this." He pointed at the rink-sized space that had been cleared and smoothed.

"You got quite a bit done yesterday," she said.

Grey smiled at her. "Yesterday was an opportunity to clean and clear. I'd done most of this work before young Master Heath arrived. He enjoyed driving the bob-cat and moved piles of dirt to the back of the lot. In speaking with your husband, he believes that he can make use of the dirt in preparing the space for your friend's new home."

"Joss and Nate?"

He nodded.

"You aren't getting off that easy." Polly grinned at him. "What if Denis Sutworth worked Saturday evening? There will probably be nothing going on and if he has any questions, he can call and you'd be back within minutes."

Grey followed Brutus as the dog tugged him forward, desperate to smell something else in the yard. "Is there any particular reason for your attempt to bring me to Sycamore House on Saturday evening?"

"Well..." Polly said.

"I gave my promise to Mrs. Donovan that my initial outburst would never occur again. She is a lovely woman and though my heart reacted upon meeting her, I find that our professional relationship is much too important to me. I will not sabotage it by allowing those feelings to erupt again."

Polly was tongue-tied. There were so many things she wanted to say to him, but found that she couldn't betray her friend. Even if it were for Sylvie's own good. "Let me encourage you to make every attempt to come. We have a wonderful time, you'll meet more people from Bellingwood, the costumes are great fun, and..."

He put his hand out to stop her. "Denis, Mrs. Morrow, and I will discuss his comfort level in attending the desk by himself. That boy is doing much better at spending time alone. We are, by no means, finished with his treatment, but he has come a long way and should be proud of the work he's done in the last two months. As I understand it, his orthopedic surgeon is also quite pleased with the progress he's made."

"That's all on you and Evelyn," Polly said.

"Denis has an extraordinary team of caregivers dedicated to assisting him find a return to health."

Polly scowled. "From what I hear, I don't know that it's so much a return as it is new-found health. Here's hoping he can maintain the progress."

"Every day that he is able to move forward is a good day for the world, don't you think?" he asked with a smile. "We always look for big transformations to prove that the world is getting better, but sometimes we need to see the small steps that individuals take and realize that their little world is just as important." He bent down to pick Brutus up. "And we never know which person's little world might be the one thing that changes the entire world for the better."

They walked back inside the apartment and Grey put Brutus down on the floor. "This is your home now. What do you think?" The dog burst into a run, dashing through the rooms before coming back to Grey's feet. He yipped.

"I have sliced roast beef," Grey said.

Polly took in a quick breath. "I'll run up to the grocery store and get a bag of dog food for you." She laughed. "Every time I take one of the animals to the vet, they always ask what I feed them and write it down on their chart. I'll call Marnie so that I buy the right thing for Brutus."

"That's quite a lot to ask of you," Grey said. "Brutus and I can take care of it after lunch. Things generally slow down enough that I can get out of here for an hour or two." He glanced at the front door. "But this week is different than most. I've had more drop-in business due to the haunted house."

"Let me take care of this. You are doing me a huge favor by taking Brutus in. He's already happier here with you than he was at my house," Polly said.

"It seems I shall be grateful for Master Sutworth's upcoming employment," Grey said. "It is uncomfortable for me to ask for help when I could so easily do things for myself."

"I'm the one who asked you for help. Please believe me. You two get more acquainted and I'll be back soon with food for your boy." She put her hand on the door leading to the lobby and when she didn't hear any more protests, turned back to see Grey pick the dog back up and nuzzle his neck. This was a great decision.

CHAPTER TWENTY-TWO

Running errands for someone else was much more fun than buying things for herself. Polly drove away from the inn a second time that morning after dropping off dog food and a couple of toys she'd picked up at the grocery store. As she turned onto the highway, her phone blew up with notifications.

"What in the world?" There was enough traffic that she bristled with curiosity all the way to Sycamore House, but as soon as she pulled into her garage, she swiped her phone open to find a slew of texted pictures from Beryl. She'd been taking numerous pictures of her two new residents for the last two days and had finally figured out how to send them via text message.

"Meet May and Hem," Beryl announced. She'd also figured out how to text a group of people. Polly wondered who was coaching her. "Polly made me keep them and if I'm distracted because of so much cute during the next few months, you can all blame her. The *mayhem starts every morning at dawn. Well, to be honest, that's Miss Kitty's time to be awake. The kittens still snuggle in bed with me. Yes, they are all in my bed. It's the best way I've found to keep warm on these chilly fall nights. Unless of course, one of you would like to send your..."*

The texting stopped and pictures began coming through, one after another. They wrestled, they slept a lot. They snuggled, they were absolutely adorable. Polly had forgotten how much fun it was to have a pair of kittens in the house, but she wasn't in a hurry to return to that. Luke and Leia were still playful, but not quite as frenetic.

After a few minutes passed and no more pictures came through, Polly texted back. *"I'm in love. When is the next party at your house?"*

Another text came through and Polly scrolled back, only to find that it was from Jeff, not Beryl. *"Where are you? There are some people here that want to speak with you."*

"I'm in the garage. I'll be right there," she replied.

She checked her calendar to make sure she hadn't missed an appointment. Jeff and Stephanie had finally shamed her into taking the time to learn how to use the Sycamore House calendar. It wasn't that she couldn't, but she certainly enjoyed making them work for it.

Polly walked through the kitchen and smiled at Rachel. It felt right to have the lights on and the ovens working. She pulled back the heavy, black curtains hanging in the hall, meant to block light from the kitchen. There was a full crew of people working with Lydia to build the Haunted House. All of this work for one night. There were some big haunted houses throughout the area, but Polly hated those things. She always felt out of control while walking through them. 'Always' meant the one time that she'd been dragged into one by Sal when they lived in Boston. That was the last one she ever wanted to experience. Fortunately, Lydia ensured that this haunted house, though it be frightening and spooky, was G-rated for younger kids ... which meant that wimpy adults could enjoy it as well.

They'd moved things so that it would feed out the side door, rather than turn back on itself and send people out the front door. With the number of people coming in for the masquerade ball, Lydia and Jeff had worked out a plan to make traffic patterns as smooth as possible.

Wending her way through props, tarps, and scenery flats, Polly finally got to the front door of the office. Six people of all ages were sitting in the main office and Stephanie stood when she entered. "Could I speak to you in your office?" she asked.

Polly nodded, smiled around the room and followed Stephanie who shut the door behind them.

"What's up?" Polly asked.

"Jeff's naughty. I don't think he knew what was happening here. If he'd stopped and listened to me, I would have waved you off."

Polly pointed to the door. "Who are those people?"

"Haunted house kooks. They want to talk to you about finding dead bodies and how you do it and about finding Jim Bridger and Jeremy Booten. They made some noise about interviewing you regarding the Sycamore House Haunted House and Masquerade Ball, but that's not what this is about."

"I see," Polly responded. "Where's Jeff now?"

"That's the thing," Stephanie whispered. "As soon as he texted you, he got a call and had to leave. So you can't even pass them off on him."

Polly chuckled. "That was fast. I was just in the garage. Show them into the conference room and I'll be right there."

"You're sure?"

"I can't be rude. They've already seen me. Maybe they can tell me how so many people from out of town heard about Bellingwood's ghost."

Stephanie put her hand on the door handle and Polly stopped her. "Let's kill 'em with kindness. Would you and Rachel mind bringing in coffee and tea for them? And if Rachel has anything sweet to eat, that too?"

"We'll take care of it," Stephanie said. "Good luck." She left and pulled the door shut again. Polly heard her speaking to the group and saw people moving around the main office as she dropped into her chair.

"You're in trouble now, you know," she texted to Jeff. *"I just wanted you to be fully aware."*

"Sorry. Got a call from the Mayor's office. There's some kind of emergency meeting about Halloween."

Polly creased her brow at the phone. *"Are you serious? What's going on?"*

"I'm not sure. I'll let you know when I find out."

"They can't cancel it."

"I don't know anything yet. Don't panic."

"Okay then. You handle this and you're forgiven."

He sent back a smiley face and Polly took a deep breath. This had to be the weirdest Halloween season ever. The rest of the world was worrying about Christmas invading retail stores and all she could think was that she had too many dead bodies and at least one of them wasn't ready to move on.

Steeling herself, Polly stood up, walked out of her office and into the conference room. "Hello," she said. "I'm Polly Giller. How may I help you today?"

Everyone started speaking at once. Polly remained in place and waited, hoping they'd realize how rude they were being. It was a technique she'd first seen used in junior high band. The band teacher had told the class that they were no longer children and if they couldn't conduct themselves better than common hooligans (that had been the first time Polly had heard the word used outside of her books), then they would face the consequences.

She grinned to herself, watching as they looked at each other and then at her. "That was my fault," she said. "I must have invited chaos with my question. Are you all together?"

It was interesting to see them physically separate themselves from each other, moving into smaller groups.

"We're not together," one of the older men said. "This is my wife, Mary, and our friend, Jean. We've come from Missouri."

A young woman pointed at the girl with her and said, "I'm Gina Cates and this is Angel West."

Polly nodded. "Where are you from?"

Angel spoke up. "We're here from Idaho. We want to see Muriel Springer." She had a soft, lush voice, one that Polly was sure attracted the attention of both men and women alike.

"And you?" Polly asked the last person, a middle aged man wearing a blue pea coat. His hair seemed prematurely gray and looked as if he'd cut it himself, sharp lines and angles around his face. He wore a pair of rectangular glasses and had a look she identified with academia. He had to be a professor somewhere.

He stood to shake her hand and said, "Marty Evensong. I've come into town to investigate your gift as well as the rumored paranormal activity."

"The ghost," Polly said.

"Well, yes," he replied.

A light tap on the door preceded Stephanie and Rachel coming in with carafes and trays. They placed them on the table and brought out napkins, cups and glasses from a cabinet.

"There is coffee, tea, and ice water," Stephanie said. "The baked goods come from Sweet Beans Coffee Shop and Bakery."

"That means they're amazing," Polly interjected. "I hope you enjoy them." She reached forward and pushed the two trays closer to the six and looked at them expectantly, then took up the coffee carafe and said, "Would anyone like coffee?"

The looks on their faces were priceless, but it only took moments for them to regroup.

"Tell us what comes over you when you go out to look for a body?"

"Did you sense the ghost's presence since you are Bellingwood's resident dead body finder?"

"What kind of tools do you use when you find bodies? Do you have, like, a divining rod or something?"

"Do you ever get used to seeing death?"

"Did you know that you would be doing this when you were a child? Did you find bodies then?"

"What about your husband? Does he approve of your side business?"

"Was Jim Bridger's body as decayed as the other young man?"

"I heard that your dog has ESP too. Is he the one who leads you to bodies?"

Polly finally put her hand up to stop their questions. They'd bombarded her and most of the talking had overlapped. In fact, she knew that she'd missed some of their questions because they'd hurled them so quickly.

"I'm sorry that I misled you," she said quietly. "I'm not here to answer questions about my life or my family. I don't know you people and you don't know me. Any rumors that you might have heard in town or online are simply that. Rumors. Whatever truth there is in those rumors is none of your business."

"But Miss Giller," one of the men said. Polly had already put their names out of her head. She didn't care to get to know any of them personally.

"I'm sorry if you thought you could trap me into telling you anything," Polly said. "It's just not going to happen. I'd hoped we could have a cordial conversation about the ghost of Springer House and events here at Sycamore House, but the rest of this is sensationalism at its finest. Please enjoy the coffee and goodies my team has provided and then, since this is a business, I'll ask that you leave."

"But Miss Giller," he pressed again. "Surely you can understand our interest."

"No," she replied. "I don't understand. What's it to you? What is any of this to you? Does your life change today if I tell you personal information? No. But mine does. You don't respect me enough to be polite in my own building. You barged in here, expecting to find juicy bits of gossip to spread, so why in the world would I trust you with my life? Do you want me asking about your children? Your families? Your pets? No." She put her hand on the door handle. "I'm sorry that we couldn't have a conversation."

Before they could speak, she walked out and pulled the door shut behind her. Polly sagged against the closed door and Stephanie gave her a worried look.

"Are you okay?"

"I'm fine." Polly walked over to Stephanie's desk. "I forget how much protection Bellingwood offers me. People accept me for who I am, even my eccentricities. Outsiders want to make a big deal out of those things that are odd about me; they want to try to expose me. It's disgusting."

The individual man, Marty something, came out of the conference room first. "Miss Giller, I am a trained paranormal investigator. I would like to..."

She put her hand up again. "Stop right there. I will not be a target of any investigation of yours. I've asked you to leave. Up to this point I've been polite. Please leave."

"But you don't understand the importance of understanding what it is that you do."

Polly looked down at Stephanie. "If he hasn't turned and walked out of this office in fifteen seconds, please dial the police station. I will not be harassed in my own home."

Stephanie put her hand on the phone, Polly turned back to the man and straightened up. "I wanted to be polite, but that's over. I won't be the subject of any investigation." She pointed to the door. "You can either leave on your own, or I will call for help."

"You're making a huge mistake," he said. "Don't think for a minute that I'm the last person who will come to Bellingwood in search of answers. Your story is getting out there and others will find you."

Stephanie started dialing the phone.

"I'm leaving." He strode to the front door. "Don't say you weren't warned. It would have been easier if you just talked to me."

Polly reached out to take the phone from Stephanie and he bolted for the front door.

"Who did you dial?" Polly asked.

Stephanie laughed. "Just random numbers. I don't actually know the police station's phone number by heart."

"That's hilarious," Polly said. "Let's hope we can get rid of the rest of these people as easily."

"You know they're asking questions around town, don't you?"

Polly shook her head and then dropped it in frustration. "Of course they are. We try to be gracious hosts and they create chaos because they think they have a right to be all up in our business."

The conference room door opened again and the rest of the group came out into the main office.

One of the women started toward Polly, who backed away. She reached out to try to touch Polly. "We're sorry for putting you on the spot, Miss Giller. I hope you understand that we have a great many questions."

Polly backed up again and pointed to the front door. "Thank you for stopping by. I hope you have a nice visit in Bellingwood."

"Could we at least speak to you about Muriel Springer?" one of the others asked.

"Thank you for coming," Polly said again and turned into her office. She shut the door and stood behind it, hoping that they wouldn't take long to finally leave.

In a few moments, a soft knock came at her door and Stephanie said, "It's safe to come out, Polly. They're gone."

Polly opened the door and pulled Stephanie into a hug. "Thank you. I'm sorry I made you sit there alone, but I couldn't be polite any longer."

Stephanie hugged her back. "You were wonderful. You're kind of my hero, you know. I wish I could be as smart as you when you're in the middle of a confrontation. I always scream and lose my cool."

"I've had to get better since coming to Bellingwood," Polly said. "And still - sometimes I can be just mean, but I didn't want to give those weirdos any more fodder for their blogs and websites."

"Have you ever done a web search on yourself?" Stephanie asked.

Polly's entire body shuddered. "I don't want to. Especially after today's encounter. I'm much happier living in my cocoon of ignorance about what people say about me. If I've become infamous, that scares the hell out of me."

"Was that man right?" Stephanie asked, her face reflecting concern. "Are more people going to come to Bellingwood to investigate you?"

Polly pursed her lips and then said, "I hope not. But we'll deal with them as it happens."

Stephanie chuckled. "Maybe we need to hire a good looking bodyguard for you. He could hang out here in the office all day if you like."

"Except when I need to be guarded?" Polly asked with a smile.

"Okay. I'd let him out of my sight for that," Stephanie said. "But just for a short period of time. Deal?"

"Deal." Polly headed for the front door. She turned back. "If any more psychos come..."

"And they will," Stephanie said.

Polly grinned. "If anymore show up, tell them that I moved to Oregon or something. But I'm not available. And when Jeff comes back, tell him that he's in big trouble."

Stephanie waved her away. "I can't wait."

No one in Bellingwood had said anything to Polly about being questioned regarding her talent for finding bodies, but they probably wouldn't. Her friends would try to protect her, but innocent questions wouldn't make them wary. For the most part she trusted people, but in one short conversation, it hit her that she had to be more careful. That wasn't the way she wanted to live her life.

"Watch it, Polly!"

A hand reached out to grab her and she looked up to see Len Specek standing there, ready to stop her from falling over the stack of two-by-fours on the floor.

"I'm sorry," she said. "I wasn't paying attention."

Lydia rushed over. "That was obvious. Did it have something to do with those people in your office? What did they want?"

Polly felt her face flush and gulped back tears that suddenly hit her. Lydia could always do this to her. She gulped again and felt tears fill her eyes.

"Oh, dear Polly, what happened?"

"I'm okay," Polly said. "I really am."

Lydia took Polly's arm and led her away from the construction and into the quiet auditorium. "What in the world happened?"

"They scared me, Lydia," Polly said, feeling her emotions take over.

As she started to cry, Lydia pulled her into an embrace and held her.

"They scared me to death. All they wanted to do was talk about how I find dead bodies. One man came to Bellingwood to investigate how I do it. He said that he wouldn't be the last." She snorted back tears. "And I know they're all over town asking questions about me. They wanted to know if I sensed Muriel's body. So now I've been associated with that, too. I don't want to be scared of people in my home."

Polly sniffed again and rubbed tears away from her eyes, then backed up. "I'm sorry. I thought it was no big deal. But you do this to me every time."

Lydia smiled at her. "What do I do?"

"You always make me feel safe and that's when I can fall apart. Even when I don't know that I need to."

"I'm not going to apologize for that," Lydia said, gathering Polly back in and holding her tight. "I'll never apologize for that," she whispered into Polly's ear.

CHAPTER TWENTY-THREE

"Everybody's home. Where are you, Brutus?" Rebecca called out when she came in the front door of the apartment.

Polly walked into the living room from the kitchen. Dinner had been such a wonderful time with everyone the other night, she wanted to see if they could pull it off again tonight, so she'd been cooking.

"Hi kids," she said to Andrew, Kayla, and Rebecca.

"Where's Brutus?" Rebecca asked. "I love that little rug rat."

Polly chuckled. "Brutus is gone."

Rebecca's face fell. "Gone? Did you have to put him to sleep or something?"

"Oh no, honey," Polly said. "He's living with Grey over at the inn now. Those two fell in love with each other and since Grey didn't have a pet, it seemed like the perfect match."

"I knew it was too good to be true," Rebecca whined, flopping down on the couch, a sulk about to happen. "I never get anything that's my own."

Polly walked back into the kitchen. She wasn't going to feed into that. Andrew followed her.

"Rebecca talked about him all day. She thought it was so cool that he belonged to Mr. Bridger and had probably seen the ghost."

A flashback of running through the Springer House yard with that little dog threw Polly for a split second. This had been a rough day and suddenly she remembered that she'd promised to take Rebecca shopping for a Halloween costume.

"Damn it," Polly said under her breath.

Andrew rushed ahead. "I told her that the dog wouldn't know whether it was seeing ghosts or not and that she had a lot of animals here to love. You didn't promise to keep him. It's going to be okay, I know it will."

Polly put her hand on his arm to stop the flow of words. "I'm sorry. I forgot that I promised Rebecca we'd look for costume ideas tonight and I've already started supper."

" Yeah," he said. "She talked about that today."

"I guess it's her day for disappointment," Polly said with a deep breath. "It's a good thing we all live through these horrible, awful days."

Andrew looked at her like she had lost her mind.

"Yeah, yeah," she said. "I'm weird. Live with it."

"I'm used to it." He went over to the refrigerator. "Do you care if I get something to drink?"

"That's fine." Polly waved at the fridge. "Whatever you can find. There are chocolate chip cookies in the freezer if you want any of those."

"I didn't know how much I liked frozen cookies until I met you," Andrew replied.

Polly went back into the living room and found the two girls sitting on the sofa with Obiwan between them, his head in Rebecca's lap. "Did you find a good substitute?" she asked.

"He's not a little lapdog like Brutus," Rebecca said.

"Honey, you knew we weren't keeping him. I told you that."

"Well, I hoped."

Polly sat down in a chair next to Rebecca. "I totally forgot about taking you girls to look for costumes tonight. Can we do it tomorrow?"

"We're kind of running out of time," Rebecca said, more than a little snotty.

Even as it came out of her mouth, she must have heard herself, because her eyes looked as shocked as Polly felt.

"Do you want to try that again?" Polly asked.

"Well, we are," Rebecca said, not relenting.

"Okay," Polly said. She pursed her lips and stood up to go back into the kitchen. "We'll talk about this later."

As she turned the corner, she heard Rebecca say under her breath. "We're always talking about these things later. That means I'm in trouble."

She bit her tongue. Whatever was up with Rebecca was not going to splatter all over her right now, especially with the day she'd already had. Some of this had shown itself the last few months as Rebecca was feeling her way through adolescence. But Polly refused to lower herself to base emotions in front of the kids. If Rebecca wanted a fight, they'd do it in the privacy of her room.

Andrew was at the dining room table with a book, eating a cookie.

"Why are you in here reading and not out there?" Polly asked.

He rolled his eyes. "She's in a bad mood. This is easier."

Polly wanted to laugh out loud, but she nodded and made it into the kitchen, turning her back on him before letting her face split into a grin. "Do you have much homework for tomorrow?"

"Some. We're supposed to come up with strengths and weaknesses of the North and South during the Civil War." He looked up from his book. "Got anything for me?"

She thought for a moment. "Well, the North was fighting in Southern territory. They didn't know the land."

"Yeah. I got that one," he said. "Oh well. It won't take too long."

"Good," she replied. "Anything else?"

"There's that big paper due in two weeks."

Polly spun around. "Big paper?"

"Got'cha," he said with a laugh.

She tossed a dish towel at him, but it floated over the peninsula and landed limply on the floor.

"You aren't any better now than you were before," he said.

"Whatever." She pointed at the living room. "Do you want to take the dogs out before you start your homework or after?"

"I'll take 'em now. The girls don't have to go. It's easier without them. They'll just complain about me deciding for them when we're going outside."

"Girls," Polly called. "Andrew is taking the dogs out. You can go with him or start your homework. Your choice." She winked at him. "You just have to know how to say it."

When she didn't hear any response, Andrew looked up at her and shrugged.

"Girls?" she called again, walking toward the living room.

Kayla was looking at her, trying to decide what to do, but Rebecca hadn't moved.

"Either go out with Andrew and the dogs or get your backpacks and start on your homework in the dining room," Polly said. "You have two choices, make one now." When no movement occurred, she said. "I'm not kidding. Now."

"Fine," Rebecca snapped. "Homework."

"Let's go then. I have chocolate chip cookies on the table already," Polly said.

Kayla jumped up and Obiwan followed her into the dining room. When Rebecca didn't move, Polly walked over behind her on the sofa and bent over. "I don't know what's gotten into you, but get rid of it right now. You will paste a smile on your face, quit sulking and act like a decent person. Do you understand me?"

"You just don't understand," Rebecca said dramatically, throwing her arms up in the air. She got to her feet and then slid them across the floor as she slowly walked into the dining room.

"Maybe you can help me understand later," Polly said in low tones, walking beside her. "But for now, you're going to fake it until you make it. Do you understand what I mean? Lose the pout and find a smile to plaster on your face. Straighten out your attitude immediately."

~~~

While Polly was proud of the dinner she made, the entire evening fell apart when Henry called to tell her that he wasn't going to be home until after eight o'clock and he'd pick something up in Boone so she shouldn't wait. Then Heath called to tell her he'd be late and Rebecca went to her room and slammed the door.

Polly put the artichoke chicken dinner she'd made into a couple of containers, put everything back into the refrigerator, toasted a slice of Sylvie's bread and slathered peanut butter on it. She opened the refrigerator to see if there was anything interesting to drink and tried to convince herself that the day had been awful enough she could afford to drink an entire bottle of wine, but instead, filled a glass with water and ice, walked into the media room and turned on the television. She didn't care what she watched, it just had to be mindless.

"Polly?"

She turned to see Rebecca standing in the doorway. "Yes, honey?"

"Can we talk now?"

Polly sat up, turned off the television and patted the sofa. "Sure. Are you hungry?"

"Maybe later. Your dinner smelled good. I'm sorry we screwed it up."

"It's fine. Sit down."

Rebecca sat down at the other end of the sofa, then crossed her arms and turned to Polly. "I was mad at you for giving Brutus away."

"You knew we weren't keeping him."

"Yeah, but I thought I could talk you into it. Why didn't you tell me before it happened?"

Polly cocked her head and looked at Rebecca quizzically. "I'm sorry, what?"

"I had a right to know."

"Honey, I love you so much," Polly said. "But you already knew that he was only here until I could find another home for him. And I'm sorry, but I won't be consulting you on every decision I make."

"Even when they affect me?"

This wasn't the conversation Polly had planned to have with Rebecca. Especially not at this age. She remembered her father having it twice with her. Once when she was in eighth grade and had gotten too big for her britches and then again the summer after her senior year in high school.

"I'm sorry you felt as if you have been slighted in the decision-making process about Brutus, but there are going to be a lot of decisions that I make and that Henry and I make together over the next few years regarding what happens in your life. You will not always be consulted."

Rebecca harrumphed. "But that's not fair. Mom and I always made every decision together."

"Oh, I doubt it," Polly said with a smile. "That's not how parents work. See, it's our job to make tough decisions, not yours. You aren't always going to like the choices we make, but we do it because we feel that it's the right thing to do for everyone."

"Why was this the right decision?" Rebecca's tone had gotten snotty again and Polly put up her hand.

"Lose the tone, Rebecca. You have no right to talk to me that way. And let me assure you that with this attitude you're giving me, you are proving that I made the right decision. Now, I don't know why in the world you've started getting mouthy and snotty with me, but it has to stop and it has to stop now. This is completely unacceptable."

The girl wilted in her seat. "I'm sorry. I just don't understand why he's gone."

"Honey, I don't understand why it's that big of a deal. He wasn't here that long."

"Because." Rebecca turned toward the outside of the couch, away from Polly.

"Because why, honey? Why is this thing making you so angry?"

Rebecca flung herself back to face Polly. "Because he was Mr. Bridger's dog and I know that he saw that ghost too so he was just like me. Nobody believes that I saw her, even though I was able to draw a picture of her. You don't believe me, Henry doesn't believe me; Andrew and Kayla don't believe me. But Mr. Bridger believed. I just wanted someone here who didn't think I was crazy."

"I don't think you're crazy at all, sweetie," Polly said. She took a deep breath and patted the sofa beside her again. "Come here and let me tell you what happened to me today. And maybe I should tell you what happened when I found Brutus yesterday."

Polly spent the next few minutes telling Rebecca the truth of the photograph she'd taken from Jim Bridger's house as well as the mad dash through Muriel Springer's front yard. The girl never blinked and at one point, Polly reached over to lift her lower jaw closed.

"I want you to understand, though," Polly said after re-telling the story. "I'm not comfortable with the idea that there's a ghost in that house, though I can't give you any other explanation right now."

"But you saw her," Rebecca said, breathily. "You really saw her."

"I saw something," Polly agreed. "And yes, so did Brutus. He was upset about whatever was in the backyard of that house. I was nervous enough that I didn't investigate it and by the time I heard the screams, I knew it was time to just get out of there. I was already trespassing and between not wanting to get caught and being scared out of my head, all I could do was run away.

"But if my drawing and that picture are the same person, then it has to be her ghost," Rebecca said again. "I'm not crazy."

"No, you aren't crazy," Polly agreed. Then she turned to Rebecca, "But you're out of your mind if you think throwing out bad behavior because you didn't get your way will cut it with me. I don't understand why you weren't embarrassed to act that way in front of your friends. I was embarrassed for you."

Rebecca dropped her head. "Kayla always likes me no matter what I do and Andrew is in love with me, so he doesn't care."

"And it's appropriate to treat your friends and family like that?"

"You all have to love me, don't you?" Rebecca asked.

Polly smiled. "Yes, we have to love you, but I didn't like you very much. And throwing tantrums isn't a good way to keep friends. Did your mother let you get away with that?"

Rebecca gave her a small smile. "She made me do extra chores when I got lippy. She always said that we'd never have a dirty house because I was always going to be working off something I said."

"I like it," Polly said. "We'll put that into practice right now."

"What? That's not fair."

"And your attitude was?"

"Well..." Rebecca slumped down again. "Okay. What am I cleaning?"

"Your bathroom. I was in there the other day. You and Heath have made a complete mess out of things. Bring the dirty clothes and towels out and start them in the laundry, then I want you to wash down the sink and wipe the mirror clean. You know where the Windex is, right?"

"Yeah."

"I'll come in and scrub the toilet, but I'm going to show you how to do that, too. If being lippy and disrespectful to me is something you plan to do on a regular basis..."

"I won't. I really try," Rebecca said.

"I know you do." Polly reached over and drew her daughter close for a hug. "And I will always love you no matter what you do or say. But like my father always told me: I love you too much to let you get away with bad behavior. I want you to learn how to control your anger. I won't tolerate it and you shouldn't either."

"That's what Mom said, too." Rebecca pulled back. "She also said that I had to apologize. So I'm sorry for being a brat."

"Thank you. Now, you get a choice. You can either go in and start on the bathroom now and come out when Heath and Henry get home or we can get something for you to eat now and you can work on the bathroom later."

"Are you really coming in to do the toilet?"

"I am," Polly said.

"Then let's do it now so we can talk to the boys when they get home."

~~~

They'd gotten the bathroom much cleaner by the time Heath and Henry got home. Rebecca hadn't complained about the fact that much of the mess in the bathroom had been Heath's and Polly knew that one of these days, she was going to have to end up using the same punishment on him. It would only be fair. The two kids shared the bathroom pretty well; each had their own cabinets and sink. Polly had considered letting Heath have the bathroom off the media room and Henry's office, but liked the idea of having a relatively clean place for guests. It was working so far.

Heath was starving when he came in, so Polly pulled the artichoke chicken and rice back out of the refrigerator, heated it up and served everyone. Henry came home, sat down and ate with them, telling her that he'd had a long day and an extra meal was welcome. She wanted nothing more than to curl up with him on a couch and tell him about everything that had happened to her that day and then listen to him unwind his day on her, but Heath had homework and Rebecca was wound up after an emotional afternoon.

They left the kids to do their things and Polly took Henry into the bedroom.

"What's up?" he asked. "Don't tell me you're getting frisky while they're still awake."

She hugged him close. "I missed you so much today."

Henry held her tight and they stood in the middle of the room for several moments, relaxing in each other's arms.

"Come into the bathroom while I take a shower," he said. "You can tell me all about your day."

"Tell me about yours first," she replied. "Why in the world were you so late?"

Henry shook his head in disgust. "Wrong deliveries, mistakes on-site. It was one of those red-letter, awful days. It felt like everything I touched fell apart. Heath was great, though. When he showed up, I told him where he needed to go and who he needed to see and he took off and did it." He scowled. "Better than some of the other rummies I have on the crews."

She took his hand. "I'm glad he's working out for you."

"I know I shouldn't keep him out so late," Henry said. "And I had no idea the kid hadn't eaten. I'll make sure that never happens again. Any of the other guys would have demanded their time to eat. But the poor guy is so new that he didn't think he dared."

"He's nothing like that boy we met in August, is he," Polly said.

Henry kissed her forehead before stripping off his t-shirt. "I doubt that he'll always be this good, but he's glad to be safe and in a happy environment."

"Yeah," she said with a laugh. "Even with that, they tend to be normal kids, all belligerent and stuff."

He raised his eyebrows.

"A little altercation with Rebecca. It's fixed and their bathroom is clean due to her punishment. She's going to be a trip, that's for sure."

"Sit," he said. "Tell me what happened today and where's Brutus? Did you already find him a new home?"

"Well, there's a story there," she said. "I should probably start from the beginning."

CHAPTER TWENTY-FOUR

Standing on a stepstool, Polly held a black scenery flat while Len Specek anchored it into place. Everything was coming together. Lydia wanted to have the Haunted House portion finished Friday afternoon so Jeff could focus on decorating for the Masquerade Ball all day Saturday with them out of the way. There were still plenty of items stacked in the auditorium that needed to be put into place, but they'd not had all hands on deck yet. She had scheduled a bigger crew to come in this evening to work so tomorrow all they would have to do is put finishing touches on the scenes.

Len nodded at her and Polly let go, standing close just to make sure it would hold. He grinned and said, "I got it."

She felt sheepish. Of course he did. "Sorry."

"It's okay." He smiled at her and turned back to his task.

She'd wanted to help today since she hadn't spent much time working on the Haunted House this last week. Lydia tried to assure her that it wasn't necessary, but Polly couldn't help herself.

Stephanie walked through toward the kitchen, carrying a coffee mug. When she saw Polly, she stopped. "I didn't realize you were down here. Do you have a minute?"

"Of course," Polly said. "What's up?"

"Kayla said you're taking Rebecca to Ames this afternoon to look for costume ideas for Saturday night."

Polly hadn't even thought that far out. She was beginning to feel like a lousy parent. These holidays were going to make her crazy. Wasn't it enough that she got the kids off to school every day? "Yeah. If I remember. I was supposed to do it yesterday, but I completely forgot. Would you like me to take Kayla, too?"

"Well..." Stephanie edged her way toward the kitchen and Polly followed. "I talked to Sylvie this morning and she said that Andrew didn't know what he was going to do either."

"I can take all three," Polly said. "It's no big deal."

"The thing is, I don't have a costume for myself."

Polly chuckled. "I'm running out of space in the truck."

"That's the thing. I also talked to Jeff and he said I could leave early. Is this something you want to do with Rebecca or would you care if I took the three kids to Ames and we looked for costumes?"

"That would be wonderful," Polly said. "I'd love to let you do that. Could I send money so you can all go out for dinner when you're done? You're doing me a huge favor."

Stephanie poured out a cup of coffee and then looked at the ground. "I hate to let you. I can afford to take the kids to McDonald's or something."

Polly took Stephanie's arm. "I know you can. But if I don't have to do this today, I'd be grateful. Take them somewhere nice. Don't even tell them that I'm paying for dinner. Just let me, okay?"

Stephanie nodded her assent. "Okay. Thank you. We'll have a good time. We always do."

"Poor Andrew might be overwhelmed by the girls. Don't let him whine too much," Polly said.

"Do you think he really minds it?" Stephanie asked.

"Of course not. He just likes everyone to think so. But wow, Stephanie, thank you. And Rebecca will have so much fun with all of you."

It had been fun to watch Stephanie come alive in the last months. Much of the fear was gone from her eyes and she took pride in her job. Jeff and she had a great relationship and little by little, her sense of style had transformed into that of a young woman who cared about her appearance. Her clothes fit and she began wearing brighter colors, leaving behind the dull browns and grays that she'd hidden in when she first came on board. There had been several all-girl makeup sessions at Jessie's apartment with Kayla and Rebecca dragging Stephanie along. Polly had hoped that Jessie had a light touch and she did, showing the girls how to use makeup to enhance their beauty, not change it. With Stephanie, the changes had happened slowly over time, but she exuded much more confidence now. Polly watched Stephanie walk back to the office, her back straight and head held high. The things that girl had gone through before escaping with Kayla would always be part of who she was, but Stephanie was learning to accept that she was worth so much more than her father ever allowed her to believe. She still met with a therapist regularly, and maybe she would for a long time to come, but seeing her embrace life was pure joy for Polly. She wished she could give that gift to so many people.

"Hey Polly," Rachel said, coming in the back door of the kitchen.

"Hey girl, how are you doing?"

"Good. I catered a meeting over at the Lutheran Church."

"The ladies didn't serve it themselves?"

"No, this was a bunch of pastors." Rachel dropped two totes beside the sink. "I drove by the Springer House. There are a ton of cars over there now and it takes forever to get through the street. They're going to have to do traffic control or the people who live there are going to be mad."

Polly sighed. "It's got to be getting worse. Saturday's the big day, isn't it?"

"Yeah," Rachel said, nodding. "The neighbors should totally charge for food and drinks. They could make a killing."

"What a racket. I'll be glad when this is all over and the weird people leave Bellingwood," Polly said. "But I hope Aaron discovers who killed those two men soon. Unless the killer already left town."

"I drove by Mr. Bridger's house, too. His daughter or granddaughter must be there or something."

Polly's head snapped up. "His daughter?"

"Or granddaughter. That's what she said."

"Who?"

"I was talking to one of his neighbors - Mrs. Cooley. She was outside raking up leaves. She was my second grade teacher."

"And she told you that his granddaughter was there?"

Rachel put the last pan into the dish washer and turned it on. "Yeah. She's come into town to take care of his estate."

"Did Mrs. Cooley say where she was from?"

"Indiana maybe? Or Illinois? She wasn't sure which."

Polly walked through the kitchen to the back, lost in thought.

"Is something wrong?" Rachel asked.

"What?" Polly turned and smiled. "Oh. No. It's cool. Thanks for everything you do here." She went upstairs and waded through the animals to get to her dining room. They'd done a quick cleanup this morning after breakfast, so she dropped into a chair. Leia and Luke jumped up on the table, and one by one, she put them back on the floor.

"Not now, kids. I need to decide whether I tell Aaron what's going on and fess up to all that I've done or get myself in further trouble before calling him."

Leia rubbed against Polly's leg and then sat down to clean her back paw.

"Thanks for the advice," Polly said. "I'm glad I can count on you."

When she'd told Henry about her day yesterday, he'd not been surprised, though the screaming episode at the Springer House unnerved him. His first thought was that as soon as someone could get in there and clear out brush, overgrowth and any trash, the place would start looking more normal. Fixing windows and the sagging foundation would be another step toward bringing it back, too. Polly didn't dare ask why he was even considering these things. They had no need of another house - especially one with the history that Springer House had. When Henry was ready to tell her what was on his mind, he would. Until that point, she was hoping to ignore the whole thing.

Luke jumped up on the table, nudged Polly's arm and when she scooped him up, purred against her chest. Then she said, "You're right. That's what I'll do." Polly put him on the floor and headed for the back door. Obiwan followed, looking hopeful. She smiled and bent over to hug his neck. "I'm sure she'll love seeing you."

Han was out with Henry again today. Those two couldn't get enough of each other. For as much as Henry hadn't been a dog person, he certainly liked having a buddy in the truck. Polly teased her husband about the additional blankets he carried, making a nest for Han wherever they were. The young dog was still enough of a puppy that he didn't spend much time sleeping whenever they were at a work site. He followed Henry everywhere and was up and running at a moment's notice.

Polly let Obiwan run in the back yard before loading him into the truck. He spent a few minutes checking out the tree line at the edge of the creek behind Sycamore House. The leaves had been steadily falling and the dogs loved playing in them, digging down to the ground, hoping for some new, exotic scent. She looked over to her sycamore trees. They'd lost their leaves and the bark was giving way to their white winter trunks. It was quite beautiful now, but Polly had planned for long into the future, when those gorgeous trees would spread their branches across the driveway.

"Let's go, Obiwan," she called and the dog gave one last look to a pile of leaves and then dashed toward her. She opened the truck's door and after he jumped up and in, she followed him, then shut the door. Obiwan climbed into the back seat and settled down on his blanket. Polly looked over her shoulder and smiled. "You are such a good boy. I don't know how I got so lucky."

She backed out and headed down the street. They weren't going far and Obiwan stood up and wagged his tail when she pulled into the driveway. He had his front paws on the console between the two front seats before she unbuckled her seatbelt. "Look," she said. "I know they give you treats here, but you're almost embarrassing."

He licked her cheek and she giggled. "I love you, too."

They got out of the truck and before she knocked on the back door, she opened the door to the shop. Bill Sturtz looked up and waved, then bent forward to turn off his dust collector. "Hi there, stranger. You've been too busy for your favorite in-laws?"

Polly dropped her head in shame. "I'm a bad daughter-in-law. Bad Polly, bad Polly."

Bill strode over and gathered her in his arms. "Marie and I were talking about you last night. We need to have you come for dinner." He poked her shoulder. "But the thing is, you never have to wait for an invitation. You're always welcome."

"I know," Polly said. "But my crazy family keeps growing and I'd hate to surprise even Marie with all of us."

"Aww, she loves it. Your young Heath is a good boy."

Obiwan had sat down at Bill's feet and looked up at him expectantly. Bill reached over and scratched the dog's ears and Obiwan's tail brushed across the sawdust on the floor.

"You have him well-trained," Polly said. "Do you mind if he hangs here for a while so I can talk to your wife?"

Bill walked over to his desk and opened the top drawer. Obiwan followed, his tongue hanging out. "This is why he likes coming to see me. If I thought it was my great personality, I'd get a big head."

Polly smiled and waved as she left and went over to the house. She rapped at the back door and opened it, calling out. "Hello? It's me, Polly!"

The sound of little feet on hard wood made Polly smile. Jessie's daughter, Molly ran into the kitchen, tumbling onto the floor in her hurry to get to Polly. She stood back up, ran a few more steps and then put her arms out.

"Up," she said, reaching for Polly.

This was the age Polly started having fun with children. Two more years and it would be even better, but at least now she could make sense of things with the girl.

"Hello, Molly," she said. "How are you today?"

"Tiss." Molly turned her cheek for a kiss and Polly obeyed.

"Is your mama here?" Polly hadn't seen Jessie in the office of the shop, so assumed she must be at the house.

Molly screwed her face up into a scowl. "No."

"What's wrong?" Polly asked. "Where did she go?"

"She's running errands," Marie said, coming into the kitchen. "Somebody is supposed to be taking a nap right now and she's decided to be strong-willed."

"No," Molly said decisively.

Polly winked at Marie. "If you take a good nap, I'll leave a present for you with Marie."

Molly reached out for Marie. "Nap!"

"You're terrible, Polly," Marie said. "Bribery isn't the best way to get a child to do what you want."

"But I interrupted her schedule. And I do have a silly little gift for her."

"Come on in. Pour yourself some coffee if you like. I'll be right back after I put her down." Marie left the room, smiling down at Molly, but shaking her head at the same time.

"Whoops," Polly said to herself. "I'll learn that lesson for next time." She poured a cup of coffee and went on into the living room. The place was a disaster. Molly had been all over the place and every single toy that resided at this house was scattered on the floor, the sofa, and even in each chair. She put her coffee down on an end table and grabbed a bright green basket. Starting at one end of the room, she picked toys up and dropped them in. When it was full, she collected more toys into a second, yellow basket and by the time Marie came back, the room looked more like a living room and less like a child care center.

"Thanks," Marie said, handing Polly a doll before dropping into her chair. "That little girl had a huge burst of energy this morning. I don't know where it came from, but I'm very glad for her nap time."

"Won't it be worse when she gets rested up?" Polly asked with a laugh.

"Probably, but at least I'll have my second wind by then." Marie started to stand.

"Stay put," Polly said. "What do you need?"

"I was going to get a cup of coffee."

"I'll get it."

"There are cookies in a tub in the fridge. Bring those out, too," Marie said.

When Polly finally settled in on the sofa, Marie smiled at her. "What's on your mind, dear?"

Polly looked down. "You've heard all about this stuff with the Springer House and the ghost and Jim Bridger?"

"I have," Marie said. She reached out and patted Polly's arm. "I wish you didn't have to experience death like that, but I'm glad you handle it so well."

"Some weird things are happening and I don't know who to talk to about this. I should probably go to Aaron, but he's going to kill me when he finds out what I've done."

Marie took a long, slow drink of her coffee and shut her eyes. "Ohhh, that's good." She looked back up at Polly. "Sorry. I needed that. Tell me what awful things you've done."

Polly told her about going into Jim Bridger's house and then about venturing onto the Springer House lot. When she finally told Marie what Rachel had said about Jim Bridger's granddaughter, the woman's brow creased. "I didn't know he had kids. I didn't know that he was married."

"So nothing about me breaking and entering or trespassing?"

Marie chuckled. "Nope. Whoever screamed and scared you to death at the Springer House did more damage to your heart than any kind of shame."

"It was awful," Polly said. "I don't even believe in ghosts and that was horrifying."

"That's the thing with the supernatural," Marie said. "We say we don't believe in it, but there is a tiny part of us that hopes it might be true. Science will never truly eliminate our search for magic and though we know that everyone dies, we hold out hope that there is something more than nothing at the end of this life."

"I believe in heaven," Polly said. "Just not ghosts."

Marie smiled and took another drink from her coffee cup.

"Do you?"

"Do I what?" Marie asked.

"Believe in ghosts?"

Marie took a breath, shut her eyes again in thought and then opened them and said, "I've learned to never say never. Do I believe that Springer House is haunted?" She shook her head. "No. I've lived in Bellingwood a long time and every once in a while, this story gets stirred up and rumors fly. But the truth is, no one has ever seen a ghost there."

"Rebecca said she did and Jim Bridger insisted that Muriel Springer was still there."

"Jim Bridger had a vested interest in that story," Marie said. "He's been re-telling it throughout his lifetime, exaggerating and enhancing it with every telling."

"What do you mean, vested interest?"

"He started bragging about it last year. Television shows and book authors were finally paying attention to him after all these years. He'd spent a lifetime creating the story and now he was about to sell it."

"I didn't know that," Polly said. "I just thought he was the guardian of the story, not wanting to let Muriel's tale get lost in history."

"No," Marie said. "It's no coincidence that he found someone just before the house went on the market. He was getting desperate. Because once someone bought that property and either renovated the house or tore it down, his opportunity for profit would be gone."

"But why him?" Polly asked. "What made him the curator of Springer House's ghost?"

"I'm sure he knew Muriel when he was young. He's lived in that same house his entire life, so he would have been around when she lived down the street."

"There's so much to unravel here," Polly said.

Marie leaned back. "Once you find all the threads, you will discover that the entire tapestry makes sense. It's as paranormal and spooky as the Haunted House your friends are building at Sycamore House. Once you see it all in the light of hindsight, you'll feel ridiculous for trying to create a story where there is none."

"Henry didn't try to talk me out of this last night."

"Believing in the paranormal?" Marie asked.

"Yeah. He couldn't come up with a good reason why the photograph matched Rebecca's drawing or why I was scared by haunting screams."

"Give it time," Marie said. "It will all come out into the light and be revealed. Trust me."

Polly let out a breath she hadn't realized she'd been holding. All she needed was for someone to tell her that she hadn't lost her grip on reality.

CHAPTER TWENTY-FIVE

Even though she enjoyed the quiet house, by the time Henry got home from work Friday night, Polly was ready to do something. Rebecca and Kayla were spending the night with Jessie and Molly. They had great plans to finish up their costumes for the Masquerade Ball, stay up late watching movies and eat all the junk food they could stomach without getting sick. Beryl had canceled Rebecca's lesson for Saturday morning, saying that she was busy with other things for the holiday.

Hayden arrived about four o'clock, unloaded his things into Heath's room and when his brother got home, they headed out for the evening. There'd been talk of going to the football game, but Polly didn't care what they did, only that they had a good time. Heath couldn't wait to take his brother over to see Grey and the hockey rink, so she thought they might end up there before the evening was out.

She wasn't sure how she'd managed to get so many great men in her life - all with disparate leadership talents. For that matter, she'd also surrounded herself with incredible women, each bringing something different to her life. This was the perfect place to mentor young people. Jessie was finding confidence in herself because of the unwavering love and trust that Marie Sturtz offered the girl and her daughter. Stephanie was growing into a beautiful young woman due to Jeff's care. Sylvie's oldest desperately needed a strong man to guide him because of his own desire to be a protector and Eliseo stepped into that role with ease. Now, here was Grey - opening up new worlds to Heath and to Denis Sutworth. All Polly had to do was stand back after she'd helped people find each other. None of them needed her any longer, other than to be a friend. She could do that.

Henry came out of the shower. "That feels better," he said. "What do you want to do for dinner tonight?"

"I want a burger and fried appetizers and something crazy to drink," Polly replied. "Can we go up to the Alehouse?"

"That sounds great. Do you want to call someone to meet us there?"

She stood up from the sofa and hugged him. "You're good to me. Let's just go by ourselves, though."

"With the kids gone, we could stay here and not eat." He reached down and patted her bottom.

Polly grabbed his hand and spun out of the hug. "You know they'd just walk in on us."

"We should go away for a night. Down to that fancy hotel in Perry. Heath and Rebecca can take care of themselves and the animals."

"You're right," Polly said. She reached up and kissed his cheek. "You find a date and I'll make the reservation."

He stepped back and looked at her. "I am? You will?"

"Sure," she said with a shrug. "One night would be perfect. Maybe even a weekend. Just tell me when."

When they got to the Alehouse, Henry opened the front door for her and they were assaulted with noise. The place was packed. A hostess came up to them and said, "Two?" She picked out two menus from under the counter and waited expectantly.

Polly looked at Henry and he nodded. "Sure," she said. "What's going on here?"

"It's all the crazies from that ghost story," the girl said. "That's all we've heard about this week. They're going over for a viewing or something at nine o'clock. Everyone is sure the ghost will be there."

Henry put his hand on Polly's back as they wove their way through the crowd. "I'll be glad when this week is over."

"Me too," the girl said, putting their menus down on the table. "Can I bring you something to drink?"

"I'll have a Guinness," Henry said and looked at Polly.

She looked back at him in panic.

"Bring a Bloody Mary for Polly and would you have them start an appetizer platter for us?"

The girl smiled. "You're smart. I'll get that in and Angela will be your waitress tonight."

"Are you sure you're okay with the noise here?" Polly asked.

"It's fine. You okay with what I ordered?"

She chuckled. "Maybe I'll get to actually drink it tonight. It looked good the last time we were here. I wish I hadn't needed to send it back."

It had been two months since they'd come across Alistair Greyson drunk in the Alehouse. Polly hadn't heard any more from him about it and hoped that he'd found a good place to deal with whatever he needed to deal with. She needed him.

Another girl came up to the table, gave them a weary smile and put pen to a notepad. "Hi, I'm Angela," she said. "I'll be your server tonight. What can I get for you?"

Polly picked up her menu and looked at it guiltily. "I'm sorry. I haven't even looked yet."

"Your hostess took our drink and appetizer order," Henry said.

Angela glanced back in the direction of the hostess table and her shoulders sagged. "That's great. I'll give you a few more minutes?"

He nodded and she walked away, stopping at tables to pick up empty pitchers and dirty dishes.

"I have no idea what I want," Polly said, flipping through the menu.

"You said a burger." Henry reached over and pointed at the page. "Eat a burger. It does a body good."

"But there are other things on here like tenderloins and pasta. The Iowa pork chop looks good too." She grinned at him. "They have walleye." Henry wasn't terribly fond of fresh fish.

"Yes they do," he said patiently. "Is that what you want?"

"Nah. I want a burger. A whiskey burger. I can't drink the stuff, but I like how it tastes in a burger."

Henry sat back. "When have you tried whiskey?"

"Oh. Uh." Polly stammered and then bit her lip. "Never. Nope. Not ever."

"Is there a story here?" he asked.

"Nope."

"Polly," he said quietly.

She was saved from having to respond by Angela returning with their drinks. "The appetizers are about up. Do you want to order now and or when I bring them?"

"I'll have the whiskey burger with a salad," Polly said. She grinned at her husband.

"Black and bleu burger with cottage cheese." Henry handed Angela their menus and pushed Polly's drink closer to her. "Taste it and tell me what you think."

She picked up the glass, put it to her lips and then put it back down on the table. "Look over there," she said quietly.

"No," he moaned. "Not tonight. Who am I looking at?"

"In the corner by the bar. That blonde girl."

Henry started to turn and Polly stopped him. "No. Not so fast. I don't want her to think we're staring at her. Be casual."

He scowled at her. "Seriously? Either I'm looking or I'm not. Why am I looking at the blonde girl in the corner by the bar?"

"She's not a ghost."

"Yeah. They don't usually come into bars to eat and drink." He took a drink of his beer and put it back down on the table. "Okay. I give up. Who's not a ghost?"

"Muriel Springer."

Henry raised his eyebrows. "We all know she's dead, Polly.

What are you talking about?" He started to turn again and Polly grabbed his hands.

"No, don't," she said. "She's looking over here. Just act casual." Polly picked up her Bloody Mary and took a drink. "Wow. That's good."

"I thought you'd like it."

Angela stepped in with the appetizer platter and put it between them. "How's the drink?" she asked Polly.

"I like it," Polly said with a smile. "If I finish this one, can I have another?"

Angela giggled. "I suppose so. Just let me know. I'll bring your sandwiches when they're up." She walked away, laughing and shaking her head.

"You're messing with me," Henry said. "So far tonight, I know that Muriel Springer has come back from the dead and you have a whiskey story you haven't yet told me. Neither of those pieces of information is satisfying. Now which are you going to expand on so that I don't fall apart on you?"

Polly pursed her lips. "That girl looks exactly like the picture of Muriel Springer I took from Jim Bridger's house and like the drawing that Rebecca did of the ghost at Springer House." She dipped an onion ring in ranch dressing. "Your mom told me that it would make sense - that more than likely there wasn't a ghost. But who is she and why is she here?"

"So there'd be more mysteries for you to have to solve?" Henry smiled. "It's good for our marriage to have mysteries happening around us. We're interesting without having to be weird."

She chucked and snorted at him. "You are weird."

"Do you think she's the ghost?" Henry asked. "Because if that's true, then she's ..." he grinned across the table. "Got some 'splainin' to do."

Polly glanced at the girl again. "I don't know. I wish I had the whole story."

Angela brought their sandwiches to the table and as she walked away, Henry brushed his napkin to the floor. He bent over, picked it up and tried to look casually around the room.

The girl caught his glance and in a flash, threw money on the table and stood up.

"She made us," Polly said. "And now she's leaving."

Polly put her napkin beside her plate and stood up.

Henry was in shock. "What are you doing? You aren't planning to follow her. Our food just got here."

"I can't let her get out of here without knowing where she's going," Polly said. "I just found her. Come on."

"But ..." he looked down at his plate, took a deep breath, and drew out his wallet. "You owe me dinner, woman." He tucked several twenty dollar bills under his plate and stood. "It's never boring with you, is it?"

"Hurry. She's probably gone by now." Polly took his hand and pulled him through the crowd. She'd lost sight of the girl and pushed the front door open, checking out the sidewalk on either side of the Alehouse.

Henry walked to one end of the block and looked up and down the street while Polly went to the other.

"Henry," she whispered, stepping back from the corner. "This way. Come on!"

Polly was in the truck before he was and he ran to catch up. By the time he'd started the truck, she was tapping her foot on the floorboard. "Hurry, hurry, hurry."

"I feel like I'm a sixteen year old with you sometimes," he said, backing out of the space and driving around the corner. They caught sight of someone running down the street and turning a corner heading east.

"Now, don't go too fast," Polly warned. "We don't want to spook her."

Henry laughed out loud. "Hurry, hurry. Slow down. Don't spook her. You're not helpful."

"Just be casual," she said. "I want to see where she's going."

"Tell me you already have an idea," Henry replied. "Surely we're going to the Springer House."

Polly shook her head. "I don't think so. You're close, but not there yet."

He turned the corner and they saw the figure dart through a yard.

"Stay back a ways," Polly said. "It's a good thing Bellingwood isn't very big. At least she doesn't have far to run."

Henry slowed down and then Polly pointed. "There. See her? She's still going."

"Just tell me where we're going to end up," Henry commented. "She's headed for Springer House."

"No, she's headed for Jim Bridger's house. I think she's staying there."

He turned to look at her, stopping at a stop sign. "Jim Bridger's house? Why?"

"Because he's dead, you nut."

They waited for a car to cross in front of them and Henry drove forward again. "I know he's dead. Why is she at his house?"

"I don't have all the answers," Polly said. "Just trust me."

"Trusting you made me miss dinner tonight. My stomach is mad at you."

Polly leaned forward in her excitement, but took a second to swat his arm. "You'll live. I promise. Isn't this exciting?"

"Not if we end up like Jeremy Booten and Jim Bridger." Henry stopped at another stop sign. "This is why I don't like driving back here. Why did the city think we need all of these stop signs? It's not like we have a ton of traffic in the back streets of Bellingwood, Iowa."

"There," Polly said, pointing. She was nearly breathless in anticipation. "Did you see that?"

Henry looked back and forth. "See what?"

"She ducked into Jim Bridger's back yard. Go ahead, pull in."

"To his driveway?" Henry asked.

"Yes, to his driveway. Pull in."

"We're not going into the house. You've already broken in once. I won't be party to your life of crime." He rolled into the driveway and stopped.

Polly opened her door and before she could jump out, Henry grabbed her arm. "What are you doing?" he asked.

"I'm going to find her. She's not getting away from me."

He shut his eyes, took a deep breath, all while keeping a firm grip on her forearm. "I'm not letting you go back there by yourself. What if she has a gun?"

Polly relaxed in the seat. "I didn't think about that. But she has no reason to shoot at us."

"What if she's waiting around the corner for you to show up so she can bash your head in?" he asked.

"She's going to be long gone if we don't do something," Polly said. She waited until he relaxed, pulled her arm away and hopped out and onto the driveway. "I'm going to look. I'll be careful. If you're scared, call Aaron."

With that, she turned her phone's flashlight on and hesitantly walked around the side of the house. Just as she started to turn the corner, something touched her shoulder, and Polly jumped and squealed.

"Sorry," Henry said.

"Tell a girl you're there," Polly gasped. "I could have wet my pants."

He handed her a big mag-lite flashlight and turned a second one on. They swept them over the back yard and found nothing.

"That's just weird," Polly said, her eyes darting around the yard. "Where did she go?" She stepped into the yard, her phone's flashlight in one hand and the mag light in the other.

It wasn't a large yard. They walked along the back of the house to the fence.

"This is weird," Henry said. "There's no house on the other side of that fence and it doesn't go all the way around to enclose the back yard. It looks old." He rapped his hand on the wood. "But it's in great shape."

He ran his flashlight up and down the wooden fence as he followed it around the back yard until it stopped about two feet before the garage. He ducked behind the fence and came back.

"Nothing there, just field. That's strange."

Polly followed his path, pressing on the fence. "Henry, come here," she said. "I found something."

They both shone their flashlights on the area that she indicated. "It's newer wood," Henry said and pressed against it. He patted up and down the new pieces of wood, reaching his fingers over the top. "Got it." He stepped back and a hidden gate opened.

"Where are we?" Polly whispered.

"This must be the border of Springer House's property," he said.

"But that back yard was horrible. It was worse than the front yard. All grown over with big bushes and stuff. Even Brutus was scared of it."

Henry aimed his flashlight through the gate and said, "It *is* a little creepy. Look at that."

What had once been an arbored walkway was obviously still in use. Leafy vines covered the frame and had recently been cut back inside the walkway. An old brick path curved to the right.

"I don't know if I want to go in there," Polly said. "At least not at night."

They heard rustling on the path ahead of them and hurried to close the gate. When she heard the lock catch, she stepped away. "I'm going to have to call Aaron."

Henry peered at her. "What are you planning to tell him?"

"I need to tell him everything. About the girl who is staying here and calling herself his granddaughter and breaking into his house and the picture. Everything."

She turned to head back to the truck just as the gate flew open and the girl they'd seen in the restaurant came flying out. "Help!" she cried. "He's going to kill me." She ran into Henry's arms. "You have to help me. Get me out of here. Now!"

Polly didn't know whether to run away or stay and face whatever was coming, but something inside her told her to get moving, so she grabbed the girl's arm and pulled her toward the driveway and the safety of their truck. Henry ran behind them, turning every once in a while to make sure no one was coming.

The girl ran for the front door of Henry's truck and jumped in, leaving Polly to climb in the back seat. Henry got into the truck, turned it on, locked the doors and said. "Who are you?"

"Get out of here. He'll kill us all."

"Who's going to kill us?" Polly asked.

"I'll tell you later. Just get me out of here!"

Henry backed the truck out of the driveway and Polly watched to see if anyone followed. She wondered if everyone who lived on this corner was just a little insane. Henry drove slowly away from the house, glancing into his rear view mirror, while Polly turned in the seat to keep an eye on the house.

"You have to take me somewhere safe," the girl said.

"Go to Sycamore House," Polly said. "I'm calling Aaron."

"You can't tell anyone where I'm at," the girl said, spitting her words out through fast breaths.

"It's the sheriff. He's safe," Henry said.

"Not the sheriff. Please, not him." The girl dropped her head into hands and started to cry. "It's all just gone so bad. None of this was supposed to happen."

"Front door," Polly said to Henry. "We'll go into the conference room."

He nodded. When he pulled into the driveway, the girl looked up. "Everybody's talking about this place. You have a haunted house or something tomorrow night."

Polly jumped down and opened the front passenger door. "Let's go inside. It's safe. There's nothing happening here tonight and the building is all locked up. No one can get in."

"Are you sure?"

"Absolutely. Then you can tell us what's going on."

CHAPTER TWENTY-SIX

No cars passed Sycamore House when they walked inside and Polly was sure they were safe. As soon as they got into the conference room, Polly realized the girl was still shivering. "I have a sweater in my office. I'll be right back."

She left and went into her office and sat down to make a phone call.

"This is my patient voice," Aaron Merritt said. "Do I need to choose a different one?"

Polly chuckled. "No. No body. I promise. However, I have a young woman in my office that looks an awful lot like Muriel Springer."

"You what?" he asked - a bit more loudly than Polly would have liked, but she knew he'd been frustrated with this case. With so many people coming in and out of Bellingwood, it had been difficult to find any connections.

"We picked her up at Jim Bridger's house."

Aaron lowered his voice and said, "I'm back to my patient voice. Would you mind telling me what you were doing at Jim Bridger's house?"

"We followed her there?" Polly said tentatively. "We saw her at the Alehouse and when she bolted, I made Henry follow her." Her words got slower as she finished the sentence, realizing how crazy this had to sound.

"I have a lot of questions, but maybe the next one you should answer is how you knew that she looked like Muriel Springer."

"Well..."

"Tell me," he said.

"I might have gone into Jim Bridger's house the other day when I found his dog and I saw a bunch of pictures in his dining room." Before Aaron could respond, Polly said, "And Aaron, they looked like the sketch Rebecca drew of the ghost. I've been trying all week to find ways to tell you, but it sounded ridiculous. And then I poked around the Springer House and somebody screamed at me and scared me to death. Brutus was growling at the back yard, so it was like he knew the ghost was there."

"Slow down, Polly," Aaron said. "You broke into Jim Bridger's house and then you trespassed at Springer House?"

"It sounds terrible when you say it out loud."

"It didn't sound terrible before?"

"Maybe."

Henry stuck his head in her office door and Polly mouthed "Aaron" at him, pointing at her phone. She reached behind her and pulled the sweater off the back of her chair and held it out. He took it, grinned at her and left.

"Am I in big trouble?" she asked Aaron.

"You probably should be," he replied. "Now tell me about this person you have. Who is she?"

"I don't know. Okay, there's more you don't know."

He sighed. "Of course there is. Go ahead."

"So, Rachel told me that she stopped at Mrs. Cooley's house. Do you know where that is?"

"Across from Jim Bridger's. Everybody knows Mrs. Cooley," he replied.

"And Mrs. Cooley told Rachel that Jim Bridger's granddaughter was in town to handle his affairs."

"He doesn't have any children."

"I know that," Polly said. "So that made me suspicious. And tonight when I saw this girl at the Alehouse, I started thinking that maybe there was something going on, so we followed her. And when we got there, she disappeared into Mr. Bridger's back yard." Polly paused for effect.

"Okay?"

"Aaron, there's a secret door in the fence that leads to an old arbor on the Springer House lot."

"Really!"

"We opened it and then heard a noise and I got weirded out, so we left. Then all of a sudden, she came bursting through that secret gate and begged for help because she said he was going to kill her. She was scared, Aaron."

"Who was going to kill her?" he asked.

"I don't know. We just got back here and I came in to get my sweater for her and then I called you."

"You're in the office?"

"She's in the conference room."

Aaron took a deep breath. "I seem to do an awful lot of interrogations in your conference room. Maybe we should consider making Sycamore House a satellite office."

"You're funny," Polly said flatly.

"I know better than to tell you to wait for me, but I'll be there in a few minutes. Don't let her leave."

Polly grinned at the phone. "She's not going anywhere. If she's not lying to us, then she's terrified of someone."

"Do you have that photograph of Muriel Springer?" he asked.

She reached into a drawer and pulled it out. It was hard not to feel guilty about keeping it, but there it was, right in front of her. "Uhhh."

"It's okay. I'd just like to be able to have it when I talk to her. It will be easier than going to Jim Bridger's..." He stopped and chuckled. "I guess that's not true. Apparently anyone can come and go at his house and no one's the wiser."

"I have the photograph and Rebecca's drawing right here,"

Polly said. She was so relieved that this was finally all out in the open. Secrets weren't something she was comfortable with.

She heard a car door slam and his SUV start up. "I'll be there in five minutes," he said. "Please stay safe for that long."

"I'll do my best." Polly swiped the phone call closed and gathered up the photograph and sketch pad, then put them on Stephanie's desk before going back into the conference room.

Henry had turned the television on and they were watching Charlie Brown's "The Great Pumpkin." The girl had wrapped Polly's sweater around her and was huddled in the chair, her knees up to her chest.

"Would you like something warm to drink?" Polly asked. "I can make hot cocoa or coffee or tea."

The girl looked up. "Hot cocoa?"

Polly smiled. "It will only take a few minutes. But first, will you tell me your first name? I'd rather not keep thinking of you as 'the girl.'"

"Kitty."

"Thanks. I'm Polly and this is Henry."

"He already told me."

Polly glanced at her husband and he grinned at her. "I'll be right back," she said and walked out into the main office. She sorted through the small cups until she found hot cocoa, popped it in and turned the machine on. During the day, they generally drank whatever Rachel brewed in the kitchen, but this was convenient for Jeff's meetings. She soon had a nice hot mug of cocoa and returned to the conference room. Kitty hadn't moved; she was still huddled in on herself, but her eyes lit up when she smelled the chocolate.

"The sheriff is coming up to talk to you, Kitty," Polly said as she put the mug in front of the girl.

"What?" Kitty yelped.

"It's okay. You said someone was going to kill you. It's the best way to keep you safe."

Kitty looked around. "I can't stay here. I need to get out of town."

"I believe you need to answer quite a few questions," Polly said.

"I didn't do anything wrong. It was all harmless."

"Portraying a ghost?" Polly asked. "Telling people you were Jim Bridger's granddaughter?"

Kitty looked at Polly in shock. "You know about that?"

Henry let out a huff and a chuckle behind Polly.

"It had to be you. What I don't understand is why."

"Money," Henry muttered under his breath.

"Is that it?" Polly glanced back at him and then at Kitty. "Was this all about money?"

"Uh huh," Kitty said and unfolded her legs. She sat forward and took a tentative sip from the mug, then blew across the top and took another. "It was a lot of money."

"From who? Who paid you to come to Bellingwood?"

"That old man. Mr. Bridger."

Polly sat down at the table. "I hate to ask, but how much money are we talking here?"

"Five thousand a week and a cut of his take from magazine articles and books and stuff. It was easy money."

"Old Jim Bridger paid you to look like Muriel Springer and scare people."

"I already look like her," Kitty said in a whisper.

As Polly tried to absorb that piece of information and process on what it might mean, she heard the front door unlock. Aaron Merritt had long ago been given an electronic key to Sycamore House. If she couldn't trust the county sheriff, she might as well move back to Boston.

"That's Sheriff Merritt," Polly said. "He's a good man and you can trust him."

"Mr. Bridger said we'd get in trouble if anyone caught us," Kitty replied. She held the mug in front of her face as if using it as a mask.

"I don't know about that. The most important thing tonight is finding whoever is trying to kill you."

Kitty put the mug back down and as if by reflex, pulled her

knees up and wrapped her arms around her legs again. Whoever it was, did frighten the poor girl.

Aaron tapped on the door and strode in. He was a big man, over six feet tall, with a barrel chest. His face was kind, but Polly had seen him get angry and he was intimidating when that happened. This evening he was wearing his uniform, which probably accounted for the extra time it took him to get to Sycamore House.

Henry stood up and shook his hand, then, using the remote, turned the television off. Poor Linus. He was still waiting for that pumpkin to show up.

"Polly," Aaron said and put out his hand.

She shook it and said, "This is Kitty. She has quite a story. It seems that our Mr. Bridger paid her to come to Bellingwood and play the part of Muriel Springer's ghost."

"Before I hear that part of it," Aaron said. "I'd like to know who's trying to kill you."

Kitty set her jaw defiantly and looked past Aaron to the door.

Both Polly and Henry glanced at the doorway, thinking someone was there, but Aaron didn't flinch. "If you don't want to talk here," he said, "I'll gladly place you in protective custody, make you a material witness." He paused and crossed his hands behind his back. "Whatever it takes. I'll put you in my car right now and transport you to our offices in Boone. This was potentially a friendly conversation, but it's up to you."

"What if he finds me?" Kitty asked.

Aaron turned to Henry. "Did anyone follow you here?"

"I don't think so," Henry said.

Polly jumped in. "I watched the house as we left and no one came out of the yard, much less followed us in a vehicle."

"We have a team arriving at Springer House any minute now. They'll be combing through the house and the property. Who do you expect them to find, Miss …?" He left it up in the air, waiting for her to give her last name.

"Hoffen," she said, her voice barely perceptible.

Polly stepped forward. "What did you say?"

"Katherine Hoffen. There. That's my name. Does it surprise you?"

Aaron put the photograph and the drawing on the table in front of him. He looked down at them and up at her. "You're the spitting image of Muriel. How in the world?"

"I colored my hair and styled it different, but grandpa always says I look just like her."

"Your grandpa?" Polly asked.

Kitty nodded. "He's one of Muriel's younger brothers."

Polly heard the tense. "He *is*? Does that mean he's still alive?"

"Sure," she said with a shrug. "He's in assisted living, but he's still alive. So's my Uncle Nick. He was the baby of the family."

Aaron took his phone out and swiped it open, read whatever had come into him. "They've been through the house and are working through the back yard and the garage. Another team is at Jim Bridger's house. They haven't found anyone yet, but there are signs of someone having lived there. Is that you?"

"Yeah."

"So who's trying to kill you? Is it the same person that killed Jim Bridger and Jeremy Booten?"

Kitty looked down at the floor. "Mr. Bridger killed that photographer. He was going to expose the whole thing." She pursed her lips and looked at them. "And that's what's so bad. He was only here because it was part of the scam. But he was going to expose everything, and I mean everything. He had the goods on Mr. Bridger.

Polly and Henry had taken seats across from her by this point and Polly put her head in her hands. "So let me get this straight. Jim Bridger brought Jeremy Booten into town so he could write about the haunting, but when the kid found out the truth, he killed him?"

"That old guy was crazy nuts," Kitty said. "He thought everybody should believe his story and when they didn't, he was pissed off. He was always muttering about how the whole town laughed at him, but he'd show them. And this was the last year he could do anything about it because it was going to be up for sale next week. He was always going back and forth between the two houses. He thought that if he could prove there was a ghost, nobody would buy the house and he'd be safe."

"Be safe?" Aaron asked. He took his phone out of his pocket again. "Yes?"

He listened and chuckled. "Well, I'll be. That old dog. Right here in Bellingwood, huh? Okay. Thanks."

"They found it, didn't they?" Kitty asked.

Aaron nodded. "Sure did." He turned to Polly and Henry. "What you thought was a raggedy back yard was actually a very well-cultivated marijuana plot. He let weeds grow up at the edges to act as camouflage."

"He said he's been growing it and selling it for years," Kitty said. "He never had to work because of the money he made. Since nobody could live in that house and it had all of those fences, it was the perfect place. That's why he could pay me so much money. Apparently it's high grade stuff. He earned a horticulture degree in college and spent a long time breeding good seeds. He bragged that people all over the country bought his seeds to grow their own. That photographer figured it out. He had lots of pictures and when he took a picture of me one night without my getup on, Mr. Bridger was pissed off. The kid tried to blackmail him."

"And when you heard the kid was killed, that didn't scare you?"

"It probably should have, but we had a deal and I already knew what was going on. I wasn't trying to take more than Mr. Bridger gave me and besides, he kept saying that I was family."

Henry put his forehead in his hand and laughed. "The Springer House is a drug house. That's priceless."

"At least it's not meth," Aaron said. "That wouldn't have surprised me either. There are too many of those operations in the county. This is new. I can't wait to tell Ken this was growing in his little town."

"It's your little town, too," Polly reminded Aaron. She looked at Kitty. "How did Mr. Bridger find you?"

"I don't know. He's always known where my grandfather lived. They stayed in touch for a while. The old guy had a weird crush on Muriel. Nick was a couple of years younger than him and Grandpa was a year older or something. One day he sent me a message on Facebook asking if I'd like to play a Halloween prank on the town and dress up like Muriel and act like her ghost. He made up this whole story about how Bellingwood still believed in the ghost and that it would be cool to bring in reporters and photographers. All I had to do was wear a white dress and glide around up in that solarium."

"How did you glide?" Polly asked.

"Roller skates. And when I was done scaring people, I got down on my hands and knees and crawled out of the room."

"Was that you screaming?" Polly asked.

"I saw you with his dog and that stupid animal knew me. So yeah. I screamed. You went away, didn't you?"

Polly knit her brows together. "Then why did Brutus growl at the back yard if you were upstairs?"

"Because he was there. He's not a nice man. He hit the dog with his stick a couple of times. Brutus hated him."

"We've talked around and around this," Aaron said. "Who is this man that hits dogs and threatened to kill you?"

Kitty looked up. "You aren't even going to believe me," she said. "I hardly even believe it."

"Try us," Aaron said.

"Gregory Springer. He said that the house is his and he's going to claim it before it can be sold."

"Who's Gregory Springer?" Henry blurted out. He put his hands up. "No, I know that he's got to be John Springer's descendant, but how?"

Kitty shrugged. "He said his grandfather owned this house and just because he ran away from Bellingwood didn't mean that the family didn't have some rights. He's bitter about everything. I think his family is totally broke."

"This is so convoluted," Henry said to Polly. "Ghosts, drugs, long-lost heirs. What in the heck?"

"Mr. Bridger contacted them too," Kitty said. "He wanted to stop the sale of this house. Gregory didn't even know it existed until the old man found him."

"So why did he kill Mr. Bridger and why is he trying to kill you?" Polly asked.

"I don't know," she said. "Maybe the marijuana. He tried to talk Mr. Bridger into making him a partner because the house was going to be his and if Bridger wanted to keep growing his weed back there, he'd have to get permission. They had a bad fight that morning. Gregory wanted to talk to some guys he knew in Chicago, but Mr. Bridger said that he had a good thing going and didn't want to mess with it. I just left. I wasn't part of that and I already had my money. All I needed to do was show up and scare people. But then when Mr. Bridger didn't come back and I heard that he'd been killed, I knew Gregory did it."

"Mr. Bridger has been dead for several days," Aaron said. "Why did you continue the ruse? Why didn't you just leave?"

"Because Gregory said he'd come after me and my family if I did. He told me that I had to stay through Halloween just like my contract said or I'd be a real ghost. He's mean. Really, really scary."

"I need you to describe him," Aaron said. "Do you know what kind of car he's driving?"

"Oh," she said. "Here. I have a picture of him. I snapped it one day when he was outside. He didn't see me do it, but after he threatened me, I thought I should have something to tell people who he was." Kitty swiped her phone open and showed Aaron the picture. "Want me to send it to you?" she asked.

He chuckled. "That would be great. Good job, there. We'll take it around town and ask questions. Do you know where he's been staying?" He grimaced. "That's ridiculous. I suppose he's staying at the Springer House."

"I don't know. He wouldn't tell us," Kitty said. "And he had a silver rental car. I don't know what it is."

"We'll check," Aaron said. "You need a different place to stay tonight. I can't let you go back to Jim Bridger's house."

"I don't have any of my stuff."

"We have an extra room upstairs in the addition," Polly said. "And I have clothes that will fit her until you get her things out of the house."

"Are you sure?" Aaron asked.

Henry stood up. "You know better than to ask, Aaron. Of course she's sure."

"You stay inside tonight, Miss Hoffen," Aaron said, pointing his finger at Kitty. "Stay away from windows, don't go outside. Just watch television or something. No more haunting, no more living in Jim Bridger's strange world. Got it?"

"It almost seems a shame," she replied.

"What?"

"People were looking forward to seeing me tomorrow morning. You know, on the seventieth anniversary of her death? It was going to be a big deal."

"You're just going to have to disappoint them. Got it?"

"It would be nice to sleep in," she said with a grin.

Aaron picked the photograph up and looked at Kitty, then back at the photograph. "I wouldn't have believed it if I hadn't seen you with my own eyes. You're the spitting image."

CHAPTER TWENTY-SEVEN

The main kitchen was the only place Polly could imagine preparing this big of a breakfast. She and Henry got up early Saturday morning because she'd invited practically everyone in town.

Henry fried sausage while she put bacon in the oven to crisp. Bags and bags of hash browns, dozens of eggs, more bags of shredded cheese, pounds of butter, sausage and bacon. Once she'd melted butter in the bottom of the pans, she added the hash browns. As soon as Henry finished with the sausage, she stirred it into the egg mixture and poured it over the top. Everything went into the ovens and she grinned at her husband. "We're getting there," she said.

He wiped his hands on the white apron and nodded. "What's next?"

"More sausage?"

He slumped his shoulders and put his hands out, waiting for her to put packages of meat in them. "What's this for?"

"Gravy. It will be great over the egg casserole and I'll whip up biscuits, too.

"It's been a long time since we've done this," he said.

"I miss it," Polly replied. "It's a lot of work, but I like having our friends all together."

"Is Lydia coming and not bringing anything?" he asked.

Polly stopped what she was doing and glared at him, then laughed. "That's the funniest thing I've ever heard. She's bringing muffins and Andy's bringing fruit. Beryl said she'd bring orange juice and milk." Polly changed the timbre of her voice and danced around. "Both chocolate and white because life needs a whole lot of color."

"Her words?" Henry asked.

"She makes me laugh. Your mom is bringing coffee cake."

"It's to die for," Henry said. "I love that stuff. I could eat the entire cake but she never lets me."

"You never told me that. I'd make coffee cake for you."

He stepped away from the stove top and kissed her nose. "Let Mom make the coffee cake, you just keep doing what you do."

"You're right," she said, nodding. "I have plenty of other things to worry about."

"Do you think that Springer guy will be smart enough to leave town?" Henry asked, stirring the sausage. "The last time we had a murderer in town during the Masquerade Ball, things got a little out of hand. I don't want you stepping in front of a crazed psycho tonight, okay?"

"I promise nothing," Polly said. "All I can tell you is that I'll try to be good."

"That's all I can ask. What do you want me to do now? This is done."

"Maybe pull tables out?" Polly said. "I need to make the roux for gravy and when you come back in, I'll have you help me drop biscuits."

"You won't let me stir them up?" he asked, laughing. "I'm good at making bricks."

She waved him out of the kitchen. "That's why you're in construction. Go ahead. We're in great shape."

"Halloo," a voice called from the front door.

Henry turned back to a smiling Polly. "Lydia couldn't stand it. She's here to help."

"I'm not surprised."

~~~

By four o'clock, Sycamore House was filled with people. Many had been here for most of the day. Jeff's crew finished decorating the auditorium and Lydia's made sure that everything worked and everyone knew where they needed to be. The sun would be down by the time they opened the Haunted House at five thirty when Polly, Jason, his friends and Eliseo planned to hit the streets. She wore a heavy black sweater and lined black pants on under the Grim Reaper robe. It was chilly and that robe didn't offer much warmth.

Rebecca, Andrew and Kayla had been quite adamant that she not see them until the Masquerade Ball, so they left with Jessie and Stephanie.

Excitement was building in the air and infected everyone. Heath and Hayden Harvey had been part of Jeff's decorating crew and Polly loved watching the two brothers laugh together as they worked. They'd gone out to the inn once things were finished and promised to be back for the ball. Hayden had poked his younger brother when Heath told Polly he was bringing a date. She hoped it would finally be a chance to meet Libby, the girl he'd talked about.

Polly had gone through the Haunted House during one of its last run-throughs since she wouldn't be able to do so during the evening. The big addition this year had been a cocoon and spiders. The cocoon had been shaped to young Skylar from the coffee shop. He was having a blast. They'd spun it around him, making it relatively solid but with an opening in the back for him to enter. Then, where his face was, it was transparent, so guests could see him in zombie makeup, screaming for help - trying to claw his way out. Spiders covered the cocoon and hung from the ceiling of the lounge around his scene.

At breakfast that morning, Lydia had convinced Kitty Hoffen to wear her Muriel Springer costume and dart in and out of the Haunted House often enough to keep people talking. Kitty also planned to come to the Masquerade Ball in full costume, yet wearing a mask. Everyone agreed that she should just own what she'd participated in and have fun with it.

Polly hurried to the barn to help saddle the horses. Eliseo and Jason hitched Nat and Nan to the cart and Jason climbed into his costume after the horses were ready to go. Jean Gardner had been put to work by Eliseo, sewing costumes for Demi and Daisy - long, flowing black capes that billowed out from under the saddle. Eliseo and Jason had worked with them since last Halloween to make sure the waving fabric wouldn't upset them. With their black masks and the capes, the horses were eerie and foreboding.

A line of people had grown outside Sycamore House by the time five thirty arrived.

"I feel like we're at Best Buy on Black Friday," Polly whispered to Jason. "This is nuts."

"It's kind of exciting," he said. "I think it's cool."

"Of course you do." She turned back to Eliseo. "Are you ready back there?"

He lifted his hand in a wave and Polly led off with Jason beside her. "Let's start the parade," Polly said, reaching forward to pat Demi's neck. As frightening as this all had to look to others, she still couldn't believe that one of her best friends was a horse.

They rode slowly past Sycamore House, Polly pointing her staff at those who had waited to see them. They rattled chains in the cart and the clopping of the horse's hooves echoed in the silence of the night.

She led them downtown first. Those who were beginning their evenings stepped back up onto the sidewalks before realizing the people behind the masks were familiar. After that, they rode through several of the more active neighborhoods while children ran from the street. Kids peered out from behind trees and around their parent's legs, squealing and screaming in horror and excitement all at the same time.

Polly finally led them to Beech Street and past those who gathered to wait for Muriel Springer's arrival. She was absolutely furious with herself for not putting Kitty in the coffin and let her rise up and scare the stuffing out of everyone.

Because of the number of cars driving through the neighborhood, the police chief, Ken Wallers, had assigned two of his men to direct traffic. Bert Bradford waved Polly and her parade through, grinning as he did. The fire dancers were chanting and had gathered quite a crowd; people watched the event and continually shone flashlights up into the solarium windows, hoping for Muriel's return. Polly hated to tell them that she wasn't going to be there. Old Jim Bridger would have been happy to see that so many people believed his decades of telling stories.

The sight of the horses, the Grim Reaper and its minions stopped all activity while they passed through the crowd. Polly breathed a sigh of relief when they finally left the neighborhood. From there they progressed to Sycamore Inn. Just before they turned onto the street leading to Secret Woods Winery, Polly texted J. J. Roberts to let him know she was close. They were hosting a corporate party and asked if she'd consider passing by. If there was ever an opportunity to show off her horses, Polly took it.

They rode back to Sycamore House and took another pass through the parking lot before heading to the barn. They'd been out long enough that Polly was going to be late to the Masquerade Ball. Eliseo drove the team out back to unhitch the cart while Polly and Jason rode into the barn.

"What were you thinking about tonight?" Jason asked. "I've never known you to be so quiet. You didn't talk at all and that's weird."

"Stop it," Polly said. "Really? I didn't talk?"

"None of us did, but it's weird for you."

"I must have been deep into character. The Grim Reaper never says much. He just gathers souls. It's fun watching people respond to us and I had a good time driving past the Springer House."

"Did you see that there were even little kids there?" Jason asked. "They were scared of us, but I don't understand why parents would take them to a little town in the middle of Iowa to see a non-existent ghost. They're just little. They don't understand."

Polly shook her head and pulled the saddle off Demi. She and Jason carried both back to the tack room. "I don't know. These days people are always looking for something that proves there is more to life than what we are dealing with day to day."

"You mean, like God?" he asked.

She nodded. "Yeah. Like God."

"So it's easier to believe in ghosts than God?" Jason was stymied.

"Many believe in both. You just never know," Polly said.

Jason followed her back to the horses. "I'll stick with God."

Polly grinned. "That's a good idea."

"Here, give me your robe and mask," Jason said. "If you sneak up the back way, you can change for the dance. I'll take care of things down here."

"Really?"

He scowled at her.

"Okay, sorry," she said. "What was I thinking? Are you coming up later?"

"Mom would kill me if I didn't."

Polly gave him a quick hug and then ran out and up to the house. Cars were pulling in to the parking lot and as she darted to the back, she saw people getting out in gowns and costumes. She was late.

The apartment was empty except for her animals and Polly dashed into her bedroom. After riding for the last hour and a half, she knew a shower was in order, so turned on the water to warm up while she stripped down. Hurry, hurry. She couldn't seem to make the world slow down or her actions move any faster, so finally she took a deep breath while putting her makeup on. It would be fine. Her friends would take care of things until she got there.

She'd been smart enough to set everything out. Not on the bed because the cats would have found her dark blue velvet gown to be perfect for snuggling. Pulling the zipper up her back was an interesting feat of acrobatics, but she finally got it into place and pulled her shoes on. Polly walked over to the mirror to make sure everything was in place and tears filled her eyes when she picked up the mask she planned to wear.

Sitting under her mask was a sterling silver rose pin. Polly pinned it to the lapel of her jacket and slipped her mask over her head, tucking the band behind her ears and under her hair. One last glance in the mirror and she spun, the skirt lifting in the breeze. From the Grim Reaper to a mysterious lady, today brought wonderful costume changes. There were never enough opportunities to dress up and Polly enjoyed every single one.

"Okay," she said to the animals watching her from the bed. "I have to hurry. No more dawdling."

Polly ran out of the bedroom, gathered her composure and quietly opened the front door, smiling at the noise coming up the steps. She was ready for this party.

Black curtains hanging from the ceiling separated the foyer. The haunted house was over, but no one was doing any teardown until tomorrow and Monday. People were still coming in the front door, but most of the party was already happening in the auditorium.

Polly put her hand out to take Sandy Davis's as they walked in.

"Hi Polly, this is my husband, Benji," Sandy said. "Benji, this is Polly Giller."

He shook Polly's other hand. "I haven't been to a Sycamore House party yet," he said. "But I hear they're fun. Is Henry here?"

"He's already inside," Polly said. "It's nice to meet you." She turned to Sandy. "You're getting out a lot these days."

"Thank goodness." Sandy broke away when they crested the door and were greeted by Henry.

"There you are," Henry said. "I was getting worried."

Polly reached up to kiss him. "Thank you." She patted the rose. "That was sweet. Made me cry."

He chuckled. "Of course it did." Then he put his hand out to greet Benji. "Benji Davis, old man. You've been back in town for months and I have to find that out from my wife? What's wrong with you?"

The two men walked over to a table where several other men about their age stood up.

Sandy grimaced. "That doesn't bode well for me."

Polly grinned and took her arm. "Come on. We have our own friends. They'll find us when they need something." She stretched her neck to look around the room and found Mark Ogden and Sal at a table on the other side of the auditorium. "Over here."

"Hi lovely," Sal said. "You look stunning tonight."

In fact, Sal was the one who was stunning. The woman could wear scarlet red like nobody's business and tonight's dress was a skin tight affair with slits up both sides of the dress. The back draped open nearly to her bottom and she was showing plenty of cleavage. Her mask was filigree made of black and silver rhinestones, but like the Phantom of the Opera, only covered one eye.

Polly coughed. "Old ladies are gonna be chattering tomorrow in church," she said with a laugh.

Mark shook his head. "I can hardly wait to hear about this one from the fellas. They're always teasing me about my hot East Coast babe."

"That's me," Sal said. "Is your husband here, Sandy?"

Sandy nodded toward the entrance. "Over there somewhere with high school buddies."

"He and Henry left us in a lurch," Polly said. "Have you seen the kids?"

"Which kids?" Sal asked. "I think your young man is there." She pointed toward the front of the room. "And Rebecca was at their table, but I don't see her now."

"I'll be back," Polly said. "Are you okay here, Sandy?"

Mark pulled out a chair and motioned for Sandy to sit with them. "We were headed to get some food. Would you join us?"

Polly smiled and took off across the room toward Heath and

Hayden, laughing as she realized who they were. "You two are awesome," she said.

They'd found similar brown striped suits with crazy vests, wild ties and colorful shirts, then colored their hair orange. Hayden drew out a wand. "I'm Fred," he said.

Heath echoed. "And I'm George."

A young girl dressed in a grey cape with her brown hair pulled into pig tails smiled from behind Heath.

"And you're Moaning Myrtle," Polly said. "Introduce me?"

"This is Libby Miller," Heath said. "Libby, this is my ... uhhh ... guardian, Polly Giller."

Libby put her hand out and Polly took it.

"It's nice to meet you. No date for you, Hayden?" Polly was sure he blushed.

"Not tonight, ma'am. I'm too busy for that."

"I'm glad you're here this weekend. Have fun." She took Heath's sleeve. "Have you seen Rebecca? I think she's hiding from me."

He leaned in. "That's because she's proud of her costume and wants to surprise you. Do you want me to go get her?"

"Either that or tell me where to find her."

"They're awesome," Hayden said. "They went toward the kitchen when you came in."

Chitters and whispers behind Polly made her turn around and she chuckled as Kitty Hoffen danced into the auditorium. The noise soon gave way to hesitant laughter and the mood changed when people realized that she wasn't a ghost, but a very alive young woman. She found Lydia and dropped into a chair beside her, causing no small amount of consternation in the room. It didn't take long for Lydia's friends to approach the table to ask what was going on. They'd pulled it off.

"I'll be back," Polly said. "I have to see what they came up with." Heath nodded and pointed to the kitchen.

Polly was nearly there when the three kids came in the door and waited for her reaction. She stopped, allowed her mouth to drop open and then laughed out loud. "You're perfect," she said.

They'd chosen three characters from the movie "Young Frankenstein." Rebecca's hair had been fluffed up into Madeline Kahn's bouffant, white stripes and all. She was dressed in a white satin gown with a robe. Andrew wore a tuxedo and top hat, lines drawn on his neck and forehead where he'd been stitched together. Kayla's was the funniest costume of all. She wore a young man's suit with a black hat. They'd penciled in a mustache over her lips and fluffed her hair to look as out of control as Gene Wilder's.

"I don't know how you pulled this off, but it's amazing," Polly said. "Have you taken lots of pictures?"

Rebecca rushed over, holding her hair as she walked. "Marie did. She helped us. We found the clothes Thursday night, but she had to sew some things to make them fit. Jessie took us over there this afternoon and we worked on putting it together. Isn't it great?"

"It really is," Polly laughed, trying not to think of Madeline Kahn singing "Oh Sweet Mystery of Life." No, she had to get that scene out of her head. The kids were perfectly innocent in their choices of characters and all she could do was laugh. So she did.

"So you like it?" Kayla asked.

Polly reached over and touched her mustache. "This is creative. You guys are terrific. You have the best costumes here."

"We only paid five dollars for this tuxedo," Andrew interjected. He lifted the jacket and pointed at the safety pins pulling it together in the back. "The pants were too big and Mrs. Sturtz didn't have time to fix them, but this is fine for now. Mom says I might even grow into them someday."

"Let's hope not," Polly said. "By then she can buy you a real one."

He straightened up. "I like looking good in a tux."

"You do look good," she replied. "Are you sitting with Heath and Hayden tonight?"

"We were." Rebecca pointed. "Did you know they were friends with Doug and Billy?"

Polly turned. Of course they'd know each other. The older boys were all about the same age. She remembered Rachel saying something about a friend of hers dating Hayden at one point.

The lights dimmed, leaving the room mostly lit by the ropes of orange and yellow lights hanging from the ceiling. At the same time, the curtains on the stage pulled back and the band Jeff had hired for the evening began playing their first song.

"Go on over," she whispered to Rebecca and watched as they headed over to join the other part of her family.

"We should take the first dance, shouldn't we?" His hand on her back spun her into Henry's arms.

Polly brought her right hand up and put it on his shoulder. "You're quite the dashing young man tonight. A rose? Dancing? What's this all about?"

"Maybe I'm happy to be married to the most interesting person in Bellingwood."

"Hagatha Dromvinica?" she asked.

"She's pretty amazing." He pulled her close and then pushed her away. "What's that?"

Polly reached into an inside pocket of her small jacket. "My phone." She looked down at it. "It's the inn. I wonder what's going on. Have you seen Grey?"

Henry nodded toward the kitchen. "He was in the kitchen talking to Sylvie earlier."

She answered the phone. "Hello? Yes, Denis, what is it?"

"I'm sorry to bother you," Denis said, "but I think that Springer guy just drove in."

"How do you know that?" she asked, then whispered to Henry. "Go get Aaron, would you?"

He nodded and walked away.

"They left a description of his car for us. I didn't know he was staying here. He's not on the register. Should I have called the police? Mr. Greyson said I should call him if anything went wrong, but he didn't answer."

"You did just fine, Denis," Polly said. "Did the car pull into a parking space?"

"Just a minute," Denis replied. "It takes me time to get around."

Aaron stepped in next to her. "What's up?"

"I think your Springer fellow is at the inn. Denis is on the phone and recognized the car from the description you left there."

He took out his own phone and headed for the front door.

"Miss Giller?" Denis asked. "He's parked down the way a bit. I can't tell which room. What should I do?"

"Don't do anything. Sheriff Merritt is on his way. Go back to the desk and act like you know nothing. Are you nervous?"

"A little."

"If you get worried can you make it into Grey's apartment?"

"He left it unlocked so I can play with Brutus."

"Then go on in. We'll have people there in just a few minutes."

"Thank you, Miss Giller."

"It's Polly. It's always Polly," she said. "Go on back and stay safe. You've done a good thing."

She'd made her way into the kitchen. "Is Grey in here?" she asked Rachel.

"Mr. Greyson?" Rachel called out.

He stepped into the kitchen from the back storage room. "Yes? Oh, hello Polly. You look absolutely entrancing."

"Denis called," Polly said. "I think he found our murderer at Sycamore Inn."

"He called you?" Grey was perplexed and patted the pockets of his suit coat until he found his phone. "It's on silent. That poor boy. I'm so sorry that he bothered you."

"No, it's fine. But he's nervous," Polly said.

Grey nodded. "Of course he is." He stretched his hand out back toward the storage room and Sylvie came out.

Polly stared at the two of them.

"What?" Sylvie said. "We were just having a conversation."

"Of course you were," Polly readily agreed. "And I'm sorry that I interrupted."

"Stop it," Sylvie scolded. "It was only a conversation." She turned to Rachel. "Do you have enough help if I leave?"

Rachel nodded. "Yeah. Everyone's in the other room right now, but we'll be fine."

"Then I'll take Grey over to the inn to make sure that Denis is okay," Sylvie said. "My car's this way." She took Grey's hand and led him back the way they'd come.

"What in the...?" Polly said. She looked at Henry who shrugged, surprise on his face.

In turn, they both looked at Rachel.

"I've got nothing," Rachel said. "And she's never walked out on an event. This is a big deal."

"Are you sure you're okay?" Polly asked.

Two girls in white aprons came into the kitchen carrying empty dishes. Rachel nodded. "I have plenty of people here. We'll be fine. Sylvie had the whole thing put together anyway and you know how organized she is."

"Let me know if you need anything." Polly took Henry's arm and walked back into the auditorium. "What was that all about?" she asked.

"The universe fixing things without your intervention?" he asked with a grin.

Polly swatted his arm. "I was the one who told Grey that he needed to be here tonight."

Henry hugged her close. "You just won't let the universe work without your help, will you?"

"I didn't get Anita Baker up here for Doug. That was a miss."

He swept her back into his arms on the dance floor and kissed her lips. "Do you need to go over to the inn and help Aaron make the arrest?"

"Stop it," she said. "Now you're just being mean."

Her phone buzzed again and she pulled it out to look at the text.

"We got him," Aaron sent. *"He had the cameras, told us he hit you in the head and killed Mr. Bridger. Still insisting that Springer House belongs to him and he had a right to everything. Think the boy is a few bricks short. Enjoy your party."*

Polly showed the message to Henry and he smiled at her. "Criminals really are stupid, aren't they? Why didn't he leave town last night?"

"Who knows?" Polly tucked her phone away. "But at least there's no ghost. When Monday comes, somebody normal can buy that property and clean it up."

"About that," Henry said. "We need to talk."

HOME FOR THE HOLIDAYS

A Bellingwood Christmas Story

Bellingwood #12.5

CHAPTER ONE

Holding the blanket up so Obiwan could crawl underneath, Polly relaxed on the couch and gave a deep sigh of contentment. It had been a wonderful day ... one she'd never imagined would be hers. She brushed her cheek on the soft robe Marie Sturtz had given to her and sipped coffee out of the R2-D2 mug from Rebecca. All around the apartment, piles of gifts and empty boxes were scattered, the last remnants of a fun Christmas morning with her family. She was all alone now except for the animals. Christmas music was playing, a fire roared and crackled on the big screen in front of her, and the mess could wait until later.

Hayden was spending as much of Christmas break as possible with his brother. He had a basketball game on the thirtieth and practice every day, but came home in the evenings. The two boys hadn't spent this much time together since before Hayden had gone to college and were usually with Grey at the skating rink they'd built at Sycamore Inn. They were there now. Grey had invited the community to try the new rink. During the first weeks it had been open, it had been such a unique new opportunity that he'd had to schedule times for hockey practice, skating lessons and free skating. As the holiday season grew busier, people found more to do with their days and the schedule wasn't quite as tight. He anticipated a good crowd today though, since several young people had told him they were asking for skates for Christmas.

Denis Sutworth was working more and more at the inn, giving Grey time away from the desk. It was fun to watch things come together out there. Polly had been concerned when Evelyn told her their time at Sycamore House was finished. Denis's mother was such a nut and he didn't want to move home. With help from Evelyn and Grey, he'd found an inexpensive apartment in the basement of someone's home.

Henry should be back any minute. He'd taken Rebecca over to Jessie's apartment for the day. Polly was grateful for the girls' relationship. They were good for each other. Rebecca was so pragmatic. When Jessie worried that she didn't have a boyfriend or a father for Molly, Rebecca reminded her it wasn't worth the stress unless he was perfect. Jessie talked to Rebecca like a sister and gave the young girl another outlet for her worries about growing up.

He had also picked Kayla up on the way. Stephanie and Kayla had been looking forward to their first real Christmas in years. Even though Polly invited them to spend the night of Christmas Eve and get up early with her family, they'd chosen to do Christmas by themselves. They'd gotten a tree and one evening, Andrew and Rebecca went over to string popcorn and make ornaments. Kayla's face lit up when she described how beautiful the tree was and how pretty all of the Christmas lights were in their house. She'd even strung lights on the window in her bedroom. They deserved to have a fabulous Christmas.

Polly's coffee was growing cold and she knew she was going to have to get up and move. They were planning for a houseful this evening. Many of their friends were gone for Christmas which meant there was enough room in the apartment for those still in town. She did need to clean and start preparing for the influx.

Andy and Len Specek were in Barcelona, Spain, with Len's daughter, Ellen. Beryl had given them her travel miles as a

Christmas gift, and though Andy was traumatized at leaving her grandkids for the holidays, her sons assured her they would celebrate again when she returned.

Joss and Nate took the twins to Indiana and would be gone until long after the New Year. With two families who didn't get to see Cooper and Sophia often enough, it was going to take time to make them all happy. The new house was framed and enclosed and Henry's crew was working on the inside. Before they left, Joss took Polly over for a tour. It was great fun walking through the rooms, with only framing for walls. Polly had never gotten to see a home in this stage of building. She and Joss spent hours talking about where furniture would fit.

Sycamore House had been quiet. Jeff left for Ohio last Sunday and most meetings were canceled until after the first of the year. He'd be back tomorrow for a wedding.

Sweet Beans was closed for the next week. When Camille and Sal had approached Jeff about taking the week between Christmas and New Year's Day off, he agreed that it was a good idea. The college kids had all gone home for winter break and Camille deserved a vacation. This was the start of their tradition, giving everyone time to travel and see family. Sal and Mark were in Minnesota and Camille had gone home to Omaha.

The dogs jumped down from the sofa and ran to the back stairway before Polly heard the garage door. Leia had been asleep in Polly's lap and looked up as if to ask whether or not she should bother.

"It's just Henry," Polly said. "You'll see him in a few minutes." She reached forward and put the empty mug down on the coffee table. Leia took the movement as a signal to leave, so Polly wrapped the blanket a little more tightly around her and snuggled down deeper into the sofa.

Henry stopped in the doorway. "You look comfortable."

"I am. You should join me."

He pointed at her coffee cup. "Do you need more?"

"Nah. I'm good. Did you get everyone where they're supposed to be?"

"Kayla and Rebecca wanted me to see the Christmas tree. The kids did a nice job. I would like to find a way to get those girls out of that trailer," he said. "It's an old one and the insulation is awful."

"Luckily we haven't had a horribly cold winter."

"I had a thought."

Polly chuckled. "Of course you did. What are you thinking about now?"

"I want to buy the Springer House." He sat down at the other end of the sofa and slid his feet out of his shoes.

"We talked about this when it went on the market. You said there was no good reason for us to own that house." Polly patted her leg and Obiwan jumped back up on the sofa and dropped his head onto her lap.

"I know. But it's killing me that the house is just sitting there and falling further into disrepair. I could fix it."

She stroked Obiwan's head, waiting for Henry to continue.

"It's got good bones. The foundation is still in good shape."

"But..." she started.

"I know. I know. It was me that said it was a bad idea. But Polly, we could turn that into four really nice apartments."

She slowly turned to face him. "Apartments? Now you want to become a landlord?"

"Is that any different than renting rooms at the inn?"

"Yes!" she said. "At least those people go away. We can fix things on a regular basis, but in an apartment, we're responsible for all of the idiots that rent from us."

He scowled at her. "We wouldn't rent to idiots. It's just something to think about."

"It really is killing you not to clean that place up, isn't it?" Polly asked.

"Kinda." Henry shrugged. "I've tried to put it out of my mind. I think I can negotiate the price even lower since absolutely no one has expressed any interest in it."

"It's already stupid-low," she said. "We should have bought it just for the land."

"That's what I thought would happen," he replied. "But no one is interested. Maybe because it has history or maybe because the government impounded all of the marijuana or maybe because it looks out over the cemetery."

"You know I wanted it," Polly said. "But since you're the one who would do all of the work, I'd never do that to you. But if you think it's a good idea, I'm all in. Now, as for renting out apartments, you're going to have to talk me into that."

"But what if you could rent to Stephanie and Kayla?" he asked. "And ensure that they have a nice home and a safe place to call their own. And what about Camille? She has to be tired of living here at Sycamore House. And even Jessie and Molly. They could get out of that apartment building and into something that's a little more like a home."

"Where did this ooey-gooey stuff come from?" Polly asked.

He grinned at her. "It's your fault. You got me paying attention to people. I just think we can do something more."

"Call about the house on Monday. If you want to buy and work on it, I'm with you. We'd have a good sized crew of people that can tear into that yard next spring when the weather gets nice."

"That's a good idea. There's a lot of cleanup that has to happen. But you'll want to go through the house first and tell me what we should keep. It's filled with old furniture and the cupboards even still have dishes in them. The Springers didn't take anything and the house was locked up until Jim Bridger opened it for that girl before Halloween."

Polly leaned over and loudly whispered into Obiwan's head. "Your dad is a nut. I just knew he was going to rescue that house. It took longer than I expected, but I'm not surprised at all."

She brought her hand up when he lobbed a pillow at her, deflecting it away from her head and right into the coffee mug on the table, knocking it to the floor.

"Oh no," Henry said. "Did I break it?"

Polly reached over and picked it up. "It's fine. But you would have had some explaining to do to your daughter if you had."

CHAPTER TWO

A very excited Rebecca was on door duty for the evening, something she loved to do. She'd dressed up in her new Christmas dress. It was as close to Polly's blue velvet gown from the Masquerade Ball as Rebecca could get without copying it exactly. A full length dress and a midriff jacket with rhinestones in poinsettia leaf patterns. She'd worn it to the school's winter concert, the Christmas eve service, and she told Polly she wanted to wear it one more time to the Winter Ball in late January. Jessie had curled her hair and pulled it back, using a rhinestone studded barrette to hold it.

"She's beautiful," Sylvie whispered to Polly as Rebecca ran to answer the door.

"And growing up too fast. I signed on to raise a little girl, not a young woman," Polly whispered back with a smile.

Andrew's adoration of his best friend had risen to new heights. He stared at Rebecca everywhere she went. Fortunately, most of the time, she didn't stray too far so he didn't have to embarrass himself.

Stephanie and Kayla came in, both dressed in holiday finery.

Kayla hurried over to Polly and pressed a bag in her hand. "You aren't supposed to open this until later. Okay?"

Polly smiled. "I promise." She gave the girl a hug and said, "Merry Christmas."

"I made pumpkin bars," Stephanie said, putting a plate on the peninsula. She looked at Sylvie. "It's a little intimidating baking treats to serve you, but it's my mother's recipe and I've always loved them."

Sylvie picked one up and took a bite. "These are great," she said. "And don't ever feel intimidated by me. I follow recipes the same as everybody else. When someone bakes for me, I enjoy it even more than eating my own food."

"Are you sure they're okay?" Stephanie asked.

"Oh honey," Sylvie replied. "They're wonderful. You can make these for me any day."

Stephanie gave her a grateful smile and followed her sister back into the living room. Jessie and Molly were already in place, the baby crawling all over the big dogs and playing with everything she could get her hands on. The cats had retreated to Polly and Henry's bedroom as soon as people started arriving. They were smart enough to come and go as they needed.

"Are they really good?" Polly asked.

Sylvie handed her the bar. "Try it. They actually are. Perfect texture and the flavors are great. She didn't use cheap ingredients."

"I'm going to be so sick tonight," Polly said, after taking a bite. "I can't hardly stop myself from trying everything."

Another knock at the door and Grey, Heath, and Hayden came in. The two boys dashed into Heath's room, while Grey came on into the dining room after saying hello to everyone. He pulled Polly into a hug and said, "Merry Christmas" in her ear. He handed her a platter, then turned to Sylvie. "You look extraordinary tonight."

Sylvie had the grace to blush. "Thank you," she said. "You cleaned up nicely too."

He wore jeans and a white button-down shirt with a dark blue sport jacket. A bright red and green plaid handkerchief poked out of his breast pocket.

Polly knew the two dated a few times after the Masquerade Ball, but couldn't get any information out of Andrew or Jason. The boys insisted that they didn't know anything. Whether they were just being good sons or Sylvie was that good at hiding her personal life from them, Polly didn't know. And Sylvie wasn't talking about it.

Another short rap on the front door announced Marie and Bill Sturtz. Coming in behind them were Jean and Sam Gardner. Jean had asked Polly if they could bring Sam's brother, Simon. He owned the Antique Shoppe downtown. The few times Polly had been in there, she really liked the man and was surprised to discover that he and Sam were brothers. When she'd mentioned it to Henry, he laughed and said that people all over town were related to each other. She'd find all of the families eventually.

Before the door could close, Sandy and Benji Davis came in, followed immediately by Eliseo, Jason Donovan and Evelyn Morrow. Now Polly's family was starting to feel like normal. She'd practically invited everyone who was left in Bellingwood. She missed Lydia and Aaron, but all of their family was planning to be at their house for the weekend and Lydia had managed to coerce Beryl into helping her with dinner this evening.

Doug Randall was with his parents, while Billy and Rachel were trying to make their families happy by spending time in each home. When Billy had told Polly what they were doing, Doug laughed at him, telling him that he was going to have to put his foot down someday and make sure that the parents knew they were going to have their own Christmas and then make decisions about where they would go after that.

Billy just shook his head and said, "When you finally get a girlfriend, you'll understand that there are certain things you do and don't do. One of those things that you don't do is put your foot down about anything unless it's a big deal."

After Heath and Hayden came back into the main living room, Polly coughed loudly - twice - to get everyone's attention.

"I'm so glad you are here tonight," she said. "Merry Christmas!"

Smiles and echoes of "Merry Christmas" greeted her.

"I could do a big long speech about how you are all gifts to me, but after a while I bore even myself, so dinner is on the peninsula. Help yourself and thank you all for bringing something to add to the meal. You can sit wherever you want. The dining room table is available and you'll find little tables and sofa tables scattered around. Just grab one and set yourself up. After dinner, I thought we could play games."

A few moans from the kids started until they were glared at by their parents and guardians.

Polly continued. "I'm just glad you're here." She looked around, trying to catch each person's eyes. "You really are gifts to me. Kids, why don't you start through the line. It's the only way I know to get the rest of you moving."

When the room fell silent and no one moved, she crossed over to Rebecca. "You go first. Please. And take your friends."

They'd already discussed this, so Rebecca knew it was coming. She huffed and then took Kayla's hand and walked into the dining room. Polly put her hands out to Jessie, who gave Molly to her. "Go on, Jessie. I'll play with her until you get back." With that invitation, Jessie could do nothing but stand up and go toward the food. She gave a pleading look to Stephanie, who followed her.

Molly reached around Polly's back and grabbed her ponytail, pulling on it. Polly chuckled helplessly and tried to pry the little fingers out of her hair. She was having no luck when, much to her surprise, Simon Gardner stepped in behind her and Molly became entranced with the man. Polly turned slowly so that the little girl could keep her eye on him and laugh at the faces he was making.

He took a bright red ball out of his suit coat pocket, showed it to Molly and then, it was gone. The child's eyes grew big, wondering what he'd done with it.

"Where is it?" Polly asked her.

Molly looked at her and then pointed at him. "Gone. Where?"

Simon reached up and stroked Molly's hair behind her ear and produced the ball.

She squealed and rubbed her ear. "Again!" she said. "Polly."

He laughed and caught her attention, then in a flash, the ball was gone. Molly turned in Polly's arms and pointed to Polly's right ear. "There?"

Simon shook his head. "Not in Miss Giller's ear." He bent down and brushed Marie Sturtz's hair and produced the ball again.

"Again!" Molly shouted. "Mommy!"

"Mommy's getting supper," Polly said.

Molly pointed at Bill Sturtz. "Bill!"

Simon shuffled across the room to his brother, making sure that Molly's eyes followed him. He showed her the red ball and then in an instant it was gone again. Molly peered at Sam Gardner, waiting for Simon to do his magic trick. He ran his hand up Sam's left arm, lifting his fingers as if the ball was under Sam's shirt sleeve. When nothing happened, Molly's face fell.

"Ball?" she asked.

Simon tapped the top of his brother's head and Sam dropped his jaw, his eyes filled with laughter. Simon put his hand up to Sam's mouth and with a loud popping sound, the ball was in his hand again.

Molly clapped and squealed, then caught sight of her mother. "Mommy!" she said. "Ball!"

Jessie had seen the last few moments of the act and said. "That's magic."

Molly tried to shape the sounds of the word and Polly repeated it quietly. "Magic. Can you say that?"

"Mack," Molly said.

"That's pretty close," Polly said.

Jessie nodded. "She can get it. We've been working on that soft gee sound. Try it again, honey." Jessie drew out the syllables. "Ma-gic."

Molly looked around the room to find everybody watching her, then turned and flung herself into Polly's shoulder.

"Y'all need to go get some food. I don't think Molly was ready to be our evening's entertainment," Polly said.

When Simon started past her, Polly put her hand on his arm. "I had no idea you did magic. Thank you for helping to distract her. I'm glad you're here."

"It's just a little sleight of hand," he replied. He put his hand on Molly's back. "I've had a wonderful life, but sometimes I regret not having children and grandchildren to keep me young." He gestured around the room. "You have plenty of it all and this is a beautiful home you've created. Thank you for allowing me to tag along with my brother and his wife."

CHAPTER THREE

Polly felt like things were completely out of whack when Monday morning arrived. She couldn't run up to Sweet Beans for coffee, the kids were sleeping in, there wasn't much happening at Sycamore House this week and even Henry was running late. He planned to call the realtor for the Springer House this morning and didn't want to do it from his dad's shop or his truck.

After he took the dogs out, he'd shut the door to his office.

She stared at the coffee selections in her cupboard, trying to decide which would give her the energy she needed for the day. Rebecca was itching to spend some of the money she'd gotten for Christmas. Last night she'd told Polly that she had never had so much fun.

When those words came out of her mouth, her eyes grew big and she stammered all over herself. "I loved Christmas with my mom," Rebecca said. "We always had fun together, but now there are so many people who know me."

"It's fine." Polly put her arm around the girl while they sat together on the couch. "I believe you should enjoy every experience you have and each year should get better and better."

Rebecca fingered the necklace she was wearing. Kayla had found a heart that when put together read "Best Friends." "I've never had a best friend who bought me presents before. I'm going to wear this forever."

Polly had just hugged her. Sometimes she missed the innocence of being so young.

She'd waited until after everyone had gone home last night before opening the gift from Kayla and Stephanie. They'd given her a beautiful grey scarf which made Polly smile. Stephanie knew that Polly had lost one of her favorites sometime between last winter and this fall.

This morning, she felt like she was missing part of her brain. "Just make a decision, Polly. It's not that difficult." She took down a bag of regular breakfast blend, filled the pot and turned it on. She wasn't sure why she was so fuzzy. They'd gone to bed at a normal hour last night.

Hayden came into the kitchen. "I smelled coffee," he said. "Can I help you make breakfast?"

"It might be a sin that you are so alert in the mornings." Polly opened the refrigerator. "Have you always been a morning person?"

"Dad used to say that if you didn't get up early, you lost the best part of the day. When I lived in the dorm, they tried to cure me of it, but I escaped their clutches." He grinned and put his hand on the refrigerator door. "I'll cook. Can I make pancakes?"

Polly waved him toward the stove. "It's all yours. Tell me if you want me to do something. Otherwise, I'm going to sit here at the table and wait for my coffee."

Heath came in, rubbing his eyes. "It's vacation, bro. Tell me again why we're getting up so early?"

"We promised Grey we'd fix that broken closet door this morning."

"A closet door is broken at the inn?" Henry asked, coming out of his office.

Hayden looked up from mixing batter. "No big deal. Easy stuff."

"I'll be done in time to check the worksites this afternoon," Heath jumped in. "Sam said something about me needing to make a run to Ames for some hardware he'd ordered. It's supposed to be there today."

Henry grinned. "I'm not checking up on you. This week isn't as stressful as the last two have been. Everybody wanted us to get things as far as possible before the holidays. I have no idea why. It isn't like they're doing anything, but it's easier to just smile and agree since it happens every year. We'll be back at it next Monday."

"Why do you even have them working this week?" Polly asked.

He smiled. "Because some of the guys need the work. I wasn't going to lay them off for a week. If they had vacation, they could use it, otherwise we just take it a little easier and put in some hours. Jimmy and Sam are taking care of the apartments and Ben Bowen's keeping things moving at the Mikkels's place. It's cool."

Polly reached out and took his hand. "I should trust you."

"Yes you should," he said. "And my boy, Heath, here, takes all of the hours I'll give him."

"I want a car," Heath said, dead-pan.

Polly laughed. "Like any good, red-blooded, American boy." She'd gotten him new sweaters and jeans for school. He insisted that he didn't need anything else, so she and Henry had started a small savings account at the bank for him. When they'd given him the account information so he could log in and keep an eye on it, he'd done his best not to cry. She couldn't imagine the pain he faced, alone without parents to back him up and support him. He was starting to learn that he always had a home with them, but it would take a long time for him to know it deep in his bones.

He'd given Rebecca a beautiful cut glass sculpture of a dancing fairy. When she opened it, he told her that was how he saw her. It nearly killed Polly. He'd found an adorable figure of two cats wrapped around each other for Polly, and Henry received a miniature teal Thunderbird. The boy had been tentative about giving gifts. Polly was sure that the last couple of years at his aunt and uncle's home had been bereft of any holiday celebrations.

Rebecca's gift to Heath had been a pencil drawing she'd made of him and his brother. She and Polly had taken it to Ames and had it framed. Rebecca had done several sketches as gifts this year. For Polly, she'd sketched her on Demi's back and for Henry, she'd managed to capture him walking with Han. She'd given Stephanie a drawing of her and Kayla, and had used a portrait that Sylvie had taken with her two boys to draw that family.

Polly and Henry had hung theirs on the living room wall above the little table just before entering the dining room. Every time Polly walked past it, she smiled. She really had a family now.

~~~

Kayla and Andrew were spending the day at Sycamore House. That much was back to normal.

After breakfast, Polly went back to her bedroom for a shower and Henry followed her in.

"Do you want to meet the realtor up at the Springer House this morning?" he asked.

She slowly turned her head. "That fast?"

"They want to dump this thing. She's willing to negotiate."

Polly shuddered. "I'm still a little creeped out by it. The last time I walked onto that property bad things happened."

"I think they've cleared some of the rubble from the front yard and the back yard was cleaned out by the state."

"But the house and the..."

"Don't say ghost," he said with a laugh.

"You're holding my hand all the way through, then," Polly replied.

He gave her a push down the short hallway to the bathroom. "Go get cleaned up. And I'll always hold your hand."

Polly hurried through the shower, getting more excited by the minute. It still scared her to think of walking through the house that had been so terrifying, but at the same time, she loved the idea of fixing it up. No one had really seen the inside except old Mr. Bridger, Kitty Hoffen, the Springer kid, and then the realtor. If they bought that house, it was also going to give people in Bellingwood something else to gossip about.

By the time they got into Henry's truck, she was moving past her fright. "I hope this works out," she said. "It would be so pretty to paint it a beautiful gray with dark blue trim. Something really different than what's there. Make people forget all about it being haunted."

"Wait until we see what we've got to work with."

"But even if the house has to be torn down, the lot alone is worth it, right?" Polly wasn't ready to let this go now that he'd gotten her thinking about it.

"Yes it is," he agreed. "But it's going to be in pretty bad shape inside. Don't get your hopes up."

"I'll try not to," she said. "They really don't have anyone else looking at it?"

"Not yet. She was already trying to figure out what my price needed to be."

Polly furrowed her brow. "But it's only been a couple of months. You'd think they'd give it more time than that."

"It sounds like somebody wants to close out the estate for good and this is one of the last things hanging out there. Just be patient, okay?"

"I'll try."

Henry turned onto Beech Street and Polly shook her head at the memory of the last few times she'd been here. She hadn't come near the house since Halloween. The main gate was open onto the driveway and Henry pulled in behind a small red car. He was right. A lot of the brush and bramble had been removed, opening up the yard and the big front porch. Someone had mowed over the grass that had sprung up between cracks in the driveway and cleared a path to the side door. It was in much better shape even with that little bit of cleanup.

A woman in her mid-fifties got out of the car and came to greet them. "Is this your wife?" she asked Henry, smiling a big, fake smile.

"I'm Polly Giller and you are?"

"Mary Mueller. It's so nice to meet you. I understand that you've purchased other properties in Bellingwood and restored them. It's the only reason I agreed to meet you today. At least you understand what goes into bringing a beautiful building back from deplorable conditions."

"Polly is the one who sees the possibilities," Henry said. "I just do the work."

"I believe there are a great many possibilities in this home," Mary said. "Have you seen the entire outside yet? It's much bigger than you think."

Polly shivered. It was chilly and though she had a coat on, there was enough wind to make her want to get inside. "Let's start on the inside. It's cold out here."

"Right this way, then. We're going to enter through the side door. The front door is still boarded up. We didn't want to take any of the boards down and expose the house to the elements. You'll be surprised at how well things have been preserved."

CHAPTER FOUR

Polly felt a little trepidation as Mary Mueller pulled the side door open. She giggled at herself. It was just an old house.

Henry stepped in and turned around to look at her. Polly nodded. She wasn't sure if she was reassuring herself or him. He put out his hand and just as she prepared to cross the threshold, her phone rang. Both of them jumped and Henry chuckled and shook his head.

Polly stayed on the stoop and swiped the call from Stephanie open.

"What's up?" she asked.

"Ummm, what are you doing?" Stephanie asked in return.

"Well, you scared me to death," Polly replied. "I was just about to walk into the Springer House when the phone rang. Is everything okay?"

"I don't know," Stephanie whispered. "I'm in your office and there are some people here that want to talk to you. One of the guys, well both of the guys are really scary looking. They're with a girl who looks nice, though."

"Did they give you a name?" Polly walked back down the steps into the breezeway.

"He said his name was Don Dobler and the girl said she wants to surprise you. They say you know them."

Polly shut her eyes to think. The name was familiar, but she couldn't place it. "That's all they said? What does he look like? And where are you?"

"I'm in your office. I didn't know what to do with them. She's wearing sunglasses and a trench coat and Polly, I swear one of the men looks like that actor on NCIS."

"There are three," Polly said with a smile. "Which one?"

By this time, Henry had come back outside and was standing beside Polly, trying to coax her back into the house. She put up a hand to wave him off, then covered the phone. "It's Stephanie. There are people at Sycamore House looking for me. She says they're scary-looking, but they know me."

His eyebrows rose as he looked at her in disbelief. "In Bellingwood?"

"Do you know somebody named Don Dobler?"

Henry thought for a minute, then shook his head. "No. I don't think so. Do we need to head back? I can reschedule with Miss Mueller."

"Do you mind?"

"Head for the truck. I'll explain it to her. We can look at the house later." He chuckled. "This probably works out for the best anyway. Give her a little something to worry about."

"You're rotten." Polly put the phone back to her ear. "I'm sorry. Henry doesn't know them either. But he's rescheduling the walk-through." This time Polly whispered. "I have to tell you that I'm in no hurry to go inside this house. I'm totally fine with running away today. Tell them to wait in the conference room and we'll be right there."

"Okay, thanks. I'm sorry to bother you, but they aren't from around here."

"We'll be right back. Ask if they want coffee or something."

Polly stuck the phone in her pocket and looked up to see Henry and Mary Mueller leaving the house. She went ahead to the truck and climbed in the passenger side and put her seatbelt on. Things looked much better, but she wasn't ready to take it all in. At least not yet.

"Do you have any idea who this could be?" Henry asked as he backed out of the driveway.

"None." She turned to look at him. "You know, I don't really ever think about the fact that Stephanie might not be safe in the office there."

Henry put his hand on the console and when she rested hers on top, gently squeezed her fingers. "Stop that. She's perfectly safe. Don't create problems when there aren't any. That's just being paranoid. If you worry about everything, all it does is wreck your peace of mind. Jeff is usually there, Rachel and her crew are in the kitchen. Eliseo is down at the barn and this week, the kids are in and out all day long."

"You're right," Polly said. She squeezed his hand. "You always are. I just wish I knew who was scaring her so badly."

"In less than five minutes you will. It's going to be okay."

She chuckled. "You know I don't wait well."

Henry drove into the front driveway of Sycamore House and pulled in behind a brand new, black Ford Expedition with Illinois plates. He pointed at the vehicle. "Illinois. Anything?"

Polly shook her head and opened the truck door. "Nope. You'd better hurry, though, if you want to keep up with me." She was at the front door before he was out of the truck. She turned and looked at him with a smile. "Come on, big boy. Don't make me wait all day."

He caught up, took her hand and they went into the office together.

Stephanie pointed at the conference room. "I offered coffee. They said maybe later. Thank you for coming back."

Henry opened the door to the conference room and allowed Polly to enter first. She didn't recognize one of the men, the woman was seated with her back to the door, and the third person was familiar, but only at the fringe of her memory.

"I'm Polly Giller," she said. "How can I help you?"

The young woman slowly turned her chair around and stood up. "Polly?" she said hesitantly.

"Elise!" Polly rushed forward and pulled the girl into a hug. She stepped back and grinned at the tall, gorgeous black man standing behind Elise. "That's why your name was familiar. Hi, Don. It's good to see you again."

Polly reached around to shake his hand and then turned back to Henry. "You remember Elise Myers, don't you?"

He stepped forward. "How could I forget? You had a rather harrowing experience in Bellingwood."

Elise dropped her eyes. "It was a bad time. I still feel awful that I brought all of that trouble to you here."

"Is it Elise?" Polly asked. "Or Linda ... Marberry, right?"

At least two years had passed since Elise had been hunted down by murderers from Chicago. She'd been kidnapped right out of Polly's apartment and then once rescued, had gone into witness protection. That traumatic experience had been one of Polly's first in Bellingwood, coming right when she was beginning to meet people in the community. The day Elise and her Federal Marshall came through on their way to wherever she'd be hiding was the day of the barn-raising and hoedown. By now, most of the people in Bellingwood had learned to accept the fact that Polly wasn't their normal every day citizen.

"Elise is fine. I've left Linda Marberry behind."

Don Dobler put his hand on his cousin's back. "She's still little Linda to all of us. We're just glad to have her with us again."

Polly took Elise's hand and they sat down in two chairs close to each other. "You're back? Is it all over? Are you safe now?"

Elise nodded. "It's all over and they say that the threat to me is essentially nil. One of the people who threatened me was killed in prison."

"I'm so glad." Polly sat back in the chair and a little part of herself that she didn't even realize existed, relaxed. "What are you doing in Bellingwood?"

"I'm moving here."

"You're what?" Polly leaned forward and hugged Elise again. "You're what? How? Why? When?"

Don bent over. "You two are going to blether about for a while, aren't you?"

"Stop it." Elise swatted at him. "But yes. Do you want to get going?"

"No, that's not it," he replied. "But Ron and I could use some lunch and a whole pot of coffee."

Elise shuddered. "I can't do one more restaurant. Too many people."

"Why don't I take you two up to the diner for lunch," Henry said to Don. "We'll let the girls talk. Polly, what can we bring back for you?"

She pursed her lips in thought. "Elise and I will go upstairs and make lunch for the kids. You guys come find us when you're done." Polly stood up and hugged her husband, then whispered in his ear. "You're the greatest. Thank you."

"Come on," he said to the men. "Best diner food around. And if their coffee isn't strong enough, I'll take you over to our new coffee shop."

They started out the door. "Do you girls want anything from Sweet Beans?"

Polly looked at Elise, whose eyes had lit up. "What do you want? A friend of mine owns the coffee shop and we own the bakery that goes with it."

"I want a huge caramel macchiato," Elise said. "Iced."

Henry turned to leave and then stepped back in. "We forgot. They're closed this week. Will you be able to live without coffee?"

Polly dropped her head and laughed. "I'm going to die before they reopen. We'll make coffee upstairs. Thanks anyway." She reached out and grabbed Elise's hand. "It's so good to see you again. I worried you were gone from my life."

"Like a bad penny," Elise said. "Henry is still around?"

"We're married." Polly chuckled at Elise's big-eyed response. "And we have two kids. One in seventh grade and the other is a junior in high school."

Elise gave her a skeptical look. "I know I wasn't gone that long!"

Polly smiled. "We adopted our seventh-grader after her mother died last spring. And we're guardians for the high-schooler. We turned the upstairs into our home and then added rooms to the other side of the building for guests." She thought for a moment. "Oh, and we bought a hotel."

"Everything has changed so much," Elise said. "But you still look the same."

"I never change," Polly said. "I have three kids upstairs right now. Are you okay with meeting them? One is my daughter, Rebecca. I don't know if you remember Sylvie's son, Andrew, and then another friend of Rebecca's - Kayla. Her sister is our receptionist."

"She's a nice girl. That would be fine."

"I want to hear why you're moving to Bellingwood and what you've been doing for the last two years. Do you have a place to live yet? Were you home for Christmas?" Polly laughed. "I have a million questions."

Elise smiled. "I can't wait to tell you everything, but first of all, the reason I'm moving to Bellingwood is because of you."

"Me?"

"I didn't have anyone I really considered a friend until I met you," Elise said. "I have a lot of family, but I don't want to live with my parents. I've been on my own for too long now."

"Then I'm so glad you're here," Polly said. "Come on upstairs and while we figure out what to do for lunch, you can tell me everything. Do you have a place to stay yet?"

"Not yet. I figured I would just get a hotel room in Ames until I found an apartment."

"You're staying here. How long are Don and..."

"His brother Ron. They wouldn't let me come to Iowa by myself. We're staying in Ames. I can go back with them."

"No way," Polly said. "We have plenty of room for all of you. The only person staying in the addition right now is Camille. She runs the coffee shop."

"That would be great," Elise said. "I have to find an apartment and then I need to buy a car. I need everything."

Polly stood up and reached out to take Elise's hand. "You've come to the right place."

They walked out of the conference room.

"Hey Stephanie," Polly said. "This is an old friend of mine - Elise Myers. She's moving to Bellingwood. She and her cousins are going to stay in the last three rooms in the addition."

Stephanie smiled shyly. "I'll take care of it and email you with the details."

"Thanks. We're going upstairs for lunch."

"Nice to meet you," Elise said.

CHAPTER FIVE

"You tell me how she's going to do it," Polly said.

She and Henry were alone in the apartment. Eliseo had called the kids down to the barn for a late afternoon wagon ride. Andrew wanted to take the dogs, but Polly wouldn't let him. It would be enough for Eliseo to keep an eye on his own dogs, the horses, and all of the kids.

"How who's going to do what?" Henry asked. He hadn't been paying attention and was scrambling to catch up.

Polly put her feet up on the coffee table and leaned back into the sofa. "Elise. Teaching. She was absolutely exhausted after interacting with Stephanie, me, her cousins, and three kids. I think she's spent the last two years as a complete hermit. She didn't know anyone or make friends. She just stayed inside, took online classes and did..." Polly looked frustrated and put her hands up. "Math and physics stuff. She said she wrote a few papers and now that she's been hired at Iowa State, she can start submitting them for publication. That girl will have to have a dark office where she can hide between classes."

"The truth is," Henry said, "unless she has a lot of undergraduate courses, she'll be working with students as intense about the work as she is. They'll be more interested in numbers than each other."

"I suppose. What did you think of her cousins?"

He laughed. "I don't know what to think. They're good guys, but I have no idea what they do for a living. It sounds a little nefarious. Don talks about his crew and taking care of problems." He shook his head. "I quit asking questions. His brother doesn't talk very much. He's kind of just there, an ominous presence."

"He doesn't smile very much either," Polly said.

"And he eats like crazy. They asked about a gym." Henry flexed his arm. "Maybe there's something in Ames they can use. I told them they could come work construction with me and Ron finally laughed."

"What did you guys talk about?"

"Food," Henry said. "And Iowa and you. They asked questions about you and us and the people in Bellingwood. Elise must have told them stories. As we talked it hit me how much has changed since she was here. You and I had only had that one date and you were still giving me a lot of grief."

He flinched away before Polly could react. "I knew you'd come around, but you didn't know it yet."

She smiled and thought back to Elise's arrival in town. They were just putting up the barn. "The horses weren't even here yet," Polly said. "How can that be? It feels like they've always been with me. Leia had just been spayed and she spent a night or two with Elise so Obiwan and Luke wouldn't hurt her. She was so little then and now look at her." Polly reached up to the back of the sofa and ran her hand down the cat's back.

Leia stretched and purred, then snuggled closer to Polly. "The additions weren't built, Eliseo wasn't here, Sylvie was just beginning to think about going to school." She pulled the cat down and Leia tucked herself into Polly's arms.

"It's strange to think about all of these changes from someone else's perspective," Henry said. "For us, it all just happened."

"What did that realtor chick say about rescheduling?" Polly asked.

He smiled at her. "We have another appointment with her tomorrow morning."

Polly's shoulders drooped. "Oh. Okay."

"Don't you want to do this?" he asked.

"That's not it. The place creeps me out."

Henry gave her a quizzical look. "This school was in much worse shape when you bought it. The Inn was a complete mess. You didn't have any trouble with either of those purchases."

"I know that I'm not making any sense," Polly said. "When Kitty scared me off the property with her screams, I ran like a frightened child. I knew better, but I still ran. Rather than facing down whatever was there, I ran away. And I don't know if I'm ready to face that house yet."

"We don't have to do it at all." Henry scooted closer to her and put his arm around her shoulders. "I don't want to push you into something that scares you."

"I know," Polly said. "And I also know that I'm being ridiculous. The house is gorgeous and if I didn't buy it, I'd be angry if someone else fixed it. I already see what I want it to look like on the outside. I'm just playing mind games with myself." She felt his laughter against her body. "What?"

"I don't know what to say."

Polly turned to look at him, face to face. "What do you mean? What can't you say?"

"No, I really don't know what to say," he protested. "I could tell you to buck up and get over yourself, that once you've faced this fear it will be behind you."

She nodded.

"But I don't want to force you to do things that scare you. I'll walk away from this deal right now if that's what you want."

"But I *don't* want that. I want to buy the house. Especially since it's such a great deal. What I don't want to do is walk through it with some strange realtor lady watching me jump at every creaking door or hesitate before I turn a corner."

He burst out laughing. "That's easy. I'll meet her there, have her open the house and then tell her that we're going through it alone. We don't need her to walk through it with us. What's she going to say, anyway? 'Look at these beautiful rotten baseboards. All they need is a little paint and they'll be good as new.' Or maybe, 'The house comes with a full set of spider webs and mouse turds.'"

"If you like the smell of pine, we have fresh boards across all the windows and outside doors," Polly continued. Then she patted his hand. "Okay. I'll walk through it with you. At least you won't laugh at me when I get the creepy crawlies."

He rubbed her arm. "Yes I will. You know I will."

"Because you're a rat."

"And proud of it," he said. "So are we responsible for dinner tonight?"

Polly took a deep breath. "I suppose I need to think about food."

"We can't go out?"

"I don't think Elise could take it. You know this is going to kill me, right?"

He chuckled. "You want her to meet everyone, don't you?"

"She already knows Andy, Lydia, Beryl and Sylvie, but I think she'd really like my other friends, too. If she just wasn't so staggeringly shy."

"She wouldn't be happy, though."

"I know that," Polly said. "This is going to require patience. I hope I have enough."

"Or you can decide that you don't have to fix her."

Polly looked at him in mock horror. "You have to be kidding me. I fix everyone."

"Maybe she's not broken. Maybe she's just different."

"When she was here the last time, she told me that she didn't want to be so lonely all the time - that she wanted to have more people in her life."

"I love you, Polly, but this girl spent the last three years by herself. I think it's a big deal that she came to Bellingwood because you're here. One friend might be all she can take right now."

"I hate it when you're right." Polly lifted the corner of her upper lip. "I'll try to be good." She put the cat down on the floor and stood up. "This means I need to figure out what to cook for supper."

"We could order pizza," Henry said.

Polly scowled down at him. "They're from Chicago."

"Now *you're* right. Our convenience store pizza won't hold a candle to that."

She wandered toward the kitchen. "I don't have enough meat to serve all of us, especially if those boys eat a lot. I have to go to the grocery store." Polly started talking more to herself than Henry. "I wonder if they have flank steak. I could make beef burgundy and mashed potatoes. That would be good."

"What?"

"Just thinking out loud." Polly opened the cupboards and the refrigerator and then closed them. "Yeah. Gotta go buy food. I'll be back in a while."

Henry stood up, causing the dogs to scramble. "I'll walk the dogs before I head over to the shop."

"Are your parents really okay with not going to Arizona this year?" Polly asked.

He grinned at her. "Mom refused to leave Molly for six months and Dad is having too much fun working. He's having a blast at that new quilt shop. The ladies there just love him."

The only way Henry could take on the renovation of the storefront next to Sweet Beans was if his Dad and Len Sturtz did most of the interior work. The company had too many projects going on all at once and while it was great for business, the last several months had been stressful for everyone. This week was the only slow time Henry would see for several months. And they knew that spring would bring more projects.

Polly grabbed their coats from the coat rack and followed him to the back steps. The dogs wagged their bodies with excitement and Henry called them to go downstairs.

They stopped inside the garage and kissed each other goodbye, then Henry opened the door and went out with the dogs.

Instead of heading for the tree line like he always did, Obiwan cut across toward the drive that led around to the front of Sycamore House.

"Obiwan," Henry called. "Come back here."

The dog stopped and looked at him, whined and turned back to the drive.

"What's going on?" Polly asked.

"I don't know. Maybe a dead animal or something?" Henry crossed the cement pad and headed for the dog. Polly came out of the garage and trotted to catch up.

"What's going on, Obiwan?" she asked.

The dog whined again and Han ran after him.

Obiwan stopped in front of a cardboard box that had been taped closed.

"What in the hell?" Polly asked. "Who would have dropped this here? Stupid kids."

Her heart leapt when the box moved.

"What's in there?" She dropped to her knees and using her fingernails, tried to pull the tape off the sides of the box. It was cold enough that her fingers wouldn't work.

"Here," Henry said. "I've got it." He'd taken out a pocket knife. He slit the tape on the sides and then pulled the box open.

Polly gasped. "Not again." And with her next breath, reached in and pulled out two puppies. "Why do people do this? Just take them to the Humane Society. What if we hadn't come outside? What if no one saw them until they'd frozen to death? Oh, you poor babies. Who would do this to you? You don't have a blanket or food or anything in there. And taped up so you can't escape? I hate people. I hate them." She tucked them inside her coat and grimaced when she felt something warm and wet soak her shirt.

"Oh Henry, what am I going to do with them?"

He shook his head. "You're going to take them upstairs, clean them up, give them food and water, and make them comfortable. I'll go to the grocery store and pick up food for dinner and puppy food. Can they wait until tomorrow to see Doc Ogden?"

Polly's eyes filled with tears and she reached over to kiss him again. "Thank you." She kicked the box they'd been in. "Damned horrible people. Who would do this?"

Henry pointed up at the security camera. "We can find out if you really want to know."

"First we take care of the puppies. Then we decide."

"Go on in. I'll walk the dogs and you can think about what you want from the store."

CHAPTER SIX

Polly swung her legs over the side of the bed and looked down at the two puppies in the kennel on the floor. She'd woken up several times throughout the night to check on them. Once they'd eaten their fill and realized that water was readily available, they'd curled up next to each other and relaxed.

Last night's events had changed, and it had nothing to do with the new puppies. She'd called Elise's phone to invite her to dinner and the girl had begged off, asking if she could find something in the kitchen downstairs. Polly hated to tell her how different things were since the last time she was here and instead, told her there would be a container with Elise's name on it. Ron and Don were going to Ames to pick up their things at the hotel and wouldn't be back until later.

Heath and Hayden had stayed at the inn and eaten supper with Grey, and Rebecca called from the barn saying that she was invited to have dinner at Eliseo's house. He was taking all of the kids out in the wagon and would have them home by nine o'clock.

They ended up having pizza after all. Henry had picked it up on his way back from the shop. He'd taken the big dogs with him, allowing Polly plenty of time to give the puppies a warm bath and make them feel at home. She'd called Marnie Evans at the vet clinic to ask about borrowing a large kennel and Henry picked that up as well.

He was already in the shower. Polly scooted down to the floor and opened the kennel door and spoke quietly to wake them up before putting her hand in. The little boy came awake and sniffed at her, then allowed her to gather him into her arms. Obiwan jumped off the bed, sniffed around the kennel again just to make sure that nothing had changed since he'd gone to bed last night, then lay down beside it and put his head in Polly's lap.

On the other hand, Han bounced around like a giddy schoolgirl, begging to play with the puppies. Polly took the little girl out and held both of them.

"Where did you come from?" she asked. She stroked the wrinkles on their forehead. "I want to say that you are bloodhounds, but you certainly aren't purebred. Your nose is too short and your ears aren't dragging on the ground." She rubbed their backs. "But you certainly look worried enough. Will you grow up and make those awesome sounds when you bark?"

The little boy licked her hand.

"I'll take that as a yes."

Henry stepped into the bedroom. "I couldn't figure out who you were talking to. I should have guessed. Do you know what you're doing with them today?"

"We're going to visit Doc Jackson. I already have an appointment. Then I'm calling Ken Wallers once Stephanie pulls the footage from the security camera. I thought about it all night and unless he tells me there's no reason to find the person who dumped them, I want them to know they can't get away with it."

"We have that appointment at the Springer House."

"This morning, right? The kids will play with the puppies until I come back."

Rebecca had found it impossible to leave them alone last night after she got home. Polly didn't want one more dog in the house, but after the fiasco with giving old Mr. Bridger's dog away, she wasn't sure if they'd make it through another experience like that with Rebecca.

"Where are you off to this morning?" Polly asked.

"I'll be over at the Mikkels' place. How about I swing by and pick you up. We'll meet Mary at the house, she'll unlock it and then leave us. Sound okay?"

Polly smiled up at him. "Sounds perfect. Do you want breakfast?"

He bent over and kissed her forehead. "Don't worry. I'll run up to the diner and get coffee. Lucy will feed me. I'm taking the big boys outside and then I'll keep Han."

"Thanks."

"Come on, boys. Let's go outside."

The word 'outside' was magic in this house. Both of the dogs raced away, losing interest in Polly and the puppies.

Polly leaned against the bed. "I'm not sure why you showed up in my life yesterday, but I'm glad you're safe. Now if we can just find good homes for you, that will make everything perfect."

She looked up and over the bed when she heard a soft tap. "Polly?" Rebecca said. "Can I come in?"

"Sure. I'm snuggling puppies. Do you want to hold one?"

Rebecca sat down beside the kennel and put her arms out. Polly handed her the little girl.

"Are we going to keep them?" Rebecca asked.

There it was. "What do you think we should do?"

"Find them good homes. We have a lot of animals in the house."

"It's hard to give furballs away, isn't it, honey," Polly said.

Rebecca nodded and pulled the puppy up to give her a kiss. "But I'm learning that however many we give away, more just keep coming in. Isn't that right?"

Polly chuckled. "I guess it is." She put her hand up on the bed for leverage to stand. "Let's take them into the kitchen and feed them. Will you be okay with me leaving this morning for a while?"

"You trust us with them?" Rebecca asked, standing up. She tucked the puppy under her arm, cradling its belly with her hand.

"I think you've got this," Polly said with a smile. "How does cold pizza sound for breakfast?"

"Awesome!" Rebecca said. "You never let us do that."

"Usually you're heading off to school and that would just make me feel guilty."

Obiwan ran up the steps and tore into the kitchen looking for his breakfast.

"Yeah, yeah, yeah," Polly said. "We're getting there." She put the puppy on the floor, filled Obiwan's dish, and poured food into the dish they were using for the pups. "Sit there with them and keep them on task, would you? I need to start the coffee."

"Can I help with something?" a deep voice asked from the doorway.

Polly still wasn't used to Hayden in the house. His height, his deeper voice and his early morning happy demeanor were startling sometimes.

"What do you want for breakfast?" she asked. "We were thinking about cold pizza. But I could make eggs and sausage. Where's your brother?"

"He was up late last night talking to his girlfriend online. I told him he had fifteen minutes before I dragged his butt out of bed." Hayden bent over and rubbed Obiwan's head. "I'm glad to make breakfast. Let me do it."

Polly shrugged. "Okay. If you insist." She smiled at him and rubbed her hand down his back. "I'm glad you're here, Hayden. And not just because you cook. You and your brother are so happy when you're together. He needs more of you."

Hayden surprised her when he turned and pulled her into a hug. "I don't know anyone else who could make me feel so welcome. This feels like home. Thanks."

The tears were going to come. Polly knew it. She hugged him back, holding on until he let go. "You will always have a home with me and Henry." Before she completely fell apart, she spun around. "I'm going to take a shower while the coffee brews."

~~~

Polly stood inside the garage waiting for Henry. He'd texted to tell her he was on the way. It was only a few minutes between their house and the Mikkels's new place, so she grabbed a coat and ran downstairs.

Rebecca, Kayla, and Andrew were playing video games and the puppies were sound asleep.

She darted out into the chilly weather and shivered after pulling the truck door shut. "Where's Han?"

"Left him with Mom and Molly. I'll get him after we're done, but I didn't think you needed the additional canine help today. Is everything okay up there?"

"The kids have this. And Rebecca is fine with letting both of them go. She worried me, but I think she realizes that if they find good homes, that means we'll have room for more rescues."

He laughed and shook his head. "At least she understands who she's living with."

When they got to the Springer House, the realtor's car was parked on the street. Henry pulled in and up to the garage. "Are you ready?" he asked.

Polly nodded. "I'm excited. I want this to be amazing, you know."

"Just remember. You and I can make it amazing. Even if we have to gut the entire thing, we can have fun with it."

Before she could put her hand on the door handle, he leaned over the console and kissed her cheek. "Thank you for overcoming your fear of this place."

Polly grinned. "I was being a wuss. I know that. Let's go see what we've got here."

Mary Mueller greeted them again and led them to the side door. She unlocked it and pushed it open, then stepped back. "Call when you're finished. I hope you like what you see. You two would be the perfect people to own this house."

After she walked away, Henry took Polly's hand. "Ready?"

"I am. Let's do this."

They had entered a large storage room. Shelves on the walls were empty but a wringer washing machine was still in place.

"Wow," she said, pointing at it. "Everything really is still here."

"I got as far as the kitchen yesterday," Henry said. "You have to see this."

She stepped into the kitchen and stopped breathing. "This is nicer than mine. Can you keep all of it?"

"If we can't keep it, we can replace it."

Every vertical surface was covered in knotty pine, the counters and accents were teal, and there was a white range with an oven in the cabinets above it. Upholstery was shredded and destroyed on the stools around the counter, but it would have been a very modern kitchen in the mid-1940s. Muriel Springer must have redecorated the room right at the end of the war to have been able to get her hands on such new appliances.

"I love this room," Polly said. She walked over to the breakfast area, a booth looking out over the back yard. Boards were still on the windows, allowing only a little light into the room. "We're going to have trouble seeing some of these dark rooms today, aren't we?"

He brandished his mag lite. "We'll be fine."

From the kitchen they walked into the formal dining room. Though the furniture was covered in dust and cobwebs, it was still intact. The window coverings were falling apart and the oriental rug on the floor was a mess, but dishes were in the hutch and two pewter candlesticks stood on the old buffet.

"I feel like I'm intruding on someone else's memories," Polly said quietly. She jumped when a floorboard creaked under her foot. "This is just weird. I can't believe everything is in such good shape."

"They sealed it up well," Henry said. "There hasn't been much in the way of exposure. Probably most of it happened when Mr. Bridger decided to try to keep the place for himself."

They went on into a living room and then on the other side of that was another living room - probably a parlor. They found a library and a game room complete with a billiards table, an office, and a back hallway that had stairs leading up. They continued on the main floor making their way around. Finally, Henry pushed a door open and they walked out into an immense foyer with two stairways on either side leading to the second floor. A huge crystal chandelier hung down and underneath it was an odd rock formation.

"What's this?" Polly asked.

Henry shook his head. "I have no idea." He walked around it several times, reaching out to touch the rocks. Then he stood up on his tip toes to see the top. "Oh for heaven's sake. It's a fountain."

"So you're seriously telling me that no one wants to buy this glorious house. Does it come with all the furnishings or are they going to have an auction?"

He grimaced. "I'd hate to lose these things. I'll ask the question and if she's planning to auction off the insides, I'll make an offer. Does that sound fair?"

Polly nodded, her eyes huge. "I want everything." She pointed up at the banister on the second floor. "Where do you suppose she killed herself?"

"I don't want to know," he replied. "Maybe we should replace the whole thing, though."

She shivered again. "That sounds like a great idea." Polly took his arm. "I want this place. Just make the deal happen. I'd thought maybe we could turn it into several apartments, but right now I don't know what I want to do with it. I just want it to be ours."

"You haven't seen the upstairs yet."

"Unless Muriel herself tells me to go away. I want it. With as many rooms as there are down here, there have to be a bunch of bedrooms upstairs. Let's go."

CHAPTER SEVEN

Leaving Springer House, Polly took Henry's hand. "I'm not ready to go home yet. I just want to sit somewhere quiet and talk this over with you," she said as they got into the truck.

He chuckled. "Not a lot of quiet at the house." He turned left at the highway, drove past the inn and turned in toward the winery. "It's quiet back here this time of day."

"Tell me about the work you have to do if we buy that place. I know that the price is ridiculously low, but it has to be more than just seventy years of being known as the haunted house."

Henry parked at the back of the lot, looking out over the vineyard and left the truck running. They both needed extra heat today to warm back up. "You're right," he said. "We'll start at the top. The roof is a mess. All of the electricity and plumbing will have to be replaced. The foundation is in better shape than I expected, but you saw how the floor in the foyer sagged. That will need to be shored up. Only one of the walls in the basement is solid. It will take work to rebuild that. The walls are all lathe construction and while I wouldn't normally worry about replacing that in a remodel, we'll have to rip everything out when we go after the electricity and plumbing."

"Even the kitchen? I love that paneling," Polly said.

"Give me time to think about whether it's cheaper to rip it out and replace or work with it as it is." He shrugged. "Knotty pine paneling is easy to find, so we can match it."

"You're scaring me with all of the problems."

"If I were anyone else, I'd be terrified of it too," Henry acknowledged. "It's a lot of work. The solarium is hanging on by a thread over that front porch. My choice would be to rip it out completely and put a new front porch on. The back porch isn't in much better shape. Vines and weeds really did a number on it."

Polly felt herself sag. "It sounds like we should buy the property, tear everything down and forget about it. You could put up a set of apartments there."

"Stop it," Henry said, turning toward her. He took her arm and forced her to look at him. "It's a great building. The solarium was added after it was built. It wasn't part of the original plans. That's no big deal. The basement and foundation work feels bigger, but once that's done, everything else becomes much easier. Electrical and plumbing? That's no worse than what we did at Sycamore House and at the inn. It's just part of bringing these old places into the twenty-first century. That's what you want to do, isn't it? Keep the feel of the old home, but make it useable?"

"We'll be investing a lot of money."

"Of course we will. That's not anything new either." He sat back in his seat. "But I'm not going forward with this unless you're completely on board. I need you."

"There are original house plans?" she asked.

He grinned. "I found them in Boone."

"Do you think we could hire Sandy Davis to work with me?"

"That's a great idea," he said. "She'd be wonderful. Talk to her and see what she says. I'd be okay with bringing a free-lance architect into the fold."

Polly rubbed her hands together, ostensibly to warm them up, but in her heart, she felt like a mad scientist planning to take over the world. "I'd have to be there a lot and I'd get to work with my friends again."

"Are you feeling better about the house?"

"Now I'm excited. I needed you to tell me that there were good reasons for it to be so cheap, but that we could overcome them."

"Of course on both counts," he said. Henry took her hands and rubbed them between his. "I've missed working with you."

"Call your realtor lady and make an offer," Polly said. She withdrew her hands and leaned forward, clasping her head. "I can't believe we're doing this. I don't even know what we'll do with that house when we're finished."

"If we have to sell it, we will," he said.

Polly looked over at him in shock. "We're not selling my dream house."

"Your dream house?" A puzzled look came over his face. "I didn't know you had a dream house."

"I didn't think it existed until I saw this." Polly shut her eyes and bowed her head. "This is going to sound ridiculous, but do you remember when Rebecca showed us the book *Little Men* by Louisa May Alcott?"

Henry nodded.

"And how Heath was like Dan?"

Henry tapped her arm. "I read the book."

"You what?"

"Well, I listened to it in the truck. I listened to all of them. Since so many things around Sycamore House came out of that series, I thought the least I could do was read it."

"I love you, Henry Sturtz," Polly said. "You're amazing." She took a breath. "Anyway. It hit me that I love having these kids around. I love that Heath and Hayden are comfortable in our house." She looked up. "Do you know that Hayden told me this morning it felt like home to him? That ripped at my heart."

"And you want to reproduce Plumfield?"

"Well not reproduce it. Not at all. I don't want to be a teacher." Polly put her hand out on the console between them. "You and I aren't going to have babies, are we?"

"Not unless you become a crazed woman and change your mind," he said. "It's not something I have a desperate desire to do."

"But I want kids around. We have the resources and Henry, there are a ton of rooms in that house. Think about how much fun it would be to fill them all up."

"I think you're going to need help."

She grinned. "That's the thing. What about Evelyn Morrow? She'd be terrific. And she could live on-site."

"You're really starting to make plans, aren't you?"

"And that huge back yard? Once it's cleaned up and all of the fencing is repaired, we'd have a perfect place for kids and animals. It's not the barn or the garden at Sycamore House, but we'd only be a few minutes away. And maybe we could build a small barn back there."

"Slow down," Henry said. "We need to take this in steps. First we buy the house and start cleaning up the yard and clearing out the inside. Then we begin renovating. It's going to take the better part of a year, maybe more depending on the other projects I get."

Polly wriggled in her seat. "I don't care if it takes ten years. It's fun just to plan."

"Can you keep quiet about this?" he asked. "Keep it from Lydia and Joss and the rest of your friends?"

"Why?" Polly stuck her lower lip out. "It's exciting. And I'm going to talk to Sandy about it."

"Because once this starts circulating around town, the gossips are going to have a field day with your life. It's bad enough that we're buying the haunted house."

"I don't care what they think."

"Okay," he said with a shrug. "Don't say I didn't warn you."

"I'll try to be good. But I have to tell someone."

"Wait until we sign the papers to buy the place and you can tell everybody that part of the plan. Sound fair?"

Polly heaved a dramatic sigh and dropped her shoulders. "If you insist." She looked at the time. "We should get back. The kids are going to wonder where we are."

He turned the truck around to leave the parking lot. "How did you keep hold of yourself when you bought Sycamore House? There was no one to tell."

"I don't know. It was all so intense. I had so much going on and I just put my head down and pushed forward."

Henry pulled out onto the highway beside the hotel and honked at Grey, who was walking back from one of the rooms to the lobby. Grey beckoned to them and Henry turned in and parked beside the entryway.

Polly jumped out of the truck and ran over to Grey. "Guess what?" she asked.

She heard Henry snort behind her. "Fat lot of good that conversation did," he said quietly.

Grey took her arm and walked with her in through the front doors. "Tell me what has you so enthusiastic."

"We're buying the Springer House. Henry says there is a lot of work to be done on it, but when we're finished, it will be gorgeous."

"That sounds quite exciting. Congratulations." He gave her a small hug and turned to shake Henry's hand. "I must say that it also sounds like a great deal of hard work is ahead of you."

Henry nodded. "That hard work is what brought us together. Polly wanted to renovate Sycamore House and I caught her dream. We invested in the inn and now look – you're even part of her dream."

Grey began humming and chuckled. "To run where the brave dare not go," he said. "What others call impossible, Polly digs in and finds a way."

"Henry's usually my way," Polly said. "Why did you wave us in?"

"Follow me." He led them through to his apartment. In the last few months, he'd done more and more decorating. In truth, much of it had happened after he'd finally purchased a used truck. But he was making the apartment his own home. There was quite a bit of hockey equipment in the living room, from helmets and gloves, to sticks, pads and skates.

"You need more closet space," Polly said.

"The basement is also filling with equipment," Grey replied. "I know that it's chilly, but do you have a moment to come outside?"

They followed him and Polly looked around, wondering where Brutus was hiding. He generally greeted any visitor with barking and yapping. She laughed when they walked through the back door and down the steps. Hayden was skating around the rink and Brutus was on a saucer, dressed in a heavy sweater.

"That's the funniest thing I've seen in a long time," Henry said.

"The dog enjoys being with his friends," Grey said with a chuckle. He waved at Hayden, who came to a stop, bent over to pick up the dog and the saucer and walked over to the edge of the rink.

"Heath got a call and had to run some errands for the guys at the Mikkels's place," Hayden said. "I have practice this afternoon, so I didn't go. Grey thought you two might stop by and wanted you to hear some of my ideas."

Polly looked at Grey skeptically. "You thought we might stop by?"

"Call it intuition."

"What are you two cooking up?" she asked.

"We need to discuss storage for equipment and supplies as well as a better place for people to rest after they've been skating," Grey said. "The picnic table and a few lawn chairs aren't good for the long-term."

Henry looked around. "What do you suggest?"

"I was thinking we could put some nice benches around the rink," Hayden said. "Heath told me you have a big shop and if you or your father wouldn't mind training me to use your equipment, I'd be glad to come home when I have extra time this spring and build them."

Grey stepped in. "We've had several people offer to pay for the benches. We could take up a collection for lumber."

"And storage?" Polly asked.

"A nice shed over there." Grey pointed toward the southwest corner of the lot. "I'd like it to be big enough that the kids could store their equipment and have space to get suited up before hitting the ice."

Henry looked at Polly and she nodded. "Put together a proposal." Then to Hayden, he said, "If you're serious about learning to use equipment at the shop, I'm sure Dad and Len Specek would be willing to teach you. Ya know old woodworkers. They're always looking for new blood."

"Thank you, sir," Hayden said.

The 'sir' raised Henry's eyebrows, but he let it go.

"I think Brutus is getting cold," Hayden said, handing the dog to Grey. "But I want to practice a while longer."

"Thanks." Grey gave him a warm smile and took the dog, tucking it under his arm.

"Do you want another puppy?" Polly asked. Henry swatted her arm. "Hey," she said. "I have to find homes for them."

Grey squeezed Brutus's nose. "We wouldn't be averse to more company. I think that I should stop at one more, though."

"Really?" Henry asked.

"Limiting yourself to one dog at a time only sets you up to be tragically broken-hearted if and when something happens. If there are two in the home, not only will they love each other and the amount of love you receive is exponentially greater, but in the event of loss, there is always one to comfort and carry you through." He held the back door open for Polly and Henry to walk through. "Is there a Cassius for my Brutus?"

"Wasn't Cassius the one who plotted against Caesar, lying to Brutus?" Polly asked.

"Yes, but my Brutus isn't quite as naive as Shakespeare's character. I believe he can hold his own against an onslaught of intricate schemes."

"If you want the puppy, I'd love for you to have him. I think he's part bloodhound."

"All the better," Grey said. When he saw the looks of confusion on their faces, he continued. "Brutus doesn't do much to keep me warm at night. One needs a large dog at his side." He chuckled. "Won't we look a sight walking down the street."

CHAPTER EIGHT

Any other day of the year, Polly could come up with a million things to do, but she and Henry still didn't have plans for New Year's Eve. She considered inviting Elise and her cousins up for dinner. Though Ron and Don might enjoy a wild party in a bar, Elise would never feel comfortable with that. An intimate dinner was much more her style. Since most of their friends were still out of town or busy with their own family plans, the holiday season had turned into a much quieter time than the rest of the year.

Rebecca was going to a party at Andrew's house.

That made Polly smile. Closing Sweet Beans for the week had been a great idea, even though she missed her friends as well as her multiple daily caffeine fixes. Sylvie needed the break. She was actually looking forward to hosting a group of kids. Since most of them planned to spend the night, Stephanie had offered to help. Polly was just as glad to not be in the middle of that chaos, but Sylvie couldn't wait. This last year had been really intense for her and she was excited about spending a holiday with her boys.

Jason and his friends were spending the night at Eliseo's house. Polly thought Jason might be worried that Eliseo would have to spend the night alone, so he'd come up with a million reasons why they should ring in the New Year together. Eliseo hadn't reacted to the news that Grey and Sylvie were dating - if you could even call it that. Everyone had wanted them to get together, but sometimes what people wanted wasn't what happened. It was interesting, though, that Sylvie had scheduled a party she needed to chaperon instead of leaving herself open to go out with Grey on New Year's Eve.

Hayden had a couple of things happening in Ames and Heath had asked if he could go to a party with his friend, Libby. They both insisted it wasn't a date. Libby's mother liked Heath, but still refused to let him take her daughter out alone. Polly was so glad he was spending time with someone his own age who wasn't a hoodlum that she agreed without hesitation.

"Polly?"

She looked up to see Stephanie standing in the door to her office.

"What's up?"

"I copied that video from yesterday for you. It shows the car, but I didn't recognize the person who dropped the box off and the plates are from Story County."

"So they had to come over here to dump the puppies? That's nuts," Polly said.

Stephanie put a DVD on Polly's desk. "Are you giving this to the police?"

"I want to. Could you tell if they were young or old?"

"Probably young, but from that angle, I couldn't even tell if it was a male or female. The person didn't even get out of the car and they were wearing some kind of hat."

Polly rolled her eyes. "I'll take it up to the police station after I'm done at the vet's office." She looked up at the clock on the wall. "I'd better get them ready to go. By the way, do you want a puppy?" She chuckled.

"Kayla would love one," Stephanie said. "I told her that we couldn't until we live somewhere that he can have a yard. I promised her that as soon as that happens, she can have a dog."

"Makes sense." Polly grabbed up the DVD. "I don't know when I'll be back. Have you seen Jeff today?"

"He was in for a while this morning, but he had a meeting with some of the business owners. It's about the sesquicentennial celebration this summer."

This was new information for Polly. She realized she had no idea when Bellingwood had been founded. Apparently in 1866. "Okay. I'll talk to him another day." Polly wanted to tell him about the possibility of buying Springer House.

Henry was right. They needed to keep this purchase quiet for a while. She wasn't ready to explain their future plans, especially plans that might include moving out of Sycamore House. That wouldn't happen for a couple of years at least and she didn't need to have people speculating about who was going to live upstairs or why she wanted a house with so many rooms or ask uncomfortable questions about how they could afford it. Sometimes people got too nosy.

Polly laughed out loud as she walked up the steps. Henry told her that *she* was nosy. "I guess it takes one to know one," she said to herself. But the truth was, when she got tired of people getting into her business it was because they wanted to criticize or make judgments. It seemed like that behavior got worse all the time. She'd even quit sharing things on social media. It was just easier to stay silent.

Bunny was the worst. Even though she lived in Boston and had only been to Bellingwood once, she had opinions on everything that Sal and Polly did and insisted on sharing them. Polly had made a comment about Beryl's new kittens and their adorable names - May and Hem - and Bunny felt it necessary to make sure Polly told Beryl that she needed to be careful about introducing the new kittens into the house with an older cat. Where did that even come from? The original post was about cute names.

Then Bunny had taken it upon herself to instruct Sal on how to interact with Mark's family in Minnesota while they were there for the holidays. She wanted Sal to understand how Christmas worked in Christian families. Polly had bought a bottle of vodka and a carton of orange juice and driven over to Sal's house after that conversation. And she'd been right. Sal was ready to reach through the Internet and strangle their helpful friend.

Mark had come home to two very drunk women that night. He didn't know what the problem was, but called Henry for help. They'd ordered pizza and had a fun dinner laughing at Bunny's sad life that Bunny, sticking her nose in everyone else's business.

Oh, what that girl would say when she found out that Polly might be buying a big old haunted mansion.

Polly gave her head a quick shake as she opened the front door to the apartment. They could take the easy road and not buy the house. She could comfortably live like this for a very long time. A nice little home where Rebecca and her friends could spend their free time. Heath would graduate in a couple of years and there was no guarantee that she and Henry would ever have any more kids in their lives. It would be easier, but it wouldn't be nearly as much fun. Stirring the pot every once in a while was just what Polly needed in her life.

"We took the puppies out to the backyard and the little girl pooped on the ground," Rebecca announced when she saw Polly. "I named her Lady. We're calling the little boy Tramp. You should see them. He loves her so much and is always laying down on top of her."

"Lying," Polly said automatically.

"What?"

"He lies down on her, not lays. You can lay a blanket on top of her, but if you do it yourself, it's lie." She waved Rebecca off. "No big deal. Lady and the Tramp? I like it." Polly sat down on the sofa and pulled Tramp into her arms. "I found you a home already. Now we just have to find great parents for your sister and my job is done."

"Where's he going?" Kayla asked.

"He's going to live with Grey and Brutus at the inn. It sounds like they need a puppy in their lives."

"These two should stay together," Rebecca said. "They love each other."

Polly smiled. "I know they do, but as long as they each have a family who loves them, they'll be very happy. I promise."

~~~

She pulled up in front of the inn and looked down at the puppies on the floor. They were passed out from the excursion to the vet clinic. Well, that and their vaccinations. Doctor Jackson had pronounced them healthy and estimated they were eight or nine weeks old. They were old enough to be placed in their own homes. There was no reason for her to keep them together any longer, even though her heart broke at the thought of separating them after all they'd been through.

Polly mentally kicked herself. She didn't know that they'd been through anything more traumatic than being dropped off. Doctor Jackson assured her that their weight was good, they weren't dehydrated, they weren't frightened of people, and they showed no signs of abuse. The pups were just fine.

She'd stopped at the police station and run in with the DVD. Bert Bradford was there and promised they'd do what they could, but he didn't have much confidence it would be much. Abandoning animals was awful, but at least whoever did it made sure the puppies were placed where they might be found.

She glanced up when the front door of the inn opened and Grey came out.

He motioned for her to roll down the window. "Hello there. Is everything okay?" he asked.

"I was just pondering things."

"Ponderings take our minds into frightening places."

"Yes they do," she said.

"Would you like to come in and have some coffee? A fresh pot just finished brewing."

Polly pointed at the floor of her truck and Grey bent over to see what she had. "You brought me a puppy," he said. "Two puppies?" He looked up at her with a grin.

"No," Polly said. "I wasn't going to do that to you. But it's going to be difficult for me to separate them. Look." She glanced down. "He's got his little paw on her neck."

Grey started humming something familiar and Polly creased her brow. "What are you singing?"

"Just an old fashioned love song."

"What is it?"

He chuckled. "Not much into seventies and eighties rock?"

"Well, yeah. Oh! That was the title."

He smiled at her. "It hit me when I realized I was about to have a lifetime of three dog nights."

"You want to keep both of these dogs? Doctor Jackson said they might get as big as eighty or a hundred pounds."

"Then it seems I will need to invest in a shovel and large bags of dog food."

Polly shook her head in wonder. "Are you sure about this?"

"I believe that we should accept serendipitous gifts without question," he said with a gentle smile. "And consider what great exercise these two will be for young Denis as he rebuilds strength in his legs."

Grey opened the truck door and scooped up one of the pups. "The name Cassius will no longer be acceptable. We can't have that kind of character in the same home as a young lady. And now that I meet you, I see that it doesn't fit."

"Rebecca suggested Lady and the Tramp," Polly said, getting out of the truck. She walked around and scooped the other out of its warm nest.

"You do look more like a Tramp than a Cassius," Grey agreed. "Tell your daughter that she has excellent taste in names. Come on inside. Denis is here. I'd like to introduce him to his new friends." He smiled at Polly. "You never know; Lady might discover that she is attracted to the boy. He could use a warm body that's filled with unconditional love."

CHAPTER NINE

No one had seen much of Elise since she'd arrived in Bellingwood. The girl was so used to being by herself, that she'd hidden away up in her room. Henry had agreed to inviting her and her cousins to dinner on New Year's Eve. He and Polly were confident that the evening wouldn't last long and they'd have the house to themselves long before midnight arrived.

She walked through the addition to the steps at the back and looked out before heading up. This really was beautiful. What was she thinking trying to find a different place to live? How would she get along not having immediate access to everybody here? And she'd miss the horses.

Henry wouldn't let her get away with any of that. Bellingwood wasn't that big and as it was, she only went to the barn three or four times a week. Wait. That wasn't true either. When she took the dogs out, they usually ended up at the pasture talking to the horses and the donkeys. She saw them nearly every day.

But moving out of Sycamore House wouldn't happen for a long time. Change was good. It was very good. Look at poor Elise.

She'd had radical changes occur in the last few years and was still willing to try new things, even if she was as frightened of social interaction as anyone Polly had ever met.

Polly walked up the steps and knocked. "Elise? It's me. Polly. Do you have a minute?"

The door opened and Elise swept her hand, inviting Polly in. "How are you? I've seen you around, but you've been busy. I didn't want to bother you."

"Did you need something?"

"No. Just to chat."

Polly stepped over to one of the wing chairs and sat down. Elise took the other. "You're never a bother. I have been busy, but I have time for you."

Elise nodded. "Why are you here?" She clapped her hand over her mouth. "I'm sorry. That was rude. You're just being friendly."

"No. I have a reason," Polly said. "I wanted to invite you to our apartment for dinner tomorrow night."

"Oh, I couldn't," Elise said, interrupting her. "Parties destroy me. I'd just hide in the corner. It will be much better for everyone if I just stay here in my room. I'll watch the ball drop on television like I do every year."

Polly smiled. "We can have you back to your room in plenty of time to watch television. But we're not having a party. It would just be you, your cousins, me, and Henry. Even the kids will be gone. And it's only dinner."

"The boys are leaving in the morning. They have families and their own parties to get back to," Elise said. She gave a tiny shiver. "I don't know where I would have gone if you weren't here. I applied for the job only because it was so close to Bellingwood."

"Tell me more about what you're doing," Polly said. "Things got busy and I didn't ask enough questions."

Elise gave her a weak smile. "I'm really looking forward to teaching. Really I am.."

Polly nodded. And then she nodded again. Slowly. "You're teaching. In front of large classes. With college kids who don't know how to control themselves and talk all the time."

"Stop it," Elise said, a burbling laugh coming from her mouth. "It sounds ridiculous, doesn't it?"

"I'll just call it surprising," Polly said. Then she looked up. "Wait. That means you were here interviewing with them and you didn't stop by?"

"I know." Elise dropped her head. "I came to Bellingwood, but it was just before Halloween and there was so much going on. I stopped at the inn and there weren't any rooms left. The nice man at the front desk said it was because of a haunted house."

"You should have called me or come here. I always have room for my friends," Polly said. "You do know that Henry and I own that inn."

"I suspected. Especially since it's called Sycamore Inn. But it was all full and I assumed that if they were full, you had to be full up over here too. I didn't know that you had gotten married and turned the upstairs into your house." Elise grinned at Polly. "Is there really a haunted house in town?"

Polly sighed. "Not really. It was an old story that grew distorted over the years, but there wasn't any truth to it. A poor woman killed herself when she found out her husband died in the second World War. But then he came back. So stories were told that she haunted him and his new family until they finally left town."

"That's spooky."

"It really was. A neighbor found the lady's great-niece and she looked just like the lady, so he hired her to come and haunt the house. This was the first year it was going on the market and he didn't want it to sell because he had a marijuana-growing operation in the back yard."

"The strangest things happen in Bellingwood," Elise said, shaking her head.

"Oh, you have no idea," Polly said. "After you left, the strange things never really stopped. We're probably about due for another one pretty soon. It's been much too quiet lately."

"This time it won't be about me. I want to be able to watch it from the sidelines."

Polly chuckled. "You've probably picked the wrong friend, then. I often end up right smack dab in the middle of things. But let's get back to you teaching at Iowa State. Undergrad or graduate classes?"

"I have one undergraduate calculus class."

"That sounds scary."

"It isn't so bad. The kids have to be pretty bright to get to that class. But Polly, I get to do research and work with some great people."

"Again with the working with people. That doesn't sound like you."

Elise whispered. "They're just like me. It will be perfect."

"Then I'm glad," Polly said. "And you managed to get in mid-year, too."

"That was one of the reasons this worked out so well. I was just notified that I could resume my regular life in September and the job came open.

"I'm really excited. I can't wait for you to meet my friends."

Elise put her hand up. "No more friends. You have too many, I think."

"We'll do it one at a time. Whenever you're ready. But first, will you come over for dinner Thursday night?"

"I don't think so," Elise said, shaking her head. "If you and your husband have the night to yourselves, you should do something special. We'll have plenty of time to spend together. I'm going to beg you to take me shopping for a car and then help me find an apartment."

"But..." Polly started to protest and Elise stopped her.

"I won't change my mind. Take Henry out for the evening. If I remember anything about you it's that you always include people in your lives. Maybe this once it should just be the two of you."

Polly chuckled. "You think you're so smart, missy."

"Yes I do. My IQ is extravagant."

"That's one way of describing it," Polly said, laughing. "Okay. I won't press you on this, but we will go car shopping soon so you can have some freedom." She stood up and then bent over to hug

Elise. "I *am* glad you're here. And please don't hesitate to flag me down whenever you want to talk. Not just if you need to, but even if you only want to."

Polly left Elise's room, wondering what she was going to do for New Year's Eve. Everyone else had a party to attend or family coming over. Henry wouldn't plan anything because he thought she was inviting Elise and her cousins up for dinner. They could just stay in and watch television, but they did that all the time.

She swiped her phone open, scrolled through her contacts and placed a call.

"Hey, J. J. this is Polly Giller. I'm really late and all you have to do is say no, but do you have any room for me and Henry tomorrow night?"

"Well, Polly Giller. You're slumming it for New Year's Eve?"

"Well, you know. Us hoity-toities have to come down and play with the common folk every once in a while. Am I too late to get a table, though?"

"I will go out and buy a table for the two of you if it comes to that," he replied. "What time should we expect you?"

"Let's say eight o'clock. Will that work?"

"Of course. We'll see you then."

"Thank you, J. J.," she said. "I'm sorry to be so late."

"It's never a problem. I look forward to seeing you."

There. Now she had a plan and no one could say that she wasn't romantic. They would dress up and spend an evening at Secret Woods Winery with great music, maybe a little dancing, dinner, and good wine. If they managed to stay up until midnight, she'd be surprised.

~~~

She was working in Henry's office later that afternoon when Andrew tapped on the door. "Polly, do you have a minute?"

"Sure, come on in. What's going on?"

He closed the door to the main part of the house and then went over to close the bathroom door too.

"This looks serious," Polly said. "What's up?"

"Tomorrow is New Year's Eve and I'm having a party at my house. There are going to be a bunch of kids from school there. We're going to eat pizza and watch the ball drop and play games and stuff."

"I know," she said. "It sounds like fun."

He lowered his head. "Can I kiss Rebecca?"

She did her very best to not laugh out loud. Poor Andrew was completely serious. She had to respect him a little for asking, so she bit her tongue and pursed her lips to hold back a smile. "You want to kiss her?"

Andrew looked up. His face had gone pale and terror filled his eyes. "Just once. I won't try anything else, but I don't want you to be mad at us. I know she'll tell you if I do it. Mom will probably be in the same room and everything. But when it turns midnight, can I kiss her and not get into trouble with you and Henry?"

"I appreciate that you've shown Rebecca so much respect," Polly said with as straight a voice as she could manage. "And you've shown that same kind of respect to me and to Henry. Yes, I think it would be permissible for you to kiss her tomorrow night at midnight."

The tension washed off him and his face brightened. "Thank you! Don't tell her I said anything, okay?"

"I promise. Now go on and do your thing. You don't want her to get suspicious."

He opened the bathroom door and then the door to the media room. "She and Kayla are looking at clothes for her to wear to the party. They're in her room and don't care what I'm doing. I'm going to play a game or something."

"Andrew?" Polly's voice stopped him and he turned around. "You haven't been writing much lately. What happened?"

He shrugged. "Nothing really. I just got busy. Junior high is different than elementary school, you know. There are bigger things to worry about." He rubbed the side of his head. "My mind has trouble sorting it all out sometimes. It's easier just to watch television or play a game."

Polly recognized that behavior. It was the best way she'd always had to avoid thinking about things that were stressful. "Are you still reading?"

"Sometimes."

"Andrew Donovan, don't you dare waste that brain of yours."

"I'm not wasting it. It's just thinking about other things these days."

"Does your mom know that you aren't reading or writing?" she asked.

Andrew shook his head. "She's been too busy. But I'm getting good grades. As long as she sees a good report card, she's happy." He heard the way that had probably sounded. "I don't mean that she doesn't have time for me. That sounded bad. But she's really busy with everything. And Jason and I talked about it. We're just going to keep things as good as possible at home for her while she's working so much. And now that she's going out with Grey sometimes, that's good too, right?"

"Honey," Polly said, getting up from behind the desk. She walked around and put her hand on his shoulder. "Your mother would worry if she thought that the two of you felt the need to protect her from your lives. You can't do that. She's your mom."

"But she'll get back to normal someday and we'll still be the same kids."

"No you won't. You're growing up too fast already. You have to involve her in what's going on in your life. She wants to know if things are upsetting you or if you're excited about something. Did you talk to her about wanting to kiss Rebecca?"

Andrew drew back in shock. "No! And don't you dare tell her. Please. That's just between you and me. I didn't want you to kick me out of your house if you heard about it from someone else. That's the only reason I said something."

"I see," Polly said. "I thought it was all about respect."

He'd walked into that trap. His mouth opened and closed a couple of times as he tried to figure out what to say.

Polly didn't have the energy to make him squirm too long. "It's okay. You're fine. But still. You need to talk to your mother. And oh by the way, you need to be reading. I don't want my brilliant daughter dating someone who can't keep up with her. Find a book and read it. Then find a story and tell it. You love to write stories. Don't let life take that away from you. Okay?"

"I'll try. But there aren't any good books to read. I've read everything."

"You're kidding me, right?"

"Well. Kind of. But I've read a lot of books. What else is there?"

She walked over to the bookshelves on her wall and took down a book. "*The Count of Monte Cristo*," she said and took the book right next to it and handed both to him. "He also wrote *The Three Musketeers*. I think you'll like them."

"Does it matter which I read first?"

"Nope. Just start reading."

Andrew sat down on the sofa and Obiwan scrambled to sit beside him. He opened one of the books and turned to the first page. Polly watched until she realized that he'd forgotten she was there. He was such a good boy. And she couldn't wait to tell Henry that he'd asked permission to kiss Rebecca. Who did that these days?

CHAPTER TEN

"Sleepyhead, wake up!"

Polly turned over and blinked her eyes. "What are you doing in here? What time is it?"

"It's nine o'clock. Henry said you had a rough night last night and we should let you sleep in," Rebecca said. "But Hayden made the best breakfast and we're all hungry." She giggled. "Henry also said that nine o'clock was late enough."

Polly pulled herself up to a sitting position and rolled her shoulders. She hadn't gone to sleep until after two. There wasn't anything stressing her out, but she hadn't been able to turn her mind off. It must have been the Springer House. She'd spent most of the evening thinking about how to redecorate and rearrange the rooms. They probably didn't need a parlor and if the solarium over the front porch was really coming off, what kind of windows would she put in that upper story so that the chandelier would light up? And was she really going to keep a fountain? How ridiculous was that? But what else would she do with that immense foyer?

And oh, those double staircases. Wouldn't they be gorgeous for wedding pictures? That had taken her off into another tangent - thinking about Rebecca getting married. And then she thought about Hayden and Heath. What kind of girls would they want to marry and would they consider her enough of a mother to want her to sit in the front row of the church at the ceremony?

It had been like that all night long. Henry had slept through most of it, but every once in a while, he woke up enough to realize that she was still tossing and turning.

New Year's Eve was another thing that had kept her awake. Polly both loved and hated the change of the year. She knew that the calendar was a man-made construct and didn't impact things, but it was always an opportunity to look back at not just the last year, but all of the years she'd lived and then, she looked forward and wondered about what was coming next. There was always a little apprehension because who knew what could happen, but mostly there was excitement ... because who knew what could happen!

She'd met a lot of great people this last year. They'd opened Sweet Beans and it was going well. Business wasn't great yet, so no one was making a lot of money, but they were paying their employees and the bills. Sal was happy being a business owner. She didn't spend quite as much time there as she thought she would, but that was okay too.

Sylvie was over the moon with her bakery. Even though the boys had to fend for themselves more often, it was an incredible time in Sylvie's life. And Grey. What a fabulous friend he was becoming. He was never not going to be odd, but he genuinely cared for people he only barely knew.

And then Heath and Hayden. How had that really happened? Polly thought back to the night that Rebecca announced Heath should be part of their family. She was absolutely right and Polly was so grateful they'd taken the risk on him. Heath still had a long way to go, but he was trying. That's all she could ask.

Polly got up on her knees and crawled over to Rebecca, then pulled her into a hug.

"What?" Rebecca said.

"I love you."

"I love you, too. What's this about?"

"Do you remember that cold, wet day I picked you and Andrew up at the school. The first time we met?" Polly asked.

"Yeah. You found Mom and she was sick."

"You're right. That did happen. But how awesome that we found each other that day. Andrew made that happen and I love him for it. I loved getting to know your mother. And I love you."

"Mom would be happy, I think," Rebecca said.

"About what you're doing?" Polly asked.

"Yes. Everything. All of these people and everything. She'd think it was pretty cool."

Polly hugged Rebecca again. "I miss her."

"Me too." Rebecca slumped against Polly. "Sometimes a lot." She looked up. "Sometimes not as much, though."

"I know. Do you ever think about all of the wonderful people you've gotten to know this last year?"

"You mean like Heath and Hayden?"

"Yeah. And Grey and Camille."

"And Kayla and Stephanie," Rebecca said.

Polly chuckled. "It seems like you've been friends with Kayla forever. Was it really just this year?"

"Yeah. Stephanie was working at the convenience store and then she started working here. It all just worked out, didn't it?"

"It did," Polly said. "Whenever the year changes I wonder who I'm going to meet next year and what kinds of things will happen."

"Will you find more bodies?" Rebecca asked.

Polly stopped to think about that. "I don't know. But if someone dies, I guess so. Are you making New Year's resolutions?"

"I should. Kayla is talking about hers. Mom and I used to do it on New Year's Day. She'd make chili and cornbread and then we'd sit at the table with our notepads and write down all of the things we thought we should change in our lives."

"Were there a lot?"

Rebecca nodded and snuggled closer into Polly's arms. "But then we picked the top ten and I made up a poster that we put on the refrigerator. We didn't do that last year."

Polly stroked her hair and leaned her face on top of Rebecca's head. "What would you think if we did something like that tomorrow?"

She had to raise her head away when Rebecca snapped hers up. "Would you? That would be fun. Would Henry and Heath do it too?"

"Sure. If we can pry them away from the football games."

"Oh yeah." Rebecca slumped back down. "Football games. That's going to go on all weekend, isn't it?"

"Yep. But that's okay. Football season will be over soon. We can let them grunt and be manly for a while."

Rebecca giggled. "I'll tell Henry you said he grunted."

"You do that. He'll agree. Now go on out and I'll be there in a minute. Pour me a cup of coffee, would you?"

Polly sat back as Rebecca jumped off the bed and ran out of the room. Even with all of the craziness that had happened this last year, she wouldn't have traded any of it away. The year had given her a daughter and a son. Neither of them had had an easy time of it, but they were here now and safe and Polly loved them as much as if she'd given birth to them. She chuckled at that thought. How would she know? But that was beside the point. She loved them with a love that she'd never realized existed. This was a good way to end the year.

~~~

The kids were gone and Henry was taking the dogs out for one last walk before he showered and dressed. Polly was almost giddy with excitement. They hadn't dressed up for a date in a few months. She and Rebecca had stopped in Iowa City early last fall and Rebecca insisted that Polly try on party dresses. There had been one that Polly had fallen in love with, all lace and chiffon. At the time, she had no idea when she'd wear it, but it had come home with her.

She pulled the dress on and looked at herself in the mirror. That was just one of those things she never really paid attention to and it felt so strange to be overly concerned with her appearance. She was just Polly. But with her hair pulled up and back, more makeup on than she usually wore, and short black pumps on her feet, she didn't feel like 'just Polly' tonight. To be honest, she had no idea who she felt like, but it was fun.

"Wow," Henry said when he walked into the bedroom. "You're kinda hot."

"Stop it." Polly dipped her head. "You're embarrassing me."

He kissed her cheek. "Then I don't say that enough to you." He ran his hands up her bare arms. "You're going to be chilly tonight. I'd better warm up the truck."

"There's a jacket." She held it up and he laughed.

"There's not a whole lot to that jacket. Like I said, I'm warming up the truck. Now go somewhere else so I can take a shower without distractions."

Polly stepped out of her shoes, bent over, picked them up and left the bedroom, followed by the dogs. She plopped down on the sofa in the living room and tucked her legs up underneath her, then pulled a blanket around her shoulders. Okay, he was right. It was going to be chilly.

Obiwan jumped up and sat beside her on the sofa, looking at her as if waiting for something. She reached out and rubbed his head. "Is there something else I should be doing for you?" she asked.

He leaned in to lick her face and she backed away. "Not tonight. Too much makeup that needs to stay in place." Polly gave his shoulders a little push and he relaxed onto the sofa. Han had jumped into the chair beside them and hung his head over, looking at the floor. "You're a weirdo," Polly said. His tail thumped against the chair.

She was glad the kids had someplace safe to be tonight. Heath's party was in town and he'd be home before one o'clock and Rebecca would be safe at Sylvie's. Sylvie promised to send the kids home completely exhausted so everyone could have a quiet New Year's Day. Stephanie picked Rebecca up at six o'clock and would bring her home the next morning.

Rebecca had nearly been beside herself with excitement. She'd packed an overnight bag and had torn through her drawers and closet trying to figure out what she needed to take. Polly knew better than to try and give advice. Especially if that advice was telling Rebecca it was no big deal and she should just relax.

Heath had tried that tack and had been dressed down quite neatly. It *was* a big deal. There were a lot of people going to be there and she wanted things to be just perfect for Andrew. Sylvie had told them to bring pajamas, but only if they covered everything and were warm. She'd sent a letter home with each of the kids, assuring parents that they would get a phone call if their child did anything to threaten the fun for everyone else. And that phone call wouldn't be a warning, they would be expected to come get their child immediately.

Polly knew Sylvie would do it, too. She'd read through that letter twice with Rebecca. There was no question as to what Sylvie expected for appropriate behavior.

"I'm almost ready. I'll be right there," Henry called from the bedroom.

"We have plenty of time," she said. "No worries. J. J. is holding a table for us."

"I can't believe you did this. Up until the minute I got in the shower, I wondered if something would come up and we'd have a crowd going with us."

"That's not fair," Polly protested. "We spent that night in the hotel in Perry before Thanksgiving. That was just us."

Henry stepped into the living room, dressed in a black turtleneck, black socks and his shorts. "Likey?" He pirouetted.

"I do," she said. "But I think you're missing something."

"You're already cold." Henry pointed at the blanket.

"I know. Let's hope they have the heat on."

"Don't you have anything warmer to wear tonight?"

Polly dropped her mouth open and looked at him in shock.

He laughed. "Sorry. What was I thinking? I'll just do my best to keep you warm. That's my job. Right?"

"I'd guess so," she said. "Sheesh!"

"At least we're only going a few blocks. If you look like you're going into hypothermic shock, I'll stop at the inn and rent a room to warm you up."

"Put your pants on."

He waggled his right leg. "You don't think I'm sexy with my black socks?"

"With or without. But come on. I can't believe I'm ready to go and you're stalling."

Henry jumped over the threshold to the bedroom. "I'm hurrying. I'm hurrying."

"He's my man," Polly said to the dogs. "But it's times like these that I'm glad no one else can see what he's like."

"Hey," Henry yelled. "I heard that." He stepped back into the living room, having added a charcoal jacket and black pants. He was slipping his feet into shoes as he walked. "Give me a few minutes and then come on down. And maybe you should bring that blanket."

Polly laughed as he ran through the house to the back door.

She waited a few minutes, stood up and pulled her flimsy chiffon jacket on, stepped toward the dining room, then turned back and looked at the blanket. It wasn't a bad idea. She grabbed the blanket, threw it around her shoulders and headed out.

"You didn't give me enough time to make the truck really warm," Henry said when she climbed in.

"I'll be fine. It's only a few blocks away. And I brought a blanket."

He leaned across the console and brushed her cheek with the back of his fingers. "I love you, you know."

"I love you too," she said, taking his hand. "It's been a pretty amazing year, hasn't it?"

His eyes puddled with tears, surprising Polly. "I can't believe how lucky I am," he said. "You and I are living a life I could never have dreamed up in a million years, but it is more exciting than anything I could create on my own. Thank you for sharing this life with me."

Polly squeezed his hand. "Thank you. I think we've only just begun."

He took his hand back, turned to look out the back window of the truck and laughed. "Maybe that should be our theme song."

"Maybe not," Polly said. "We're too young to be Carpenter's fans."

He pulled onto the highway and drove toward the inn, humming the song out loud. Polly held the blanket close around her and sat back. It was hard to believe another year was over. She could hardly wait for what was to come next.

THANK YOU FOR READING!

I'm so glad you enjoy these stories about Polly Giller and her friends. There are many ways to stay in touch with Diane and the Bellingwood community.

You can find more details about Sycamore House and Bellingwood at the website: http://nammynools.com/

Join the Bellingwood Facebook page:
https://www.facebook.com/pollygiller
for news about upcoming books, conversations while I'm writing and you're reading, and a continued look at life in a small town.

Diane Greenwood Muir's Amazon Author Page is a great place to watch for new releases.

Follow Diane on Twitter at twitter.com/nammynools for regular updates and notifications.

Recipes and decorating ideas found in the books can often be found on Pinterest at: http://pinterest.com/nammynools/

And, if you are looking for Sycamore House swag, check out Polly's CafePress store: http://www.cafepress.com/sycamorehouse

Made in the USA
Columbia, SC
11 December 2020